FOUR WEDDINGS AND A BABY

FIVE ISLAND COVE, BOOK 6

JESSIE NEWTON

JEN PUBLISHING

COPYRIGHT

ONE

Eloise Hall woke when her fiancé's alarm went off. Thankfully, the first light of day had started to seep through the curtains, and Eloise knew she wouldn't go back to sleep.

She'd had a terrible time falling asleep too, because today marked only three days until her wedding, and her dress was completely tailored and ready to be picked up.

Robin would be by at nine-thirty to take Eloise to the dress shop, and then they needed to finalize the fruit platter with the caterer as well.

She'd selected a seasonal fruit buffet, and the caterer now knew what they could offer.

"Getting up, sweetheart?" Aaron asked from his side of the bed.

"Yes," she said. "I promised Billie I'd help her with her

hair today, and I've got a call with Marge before Robin's coming."

"I can't wait to see the dress," he said, coming around to her side of the bed. He leaned over and kissed her.

"You can see it in three days," Eloise said, feeling soft and warm inside this house, this bed, the arms of this man.

"Not a day sooner, I'm sure," Aaron said, smiling.

"Not a day sooner," Eloise said. "Can you imagine the scandal that would hit the Cove Chronicles if it got out that the Chief of Police had seen his bride's dress before the wedding day?"

"If that's the huge scandal that gets attached to my name, I'll take it," he said, sighing as he sat on the bed near her knees.

"Are they going to print the article about your dad?"

"He says this kind of stuff happens every election year."

"I don't understand what would possess someone to want to run for office."

"It takes a special breed of human being," Aaron agreed, his hand moving down Eloise's leg. "You and the girls will be back in time for dinner with my parents?"

"Of course," Eloise said, enjoying Aaron's touch against her skin. "We'll be on the five-twenty ferry, and we'll be here by six."

"Great," he said. "The food will be delivered at six-thirty, and we'll eat soon after that."

"I'll make sure the girls are at nearly their best before we leave the inn," Eloise said.

"They're my parents," Aaron said. "They know what Billie and Grace are like. Right after their mother left, my mom came over. We were all a horrible mess, and I don't think I'd brushed poor Grace's hair for a week."

Eloise lay in bed and listened to him talk for a few more minutes, and then he stood. "I'm going to go shower, love."

"Okay." Eloise rolled over and closed her eyes, letting the soothing sound of the rainfall shower head lull her back to sleep. When Aaron came back into the bedroom to put on his shoes, she woke again.

"I love you, El," he said on his way out the door, and Eloise repeated the sentiment back to him.

A few minutes later, she got out of bed and padded down the hall in her nightgown, where she found Aaron making coffee and Billie shoving books in her backpack.

The silence in the kitchen meant they'd started this Thursday with an argument, and the way Billie looked at Eloise with such earnestness confirmed it.

"Make sure you have your math homework," Aaron said, turning and sipping from his mug.

"I've got it, Dad," Billie snapped.

Eloise wasn't sure what they'd argued about, and she swept into the kitchen to get a cup of coffee, her eyes on Aaron. "What's going on?"

"Billie wants to bring a date to our wedding," he said.

Eloise had not yet picked up a cup, a fact she was very glad of, for she'd probably have dropped it. Her eyes flew back to Billie, who cocked her hip and put one hand on it.

She'd matured a lot this year, and Eloise loved her fiercely. The protective streak she possessed for Billie didn't make sense to her, and she knew it was only stronger for Aaron.

"It's not a date, Dad."

"When you bring a boy to a wedding, it's a date," Aaron said.

"He's my friend."

"Who is it?" Eloise asked, placing both palms against the countertop. She stood next to Aaron, and she hoped they were a united front. She'd taken Billie's side several times in the past, and she didn't want to undermine Aaron with his daughter.

"It's Chris Knight."

"Chris Knight?" Eloise and Aaron asked together. "Oh, no," Aaron added, shaking his head. "I know those Knight boys. They're always in trouble, and I've heard enough of their name to last a lifetime."

"First," Billie said. "They're his half-brothers, and much older than him, Dad. He gets his own chance, doesn't he?"

"He should—"

"That's what you're *always* saying," Billie said. "Don't judge, Bills. Everyone gets their own chance."

"Billie," Aaron said, his voice soft but powerful. Eloise

glanced at him, hating that he and his daughter argued so much.

They didn't really, usually only when it came to Billie and the fact that she was growing up.

"He's just my friend," Billie said.

"I thought we liked a boy named Alex," Eloise said.

"I do," Billie said. "That's why it's not a date if Chris comes with me to the wedding. You said there'd be dancing, and we're in the same dance class. I told my teacher about the dancing at the wedding, and she said anyone who dances outside of class gets extra-credit."

She shoved another notebook in her bag and zipped it closed. "He asked if he could come, because he's not a great dancer, and he needs the extra-credit."

"So you didn't invite him," Eloise said.

"No." Billie stepped into the kitchen. "Will you braid my hair now?"

"Yes, dear, get the stuff."

Billie went to get the comb and hair ties, and Eloise got out her coffee mug. She said nothing, because Aaron needed to make this decision himself.

"I suppose the boy can come to the wedding."

"He'll probably step on her feet and cause a scene," Eloise said dryly. "They'll trip into the cake or something."

Such a thing would be a disaster, what with all the press that would be at the wedding. Eloise reminded herself that Aaron was only Five Island Cove royalty, and that literally no one outside of these five tiny islands in the middle of the sea would know about their wedding, whether someone tripped into a cake or not.

She braided Billie's hair and kissed Aaron good-bye, hurried Grace through eating and getting her shoes on, and sent the girls out the door to school.

She retrieved her phone from the bedroom, where she kept it plugged in overnight, and checked it on her way to the shower.

She had three missed calls from Robin. Shock and fear struck her as one giant lightning bolt.

No matter what, three calls from Robin before eight o'clock in the morning was not good. Eloise's fingers fumbled as she dialed her friend and wedding planner.

"Eloise, I don't want you to freak out," Robin said when she answered the phone.

"I'm already freaking out," Eloise said. "You called three times."

"There's been an accident at the dress shop," Robin said, and she sounded breathless, as if she'd run from her house to Beachfront Avenue, where the dress shop sat.

"What kind of accident?"

"Emma called," Robin said. "I haven't seen the dress yet, but El..." She blew out her breath. "I'm on the way right now, and I'll let you know. I just wanted you to be prepared."

"What happened?" Eloise asked again. "Just tell me, Robin. Then I can be prepared for what I might find."

The dress had taken the longest for her to find and

tailor. She had a love-hate relationship with it as it was, but in the end, she truly did love the dress, and she felt strong and sexy in it at the same time. She knew Aaron would love it, and Eloise felt the first hot tears enter her eyes as she waited for Robin to explain further.

"There was a burst pipe," Robin said, sighing again. "Overnight. It apparently gushed for hours, and some of their dresses got wet."

"No," Eloise gasped.

"I don't even know if one of them was yours," Robin said. "And things dry out, El."

"I'll change and meet you there," Eloise said. She could reschedule her call, as she understood the nature of emergencies better than most.

"Okay," Robin agreed readily. "I'm leaving now."

––––––––

ELOISE CLUTCHED HER PURSE, AS IF THE TIGHTNESS IN her knuckles would keep all of her emotions in check. Before she'd returned to the cove only a short nine months ago, Eloise had lived a fairly mundane life. She taught college students about biology, and she'd enjoyed it. Her life had been predictable, and she'd never gotten calls like the kind she'd had with Robin a half-hour ago.

She hadn't dared to call Aaron, because she couldn't stand the thought of postponing the wedding. They'd been waiting long enough as it was. Absolutely everything was in place, and Eloise just wanted to walk down the aisle and pledge herself to Aaron.

She'd packed everything in her tiny house on Sanctuary. All she needed to do was move it, something she and Aaron were planning to do after their honeymoon. He'd taken time off work, a feat not easily achieved for the Chief of Police.

"Looks like the street is closed, ma'am," the RideShare driver said.

Eloise pulled her attention from the side window where she'd been looking and toward his voice. He peered through the windshield. "I think this is as far as I can get you."

"Here is great," Eloise said, her voice steady and strong. She was not going to break down over this. It was a dress, not her health. Aaron hadn't abandoned her at the altar. Everything else would still be flawless. "Thank you." She swiped her payment card and got out of the car.

In front of her, the street had been closed, and a pair of police officers worked the scene, along with five or six people dressed in dark blue polo shirts with the Five Island Cove utility logo on them.

"Ma'am," someone said as she took her first step down the sidewalk. "You can't come this way. It's closed."

"My dress," she said, glancing around for Robin. If she couldn't get down the street, maybe Robin couldn't either. "I got a call from Judy's Bridal about my dress."

"They're down on the other end of the street," he said.

"Okay," Eloise said. "I can go around?" She could walk a block over and then down.

"Eloise?"

She turned toward the sound of a familiar voice. "Paul," she said. "The dress shop called about my dress."

He wore a sympathetic look as he approached. "I'll take you." He nodded to the utility worker. "She's okay. I'll get her down there." He reached for her, and Eloise let him put his arm around her.

"How bad is it?" she asked as they navigated past the yellow caution tape. The left side of the street had been dug into, and Eloise wished the smell didn't remind her of the sewer. An image of her dirty and stained dress flashed through her mind, but she quickly pushed it away.

"They've called the mainland for new pipes," Paul said. "This street is going to be shut down for at least two days."

"Mm." Eloise didn't own any of the shops here, but going into a weekend with good weather, she wouldn't be happy to be shut down.

"Watch your step here," Paul said, taking her onto a board that went over the hollowed-out street.

She followed him carefully, watching where she put her feet until she stepped back onto cement. Paul delivered her to the end of the street and past another barrier keeping people out. Eloise spotted the white tent where a few women had crowded, and in the next moment, she saw Robin.

"Thank you, Paul," she said, pausing to look up at him. She put her hand on his arm. "Please...don't tell Aaron anything. I'll talk to him as soon as I know what's going on."

Paul looked from the tent where dresses hung on portable racks to her. "Good luck, Eloise." He bent down and hugged her, and Eloise clung to him a little bit.

She cleared her throat as she stepped away, and Robin took the last two steps to her. She grabbed her in a hug and said, "Come see. It's not so bad."

"Really?" Eloise asked as she started walking with Robin. They arrived at the tent, where Eloise picked out her dress instantly. "Not so bad?" She took in the once-white lace that now held a shade of gray no one wanted on their wedding dress.

There was no way that would come clean. The strongest bleach couldn't take out sludge.

The bottom of the dress looked like someone had dipped it into a vat of dye the color of mud, and it seeped up the skirt until it finally petered out. Only the middle of the dress—from about the knees to the wide sash around her waist and into a few inches of the lace that covered the bodice—remained clean.

She reached out and touched the wide straps that went over her shoulders. They too had the look like someone had dropped gray ashes on them and then rubbed them into the fabric.

"This is terrible. There's no way I can get this cleaned."

"Yes," Robin said, hooking her arm through Eloise's. "We can. I've already called Mike, and he's waiting for us." She tightened her hold on Eloise's arm. "It's just mud. He can clean it."

"This isn't mud," Eloise said, drawing back her fingers from the sooty substance. "What *is* that?"

"It's debris from the ceiling," Robin said in a miserable voice. "Mike is a miracle worker, El. Let's get this over to him." She released Eloise's arm and picked up the dress. "I've got my van."

She seemed so positive and so sure, and Eloise grabbed onto her optimism as she went with Robin. That was all she could do. Oh, and pray. She could do that too, and Eloise kept up a stream of pleading as Robin put the ruined wedding dress in the back of her van.

"Do we have a back-up plan?" Eloise asked as she got in the passenger seat.

Robin looked at Eloise, pure nerves in her expression. "Let's go shopping as soon as the stores open," she said. "Just in case."

TWO

Alice Kelton bent to take the pizza out of the oven just as the front door opened. It would be Laurel, the female cop that had joined their friend group last summer. Alice had really taken a liking to her, and she found herself fiercely protective of the other woman. She thought her former abusive relationship had something to do with that, as Alice had come to view her marriage with Frank as abusive too.

In some ways, Alice was so much better off without Frank. She'd regained her confidence and control over her life, and she liked that. In other ways, though, she had quiet moments of loneliness, despite being surrounded by people she loved and who loved her.

"It's just me," Laurel called, the door closing a moment after she finished speaking. "Smells good in here." The dark-haired woman appeared from the hallway, dressed in her police officer uniform and wearing a smile.

"It's just boxed pizza," Alice said, returning her smile.

"It's better than a protein shake." Laurel sat at the bar, a long sigh coming from her mouth.

Alice watched her, her mind moving through several scenarios.

"I know that look," Laurel said, reaching for a can of soda. "Just spit it out, Alice."

"When are you going to set a date?" she said.

The *pop-hiss!* sound of Laurel's can opening filled the air, and then her eyes widened. "You didn't check your phone." She looked around as if Alice's phone would be right there, blinking that she had a message.

Alice had left it in the bedroom, because she'd used it as an alarm for when Arthur had to leave. Her face filled with heat though she tried to keep it cool. "Not for a while," she admitted. "Did you set a date?"

"September eighth," Laurel said, her face falling slightly. "It's later than I'd like, but we'll basically be taking the whole force for the wedding. And if we wait until after Labor Day, things will be quiet here in the cove, and Aaron said we could each have two weeks off."

"Wow," Alice said. "Two weeks."

"Yeah," Laurel said. "It's almost five months, but it's okay."

Alice nodded in agreement. "Are you going to move in with him before the wedding?" She turned to get out the pizza cutter. If she could keep Laurel talking about Paul and their upcoming nuptials, then Alice wouldn't have to talk about Arthur. She couldn't believe she'd kept their relationship as much of a secret as she had.

Robin asked the most questions, of course. Every time she'd asked over the past two weeks, Alice had been able to put her off with a simple, "Yes, I'm still seeing him."

It had only been three weeks, though she supposed she hadn't dated Will for much longer than that.

"No," Laurel said. "My mother would be mortified." She grinned as she tipped her head back to drink from her soda can. "What about you?" She set the can on the counter. "Things going well with Arthur?"

Alice kept her gaze on the pizza as she cut across it. "Yeah," she said, not able to hide her smile. With Laurel, she didn't have to hide as much. The woman could be very discreet, and Alice liked that. She herself wasn't great with secrets, and she thought maybe she could just tell Laurel about Arthur.

No, she thought. *Keep it to yourself a little longer.*

"Things are going well," she said. "I mean, it's been three weeks, but yeah. Good." She shrugged and finished cutting the pizza. She got out a couple of paper plates and handed one to Laurel.

"What about Charlie?" Laurel asked.

"That boy," Alice said, shaking her head and seizing the safe topic. "He's going to be the death of me."

"Why's that?" Laurel rose up onto her feet to get a

couple pieces of pizza, and Alice sat down next to her at the bar.

"He's already kissing Sariah. I caught them last night on my own front porch."

"He *is* a cute boy."

"Yeah, who broke up with a different girl only two weeks ago. If that." Alice wasn't sure how many days it had been. Maybe only ten or so. No matter what, it felt fast to her. She hadn't breathed a word of it to Robin, as it was her daughter Charlie had broken up with after almost a year of dating.

"He'll figure things out," Laurel said.

"I hope so," Alice said. "I talk to him until I'm blue in the face. I'm not sure it's getting through."

"I think it does more than you think." Laurel offered her a supportive smile, and Alice did appreciate that.

"September eighth," Alice said, lifting her pizza to her mouth. "What are you thinking? Beach? Indoors? What kind of dress?"

Laurel started to talk, and Alice simply listened to her detail her first planning session with Robin and how they'd already started looking for dresses online. "I'm not very feminine," Laurel said. "So I don't know about the dress. I honestly just want to wear a skirt with my police uniform."

"Then do that," Alice said. "Will Paul wear his dress uniform?"

"I think so," she said. "I just mentioned it to him last

night, but we got interrupted before we could talk too much about it."

Alice nodded as if she understood interruptions. In a lot of ways, she did. She could have her whole day planned, only to have everything implode by ten a.m. Nothing on her to-do list would get gone, and the hours slipped through her fingers like smoke.

"So..." Laurel said, and the hair on Alice's arms stood up. "Tell me about Robin and her mother."

Alice looked at Laurel, searching her face. "Why? What happened?" Her protective streak kicked in, because Jennifer Golden had a special way of making Robin feel two feet tall and completely insignificant. Robin had been fighting with her for decades, and Alice knew how hard she'd been trying to build a bridge between them.

Her mom didn't make it easy, that was for sure.

"Her mom arrived during our session a few nights ago, and they got in a little fight."

Alice waited for Laurel to say more, but she remained silent. "What did Robin say?"

"Nothing," Laurel said. "I waved to her and slipped out while they were arguing. I haven't spoken to her since. I mean, a text here or there about the wedding."

If Robin hadn't said anything, Alice didn't want to betray her confidence. "They've never gotten along," Alice said, trying to find the surface details that would explain but not betray her friend. "They fought like crazy when we were teens, and Robin's been trying to prove she's good enough for her mother for her entire life."

"She's literally one of the best people I know," Laurel said, her eyes wide.

"I know," Alice said. "You won't find someone who cares more."

"She knows everyone on the island, and she knows all the best deals. She's so organized."

"She's pretty, she's thin, she's been married to the same man for almost twenty years." Alice shook her head. "Nothing is ever good enough for her mom. I know Robin tries, but I think she just gets tired."

Laurel nodded and dusted her hands together, her pizza gone. "I was just wondering. She's never said much about her family—her parents and siblings."

Alice wasn't surprised by that at all. She drew in a deep breath. "I can't wait for Eloise's wedding. I think they're finalizing the fruit platter today, and then everything is set."

Laurel's eyes widened again. "Didn't you hear? Eloise might postpone. You really need to look at your phone."

Alice sucked in a breath, her heart positively stopping. "What? Postpone? Why?" She got to her feet and started toward her bedroom, her heartbeat flying through her veins.

"Her dress got ruined," Laurel called after her, and Alice cried out.

"You're kidding." She swiped her phone from the

nightstand and saw all the missed messages in the group text. "Eighty-four messages. My word." She tapped and started reading, unable to get a proper breath.

Laurel had announced her wedding day. The others had congratulated her and said they'd mark their calendars.

Robin had gotten on and said they'd had a "slight problem" at the dress shop, but that she and Eloise had taken the dress to a cleaner. AJ and Kristen had asked the most questions, and Robin fielded them all, not Eloise.

The truth was, they didn't know if the dress would come clean. They were shopping for alternatives that day, and Alice didn't have to imagine the anxiety Eloise must be feeling. It ran through her right now.

Eloise had then said, *I might push things back. I need a dress to get married in.*

Everyone had gotten on and expressed support and concern for her. Everyone except Alice, of course.

The string had gone quiet after that, and Alice cursed herself for putting her phone on silent while she made love with Arthur. The truth was, though, the phone distracted her when it went off during the brief time Arthur had in the middle of the day. She'd learned to put it on silent so they could enjoy one another, and she'd never missed much.

Until today.

She typed out a quick message of congrats for Laurel, though the woman sat in the kitchen, and then one of sympathy for Eloise, asking, *What can I do to help? I knew a woman in the Hamptons who could get the most gorgeous dresses. Maybe she could help?*

She stepped back into the kitchen, noting that Arthur had also texted since he'd left her house.

"You got it?" Laurel asked. She drained the last of her soda and met Alice's eyes.

"Yes," she said. "She can't postpone. The press will go crazy."

"Not to mention the Chief has everything set so he can be gone." Laurel wore a look of sympathy. "I don't think she'll actually postpone. She probably just feels like she needs to."

Her phone chimed, and she looked at it. "Oh, it's you."

Alice nodded as she sat back down, Arthur's message shining in her face. *I miss you already. Dinner tonight? My place after that?*

Alice only had two words for that—*yes, and yes*—and she sent them while Laurel said something about Kelli's wellness center.

"Okay," she said a moment later. "I better get going. I can see you've got someone better to talk to."

Alice lifted her head, surprised and embarrassed at what Laurel had said. "No," she said. "You don't have to go."

"Yeah, I can tell it's Arthur," Laurel said, grinning. She clearly wasn't upset. "You're glowing."

Alice's face heated again. "I am not."

"You are," Laurel said, laughing. She stood and leaned over Alice's shoulder, clearly looking at her phone. "Oh, and making plans for tonight, I see."

A message popped up, and Alice gasped as she read it. Laurel did too.

She practically threw her phone across the kitchen, really only managing to toss it a foot or so, where it slid toward the opposite edge of the counter.

"My goodness," Laurel said, sitting right back down. The barstool moved as she did, creating a terrible noise against the floor. "Alice...?" Her name was full of questions, but Alice didn't know how to answer any of them.

Arthur's message burned her retinas and she'd never get rid of the words. *I know it's fast, but I'm thinking about marriage. Can we talk about that tonight?*

Seconds ticked by, each painfully loud in Alice's ears.

"What are you going to say?" Laurel asked, her voice finally breaking the silence.

Her phone chimed, and Alice's eyes flew to it.

Slowly, as if encased in quicksand, Laurel reached for it. Alice wanted to shout at her not to read the texts—especially not the ones Arthur had sent before he'd come over that morning. She deleted his texts several times each day, because her children picked up her phone at will, and she didn't need them to see anything that would indicate her physical relationship with their school counselor.

"Oh, my," Laurel said, breathing out heavily. She put

the phone in front of Alice, who couldn't help looking at the text.

We can eat that seafood scampi from The Bridge and just talk about it. Then I'll do that thing you like at the edge of the bed.

Alice pressed her eyes closed, her whole body hot. She definitely liked the things Arthur did in the bedroom. He was an excellent lover, and Alice wasn't embarrassed of a consensual, adult relationship with him. She enjoyed talking to him, and she enjoyed kissing him.

"How long have you been sleeping with him?" Laurel asked.

"I don't think that's the most important question," Alice said, her voice hoarse.

"No?" Laurel asked. "What is then?"

She looked at Laurel, pure shock moving through her. "Who wants to talk about marriage after three weeks of dating?"

Her phone chimed again, and she and Laurel both bent over it.

You've gone silent, which means you don't want to talk about marriage. It's just a conversation, Alice. Nothing too serious.

"Nothing too serious," she repeated. "Isn't marriage serious?"

"Just tell him that," Laurel said. "Maybe you do want to talk about marriage though."

Alice swallowed, because she wasn't sure. "I haven't even been divorced for a year," she said.

"Well, you could be the fourth wedding this summer," Laurel said with a smile. "Might have to fight Kelli for the spot though. She and Shad seem to be getting pretty serious too."

"Is there a limit on the number of weddings we can have this summer?" Alice teased, flipping her phone over so whatever Arthur said next would stay secret for a few extra seconds. "And you can't even breathe a word of this to anyone else."

"I wouldn't dare," Laurel said, smiling. "And I think the limit is four. Four weddings, Alice. So if you want that spot..." She let her words hang there, though she was clearly teasing. She got to her feet and gave Alice a side-hug. "I have to jet. Duty calls."

She started for the front door, calling over her shoulder, "And answer that man. He's dying."

Alice picked up her phone the moment Laurel closed the front door behind her and re-read all of Arthur's messages.

Her fingers hovered over the screen while her mind whirred and whirred. Finally, she typed, *We can talk about marriage...if there's plenty of shrimp scampi AND that carrot cake from Shirley's.*

She grinned at her message, her smile widening at Arthur's response that came in a few second later.

Carrot cake ordered.

Alice pressed her phone to her heart, letting the fantasy of her own summer beach wedding run through her mind. Could she really marry Arthur Rice so soon?

Don't be ridiculous, part of her mind told her, while the other half thought, *Why not?*

"Mom?" Charlie called, and Alice hastened to delete the messages from Arthur as her son's footsteps came closer. "There you are," he said, stepping past her and taking a piece of pizza. "Is it okay if I go over to Sariah's after work? You never answered me."

He wore eagerness and hope on his face, and Alice didn't have the heart to tell him no. "You be safe with that girl," she said.

"I am, Mom," he said, grinning at her. He grabbed onto her and hugged her. "I won't be late since it's a school night."

"I'm going out with Arthur tonight," she said. "I won't be late either. Ten for both of us."

"Okay," Charlie said, hurrying back the way he'd come. "Love you, Mom."

"Love you too," she called, and her fantasy warped and disappeared when she thought about how she could possibly tell her twins that she might marry their counselor.

THREE

Robin Grover was not the type of woman to give up without a fight. She checked her phone, though she had the ringer set on high, and it had not made a sound in over thirty minutes. A couple of cushy armchairs sat in front of the wide wall of dressing rooms at Castle Bridal, but Robin couldn't commit to sitting down.

Energy ran through her body as if someone had connected her to a live wire, and she simply needed to stay on her feet. Eloise had gone into one of the dressing rooms with an attendant with a waist no bigger than a toothpick, and Robin worried as much about that as she did about making sure Eloise had the perfect dress to wear as she walked down the aisle.

They'd already spent hours finding that dress, trying on that dress, and altering that dress. It felt like such a huge setback to be doing it all over again.

She checked her phone, her pulse pounding when she still didn't have a text from Mike or Georgia, the only other dressmaker in the Cove that Robin trusted to make wedding dresses. Sometimes Georgia had rentals that worked well for last-minute nuptials, and Robin had already spoken to her twice that morning.

Her phone dinged, and Robin nearly dropped it she lifted it so quickly. Alice had finally texted *What can I do to help? I knew a woman in the Hamptons who could get the most gorgeous dresses. Maybe she could help?*

Robin tapped to call her, because she would take any help she could get. It was an hour flight to the Hamptons, and she'd make it herself to get Eloise the right dress. Before she could get the call off, the dressing room door opened, and Eloise stepped out.

Robin shoved her phone in her back pocket and stepped around the plush chairs, trying to see everything at once. Such a feat was impossible, but Robin sure did try harder than anyone.

The sleeves made her frown, but Robin straightened it as quickly as she could. Sleeves could be replaced. She could cut them off herself and sew under the raw edge. She would, too, if it meant Eloise had the perfect dress for her big day.

The dress didn't gape around her bust, which made Robin smile. The shiny, white fabric spoke a little bit of the eighties, and five months ago, Robin would've vetoed this dress on that fabric alone. It would cause a glare in the photos, but at this point, she couldn't be too terribly picky.

The bodice clung to Eloise's midsection, and a wide sash went around the waist. So far, so good. The skirt flared from there, dropping to the ground in layers and layers of fabric, lace on the lower half of the dress that made it look unique and expensive.

It probably would cost a pretty penny, but Eloise hadn't mentioned a budget for this impromptu and emergency shopping situation.

"What do you think?" Robin asked.

"I hate the sleeves," Eloise said.

"I can fix the sleeves."

"We can take them off too," the toothpick-sized attendant said. Robin glanced at her and took in her name. Sabrina.

"How quickly?" Robin asked.

"They're made to come on and off," Sabrina said, stepping over to Eloise and tugging on the sleeves. "We've rented this dress out before, and I know the last girl had us put them on." She twisted the fabric under as Robin caught El's frown of displeasure.

"You can rent this dress?" Robin asked, meeting Eloise's eye. Sudden understanding filled her friend's eyes, and she turned back to the mirrors that spanned the whole wall.

"I do like the lace on the bottom," she said. "It makes it look very fancy."

"It's different," Robin agreed, because she knew Eloise wanted a unique dress. She didn't want something everyone and their sister had worn.

"Yes, you can rent this," Sabrina said. "It's three hundred dollars for the day."

"That's all?" Robin asked, surprised. Why was she having her brides buy wedding dresses from Judy's when they could rent from here?

"We have rentals from one-ninety-nine to nine-ninety-nine," Sabrina said. "I've got a fabulous Jennifer Pennace for six hundred."

"The Pennace's don't look good on me," Eloise said. "She puts way too much frilly fabric around the waist. That's already the thickest part of me." She smoothed her hands down the front of her body, and Robin thought the thick fabric did a nice job of covering up the parts of Eloise's body she didn't like.

"The train is pretty long," Robin said, bending to pick it up. "Did you see that, El?"

"I did," she said. "It's not a deal-breaker, right?"

"No," Robin said. "I just want to make sure we're not taking the first one just because we can."

"Did you see Alice's text?" Eloise asked, meeting Robin's eyes in the mirror.

"I was going to call her."

"I don't know if we need to," Eloise said. "I could wear this—if the sleeves were removed and a nice, wide strap held the dress up."

"We have two more to try on too," Sabrina said, her eyes wide and eager to help. "But definitely. The straps aren't a problem. When is the wedding?"

"Sunday," Eloise said.

"This Sunday?" Sabrina said, actually pressing one palm to her heart.

"Yes," Robin said. "I'm surprised you don't have more women in here. Judy's had a burst pipe, and several dresses got...dirty."

"Ruined," Eloise said almost over the top of her.

"No," Robin said. "We're getting the dress cleaned, but we wanted a back-up plan."

Sabrina's mouth dropped open, and she said, "You're kidding."

"Not kidding," Robin said. "If you can't alter the sleeves by Saturday, I'll take it and do it myself."

"Let's try the other two dresses," Eloise said. "Maybe I'll like one of them more, and it won't be a problem." She swished into the dressing room, holding up the skirt in double fistfuls of fabric.

Robin watched her go, admiring her resilience and optimism. Eloise had always been steady and strong in the face of disaster, and Robin finally sank into the armchair and let it swallow her whole, letting her mind drift back to the day she and Eloise had gone to the high school to take the ACT.

Robin had just gotten her driver's license, and she'd picked up Eloise at the ferry station and driven them to the test. Eloise had finished way before Robin, and by the time Robin had come out, she'd been in a huge hurry to leave.

Her mother's unreasonableness stretched back decades, and she wanted Robin to have the car back by one o'clock. In her hurry to get out of the parking lot and get home before her mother's deadline, she'd cut the corner too close as she'd backed out. The entire passenger side of the car had scraped along the bumper of a truck, and Robin had slammed on the brakes and then frozen.

Eloise had not. She'd known exactly what to do, and she got out of the car and wrote down the license plate number of the truck. They'd had to wait until the owner of it came outside, and Robin had been mortified to face Jeremy Simpson.

Of course she'd had to hit the most popular boy's truck. *Of course.*

And she'd been late, and her mother hadn't let her drive the car again for another six months. She had a way of taking things too far, of overcorrecting in a ridiculous way.

Eloise had been level-headed and smart. She'd taken down all the information, and she'd remained optimistic that everything would work out. At age sixteen, Robin didn't have quite the long-range perspective she did now and hitting that truck had felt like the end of the world.

She was sure Eloise felt like that right now. She'd been waiting for this wedding for her entire life, and Robin's resolve that she would have absolutely everything she wanted hardened.

The door opened again, and Eloise didn't even commit to coming all the way out into the viewing area. "This is a no."

Robin tried to get out of the chair and couldn't quite manage it. She said, "Oof," and fell back, giving up. "No," she said, taking in the form-fitting mermaid dress. "That's not for you."

"Let me just try the Pennace," Sabrina said, squeezing out behind Eloise. "You go in and start unzipping that one. I'll be right back." She hustled off, and Robin met Eloise's eyes.

"I don't mind that other one," Eloise said.

"Yes, but we don't want a dress we don't mind," Robin said. Using both hands, she pushed herself out of the chair. "I'm going to call Mike, just to see how he's feeling."

"It's not bad."

"El, honey, the fabric is from the eighties," she said. "And everyone and their dog has worn it." Both things weren't deal-breakers, but Robin wasn't going to give in too easily.

She ignored the list of things she needed to do that day. There was nothing that required her attention more than this, as her next wedding wasn't for two more weeks after Eloise's. Whatever she'd had on her list for today after Eloise's dress pick-up and fruit platter selection could wait.

With a start, Robin realized she needed to call Betty about the platter too. She watched Sabrina hustle back into the dressing room, a gorgeous dress in her arms, and Robin did her best to estimate how much longer they'd be there.

Probably at least an hour. She'd call Betty first to set up a new time to pick the fruit, and then she'd call Mike. As she dialed, she ignored the quaking in her stomach. *Things will work out,* she told herself. *Things will work out. They will.*

If they didn't, Robin didn't have a Plan C.

FOUR

"I'm fine," AJ Proctor said as her fiancé gave her a cocked-eyebrow look. "Eloise needs help choosing a dress."

"I'll drive you," Matt Hymas said, getting to his feet.

"Alice is going to come get me." AJ started toward the kitchen to put her teacup in the sink. Matt followed her, his hand on her hip the moment she arrived at the counter-top. A small smile touched her face, and she leaned into his palm.

"How are you feeling?" he asked, ducking his head closer to her neck. "I'm worried about you. You got up really early."

"I couldn't get my legs to settle down." AJ turned in his arms and slid her hands up his chest. "I laid on the couch and fell back asleep for a little bit."

He pushed her hair back and studied her face. AJ

hated what he might find, because she couldn't erase her exhaustion. At the same time, she couldn't stay home this time. She felt completely isolated from her friends, though each and every one of them had been by the house to see her in the past couple of weeks.

Kelli came almost every day, and AJ had finally told her she didn't need to do that. AJ still felt like she'd done something wrong, but she hadn't.

Something bitter touched her tongue, and AJ swallowed against it. "I'd really like to go. The moment I start to feel overwhelmed or like I need a nap, I'll make Alice bring me back."

"Okay," Matt said. "Remember, I'm going to the airport on Sunday right after the wedding to get Justin."

"Yes," AJ said. "I'll get a ride home with Kristen. It's all worked out." Matt and his son might beat her back here to the house, and AJ would be lying if she said she wasn't nervous to start meeting Matt's kids.

Justin, his youngest, was coming first. He'd be here about two weeks before Lisa would show up, and all four of them would be living in Matt's three-bedroom house. Trepidation like AJ had never known flowed through her every time she thought about it.

Matt's other son, Derrick, had plans for a summer visit, but dates hadn't been set yet, and plans were still liquid.

The doorbell rang, and the pair of them turned toward the front door. "I'll get it," Matt said.

"You don't need to lecture her," AJ said, but she let him go. Matt would just murmur to Alice that she'd gotten up too early, and he was worried about her. He'd tell Alice to call him if he needed to come get AJ, and she took a moment to wash her hands before she turned toward the dark-haired woman she'd known for practically her whole life.

"You ready, AJ?" Alice asked, smiling at her as if everything was normal.

"Yes," AJ said, beyond grateful that Alice hadn't asked her how she felt. She was so tired of answering that question. She still had three and a half months before she'd deliver her baby, and now that she'd been on bedrest for the past month, her energy was starting to improve.

She had another doctor's appointment next week, and she was hoping to get cleared off of bedrest. She hadn't had a single spot of blood in weeks, and her boredom was leading her toward a complete mental breakdown.

"Let me grab my phone," AJ said, detouring toward the office. Matt had gone in there, and he met her at the door, her phone in his hand.

"Call me if you need me to come get you," he said.

"I'm sure Alice will bring me back," she said, leaning forward to kiss him. A quick peck, and AJ followed Alice toward the front door. Out on the porch, she linked her arm through Alice's and said, "He told you the same thing, right?"

"He's sweet," Alice said kindly. "He's worried about you and his baby."

"Yeah." AJ sighed as she reached the ground.

"You don't think he is?"

"I think he is," AJ said. "I'm just...worried all we're ever going to talk about again is how I'm feeling."

Alice pealed out a round of laughter that made AJ's heart take flight. "It feels like that, doesn't it?" She escorted AJ all the way to the passenger seat. "When I was pregnant with the twins, I was huge. Like, as-big-as-your-house huge. I couldn't go anywhere or do anything without every single human being I came in contact with asking me if I was okay." She laughed again and shook her head. "I'd get so many questions—how many babies are you going to have? Are you sure there's just two in there? Why are you out of the house? You should be in the hospital!"

AJ opened the door and eased into the passenger seat. Alice closed the door behind her and went to get behind the wheel. "I promise, AJ, I will not ask you how you're feeling."

"I noticed you didn't," AJ said. "And I appreciate that." She buckled her seatbelt, making sure it was low under her belly. "I've had so many sports injuries, and all of them were worse than this. No one ever cared how I was feeling then."

"You do want to make sure the baby's healthy," Alice said.

"Of course," AJ said, leaning her head back and

closing her eyes. *Of course* echoed in her head. Alice might've said something else, but AJ wasn't sure. Everything softened, and the next thing she knew, Alice nudged her and said, "We're here, AJ."

She opened her eyes with some effort, realizing she'd fallen asleep. "Sorry," she said, feeling a bit out of it. Her head swam, and she tried to focus through the windshield to the car in front of her.

It took ten minutes to drive from Matt's to Aaron's, and AJ couldn't believe she'd fallen asleep so fast. "My restless legs have kept me up the past few nights," she explained to Alice, though she hadn't asked. "I guess I'm just like a baby. Put me in a car and drive me somewhere, and I'm out like a light."

She smiled at Alice, who gave her a brilliant smile in return. "You sure you want to be here? I can actually drive you around Diamond while you sleep. I've got time."

"No," AJ said firmly. "I want to be here. I've missed so much this month already."

"Amelia's been coming and bringing the kids, hasn't she?" Alice asked, reaching for her purse. She opened her door and got out.

AJ copied her, stretching her back once she'd gotten to her feet. "Yes," she said. "I love it when she and the girls come. They break up the monotony of looking for another job, chasing down another lead, or writing another article."

"How was it going back to the freelance?" Alice met

her at the front of the car and hooked her arm through AJ's again.

"Good," AJ said in a somewhat false voice. She didn't have the same passion for sports journalism as she once had. She couldn't remember a time when sports didn't dominate her life. If she wasn't playing them, she was training to. If she wasn't doing that, she was watching them on TV.

She used to record the games she really wanted to watch, then wait for her father to drink himself to sleep, and watch the matches in the middle of the night.

In college, she'd played soccer and volleyball. She'd written about sports. She'd graduated and gone into broadcasting. She'd interviewed hundreds of professional athletes, and dated quite a few too.

It was all sports, all the time, and AJ was actually sick of it.

"Yeah," Alice said. "Sounds really good." She gave AJ a look that she ignored, and the went up the steps to the house. Alice didn't ring the bell or knock, and when they walked in, a dog barked once before trotting over to them.

AJ adored animals, and she bent down to pat the beast's head. "Hey, you," she said, as she didn't know the dog's name.

"Prince," Aaron said, barking in his own way. "Come on. Leave the ladies alone." He smiled at Alice and AJ as he approached. "She's in the bedroom, and I'm banned from even taking a step down the hall, so you'll have to find it yourself."

He grabbed Prince's collar and hauled him backward so Alice and AJ could get by.

"Thanks," AJ said. She walked through the kitchen, noting the absence of dinner plates on the table. A backpack sat there, with a math book open beside it, but whoever had been doing the homework wasn't around.

Alice led the way down the hall, and she did knock on this door before entering the room. AJ filed in last, and she was the very last to arrive. Eloise had brought in dining room chairs, and Robin jumped to her feet.

"AJ," she said. "Come sit here."

AJ would've normally hated taking Robin's seat, but she moved over to the chair without protest. Kelli reached over and took her hand, and AJ squeezed her fingers in hello.

"Hello, dear," Kristen said from the next chair over, and AJ smiled at her too. Laurel sat in the last chair, and Alice piled onto the bed with Aaron's girls, Billie and Grace. Robin stayed on her feet, her thumb in her mouth as she chewed the nail.

"We're all here, El," she called, and the tension in the room went through the roof.

"Did you give them the spiel?" Eloise called back, the door remaining stubbornly closed.

"No, just a sec." Robin strode toward the closed bathroom door and faced the group. "Okay, so we found a couple of replacement dresses today. Mike still thinks he can get the original dress clean, and we stopped by and saw the dress this afternoon." She surveyed the group, her expression very serious. "I personally think it's going to be fine, and she'll get to wear the original dress. But to be safe, we got these two. They're both rentals, and they both—"

She cut off as if someone had muted her. "Eloise just wants to model them both and then we'll vote. She doesn't want comments or lists of what you like and don't like. She'll tell you how she'll alter them, if she's going to. We have to decide tonight and get the alterations done tomorrow, and Mike said he'd call me the moment the dress comes out of the solution he's tried on it tonight."

"They're still open tonight?" Kristen asked. "It's six-thirty."

"He's staying late to work on the dress." Robin looked like she might throw up, and AJ felt bad for her. Being a wedding planner had to be such hard work. She didn't get do-overs. If something didn't go right, that was part of that couple's big day forever.

She'd been working like a dog on AJ and Matt's wedding, and AJ knew the details that Robin paid attention to. There was no stone unturned. No question unasked. No deal not gotten. She was very, very good at her job, and AJ knew she needed to hear it more often.

"Robin," she said, and everyone looked at her. "It's going to be so amazing. You've done so much work on this wedding, and every little detail is going to come together."

"AJ's right," Alice said. "Eloise is going to look amazing no matter what, and you really have worked magic with this wedding."

A soft smile touched Robin's face, and she said, "Thank you," in the quietest voice AJ had ever heard her use. She was so full of life, with such a rah-rah attitude about everything. She'd cheered in high school, and her enthusiasm had been—and still was—contagious.

"Okay, El," she called through the door, and then Robin actually perched on the corner of the bed to watch the fashion show.

AJ's pulse skipped a beat as she waited for Eloise to exit the bathroom and show them the dress. Finally, the door opened, and Eloise came through the door, her very full skirt bunching on the sides before it made it through.

AJ loved big, flowing, prom-style dresses, and her wedding dress was very much like that. Huge puffy sleeves with a scooping neckline to show off the best parts of her body. The fabric clung to her torso and then, from the waist down, billowed in waves and waves of fabric to the floor.

This dress wasn't quite that full and majestic, but the feathers on the bottom were stunning. AJ pulled in a breath and wondered why they hadn't bought this dress to begin with.

"I hate the sleeves on this one," Eloise said. "But they can take them off and have simple, wide straps." She turned around to show off the long train in the back, and then she headed back into the bathroom.

"That was pretty," Kelli said, and AJ smiled at her.

"I agree. Hey, whatever happened with you the other night? You said you'd call me when you two got back to Pearl, but I never heard from you."

Kelli and Shad had come to dinner at AJ and Matt's, and after a great dinner Matt had picked up at Morty's, they'd sat on the back deck with coffee and wine. AJ had sipped water, because coffee made the baby kick her all night, and she obviously couldn't drink wine.

Kelli had told her that Shad had mentioned taking a trip together, because his parents were getting older, and he always went to visit them in the summertime. They lived on Long Island, and he'd suggested he and Kelli could go for a few days, especially since she wasn't tied to a job here—or wouldn't be come tomorrow, which was her last day at the school.

She hadn't been sure she could take a trip with Shad. She'd worried about Parker, and AJ had assured her she could go with Shad, and that any number of people would watch Parker while she was gone. So they wouldn't be whispering among themselves, Kelli had said she'd call when she got home.

She hadn't.

"Oh, uh, I don't know," Kelli said. "I guess I forgot."

Her very best friend in the whole world wouldn't look at her, and AJ's stomach dropped. Not because of anything to do with the baby, but because she was fairly sure Kelli had just lied to her.

"You forgot?" she asked, but Eloise opened the door and said, "I need some help in here."

Robin jumped to her feet, and AJ watched as Kelli turned slightly toward Kristen and asked her if Rueben still went out to The Claw.

AJ pulled her hand away from Kelli, stung and a bit unsure as to why Kelli didn't want to talk to her now. *Perhaps she doesn't want to say anything in front of so many people,* AJ thought. She looked at Kelli, and she sure seemed normal.

Perhaps AJ was reading too much into things. Maybe she just needed to come right out and ask if he she'd decided to take the trip with Shad or not. Determined to do that before she went home that night, AJ let Kelli put her off for now, and she simply waited for Eloise to come out in the second wedding dress.

FIVE

Laurel Baker frowned at her phone, her fingers flying across the screen. *That can't be right,* she said, knowing she needed to put her device away and have this conversation another time. If she carried on for too much longer, Alice would notice and want the details. Robin sat only a few feet from her, and that woman didn't miss much of anything.

I'll call you when I'm done here. She sent both texts and looked up just as Eloise stepped out of the bathroom again. Her heart pounded in her chest the way it had when she'd been in her terrible relationship and subsequent bad marriage.

Her anxiety had started high tonight, because Laurel still had a lot of nerves about getting married. She glanced down at the diamond engagement ring on her had, completely distracted from the ooh-ing and ahh-ing going on around her.

She forced herself out of her mind, telling herself she *wanted* to marry Paul, and that she could deal with her troubling case later. She didn't have to take the job with her everywhere she went.

This dress had real charm, as it showed off Eloise's bare shoulders and lifted her chest in a way the other one didn't. The fabric wasn't quite as shiny either, but a softer version of the bright white—almost yellow—of the other dress.

It looked almost gauzy and lightweight as it flowed over Eloise's body. A bright blue sash went around her waist, bunching up some fabric that spilled upward in an elegant arc, and sending the rest to the floor in wavy layers of fabric, almost like the effect of a waterfall frozen in motion.

Everyone clearly liked this dress more; Laurel did, and by the glow on Eloise's face, she did too.

"Okay," Robin said, standing up, and Laurel hoped this get-together would end soon. With it being a school night and all, surely all the moms in the group would need to get home and get their kids to bed.

Laurel glanced at Alice, who spoke to Billie and Grace with a wide smile on her face. *Or go on dates with their hot boyfriends.*

Alice was very good at keeping secrets behind closed doors, and Laurel trusted her completely. She wouldn't betray Alice's confidence to anyone, and she frowned again as her phone buzzed against her thigh three times in a row.

She'd come straight from the station to this emergency dress meeting, and she needed to get back there. Thom had gotten the air traffic controller's report for the drug case they'd been investigating, and it didn't add up.

"Laurel," Robin said, and she looked up at the woman. She held out a piece of paper and a pen. "It's time to vote."

"Right," Laurel said, having missed the instructions.

"There's six of us," AJ said. "Why can't we just hold up one finger for the first dress and two for the second?"

"Just write the number on the paper," Robin said, her voice tight.

Eloise had disappeared, probably back into the bathroom to change, and Laurel told herself to *be present*. She scrawled a big 2 on the paper and handed it back to Robin without folding it.

Robin did that, as if this was some big mystery surprise, and Laurel's skin itched to get back to her real mystery. She'd been moved to the narcotics department in the last week, and while she'd need time to adjust to her new partner and new job, she didn't want to take too long. She wanted to show Chief Sherman and everyone in narcotics that she was a talented detective.

She'd been working as a regular police detective for several years now, usually assigned to property vandalism or robbery cases on the north two islands in the cove. The move to narcotics was a step up, not a lateral reassignment, and she was the only female in that department at the moment.

Weight had settled on her shoulders and around her neck the moment Chief Sherman had asked her if she could make the move. She'd held her head high and said yes, of course. She was ready to move to a smaller department, with bigger cases, and more tension.

She was.

She wanted to prove to everyone that she had the talent, the mind, and the skill to get the job done.

"Looks like dress number two," Robin said as Eloise re-entered the bedroom, now back in her regular clothes. For some reason, the women started clapping, and Laurel joined in. She smiled at Eloise, because she did love the woman, and she did want her wedding to go off without a hitch.

The entire Five Island Cove Police Department would be there, half of them actually getting paid to work the crowd and keep the Chief and his new bride, his girls, and his parents safe. They were high-profile figures in the cove, and his father was running for mayor.

Stress accompanied Aaron Sherman wherever he went, and the whole department had sat through a debriefing meeting for two hours yesterday morning where the only topic discussed had been Sunday's wedding.

Laurel wondered if Eloise even knew that. She wasn't

a stupid woman, but she did bring cookies and sub sandwiches into the station as if it were an office building full of
businessmen. It wasn't. They handled criminal cases from
big things like homicide to small things like a stolen bike.

All the cops liked Eloise, though, and Laurel couldn't
fault her for wanting to steal a kiss from Aaron in the
middle of the day. The man worked insane hours, as did
his Deputy Chief, who was Laurel's fiancé.

Second thoughts ran through her mind again, and her
phone vibrated a couple more times. Her nerves teetered
on the edge of a cliff, and she got to her feet. "Congrats,
Eloise," she said, taking the woman into a hug. "Either of
those dresses will be gorgeous."

"We're still going to see about the original dress,"
Robin said, as if Laurel or Eloise needed to be reminded.

"I'm so sorry," Laurel said, holding up her phone. "But
I have to run. My new partner doesn't understand the idea
of clocking out once five o'clock hits." She flashed a smile
around at everyone.

"Be safe," Eloise said, a worried look in her eye.

"I will." Laurel reached out and squeezed Robin's
hand. "We're still on for next Thursday?" Her schedule
had changed with her new appointment, but she should
have Thursdays off from now on. Narcotics detectives did
a lot more work on the weekends, that was for sure, and
Laurel had already started to feel that pain only ten days
into the new job.

"Yes," Robin said. "I'll have lunch in my office too, and I promise we won't get interrupted this time."

Laurel released her hand and waved it, as if Robin's argument with her mother hadn't bothered Laurel at all. It had, however, and she needed to do something about that too. She couldn't carry around the negative emotions from others, and as she hurried out of the bedroom and down the hall, Laurel knew she needed to get back into therapy.

She'd missed a couple of sessions, and she could feel herself spiraling. She didn't want to marry Paul. She couldn't imagine going shopping for a wedding dress. She absorbed the bad energy and confrontational vibe from everyone around her.

Her mind spinning, she got behind the wheel of her police car. She gripped the wheel and took a deep breath. "Slow down, Laurel," she said, looking straight ahead. She'd parked on the street so she wouldn't get boxed in when the others arrived, and as she watched a man and his wife walk their dog, the world started to come back into focus.

She breathed in slow, the way she'd learned to do, and she isolated her thoughts from one another. Alice was seeing Arthur that night, and Laurel now knew they were doing a lot more than just going to dinner.

Robin was stressed to a ten, and Laurel had the distinct thought that she should send dinner to her family. Not only was this the wedding of the year, and Robin was in charge of it, her daughter was going through a break-up, and her husband was leaving to fish the waters around Alaska in just a few weeks.

Eloise was getting married in two days, and her dress had been ruined. Laurel couldn't do much about that, but her presence tonight to vote on the dress had been good for her—and probably good for Eloise.

Kelli, Kristen, and AJ all had things going on in their lives. A new boyfriend, upcoming moves, meeting important people, and another wedding in only four more weeks.

Laurel blew out her breath and picked up her phone. She called Thom without reading his texts and said, "I'm on my way back to you. I couldn't read your texts, so fill me in."

TWENTY MINUTES LATER, LAUREL LOWERED THE paper she'd been reading. "I still don't think it's right." It couldn't be.

Thom looked up from the newspaper he held. Yes, he still read the newspaper, because he was about fifteen years older than Laurel. She remembered celebrating his fiftieth birthday right here in the station last year.

Last summer, she thought. So he was almost fifty-one. He had a head full of silver hair, with a mustache and beard to match. He kept everything neatly trimmed, and he still looked like he could bench-press more than Laurel weighed.

She had no idea if he was happy she was his new partner or not. He'd never indicated he was *un*happy about it, but he hadn't rushed at her with open arms when the introduction was made either. He'd nodded to her and thrown back another handful of pistachios.

The man adored pistachios, and at least Laurel would know what to get him for his birthday.

Thom had a wife and kids, though his two boys were grown and graduated. One had moved to the mainland to do a cybersecurity program, and one had finished his police training and taken a job on the island of Nantucket.

They'd bonded over that, as Laurel's parents lived in Nantucket. Thom was easy to talk to, and Laurel wouldn't hesitate to tell him what she thought.

"What's not right about it?" Thom asked. "That's the report from the air traffic controller."

"Who's no longer working at the airport," Laurel put the paper on her desk and looked up at the ceiling. "He could be disgruntled. He could be making it up. It doesn't feel...complete."

"We know there are drugs coming into the cove via land and air," Thom said. "Marsden was caught with it on his person and in his luggage. The stories corroborate."

"Do they?" Laurel got up and walked through the empty station. A few night cops worked near the front doors, but the narcotics department got a quiet corner far from the regular comings and goings of police activity.

"Yes," Thom said slowly. "Marsden gave us all the dates he'd been in the cove. They match up with that report."

Something niggled at her mind, but Laurel couldn't find the detail she needed. An increase in drugs—particularly methamphetamines and cocaine—had been surging in the cove for the past year, and Chief Sherman wanted to put a stop to it. Since the cove was an isolated chain of five islands that ran north to south about twelve miles off the coast of mainland New York, the only way the drugs could be getting here was through the air or on a boat.

After that, people could cook them up, and two sets of detectives were working those cases.

Harold Marsden had been trafficking cocaine into the cove for the past eight months, and an undercover officer had finally learned about him and set up a deal to buy the drugs. That had turned into a sting operation, and they'd actually arrested Marsden at the airport, with drugs sewn into his clothes and bags stowed with his toiletries in his carryon.

He'd been sitting in the basement jail for over three weeks while the case got investigated. Thom and his previous partner had interviewed him. When Laurel had been reassigned, she had too.

She went back to her desk and pulled out her notebook with the interview transcript in it. She could read her messy handwriting, though not many others could. She flipped a few pages, because she'd then interviewed all the airport personnel as well. Thom had humored her and let her do the interviews, though he had notes from the initial interrogations.

Scanning quickly, she went past Marsden's claim that he didn't know who funded his plane tickets. He made the drug drop in the library's book return, late at night, on specified dates. He always got texts from different numbers, with the code word *Dumbo* in them so he'd know he was talking to the guy above him.

He didn't know who it was. He'd been approached by the air traffic controller, a one Lucas Winters, because he'd noticed how often Marsden came to the cove. He did fly back and forth, because he owned a vacation rental on Rocky Ridge, and he came to the cove after every stay to get the house cleaned up and put back together for the next guest.

The two of them had been moving cocaine into the cove for eight months.

"Eight months," Laurel mused, picking up the paper. "This only goes back to November." She turned the report toward Thom. "Where's September and October?"

"I don't know." Thom took the paper from her, a frown on his face.

"Marsden's been coming to the cove for years," Laurel said. "Not just the past six months. We have no way to trace who bought the airplane ticket?"

"He didn't always come by plane," Thom said, his voice distracted as he studied the report.

"What?" Laurel asked. "So he...flew into Nantucket, then took the steamer? Why would he do that?" Unless he'd chartered a boat to the cove, that was the only other way to get to the islands. Plane or steamer from Nantucket. That was more of a tourist experience than something a person would use for commuting, but it was a viable way into the cove.

"Charters would have records," Laurel said. "We should request all of those from all the docks, especially the one on Rocky Ridge."

"Yes," Thom said. "We should go pay Mister Winters another visit too." He put down the paper and got to his feet. "I need to stew on this. Let's get out of here."

"There's something not right," Laurel said, scanning her documents again. She picked up the report and tucked it into her notebook. She put that in her bag to take home with her. "It's almost too perfect. Like they planned it all to keep us from finding the truth."

"They're criminals," Thom said with a sad smile. "That's what they do."

"They're protecting someone," she said. "Someone big. I can feel it." She shouldered her bag and started to leave.

Thom put up his hand. "Stop for a minute here," he said quietly. "Think about what you just said. The cove is a small place. There are only a few 'big' people here." He held up one finger. "The mayor—and this is an election year, so you've got the guy trying to unseat the current mayor."

He put up a second finger as Laurel's lungs began to ice over. Greg Sherman was running for mayor, and yes, he was one that Laurel would consider "someone big." He was also Aaron's father.

A third finger went up. "You have the Chief of Police or someone close to him." He looked at his fingers while pure horror moved through Laurel.

Aaron? It couldn't be Aaron.

Thom continued with, "Maybe one more—a big businessman like the guy who owns those four resorts, or someone who's buying up land, like the guy who just bought that golf course on Rocky Ridge to fix it up. Someone with money. A lot of money."

Laurel swallowed, because Matt Hymas and his father, Yancey, had bought the old golf course on Rocky Ridge to fix it up and add it to the one they ran here on Diamond Island.

"There are others in government," she said. "Restaurant owners who could easily distribute."

"It's not a scandal if a crab shack owner is peddling drugs out of his beach-side taco stand," Thom said. "You said someone big."

Laurel's gut didn't usually lie to her. She met Thom's eyes, and they simply looked at one another. "We need to be careful," she said quietly.

"That we do," he agreed. "I'll call Mel on the way home, and we'll meet with him in the morning. Then we need to go see this air traffic guy again."

"I'll make a list of all the ways on and off the islands," Laurel said. "Any island, from all sides."

That decided, they walked out of the station together, both of them nodding to the night secretary as they did. As Laurel pulled up to Paul's house, she realized he could probably be classified as "someone big" too. It would certainly be a scandal if the number two in the police department had been running drugs into the cove for the past year.

"Please don't let it be anyone I know personally," she prayed as she got out of her car. "And no one connected to any of my friends. Please."

SIX

Kelli Thompson stepped into the office at the junior high for the last time and lifted her lanyard from around her neck. Sadness pulled through her at the same time excitement leapt into the back of her throat.

She'd miss checking in here each morning. She'd miss working with the kids and the teachers. She'd miss feeling like she belonged to a group of people, but she told herself she had her friends—and she'd be able to attend the Wednesday lunches.

Her mom and Devon spent time with her and Parker too, and bridges were being rebuilt all over her family with her sisters.

She also had Shad Webb, the man she'd been seeing for about a month now, and he'd been a great support to her. In fact, he'd texted ten minutes ago to say he was waiting out in the circle drive whenever she was finished.

"Headed out?" Barb asked, coming out of Dr. Pratt's office. The principal followed her, and both women smiled at Kelli.

"We're going to miss you so much." Dr. Pratt folded Kelli into her arms. Kelli hugged her back, the scent of the professional woman reminding her of Alice. Always put together, with jewelry and perfume every single day.

Kelli was lucky to get out of the house with her lunch and Parker. He sometimes forgot his homework, and she was sorely looking forward to days where they didn't have to rush out to catch the ferry.

"I'm going to miss everyone here," she said, stepping back. "I have my badge." She handed it to Barb, who tossed it on her desk and hugged Kelli too.

"We got you a bread basket," she said, indicating the huge basket perched on the counter where parents came to ask questions. The main office didn't handle money or attendance issues, and that kept the foot traffic to a minimum in here.

"My goodness," Kelli said, eyeing the blueberry lemon bread. "I'm going to eat all of this by Monday." The three of them laughed together, and Kelli experienced another moment of hesitation. Then she said, "I'll send you guys free passes to the wellness center when it opens."

"June fifteenth," Dr. Pratt said. "I've already got it on my calendar."

"Me too," Barb said. "Because that's the week after

school gets out, and I'm going to need a full-body massage."

"We can do that," Kelli said, giggling with them. She looked past them to the wide windows that showed the front parking lot. A sigh filled her body. "Okay, well, I'm off."

"Good luck," Barb and Dr. Pratt said at the same time, and Kelli turned to leave. She walked out of the office, and then out of the junior high. She'd been working here for several months, and the job had given her confidence in the wake of a divorce. She'd been able to provide for herself and her son, and she loved the little twinhome where she lived on Pearl Island.

She strode toward the dark blue government car, and Shad emerged from the driver's seat. A smile rode on his lips, and Kelli laughed and ran the last few feet to him. He caught her in his arms and lifted her up. "Done," he said, not asking.

"Done." She braced herself against his shoulders and leaned down to kiss him. She didn't care if other teachers saw. Even students were fine.

Before, Kelli would never have displayed any affection in public, but today felt like the first day of the rest of her life. She felt free to do what she'd always wanted to do, and while she knew opening a yoga studio wouldn't be a walk through the park, she just knew it would bring her the happiness that had eluded her for so long.

Shad laughed as he broke the kiss. "Come on, sweets. Let's go get Parker and go to dinner to celebrate."

She nodded, her smile seemingly etched into her face as she went around to the passenger seat. The moment she buckled, Shad asked, "Dare I ask if you've thought more about going to Long Island before the wellness center opens?"

Kelli sighed before she could stop herself. "I have," she said quickly. "I just...when Eloise was getting ready to open Cliffside, she was crazy-busy. Like, all over the place. She had a lot of help, but she worked fifteen-hour days." She looked at Shad, but he kept his eyes forward as he pulled away from the curb.

"I'm just worried I'll say yes, and then I won't be able to go. I can't predict what the first week of June will look like."

"Let's go for the Fourth then," he said. "They do a big celebration, with fireworks right over the water." He glanced at her, and then looked left to check for traffic.

Kelli's stomach quaked. She didn't know how to go on a trip with her boyfriend. She had never done that before, and she had Parker to consider. She wasn't sure if she was ready to meet Shad's parents, and if she were being really honest, she wasn't sure she wanted to get so close to New Jersey again.

"Talk to me," Shad said gently. "I can't read your mind."

Kelli took a deep breath, this part of her relationship

with a man brand new for her too. Julian hadn't really wanted to know what Kelli thought. His focus had always been on his business, and the more she looked back on their marriage, the more she realized that she'd just been a helper to him. A sidenote. A second thought.

"I'm—I've never gone on a trip with my boyfriend," she said. "I'm not sure I'm ready to meet your parents. I don't know what will happen with Parker, as Julian still hasn't called me back about if he'd like his son for the summer or not. A week here. Two or three or the whole thing."

She sure would like to plan something for July, but she didn't feel like she could.

"It'll be completely innocent," he said. "We can stay in separate bedrooms. I'm not trying to pressure you into anything."

Kelli nodded and folded her hands in her lap to get them to stop moving. "I appreciate that." She did like spending time with Shad. He lit up her world and made her heart do things it hadn't done in a long time. She sure enjoyed kissing him, and when he let his hand drift down the side of her neck to her shoulder and then to her waist, she relished his touch.

"My parents won't think anything of it," he said. "It doesn't mean we're more or less serious, though I just have to say—" He cleared his throat. "*I'm* serious about this already."

Kelli's chest pinched, and she looked at Shad again, pure surprise pulling through her. "You are?"

"Remember how long it took me to ask you out?" He chuckled, and an adorable pink hue touched his face. "Yeah, I'm serious."

Kelli drew in a breath and everything tight in her chest released. She reached over and took his hand in hers, noticing how quiet hers stayed with his to hold. "I'll call Julian tonight, after we get home."

Shad swallowed, the movement in his throat making Kelli smile. "All right."

"All right," Kelli said. "If it works out with Parker—and I can ask Eloise or Alice to take him if he'll be in the cove when we go to Long Island—let's plan for July instead of June." She swallowed too, her nerves going down easier than she'd anticipated.

"July it is," Shad said, grinning as he joined the pick-up line for the elementary school. They got out a bit later than the junior high, but they wouldn't have to wait long.

The moment Shad put the car in park, Kelli leaned over and drew his face toward hers. She kissed him, the gentle stroke of his mouth against hers working up to something more passionate and fevered. Heat filled Kelli, and she slowed the kiss so she could enjoy every touch of his hands in her hair, along her face, and down her side.

KELLI GLANCED AT PARKER ON THE COUCH, A BOWL OF popcorn in his hands and his favorite dragon movie playing. She didn't want to introduce tension and conflict into this perfect evening, but she'd promised Shad she'd call Julian tonight.

At nearly nine p.m., the man should be home from work. Anything was possible, and Kelli had known him to pull all-nighters if a job required it.

She dialed and went upstairs without saying anything to her son. The line rang and rang, and Julian didn't answer until she'd reached the top of the steps. "Kel," he said easily, as if she'd be calling to offer to bring him a bread basket.

She wished she'd brought up one of the oatmeal raisin cookies to help her through this conversation. "Hey," she said, her voice slightly meek. She told herself she wasn't the meek, nervous Kelli she'd been in her marriage.

She was strong now. She didn't need Julian, but she could be civil. "We're only six weeks away from summer vacation," she said. "I need to know what you'd like to do with your son." Her voice sounded strong now. She'd phrased nothing as a question, nor had she demanded. A nice request, that was what she'd done.

"Uh, let's see," Julian said, already distracted by something else, as if his own child didn't deserve his full attention. Frustration built within Kelli, but she stayed silent.

"We'd love to have him all summer," Julian said. "He's done on June seventh?"

"Yes," Kelli said, blinking at the idea of not having Parker with her at all this summer. She hadn't anticipated Julian requesting that.

Her heart stalled completely as she realized he'd said "we."

"Who's we?" Kelli asked, her voice much too high now. She knew who it would be.

"Tiff and I," he said, clearing his throat. "I guess I better tell you. It's not like you're not going to find out."

"She's living with you," Kelli said, getting control of the squeakiness in her tone.

"We got married last week," he said, and that did cause Kelli to produce a loud gasp.

She leaned against the wall for support, the word, "Married?" escaping her mouth before she could call it back.

"Yes," he said, and she could just see him glaring at her, daring her to contradict him.

Nasty comments and questions piled beneath her tongue, and Kelli breathed deeply to keep them submerged.

"He's got to be back on August thirtieth?" Julian asked as if he hadn't just dropped a bomb.

"Yes." The word scraped her throat. "I'd like him back in time to do some school shopping and meet his teacher."

"How about we come get him on June eleventh? We'll bring him back on August eleventh. That's two months, and you'll have him for a couple of weeks before school starts."

Kelli started shaking her head in the middle of his question. "No," she said, pushing herself back to a full standing position. "*You'll* come get him in June, and *I'll* come pick him up in August. I don't want *Tiff* here."

She couldn't even imagine sending her son to live with that woman and her ex-husband for two months. Every cell in her body trembled, and tears filled her eyes. She pressed against them and added, "If she harms my son in any way, Julian, I will make sure you never see him again."

"Come on, Kelli." He scoffed. "Don't be petty and vindictive. It doesn't suit you."

"Don't lecture me," she blurted out. "I don't like her, and I don't want to send Parker to spend any time with her. I will, because the court says I must, but I'm not joking. I know a lot of lawyers, and Parker's not an infant. He knows what you've done and why we got divorced, and he'll tell me if he's uncomfortable in any way."

"He's not going to be uncomfortable in the house where he grew up."

"With another mother." Kelli did the scoffing now. Julian was so clueless sometimes. Parker wasn't grown up. He was ten years old, with plenty of childhood left. "Is she the only woman you have in the house, Julian?"

"How dare you?" he asked. "I don't have to answer that."

"Yes, you do," Kelli said. "I can go to the judge right now and say I don't want my son exposed to a brothel."

"My house is *not* a brothel," he spat out. "It's just me and Tiff."

"I'll be asking Parker," Kelli said, though the idea of putting her son between her and Julian made her sick.

"You do what you have to do," Julian said, and that only fueled Kelli's fury. He said stuff like that, but he didn't mean it. He'd always wanted her to do what he wanted to do. "I'll come alone on the eleventh of June to get him."

Kelli took a deep breath, her hands shaking as she held the phone to her ear. "I'll have him ready for the summer."

Silence poured between them, and Kelli pressed her eyes closed, wishing she could keep the memories she had with this man from flowing through her mind. She couldn't, though, and she did have good memories mixed in with the more recent bad ones.

"Thank you, Kelli," Julian said, and the call ended.

She exhaled and let her hand drop. She turned around, her mind racing as fast as her heart. Her feet took her quickly down the steps, and she called to Parker, "I'm running next door for a minute. I'll be right back," as she ran out the front door.

She rounded the short, wrought-iron fence that separated her house from Shad's and pounded on the door. "Shad," she called. "It's just me."

His footsteps approached quickly on the other side of the door, and he opened it, his eyes wide. "What's wrong?"

She stepped into his arms and let the few remaining tears in her eyes fall. "He's going to take him for the whole summer."

"Hey, it'll be okay," Shad whispered as he stroked her hair. "I'm here, and Kel, you can put it on your friends' text, and everyone will come support you."

She pulled away from him and looked into his eyes. "You're right. I'm going to do that right now."

He smiled at her and leaned down. "Maybe after I kiss you." He claimed her mouth, and Kelli's fantasies formed and went wild. Parker would be gone for two whole months, and she'd be living right next door to this stunningly handsome and thoughtful man...

He backed up, taking her with him, and closed the door before he pressed her into it, kissing her deeper and deeper before moving his mouth to her neck and murmuring, "It's going to be a great summer, Kel. You'll see."

SEVEN

Kristen Shields picked up her purse and followed her son and daughter-in-law up the steps from the subterranean levels of the lighthouse. The steps had become harder and harder for her to climb, but Rueben and Jean waited for her at the doorway, and Jean gave her a kind smile.

She'd changed so much in the past eight months, and Kristen wondered how much Parker Thompson had to do with that. She wondered if Kelli had texted Jean that the boy would be gone for most of the summer. Kristen said nothing, because it wasn't her place to spill the beans if she hadn't.

"Thanks for coming with me to look at places," Kristen said. "I'm more nervous than I thought I'd be."

"Yeah?" Rueben asked, holding the door for his wife and then Kristen. "Why do you think you're nervous?"

"I don't know," Kristen admitted. "I've never looked at houses before? I've not moved in fifty years?"

"You've cleaned out that cottage so well," Jean said. "Moving won't be too terribly hard, I wouldn't think."

"It shouldn't be," Reuben said. "You live like a minimalist almost, Mom."

She smiled at her son, but she didn't contradict him. Since her husband's death a little over a year ago, Kristen had been digging out from under a mountain of papers, books, journals, clothes, and secrets.

She had gotten rid of many, many things. Hundreds of pounds of things Joel had stuffed into the house, and every time Kristen thought about it, her shoulders sagged under the weight of the memories.

She'd been buried in that house, and now she was going to leave it behind.

"I can ride in the back," she said quickly when she saw Jean reaching for the door handle on the back door of the SUV.

"I'll move my seat forward," Jean said, opening the door anyway. Kristen smiled at her and ducked into the vehicle. With everyone in, Kristen handed her phone to Rueben, so he could navigate them to the first property.

"Linnie will meet us there," she said, settling back against the seat and looking out the window. The sky held a brilliant blue hue today, without a single cloud in sight. Sometimes the sea spray would fire up into the sky when a particularly large wave hit the rocks below. She saw nothing of that today, and she took a breath and held it for a moment.

Rueben backed out of the parking stall and headed down the curved road that led to town. It wasn't a long drive, as the islands weren't huge, but it still took about fifteen minutes to arrive at the first condo.

Kristen took in the wide, open gate, the neatly trimmed grass, and the golden bricks that marked the pillars in the fence line. Three-story buildings started, with covered carports in the parking lot they now drove slowly through.

"This is nice, Mom," Reuben said, leaning down to peer out the windshield too. "Some of the tallest trees on the island, I'd say."

The trees didn't grow very tall in Five Island Cove, because the wind didn't allow it. The roots couldn't get very deep into the rocky island, and yes, these were about six or eight feet tall, which was about as tall as trees got here.

Kristen swallowed, determined not to fall in love with the outside of the house first. She wasn't going to fall in love with the very first condo she looked at, period.

"It should be right down here," Rueben said slowly.

"Look, Kristen," Jean said. "They have a dog park right here on-sight. You could get that dog you want."

"Mm." Kristen had mentioned that she'd like a little friend to help ease the loneliness in the evenings. She'd been spending a lot of time with her girls, and with

Rueben and Jean, but when she moved, she wouldn't be as close to them as she was now.

She told herself she could get a RideShare and go to the lighthouse any time she wanted to. She told herself a lot of things, and Kristen did her best not to tell Rueben to keep going and take them all home.

"Do they have activities here?" Rueben asked.

"Yes," Kristen said. "It's a fifty-five-plus community. No yard work. I get my own parking space, and they have a big clubhouse where they do things." She'd done a little research online, and she had three appointments with her realtor to see the available units on Diamond Island.

There were only three such communities in the cove, as the fourth and fifth were full, with waiting lists.

"That must be Linnie," Rueben said, swinging his SUV into an uncovered parking spot. Kristen took a deep breath and unbuckled her seatbelt. Jean stood nearby when she got out, and Kristen reached for her hand. She squeezed it quickly before stepping to greet Linnie.

"What do you think?" Linnie swept her arm toward the nearest condo building. "There are five buildings here. It's one of the smaller retirement communities in the cove, which can be good and bad." She started toward the hallway running right through the middle of the building.

"Can we hear the ocean?" Rueben asked, looking west.

"Yes," Linnie said with delight in her voice. She had auburn hair that curled naturally and flounced against her shoulders as she walked in her heels. Today, she wore a skirt suit in dark blue, with a pink blouse under the jacket, with navy heels. She carried a brown leather portfolio in her arm, and Kristen felt like she was in good hands with Linnie.

"Isn't that great?" she asked. "They have a viewing area too. With picnic tables. It's wonderful, and we'll get to see all of that. Come on, Kristen. Your unit is right on the other side of this building."

She continued to talk about the common green space Kristen's condo would border, and how many units were in each building—twelve—so there were only sixty condos here.

Kristen had requested one on the ground level, because she didn't want to deal with stairs, and as Linnie pressed in the code on the lockbox of the unit on the bottom left-hand side, Kristen gazed at the green space her realtor had spoken of.

"It's beautiful," she said.

"It looks like it has a walking path, Mom," Rueben said, linking his arm in hers. "And the dog park is just a building down, and the picnic area she just talked about is right there." He pointed to the left, where a gate led out into an area where Kristen could clearly see a pavilion with tables.

Her heart grew and expanded, and all of her nerves disappeared. Her girls had all sent support for her endeavor today, and Robin had even offered to come. But

Kristen couldn't pull her from the last-minute wedding preparations she needed to attend to for Eloise's wedding.

She couldn't wait to tell them about this place, and she smiled as she turned to enter the condo.

"Okay," Linnie said with a big exhale. "You enter into the living room, with your dining room right here as well. It all flows right into the kitchen, and aren't those huge windows amazing?"

Compared to the cottage where Kristen had lived for the past several years, and the cramped lighthouse where she'd raised her two kids, the condo *was* flat-out amazing. It was light, airy, and absolutely huge with two bedrooms and two bathrooms.

She knew she could be happy here, and she looked in every bedroom, every cupboard, and every closet. Linnie talked and talked, and she led them down the walking path, past the grills and fire pits, and past a patch of lawn for horseshoes, cornhole, and croquet.

Kristen heard the ocean before she saw it, and her breath came in puffs by the time she caught a glimpse of the waves. The wind she loved so fiercely blew in her face, and she turned further into it, feeling the vastness of the world in front of her.

She clutched her arms around herself and tried to feel the right thing to do. "This is wonderful," she said to Rueben, and of course, Linnie heard.

"This is a very nice place," the realtor said. "But let's go look at Beach Acres." Linnie led the way back to the parking lot, and Kristen waited until she'd sealed herself in her son's SUV before she said a word.

"So?" Jean asked, turning almost all the way around in the front seat to look at Kristen, who rode behind her.

"I really like that place," Kristen admitted. "I love that it's the back building. I like that I'm close to that lookout, and I like that my view is of grass and trees and not the parking lot."

"It's bigger than where you are now," Rueben said.

"Only by a bathroom," Kristen said.

"Mom." He backed out of the spot and followed Linnie's convertible through the parking area. "No. The living area is twice as big. You could actually get a full-sized couch in there. You could never do that in that cottage."

"The kitchen is huge," Jean added. "I think I'll come there to make dinner." She grinned at Kristen, who felt so much lighter than she had twenty-five minutes ago. She hadn't been sure if this move would bring her the closure and illuminate the path forward the way she hoped it would, but she felt differently now.

Kristen smiled back at Jean. "Thanks for coming with me," she said. "I appreciate you two so much."

"Of course," Reuben said, and Jean twisted back to face the front, something quick crossing her face. Kristen wasn't sure what it was, but it didn't look good.

"It's just down the street to the left," Kristen said, though Rueben could see the bright red car in front of her.

She saw Jean reach across the console and take Rueben's hand in hers. He lifted it to his lips and gave her a quick smile before making the turn to follow Linnie.

A few minutes later, Linnie made a right turn, and they drove away from the beach for a block or two. Kristen didn't like that, but she said nothing as the homes went by the window.

"Mom." Reuben cleared his throat. "We wanted to tell you something."

Kristen tore her gaze from the landscape passing by, and as Reuben turned into Beach Acres, she noted that there was no fence whatsoever. The buildings didn't seem as plated in gold, as they bore a light brown stucco and not the golden hue of the bricks at the first location.

"Okay," she said, trying to listen and take in details at the same time.

"Jean and I turned in our adoption papers."

Kristen sucked in a breath and stared at the side of her son's face. In the front seat, Jean sniffled a little bit. "You're kidding," she said. "I thought you'd decided not to do that."

"Our case worker thought we might be a little bit too old," Rueben said. "But I'm only forty-three, and Jean's only forty. We have plenty of time to raise a child."

"Are you—?" She cut herself off, because she didn't want to ask if they'd stay in the lighthouse. She'd turned over complete control of the lighthouse to Reuben, and he could do what he wanted with the appointment.

"Yes," Jean said. "We're going to stay in Five Island Cove, Kristen."

"You are?" Kristen didn't mean to sound so surprised, but Jean had not particularly enjoyed the cove, and she'd once gone to the mainland to visit her parents for long stretches of time. There'd been a period where Kristen was sure Reuben would either have to endure a divorce or he'd leave the cove—and the lighthouse.

Kristen realized now that such a thing wouldn't be the end of the world, though she had enjoyed having her son in the cove with his wife. She thought of Clara, the daughter who'd come for her father's funeral, then promptly left the cove as if Kristen had been as bad as Joel.

Perhaps Kristen could try another invitation. Perhaps as a family, she could host a housewarming party and both of her children and their spouses and children would come. For Rueben and Jean, right now, that would include a pair of dogs as well as two cats.

She could just see them all on those picnic tables, each person carrying out a bowl of salad or a plate of hot, buttered corn on the cob.

"The cove has grown on me," Jean said.

"Well, I'm just thrilled," Kristen said, smiling at Jean, though the other woman didn't look at her. "And I'm glad to have something to occupy my mind too."

"Mom," Reuben said with a chuckle. "You have a lot going on. Finding a new house, moving, getting new furniture."

"And all your girls," Jean said. "It's almost summertime, and you'll be going to the beach or a lunch or a picnic every single day." She did finally turn and smile over her shoulder.

Kristen lifted her chin and asked, "Who said anything about new furniture?"

EIGHT

Eloise faced herself in the mirror and held the bouquet with straight arms so they made a V with the flowers right in the center.

"Head down a little bit," the photographer said, and Eloise sincerely hoped the picture-taking would end soon. "To the right, please. Yes, that light is spectacular."

Eloise couldn't find a spot of soot, debris, sludge, or mud anywhere on her dress, and Miriam had told her that even if a dot remained, she could take it out in post-production. Eloise didn't want to walk down the aisle in a soiled dress, but Mike had worked dry cleaning magic, and she currently found herself buttoned and zipped into her original wedding gown.

She didn't care about the six-hundred-dollar fee for the dress rental for the Pennace, though Robin said she'd take it back tomorrow and say they hadn't used it. Mike had needed two full days to get the wrong color out of the white fabric, and they'd needed a back-up plan.

Robin bustled into the room wearing her gorgeous gown. She'd changed into it a few minutes ago, which meant the top of the hour approached. Eloise had been waiting for months to marry Aaron, and the last few hours had felt like torture.

They'd been at the venue since right after lunch, and Eloise cursed herself for setting the wedding at four p.m. But she'd wanted a sunset-facing wedding on the beach. She wanted to serve good food, and that required a wedding that sat near a mealtime. She wanted to then leave for her honeymoon and be ready to go to bed with her husband.

Four o'clock had seemed like the perfect time—until six a.m. that morning. The hours from then until now had felt eternal, and as Robin told the photographer that their time was up, Eloise had never felt so grateful.

"Thank you, Miriam," Robin said, and the photographer stepped toward the door. As she opened it and slipped out, Eloise caught a few notes of the music piping beyond this small structure that housed the dressing rooms for the wedding party.

"Is everyone ready?" Eloise asked as she put her bouquet back in the bucket of water where it had been chilling before Miriam had wanted pictures with it.

"Yes, they're coming," Robin said. "We have five

minutes to be lined up. Duke is clearing the press right now."

"Did they get the shots they wanted?" Eloise asked, though she wasn't sure why she cared. She and Aaron had given them access to some parts of the wedding, with the clear understanding that there would be no cameras— digital or video—during the ceremony and subsequent dinner.

"I have no idea," she said. "There was quite the crew when Aaron's father arrived, and he stood and spoke to all of them, his perfect wife standing there with a perfect smile on her face." Robin spoke in a high-pitched, animated voice for the last several words, and she did her crazy eyes.

Eloise laughed, as did Robin, and she could admit that Cindi Sherman was a tiny bit fake. Fine, maybe very fake. Her husband was running for mayor, and apparently the race was heating up early this year.

She hadn't seen anything come out in the papers or on the Internet yet, and perhaps the editor at the Cove Chronicles had listened to Aaron when he'd begged him to wait until after the wedding.

The door opened again, and this time, Alice led the way as she, AJ, Kelli, Laurel, Kristen, and then Eloise's mother entered the room. Her mom held Billie's hand and Grace's hand, and Eloise had never seen her mother glow more than when she was with Aaron's girls.

Her heart warmed and expanded, and she opened her

arms to her mom and the girls first. The four of them hugged, and Eloise nearly ruined her makeup, which she'd sat so very still for only a couple of hours ago.

"Oh, my very favorites," she whispered. She crouched down enough to be the same height as Billie and Grace. "You're going to escort me down the aisle to your dad, right?"

They'd practiced last night, and Eloise had taught them to take a step—feet together—pause—another step. Step—together—pause—step.

That would give Miriam time to get the pictures she wanted of them walking toward Aaron. She could get Aaron's face as he watched them come.

The aisle on the beach was only thirty feet, and Aaron had marked off the distance in the hall and into the kitchen, and he'd stood at the end of it. They'd had a great night together last night, and Eloise almost wanted to bring the girls with them as they went to Italy.

Not quite, but almost.

"What's it like out there?" she asked, her nerves pressing against the back of her throat.

"Busy," Alice said, and Eloise stepped into her arms. "I'm so excited for you, Eloise."

"Thank you." Eloise didn't want to let go of her, but the moment she did, Kelli stood there, and she hugged Eloise too. She said nothing, but Kelli wore most of her emotions right out in the open on her face, and she shone with happiness.

"Could be you soon," she said, as Kelli had told everyone about her July Fourth trip to Long Island with Shad.

Kelli lifted one shoulder and said, "Maybe."

Eloise faced AJ. "How are you the most beautiful woman in that dress?"

She put her hand on her belly, which protruded from the front of her body. "Please." She grinned. "You chose a wine red dress for the bridesmaids, and it's my color." She laughed and drew Eloise into an embrace.

The dark red was one of her colors, and all of the dresses looked amazing on every body in the room. The dresses glinted with sequins along the bodice, with thin straps that went over the shoulders. A ruching went along the waist that hid flaws in bodies, from bony hips to extra pounds, and the color and style even looked good on Kristen.

She hugged her Seafaring Girls leader next, her arms around the older woman as tight as she could get them. "Thank you so much for coming."

"I wouldn't miss this for anything," Kristen whispered. "You're the one who includes everyone, no matter how old they are." She beamed with the power of the sun as she stepped back. Robin swooped into the space and handed Kristen a wrist corsage in a light pink carnation paired with a white one.

"This goes on now," she said, stepping back and handing the last one to Laurel.

Eloise knew she and Laurel still had a ways to go to be as good of friends with her as she'd like. "I'm surprised you're in here."

"I've got a gun in a thigh holster," Laurel said with a grin. She reached out and hugged Eloise. "I'm working the wedding undercover."

Eloise grinned as the much thinner woman gripped her shoulders. They parted, and Eloise faced Robin. The woman hadn't stopped for longer than two seconds in the past three days, and Eloise gripped her with both hands.

"Robin," she said, tears filling her eyes. "You have made everything as magical and as perfect as it's going to be. Will you take off the wedding planner hat and be my friend again?"

Robin brushed at her eyes and said, "Oh, all right." She stepped into Eloise's arms and hugged her, her chest heaving a little bit. For once, Eloise got to be the strong one out of the two of them, and she only stepped back when Alice said, "Someone just checked on us, and I think it's time."

Eloise had been waiting her whole life for this moment. She stepped back and took her bouquet from Alice. She'd be going last with Billie and Grace, and the two girls came to her side. She positioned the flowers in front of her, not too high and not too low, as instructed, and Billie put her hand on Eloise's left arm while Grace put hers on the right.

"Is Chris here?" Eloise asked in a quiet voice.

"Yes," Billie whispered back. "He's sitting with Dad's secretary. I swear she's asked him ten times if we're dating and that she knows a lot of cops if he puts one toe out of line." She rolled her eyes and huffed slightly.

Eloise stifled a giggle as Robin opened the door and led the way out of the building. Eloise stepped when it was her turn, and she couldn't wait for her toes to sink into the sand.

"Does your dad have Prince at the altar with him?" she asked.

"He wasn't out there when we came in," Billie said.

"He wasn't?" A flash of worry filled her. Surely he wouldn't leave without his children, though.

Don't be ridiculous, Eloise told herself. *He's here.* They'd arrived together, and Robin would've come and told Eloise immediately if anything had gone amiss with the groom.

The moment Eloise emerged into the sunlight, the music changed, and the breeze picked it up and brought it back to her. She stopped to take in the sight before her. Robin had been on the beach all morning, helping to set up chairs, tie bows on them, and make sure every bloom and every bottle sat in the right place.

Thirty feet away, Aaron grinned at her, his hands clasped tightly in front of him. He wore his dress police uniform in a crisp black with plenty of colored lines and squares on it. He wore a cap with a flat top, and everything about him called to Eloise—including the dog at his side.

Without that dog, Eloise might never have reunited with Aaron.

She couldn't help smiling back at him as the breeze tried to take down the arch that had been erected above the altar, which Eloise had wanted covered with pink, red, and white roses. She could see them bulging out behind Aaron, and she loved the way the long tails of the bows on the chairs seemed to be waving to her.

Since it was only the end of April, the sun lowering in the western sky hadn't heated things past comfortable, and Eloise couldn't imagine a more perfect time to get married. Not a single cloud marred the blue sky, and the bottom of it had already started to glow golden in the distance.

The bridal party moved down the aisle while Eloise took in the men, women, and children who'd come to witness the wedding. She saw Robin's mother near the front, as well as Alice's children standing with Parker and Shad. She smiled at her housekeepers and her inn manager, her tears rising higher and higher with each person she saw dressed in their very best, there to support her and Aaron on their big day.

The scent of salt, sand, and sunshine dominated the wedding, but Eloise could also smell a hint of chocolate and a bit of the balsamic she'd chosen for the fish. Aaron had insisted on steak, and the surf-and-turf dinner coming in an hour or so already made Eloise's mouth water.

Not nearly as much as the man waiting for her at the end of the altar, and she waited until Laurel and Paul had taken their spots on the outer edges of the altar and everyone looked at her, and her alone.

"Okay, girls," Eloise said, and amid all the ribbons, bows, blooms, and roses, she took her first step toward her future. "Remember, slowly now."

They moved exactly the way they'd practiced, and before she knew it, Billie had kissed her father's cheek and left Eloise alone with him at the altar.

"I'm speechless," Aaron whispered, his lips right at her ear. "I'm the luckiest man in the world."

"Just for this moment," Eloise whispered, and together they faced the altar and the pastor now standing there. She thought Aaron had gotten it all wrong, because the day she'd stopped at the beach and been knocked over by his dog and they'd been reintroduced had been the best day of her life...until today.

NINE

Robin dabbed at her eyes as Aaron said, "I love you more than anything in the world," to finish his vows. The pastor declared him and Eloise man and wife, and the crowd started to cheer as they kissed.

Eloise glowed with happiness, and Aaron lifted their joined hands as they faced the crowd together. They got separated as her mother went to hug her, and Robin loved this part of the wedding almost more than the slow walk down the aisle and all the prep. She adored seeing all the pieces come together to create the most beautiful setting.

She enjoyed watching the wonder on people's faces as they saw the way the colors came together. She'd caught the glint of joy in Eloise's eyes, and even Aaron had taken Robin by the shoulders only a few moments before Eloise had appeared and said, "Robin, I see why you're the best. Thank you for doing this for her."

She'd done it for both of them. For Grace and Billie too, because those two little girls, who weren't so little anymore, deserved an amazing start to their new family, with Eloise as their new mother. She loved those girls, and Robin did too.

Duke put his hand in hers and squeezed, and Robin looked away from Eloise hugging her mother, both of them crying, and at him. "Thanks for clearing the press, baby." She tipped up and kissed him, and the stroke of his mouth suggested his desire for her.

She pulled away after only a moment, because now wasn't the time.

"Reminds me of our wedding," he murmured. "You did such a great job, Robin."

"Thank you," she whispered back, leaning into the strength of his side and focusing on Aaron's mother as she stepped away from her son and over to her new daughter-in-law.

Robin loved watching two families coming together, and she loved watching all the celebrations from friends and loved ones. Aaron currently hugged his father, and once he stepped away, Paul Leyhe stepped in to clap his Chief on the back. Laurel lingered nearby, her smile large and genuine as she clapped. She didn't focus on Paul and Aaron for too long, her eyes constantly moving, and mostly following Greg Sherman, who was running for mayor of Five Island Cove.

She was a very good cop, and a very good friend, and

Robin hoped she could plan a fantastic wedding for her and Paul too. She would, and she took a deep breath, her resolve solid. She endeavored to put on an amazing wedding for every bride, and between now and Laurel's wedding, she had nine more nuptials to get through.

AJ's was in only a month, and Robin had made a final to-do list for it she'd start on tomorrow.

She watched as the mayor shook Aaron's hand, then his father's, which was such a political move. The two were running against one another this year, but Robin supposed even differences could be set aside for an hour during a wedding.

The City Manager, Nathan Baldwin, stepped up to Aaron and drew him into a hug. The two men laughed, and they were obviously familiar with one another. They man-clapped each other on the back, and Nathan stepped over to Eloise.

Robin really had never done such a high-profile wedding, and while most of the government officials there were already married, she hoped they felt safe, secure, and would have a good time at today's wedding.

"Maybe we should renew our vows next year," Duke said, interrupting her thoughts. "Then we can take that honeymoon we never really got."

She looked at him again, the idea one of the best she'd ever heard. "Really?"

He leaned down and pressed a kiss to her temple. "Really. We'll be caught up on everything by fall. You won't have to work yourself to death." He kept his face very close to hers, the moment intimate even among the biggest wedding the cove had seen in a while. "I'm sorry about everything. I hate that you have to do as much as you do."

"It's fine," she whispered back. "I'm glad I have the skills to be able to help our family." She would do anything for her girls and anything for Duke. She hadn't gone to college, something her mother had told her she'd regret one day.

She was still waiting for that day, just like she was waiting for the day Duke would leave her—something else her mother had told her. At some point, Robin was going to have to accept that her mother was wrong. So much of what she'd learned growing up and so much of what her mom had said had formed her. She'd once believed everything Jennifer Golden had said, and she did love her mother.

But it was time to shake off the chains weighing her down. Duke wasn't going to leave her. She didn't need to go to college to plan a spectacular wedding—and get paid handsomely to do it.

"Let's go say congratulations," Duke said, straightening. "The political crowd is clearing out. Then I'll help you check on the food."

Robin looked to her left. "They should already be setting it up." Sure enough, a waiter moved among the tables, filling water glasses with ice from a metal bucket, another following him with a tall pitcher of water.

"They are," Duke said, tugging on her hand to get her to go with him. "But you'll check anyway."

He knew her so well, and Robin didn't argue. She moved through the squishy sand, edging closer while Eloise and Aaron continued to accept embraces and congratulations. Robin stepped into both of them at the same time, barely able to lift her arms around the two of them as short as she was.

"Congratulations," she said, her smile instant. "I love you both so much, and I'm so glad I got to be part of your special day."

"You made it special," Eloise said. "I love you, Robin. Thank you."

"Yes," Aaron said. "Thank you. Everything is perfect."

She stepped back, meeting El's eyes first and then Aaron's. "Just the dinner and dancing to go, and every-thing is set."

"And the sunset pictures," El said, and Robin nodded.

"More pictures?" Aaron asked, and both Robin and Eloise started to laugh.

"*Family* pictures," Eloise said. "With the girls. As the sun sets into the ocean." She put one hand on his chest as the other moved around his back. "Don't worry, Chief. I'll use them on our Christmas cards and everything. No more pictures for another year."

"I'm holding you to that," he grumbled, and Robin

went to check on the food. With so many VIPs here, everything had to be perfect.

"YES, THANK YOU," SHE SAID INTO HER PHONE. "WE'LL be there on Wednesday morning." She smiled as if the owner of the cake shop could see her. "Ten-thirty. She'll be so excited."

The call ended, and Robin looked up as the garage door started to rumble upward. She got to her feet, wondering if she'd find Mandie or Duke coming home early. Both were equally bad. If it was Mandie, that meant something had happened at the high school bad enough to drive her back home.

Something with Charlie Kelton, no doubt. The boy already had a new girlfriend, and it hurt Mandie every time she saw them together. That, or Jamie was driving her nuts with her new crush, a boy named Damien Robinson, who she'd been "hanging out with" more and more.

Every weekend, in fact. They hadn't gone out alone, and Robin wouldn't allow that anyway, as Jamie was only thirteen years old, and far too young to have a real boyfriend.

If Duke came through the door, that meant bad news too. It meant something had happened out on the water or with the boat, and Robin's anxiety tripled when his boots sounded in the hallway outside her office.

She reached the door and their eyes met. "What's going on?" she asked, folding her arms across her stomach. She just needed to be calm and hold things together. Not everything was bad news, though Robin worried about such things constantly.

Duke smiled, and Robin relaxed a little bit. "I ran full by mid-morning, and instead of going out again, I thought maybe we could have the afternoon to ourselves before the girls get home." He nodded toward the kitchen. "I called for lunch, and I used FoodShare, so it'll be here in a few minutes."

She entered the hallway and let him take her into his arms. "You don't even have to stop working, baby. I know you're busy."

"I am busy," she said, starting to sway. "But never too busy for lunch with my husband, the one who's leaving in two weeks for Alaska." She looked up at him, smiling as he danced with her right there in their house.

They moved together slowly, and Robin forgot about the floral arrangements, the centerpieces, the gems she needed for the lanterns, the food for the anniversary party, and the appointment she'd just made on Wednesday morning to sample AJ's cake choices for her wedding.

Only her and Duke existed, and she knew she could do anything with this man at her side. "I'm going to miss you so much," she whispered.

"So let's eat and...hang out," he said into her ear. "I already miss you."

While in Alaska, Duke lived in a tiny hotel cabin only a few yards from the beach. He shared with his friend Brian, and the two of them worked and worked and worked. Last summer, he'd made as much as he made here in Five Island Cove in a year in only four months, and this year, that money would pay off his new boat and get their family back in the black.

If he went to Alaska next year, they might actually be able to buy the house from Robin's mother and take the honeymoon-trip-that-never-was. Mandie would graduate soon, and Robin wanted to give her an amazing party and send her on the trip she wanted to take—to see the mountains.

They'd been talking about Calgary and the Canadian Rockies, and Robin could admit she'd like to make that trip too. She'd heard of lakes so blue, the color couldn't even be described.

"We've come a long way, baby." Duke twirled her away from him, his grin so sexy as he pulled her back. "I love you."

"I love you too." Robin kissed her husband, and he only took a breath from that to bring in the food and set it on her desk before he led her down the hall to their bedroom.

TEN

AJ rose to her feet as Matt's car turned into the driveway. She'd been sitting at the window for the past thirty minutes, since he'd texted to say his son's flight had arrived. Justin Hymas was the youngest of his sons, having just finished his first year of college.

AJ's nerves felt like they'd been put through a wood chipper, and they vibrated and screamed at her to make sure this meeting went well. Her mind blitzed from one thought to another, and she hated how loud everything shrieked through her head.

If she could take her anti-depressants, everything would quiet. "Three more months," she told herself, reaching for the back of the chair. She'd been attending therapy every week to learn how to control her thoughts without chemicals.

She drew in a deep breath and focused on the feel of

the fabric against her fingers. She thought about the temperature of the air as it moved through her nose. She breathed out, sending the panic with it. She didn't need to panic. She was going to be this boy's step-mother, even if he was already grown.

She'd seen Eloise step into the role, and she'd spent most of yesterday listening to Matt talk about his youngest son. His daughter Lisa would be here in two weeks, and his other son, Derrick would be here the following week. They'd live all together in this small house in the quaint Diamond Island neighborhood for a week before AJ and Matt would get married.

The front door opened, and AJ focused on the sound in that moment. She couldn't spend her time worrying about what might happen in the future.

Right now, Matt's voice reached her ears, and then one slightly lower. They both laughed, and AJ smiled as she opened her eyes.

She started for the doorway of the formal living room, and Matt turned toward her, catching her eye as she arrived in the foyer. "There she is." He grinned at her and practically bounded toward her, taking her into his arms. "How are you feeling, my AvaJane?"

"Good," she said, and that was true. She met Justin's eye over his father's shoulder and cleared her throat.

Matt stepped back and turned to stand beside her. He took her hand and grinned with all the power he possessed at his son. "Justin, this is AvaJane Proctor. AJ, my son, Justin."

He had dark hair like his father, and brooding eyes when he wasn't laughing. He didn't have a beard at all, and he stood a couple of inches shorter than Matt. The shape of his nose came from someone else, as did the way his chin went to a point instead of a square like Matt's.

"Hello," she said, putting a smile on her face. She stepped away from Matt to shake Justin's hand. "I'm glad your flight wasn't canceled this time." His arrival had been postponed a few days, and while it had added to AJ's worries, she'd actually been glad about it.

"Yeah," Justin said, glancing at his father. He didn't say anything else, and that only lit AJ's anxiety on fire. She too looked at Matt, whose smile hadn't slipped an iota.

"How was the flight?" she asked next, wishing she didn't have to dig so deep into her small talk reservoir so soon. "You came from Baltimore, right?"

"The city," Matt said quietly at the same time Justin said, "No, that's Lisa. She's coming from Baltimore."

"I thought she was *going* to Baltimore," AJ said, frowning. Why was everything so jumbled in her head? Since she'd been put on bedrest, she felt like she'd lost track of her life. She barely knew what day it was, and the hours slipped by like smoke disappearing into the sky.

She'd gone back to the doctor, and she'd been cleared for anything that didn't require lifting over ten pounds. She'd taken to walking in the morning, first going north toward the ferry station, and then sticking to the shoreline boardwalk all the way to the lighthouse.

Kristen would join her there, and the two of them would complete the circuit back to AJ's house. In all, it put two miles on her step counter for the day, and AJ felt like a new person after the exercise.

She'd spent so much of her life working out or being active, and the past month had been terrible for her physically and mentally. Since she'd been getting out in the sunshine, her outlook on life had improved greatly.

Last week, she'd found and written three articles, and she'd finally started to bring in some money again. She had enough in savings to go for several months, especially since she'd been doing freelance since the beginning of the year. Matt didn't ask her to pay for anything, and while they hadn't had a specific conversation about money, AJ didn't want to lounge on the couch, re-watching the same movies over and over while he went to work each day.

She'd never wanted that life, and she thought that had definitely contributed to her aversion to marriage in her twenties.

Now, at forty-four, AJ's life very nearly mirrored those of other women's her age.

"Lisa lives in Baltimore now, yes," Matt said. "She's going back there too, baby. For grad school."

"Oh, okay," AJ said, focusing on Justin again. He reached up and wiped his hand through his hair. "How was the flight from JFK? I lived in New York City for a little bit last year."

"Yeah," Justin said again. "That's what Dad said. You lived there before he got you pregnant."

AJ pulled in a breath, and Matt said, "Justin, come on." He released AJ's hand and started down the hall. "I'll show you where your room is."

Justin bent to pick up his carryon, and he grabbed the other piece of luggage Matt had left by the door. He glared at AJ as he went by, silent.

She turned and watched them go, hearing Matt say something to his son that wasn't loud enough to reach her ears. "And he's the most forgiving one," she muttered. This was going to be harder than she thought.

Her chest stung, because while she hadn't anticipated his children to throw a welcome-AJ party for her, she hadn't expected the glaring. Nor had she thought that he would act like her pregnancy was a mistake, something a sixteen-year-old boy would do because he didn't know better. As if Matt and AJ didn't know how to not get pregnant.

Like their baby was unwanted, but they were dealing with it the best way they knew how by getting married.

She couldn't get a proper breath, and she turned and went through the kitchen and out the back door. Matt had a beautiful deck that overlooked a pristine back yard. He grew roses and dwarf Granny smith apples. He spent the weekends trimming the hedges into perfect, ninety-degree angles.

While spring still only showed her face for a few hours each day, Matt had been spending a lot of time in the yard. For one, their reception would take place right here, on the lawn and deck in front of her.

For another, he spent so much time on the grounds at the golf course, which his father owned, that he thought his yard should look just as pristine.

AJ wasn't complaining, though she'd rarely lived in a home that required her to take care of the lawn. Growing up, she'd done plenty of weed-pulling and lawn-mowing, but she didn't particularly enjoy it. She'd lived apartment buildings and condos for most of her life since leaving the cove, and not having to do the yard work was only one of the perks of such a life.

Something scraped, and AJ looked left as someone opened the window in the bedroom where Justin would be staying. When Derrick came, he'd be in there with him. Matt and AJ shared the master, obviously, and Lisa would be in the third bedroom. The house had a dedicated office space, which Matt and AJ shared, and the formal living room besides the family room, kitchen, and dining room.

The three of them would have to share a bathroom, but Matt had assured AJ they could. They'd done it before.

"...really fast, don't you think?" Justin's voice came

through the now-open window. "You should hear Mom rant about it."

"I'm not married to your mother anymore," Matt said, his voice full of bite. "Which, by the way, Justin, *she* wanted. Not me. *She* cheated on me."

"If you say so," Justin said, his voice moving farther from the window.

AJ's heart pounded really hard, because she hadn't know Matt's ex-wife. She hadn't known she'd been unfaithful. She hadn't really asked him what had happened in his marriage to end it.

Matt had told her he wasn't happy, and that he hadn't been for years. He and Melanie had talked of divorce previously, but they'd waited until their youngest left the house.

His divorce had been final in August, and AJ had run into him a month later. She hadn't caused his marriage to end. She hadn't caused him to be unfaithful.

"I do say so," Matt said. "Because that's the truth. Just because she hasn't married Theo yet doesn't mean they weren't together a year before we got divorced. A year, Justin."

AJ couldn't hear what his son said, as she walked toward the edge of the deck and down the back steps. She didn't want to overhear them. She didn't want to know what Matt hadn't told her himself.

So his kids weren't happy about the baby or the wedding. They'd all agreed to come, probably out of loyalty and love for Matt. Their mother was obviously talking trash behind Matt's back, and AJ wondered what he'd do about that.

"Nothing," she murmured to the marigolds. Matt wouldn't do anything about Melanie's forked tongue. He wouldn't call her and reprimand her. He hadn't even said anything to Justin about his behavior toward AJ.

She bent down and touched the bright yellow blooms, knowing that wasn't true. He had said something to Justin; that was why they were arguing in the bedroom.

AJ thought about the dinner she'd prepared, bubbling away in the slow cooker. She didn't have all the skills Robin or Kelli did in the kitchen, but even she could put in a beef roast with potatoes and carrots. She and Matt hadn't starved yet, at least.

She'd gotten the recipe for the onion soup the roast boiled in from her sister, and AJ tugged her phone from her back pocket and texted Amy.

He's not happy to be here. I don't know how to do this.

One moment at a time, Amy said back. *It'll just be an adjustment for everyone. Be patient.*

"Be patient," AJ repeated, and she had the distinct feeling she needed to give herself time to figure out how to deal with Matt's children, and they needed time to realize how much happier Matt was now that he wasn't with Melanie.

He'd admitted that he hadn't seen himself returning to

the cove to run the golf course, but his father had called the very day he'd been served the divorce papers.

He'd come straightaway, and they'd both admitted they could stay and live in the cove. They could raise their child here, the way they were raised here.

Matt had already joked that if the baby was a girl, he was putting locks on her bedroom window, and he'd check them every evening. AJ had laughed with him, because he used to sneak in through her window at night to be with her.

In all honesty, AJ was lucky she hadn't gotten pregnant in high school, though she had known about and used contraceptives back then. She hadn't with Matt several months ago, believing herself too old to get pregnant.

"AJ," Matt said, and she lifted her gaze from the flowers. He hadn't seen her yet, and she did adore the boyish way about him. He'd had that as a teen too, and there had always been this innocence about him that touched her heart. His kindness had been the real trigger for her, then and now, and she never felt like he was judging her.

"Right here," she said, lifting her hand.

He found her and strode across the deck. "Justin wants to go to dinner."

"That's fine."

"No, it's not fine." He wore frustration on his face. He came down the steps heavily. "Sorry about that in there. I talked to him on the way over from the airport, and he didn't give any indication that he wasn't thrilled to meet you."

"He's probably just trying to process it all," she said, smiling at him. Fragility shook her heart, and her lips felt like they might crack any second.

"He said it's because you're prettier than Melanie. He said it triggered him for some reason." Matt reached for her. "I'm sorry. I was caught off-guard. I told him he can't treat you like that. Or say rude things about the pregnancy. Or he can't stay here."

"I don't want to come between you and your son. Any of your kids."

"You're not," he said. "I told him you had dinner ready, and we don't need to go out."

"I'm fine if he wants to go out to eat." It was a pot roast, not a gourmet meal she'd spent more than twenty minutes putting together. At least not physically. "I finished my article and sent it to Zephora. She said I'd hear back by Monday morning." She reached up and put her hand on the side of Matt's face, enjoying the softness in his beard.

"Besides, the baby and I are feeling like lobster rolls."

Matt grinned at her, those dark eyes filling with love and a hint of heat that made AJ's whole world expand. "Well, the baby gets whatever she wants, right?"

"Right," she said. "*He* does." They laughed quietly together, as neither of them knew the sex of their child, and AJ didn't want to find out until the doctor handed the infant to her and said, "It's a boy."

She really only wanted a boy, a fact she had not hidden from Matt. Just to goad her, he'd said he wanted a girl. That way, he'd have two boys and two girls, making a complete set.

In all honesty, AJ didn't care if the baby was a boy or a girl, though she thought she was nothing but trouble, and a boy would be easier.

Matt put his arm around her and guided her back to the steps. "So Mort's?"

"Mort's on Saturday night?" AJ shook her head. "We better call now and just pick up. We can take it to the beach and watch the sun go down."

"Sounds good," Justin said ahead of them, and AJ lifted her eyes to meet his. She painted a smile onto her face, sure he didn't really think her prettier than his mother. He simply needed more time to accept the divorce and AJ's new role in his dad's life.

She could be kind to him, and she could be patient until he had time to process the situation. Sometimes, AJ thought she was still processing how much her life had changed in only a year, and she'd appreciated how kind and patient her friends had been with her.

"Great," she said, approaching the nineteen-year-old. "If you load up a couple of beach chairs, we can relax while we eat the best seafood in the cove."

ELEVEN

Alice reached for the triangle of garlic toast on Arthur's plate. "I'm just saying..." She trailed off, not quite sure how to say what she was trying to.

"Is it because I work at the high school?"

"Yes," she said, and then she sighed. "No. Sort of?" She took a bite of the toast, wondering how restaurants got such a crispy outside on the bread. She loved the thick slab of it, and the way it crunched between her teeth. She moaned. "I love this stuff."

Arthur smiled at her, but it didn't last long on his face. "I think the twins will survive."

"I'm sure they'll survive," she said. "It's not that I'm worried about. It's the fact that I want them to keep talking to me about sensitive things. I want them to want to come home after they leave to go to college. I want them to trust me, and if I just go off and marry you, I'm afraid that will put all of that in jeopardy."

Arthur started to nod about halfway through her speech. "I'm not saying they're more important than you, but—"

"They are," Arthur said. "I know that. It's okay with me."

Alice heard the false note in his voice, and she hated that she couldn't erase it. "You're important to me in a different way than they are. That's all." She finished the toast and dusted her hands of the crumbs. "We've only been dating for a few weeks. You do realize couples talk about marriage when they're in love." She gave him a small smile, but really, her heartbeat skipped through her chest in a quick rhythm. She'd managed to put off the conversation for a week, citing her need to get through the wedding, and then a busy week with an online conference before she'd even be willing to entertain the idea of talking to him about saying I-do.

She saw him almost every day, and she enjoyed her time with him. She liked kissing him, and she liked texting with him. Her children knew about their relationship, but Alice had a feeling she'd be dealing with a coup if she told Ginny and Charlie that she was thinking about marrying Arthur.

They'd probably be horrified if they knew she was sleeping with him already. Even for Alice, their relationship had accelerated quickly. She'd been celibate for so long, even inside her own marriage. She'd tried one other relationship before Arthur, and while there had been a spark between her and Will, it had ben an old flame and easily quenched.

With Arthur, an entire lightning storm struck her cells every time she even thought about the man. He reminded her so much of the first month of her relationship with Frank, and she couldn't put another bite of her salad in her mouth, despite the delicious crab, avocado, and lemon dressing.

"I need more time," she said, meeting his eye. She reached over and cradled his face in one hand. "I do adore you, Arthur. I don't want to end things with you at all. I like where we are, and I want to keep doing what we do." She swallowed and picked up her fork as if she would take another bite of the lettuce, tomato, and fish that made such a medley in her mouth.

"Are you happy with that?"

"Very much so," he said. He turned his face into her hand and kissed her palm before taking her fingers in his. "I've simply learned to claim what I want early so it doesn't get away from me."

"Maybe you wouldn't feel the need to do that if you tried to enjoy the time we have now."

"I do enjoy the time we have now."

"You worry too much about the future," she said, giving him a knowing glance and pulling her hand back.

She speared a square of avocado and a single craisin to go with her lettuce. "Tell me I'm wrong."

"You're not wrong," he said with a sigh. "It's just...I feel like I've been waiting for a woman like you for a very long time, and I'm tired of being alone." He lifted his shoulders into a shrug. "That's all."

"Yes, but that doesn't mean we have to get married in the next thirty days." She smiled at him softly, hoping this conversation wasn't coming across as a rejection. She didn't want to end things with him. She wanted to keep getting to know him and keep finding out if they were as compatible as they first seemed.

"How is everything?" Their waiter appeared, and Alice looked up at him.

"So great," she said.

"Are you going to need boxes? Dessert?"

"I definitely want dessert," she said, and since she and Arthur had frequented the Yacht Café several times, she knew exactly what she wanted. "I'll take that warm pumpkin spice cake."

"With ice cream?" he asked.

"Is there a better way to eat cake?" She grinned at the waiter, who chuckled and looked at Arthur. "Anything for you, sir?"

"I just want another glass of wine, please," he said.

"Comin' up." The twenty-something knocked on the table and walked away, and Alice watched him go.

When she turned back to Arthur, she took another

bite of salad while he finished his lobster ravioli. "I think I should sit down with the twins and be honest with them about what our relationship is."

That brought his gaze up. "Oh?"

"Who knows?" she said slyly. "Things could shift between us at any moment, and I'll be ready to marry you sooner than I even know."

Arthur blinked at her, and Alice trilled out a laugh. "Don't look so surprised."

"You just said you needed more time."

"I do," Alice said, shaking her head. "Time to talk to the twins. Time to see how they feel. Time to know how *I* feel. I'm less than a year out from my divorce, Arthur. I'm not like you at all. But that doesn't mean I won't get to where you are in a few months. Who knows?"

Even now, her heart did a little tap dance at the thought of facing Ginny and Charlie and telling them she was sleeping with their school counselor. A man she'd met because he'd called her in to talk to her about Charlie's chemistry performance.

"Maybe this is a bad idea," she said. "I basically tell Charlie every chance I get not to do anything with his girl-friend." She put her bite of salad in her mouth, but it tasted too bitter now.

"It's not even the same situation at all," Arthur said. "For one, we're not juniors in high school."

"But he is, which is why I have to talk to him every

single day about being careful with girls." Alice sighed. "I fear he has too much of his father in him."

"I think you'd be surprised," Arthur said. "He knows who his father is, Alice." He spoke in a quiet voice and leaned back in the booth. "He knows what his father has done, and what it cost him. You've tried to shelter your kids from that, and you've done a fabulous job of it. But they know."

Alice didn't want to believe him, but deep down, she did. She wanted her kids to think only good thing about Frank, and she wanted them to believe in love. Real love. True love.

"I know they know," she admitted. "But I want them to believe in love. The kind of love Robin and Duke have. The kind of love I saw on Eloise's face, and shining from Aaron's eyes. The kind of love every young person should hope for, that their spouse will be forgiving and kind when they make mistakes, and that they'll have this future filled with rainbows and happy endings."

She sighed, really needing her pumpkin spice cake. She glanced around for the waiter, but he wasn't anywhere in sight.

"That's beautiful, Alice," Arthur said, reaching across the table to hold her hand. "Do you believe in that kind of love?"

"I did, once," she said, ducking her head.

"But not anymore?" His fingers around hers tightened.

She looked up at him, searching his beautiful eyes.

"That's one of the things I need time to find again," she said. "Because if I'm ever going to stand at an altar again, it's going to be with a man who adores me. Who I adore. And the two of us together can make sunshine and rainbows appear, no matter what the weather is around us. It'll be the true love I've always wanted in my life."

Arthur smiled fondly at her. "Sounds like a dream come true."

"Do you believe in love like that?" she asked. "Have you had that in your life?"

"No, ma'am, I have not," he said. "But I'd like it." He pulled his hand away as the waiter arrived with her cake and Arthur's drink.

He lifted the glass of wine to toast her, and the edge in his eyes told Alice that he'd like more time with her to find out if they could have this true love they spoke of.

"So more time," she said, dipping her spoon into the ice cream and looking at Arthur.

"Definitely more time," he confirmed for her.

"Okay, okay," Alice yelled over the noise a few days later. "Tacos are here."

That got the teenagers in her living room to turn in her direction and acknowledge that she'd spoken. She made every one of them stop at the front door and tell her their name before she allowed them into her house, so they had to acknowledge her then too. After that, they did their best to pretend she didn't even exist.

Now that Alice and the twins lived on Diamond Island, Charlie and Ginny's friends had shifted a little bit. Charlie said he still talked to the the friends he'd had on Rocky Ridge, but Alice didn't have to entertain them in her house.

This crew he hung with now definitely came from a different side of the tracks than the boy who'd brought pot to the pool party last summer. Charlie's new girlfriend, Sariah Page, was a straight-A student and the president of the Academic Olympiad.

Charlie had never been the smartest student in school, but he tried hard. He worked when he was motivated, and a pretty blonde girl sure was motivating.

Alice wasn't complaining about that, but she wanted Charlie to be liked for who he was, not what his report card showed.

"Thanks so much, Mrs. Kelton," a girl named Emily said. She was Ginny's best friend, and she actually did talk to Alice like a normal person.

"You're welcome," she said, and that prompted several others to express their gratitude for the tacos and quesadillas Alice had ordered from the fast-food Mexican joint that sat on the beach, only a mile away from her house.

FoodShare had saved her more times than she could admit, and on a Sunday evening before a Monday where her kids didn't have school due to a senior college and job fair the next day was the best example.

She could feed the eight bottomless stomachs in her house with a taco dozen-by-the-box for less than twenty bucks.

"Do we have any soda pop, Mom?" Charlie asked, finally coming into the kitchen with Sariah and a boy named Tad, who he'd been spending a lot of time with this year. They'd met in Charlie's shop class, and they had history and Spanish together too, which had honestly been an answer to Alice's prayers.

She worried about moving her children all over the place, and while the islands in Five Island Cove was all the same town, it was still somewhat hard to hang out with others living on the other islands. She knew, as she'd grown up on the northern-most island of Rocky Ridge, and her only choices for some evenings was to ride the ferry back to Diamond to spend time with Robin or riding her bike around the end of the island to Audrey's, a girl who'd never really liked Alice. They tolerated each other, because they were in the same year in school and had to ride the ferry together in the mornings.

After Alice's mother had died, though, Alice did what she wanted, and it wasn't to spend any time with Audrey. She didn't come home until late at night, and she'd seen first-hand some of Robin's mother's crueler statements. Still, Jennifer Golden's house had been better than Alice's.

Now, she wanted her children to be able to bring their

friends over whenever they wanted. She wanted her house to be safe for anyone who walked through the door, and if that cost her twenty dollars in tacos on Sunday night, she'd do it.

"Thank you, Mrs. Kelton," a boy named Ray said, and he smiled at her. He had nice eyes, sort of a light color between blue and green, with plenty of dark hair that curled everywhere.

"Of course," she said, smiling back.

He reached for a taco and held it up. "Before we all go back into the living room, I have to say something."

"Taco toast!" someone yelled, and Alice knew enough to get out of the way. She'd been through a taco toast before, and sometimes lettuce and tomatoes went flying. She'd also witnessed a pizza pledge, and that was slightly less messy, depending on the toppings on the pie.

"Shh," someone said, and finally, enough people had quieted for Ray to lift another taco in the air.

"I'll never eat another taco again if Ginny doesn't go to the prom with me."

"This is not happening," a girl said. Alice whipped her attention around the group, trying to find her daughter.

She knew exactly who Ray was, and Ginny spoke highly of him. Alice hadn't asked her daughter if she liked Ray for more than a friend, but the moment she located Ginny's flaming red face, she had her answer.

"Is that an invitation to the prom?" Ginny asked, her

eyes shooting lasers at the boy holding the dual tacos. "The prom that's in literally two weeks?"

Alice started to step forward and then fell back again. She'd do what she could to help Ginny get a pretty dress for the dance.

"That's the one," Ray said, still grinning. "I just found out I'm not going to my dad's, or I would've asked you earlier." He started to lower the tacos.

Ginny ducked her head and Emily and Abby, another of her friends, created a little huddle, the three of them whispering like mad.

"She's gonna say yes," Charlie said. "Don't worry, man."

Ray had the tacos all the way down by the time Ginny's huddle broke up. She folded her arms and said, "Okay, but Ray, you owe me more than a taco toast."

"Like what?" someone asked, and it sure sounded suggestive to Alice. Her pulse beat a bit faster while she waited for Ginny to answer.

Emily stepped forward and said, "She wants ice cream every day after school this week."

"She works at an ice cream shop," Charlie said, frowning.

"Exactly," Emily said, grinning. "So she'll be expecting you to stop by and get something, then fill out the survey so she gets bonus points with her boss."

"Done," Ray said, laughing. "Now, come on. I've held these tacos hostage for long enough." He'd actually done no such thing, though he was popular enough that everyone had paused in their taco consumption for his toast.

The chatter broke out again, and Alice folded her arms while Ginny giggled with her friends. Then she came rushing toward Alice, her face definitely flushed.

"Mom, can we go shopping tomorrow? Please?"

Alice didn't say yes or no right away. She'd expected the twins to sleep late and then eat cold cereal for brunch while something played on the TV. She'd work until mid-afternoon, and then they'd go see a movie or go to the beach.

She supposed dress shopping could replace that afternoon activity. "I have to work," she said. "Arthur is coming for dinner." Even as she said it, she wondered if she should cancel. She wasn't going to disclose the true status of their relationship yet, but he'd suggested he could spend more time with the twins, and Alice had thought that was a good idea.

"And there will be a budget," Alice said. "Unless you want to call your father."

"I have two hundred dollars in my account," Ginny said, grinning. "Thanks, Mom." She threw her arms around Alice and held her. "He's *so* cute. I can't believe he asked me to prom."

"So we like this boy."

Ginny nodded as if her neck had become rubber.

"Okay," Alice said. "We can go tomorrow."

Ginny squealed and said, "Thanks," before she grabbed the remaining tacos in the dozen-box and took them into the living room, where almost everyone had re-gathered.

Alice noticed that Ray had saved her a seat next to him, and that he put his arm around her and squeezed her tight before they kept eating tacos.

TWELVE

Laurel stood on the dock, her hands in her police department jacket as the wind blew in her face. Fishing boats dotted the water in front of her, and on any other day, with any other woman, it might have looked like an idyllic, near-summer day. Blue sky. Puffy, white clouds. Salty breeze. Colorful sails, with a beach to her right where families gathered for picnics and days in the sand, surf, and sun.

She could see herself on that beach, with Paul in a pair of multi-colored board shorts and trotting toward her with a boogie board under one arm. He'd grin at her and collapse onto a towel in the sand beside her. Robin would pass out sandwiches and Alice would spring for sodas, and everything would be perfectly, completely normal.

"Normal," Laurel said, wishing she could be normal. She hadn't been operating in the realm of normal for many long years. Just when she started to think she might be edging closer and closer toward a suburban life, with a husband and children, a nice house with a green patch of lawn surrounding it, something came up that pulled her away from it.

The growl of a vehicle met her ears, and she turned away from the picture-perfect scene in front of her. Drugs found their way even into the most pristine of places, including Five Island Cove.

They could be getting onto the island via boat—a commuter boat, a private vessel...or a fishing boat. She'd put that piece into place at Eloise's wedding last weekend, when she'd seen the boats floating benignly in the water. That, coupled with Duke right there at Robin's side, had trigged Laurel's mind.

There was only one airport coming in and out of Five Island Cove, and that happened right here on Diamond Island, but there were multiple docks on every other island. The drugs could be coming in shipments to public places, like hotels, restaurants, or the golf course.

Laurel had spent every waking moment she wasn't with Paul or her new partner reading about the unique and diverse ways people moved illegal things. Money launderers used actual laundromats to move money. Strip clubs, hotel chains, anything that they could hide the money moving in and out behind real transactions.

Drugs could be no different. They could arrive in a package of new towels for an inn, or sewn inside the fish of the day on a boat selling to the most popular restaurant in the cove.

She didn't know which way to turn, and she hadn't been able to talk to anyone about the circular thoughts in her head. As she watched the man she loved, Paul Leyhe, get out of the RideShare, she knew she needed to trust him. She needed to trust him enough to tell him about her case, ask for his opinion, and then listen when he spoke.

Paul was a brilliant cop, the second in command at the department. He could help her, but only if she opened the door and let him in.

She put a smile on her face as he turned away from the car. A grin popped onto his face too, and he jogged the last few steps to her. Laughing, he swept her off her feet. "Look at us," he said, gazing up at her. "We finally have the same day off." He set her back on her feet and leaned down to kiss her.

Laurel did enjoy the intimacy that came with kissing. She almost liked kissing more than anything else, though she did like being with Paul. He treated her with love and respect, and she could lay in his arms and listen to him breathe for hours. She'd rather sleep in the same bed as him than alone, and he said she could move in with him any time she wanted.

She hadn't done it yet, mostly because she didn't want to explain anything to her mother. She also wasn't sure she wanted to live in his house and give up hers. She loved her house beyond measure, because it had been the very first thing she'd acquired on her path toward freedom.

Paul possessed more patience than anyone she knew, because he'd told her to keep the house if she wanted to. In truth, Laurel was still figuring out what she wanted.

Today, she wanted to walk the beach with Paul's hand in hers, eat lunch, and talk to him about her case.

She focused on the light touch of Paul's hands in her hair and down her back. Her mind slowed as she kissed him back, and she finally felt centered enough to get things to line up.

"Mm." Paul pulled away but kept his face close to hers. "I know we talk every day, but I've missed you none-theless."

"I've missed you too," she said. "I feel...distant from you."

"That's because you're on narcotics now." He stepped away, his eyes sticking to hers for a moment. She couldn't deny what he'd said, so she just turned back to face the wind, and he joined her.

"I want to talk about my case today," she said. "Would that be okay? I can't riddle through it alone anymore, and I trust you to tell me what I'm assuming that I shouldn't be."

"All right," he said. "How are things working out with Thom?"

"Good," Laurel said truthfully. "Yeah, good. Thom's good. He's nice, and he's smart. He works more than the Chief."

Paul chuckled and said, "I highly doubt that."

"Just feels like it," Laurel said. "Narcotics is a lot different than being in a car."

"Yes, it is," Paul said. "Going crazy behind the desk?"

"Yes, a little," she said. "It's not my strong suit. I like being out there." She waved her hand toward the horizon in front of her. "Doing things."

"Mm." He grinned at her and slid his arm around her waist. "I know, sweetheart." He took a deep breath and blew it out. "Today is gorgeous, isn't it?"

"Yes," Laurel said. "Feels like summer already, though my mother says it's still cold in Nantucket."

"In May?" Paul asked. "I suppose it rains a lot in the spring. With the wind, it could be cold."

Laurel drew in a breath that wasn't cold here in Five Island Cove and blew it out. "We're trying to track down where the drug entry point is," she said. "We've got a witness who turned over the air traffic control books, and we've got two people in custody. But." She let out a sigh.

"But what?" Paul asked.

"They're story is too perfect," she said. "It's orchestrated and well-rehearsed. It's not right."

"You think the drugs are coming in another way."

"I feel it in my gut," Laurel said.

"You always have to listen to your gut."

"So I've been exploring all the ways things are moved, and it's everything from planes, boats, regular citizens mailing things to each other, to businesses, and just anywhere. They could be coming in through the multiple docks on any island here. Someone could be shipping them via commercial boat or plane to hotels, restaurants, and the like. Thom and I are going out to Rocky Ridge this week to find out what's going on with the golf course there."

"The golf course?"

"Yeah, because it's right on the water. They have a floating green even. It wouldn't be hard to have someone motor by in a boat and hand someone a package. Drug deals don't take place in back alleys anymore. They're everywhere, and they originate online."

"Okay, true," Paul said. He paused for a moment as a mother came jogging toward them, her stroller in front of her. She took up the whole sidewalk, and Paul stepped out of the way so she could get past. He grinned and nodded at her, but the interruption actually annoyed Laurel.

"So what's the problem?" he asked, once the jogging mother had passed. Laurel's mind had gone with her, because she wondered if that could ever be her.

"Do you want kids?" she asked Paul, who looked at her with shock in his dark blue eyes. She hooked her thumb over her shoulder. "Yeah, kids. Like, if I had a baby, I could run with him in a stroller along the beach in the morning."

Paul blinked, and Laurel had never surprised him before. She smiled at him and gave him a playful push. "Did I surprise you?"

"A little," he said, grinning. "I didn't think you wanted children."

"I think I could have kids," she said. "With you."

He ducked his head in an adorable way. She'd seen the alpha-male side of him at work, but she sure did love the softer side of him that came out on their dates. "I'd love to be the father of your kids," he said.

Laurel took another breath, and things shifted for her again. In the grand scheme of things, her first narcotics case was just that—a case for work. She didn't have to dedicate her entire life to it. She wanted room for Paul too, and she wanted room for her friends.

"I think I'm so confused about the case," she said slowly. "Because it touches every part of my life."

"How do you mean?" Paul strolled along beside her, and Laurel recognized how comfortable she was with him.

The weight of her thoughts descended on her again. "For example, let's say I start visiting the hotels and inns in the cove. Who would I have to go to? I'd start with the bigger places, but then I'd be looking at hotspots that are a little bit out of the way. Places where it would be easy to get packages or guests that no one in the cove would ever see."

"The Cliffside Inn."

Laurel knew Paul would get it. She didn't even have to keep explaining, but she went on anyway. "Matt Hymas owns the golf course on Rocky Ridge. I'm already going there this week, and I don't know how to tell AJ. I don't even know if I *should* tell AJ. If we start looking at govern-ment officials or cops that are pilfering on the side, that brings in Kelli's boyfriend, and the Chief..."

Her mind spun now. "If I start investigating fishing vessels, we're talking about Robin and Duke. Waterfront properties brings in the lighthouse and Kristen. It could literally touch all of my friends, and I can't hurt them. I won't." She ran her hand through her hair, feeling her panic start to rise. "But it's my job. If they're bringing drugs into Five Island Cove, they should be stopped."

"Laurel, honey, stop and think for a second." Paul stepped in front of her and made her physically stop. "Do you really think the Chief is the one **bri**nging in drugs."

"Of course not," she whispered.

"I don't think so either," he said. "Nor do I think Cliff-side is getting shipments of cocaine with their soaps and shower gels."

Laurel shook her head, near tears now. "I don't either, but I don't know how to turn a blind eye to all those places just because they're my friends. That's not what detectives do. You have to investigate the case and turn over every stone."

She thought about the money Kelli had found only a month ago, along with the list of names her father had written on a paper with it. AJ's name had been listed, and Laurel had seen Aaron Sherman dive into the case without any prejudices at all.

She'd also seen AJ retreat from the group, and she'd

seen the way it had splintered through the other women. In the end, of course AJ wasn't involved with Kelli's father, but the words had already been said. The accusations made.

AJ hadn't left the cove or shut everyone out, but Laurel could still feel that things weren't the same. If she started making accusations left and right or even asking questions about Duke's fishing boat or Kelli's boyfriend and what he really did for the town of Five Island Cove, she'd be setting bridges on fire.

"So you're going to the golf course," he said. "See what that turns up. Look through the controller's notes again. Do some interviews of your guys in custody. What does Thom say?"

"Thom says the guys we have in custody are covering up for someone bigger." Laurel sighed again. "I agree with him, but I'm not sure who that is. Anyone big...Paul, it's Aaron or Aaron's father. I mean, think about it."

"Not true," Paul said, and he sounded like she had when she'd argued with Thom about this. "There could be any number of people connected to this that would be a big deal. Do you know how the drugs are getting to the users?"

"Harold said he was dropping it in the library night book return."

"What?" Paul asked, looking at her with shock again. "Have you interviewed all the librarians?"

"There are three," Laurel said, frowning. "And no, I

personally haven't. Thom said he and Kent followed up that lead, and they learned nothing."

"The library?" Paul asked again. "Laurel, there *has* to be something there. How many people have a key to the library? There are cameras at the library. Closed-circuit. If he was dropping the drugs there at night, how many people could really get in and retrieve those?"

Laurel nodded. "You're right. I can't just accept Thom's word that the lead didn't pan out. I need to talk to the librarians. Find out who has access to the library at night. It is connected to the courthouse, as well as the traffic school, and they run those on Thursday nights."

"Did he make drops only on Thursdays?"

Laurel's mind spun in a new direction now. "Harold didn't specify," she said slowly. "I'll be sure to ask him." She needed to figure out where the closed-circuit tapes were stored, and she could get the footage of the evenings surrounding the dates Harold and Lucas said drugs had been flown into the cove.

"Okay," she said, exhaling. "Enough about work, unless you have something."

"Nothing for me," he said, sliding his arm around her again. "Do you really mean enough about work?"

"Yep," she said. "We're going to enjoy lunch, and Robin gave me a whole list of things I want to ask you about for the wedding. Then she can start putting together our dream event."

Paul groaned, but he laughed in the next moment. "But you just said we didn't have to work today."

"Planning the wedding is *not* work," Laurel said, hipping him away from her. "It's easy stuff, Paul, like what kind of cake you want and the colors for the dresses and flowers."

"Mm hm," he said with a touch of sarcasm. "Aren't we wearing uniforms? You said you'd wear that sexy police-woman skirt." His hand on her hip tightened, and Laurel warmed from head to toe.

"I will," she said. "But I have to carry flowers down the aisle, Paul. We need centerpieces. Decorations. The colors are for those."

"Ah, I see."

"Do you?" she asked. "We should probably get our engagement pictures done too, because we're not having a long engagement."

"I guess selfies don't count," he said.

"No," she said, smiling into the wind now. "Selfies don't count." She managed to push her worries about her case to the back of her mind, but they didn't go away completely. She finally got to enjoy herself with her fiancé by telling herself she'd go over all of the notes on the case once she got home later that night.

THIRTEEN

Kelli walked up the hill toward the house on Seabreeze Shore, the sight of it glowing in the sun making her heart fill with wonder and joy. She couldn't believe she owned this house, and she couldn't believe her dreams of opening her own yoga studio lay only six weeks in the future.

That thought sobered her slightly, and she arrived at the house a few minutes later, panting and out of breath. "Better than yesterday," she told herself. She'd been riding the ferry with Parker from Pearl to Bell, where he continued on to Diamond with another mom and her son. Kelli got off and made the short, ten-minute walk around the corner and up the hill from the ferry station to the wellness center she was implementing into this house.

She'd only been doing so for about ten days, and every day, the walk got easier and easier.

She found a half-dozen packages on the porch, which had also become the norm. She'd been ordering everything from towels for the aerobics classes to plastic cups for the juice bar to scented lotions for the bathrooms.

The front door sat slightly ajar, and Kelli nudged it open with her foot to hear a couple of guys talking inside. Her construction foreman appeared a moment later, wearing his sunglasses inside the house as the light streamed through the stained glass windows. "Morning," he said, smiling at her. "I wasn't sure where you wanted those."

"I'm not either," Kelli said, entering the house with two boxes stacked on top of one another. She took them to the right, into the room where she'd found the money that funded this project, and put them on the table there.

The furniture in this room would eventually be cleared out, but for now, Kelli was using the space as an office of sorts.

Cal brought in the biggest box with a groan, and Kelli went to get the last few. "Thanks," she said, pushing her bangs back out of her face. Cutting them had been a big mistake, and she honestly had no idea what she'd been thinking.

She felt so different this week than even last week. Parker would be leaving for the summer soon. Another school year would end. She'd quit her job at the junior high. She'd been able to attend the Wednesday luncheon last week, but it hadn't been the same without Eloise there.

She returned home from her honeymoon tomorrow morning, and she'd be at the luncheon a few hours later.

"You wanna come look at the changes upstairs?" Cal asked.

Kelli gave him a smile, because he and Ian had been here every day for the past week. "Sure," she said. "The pipes were okay, you said?"

"Yes," he said, heading for the stairs. He took them two at a time all the way to the top, but Kelli had just climbed that hill. She'd been doing her aerobics routine in the afternoons, and her stamina would be back where it needed to be before she had to start teaching classes. Right now, though, she took the steps one at a time like a normal person.

The scent of coffee reached her nose, and she perked up as Ian came out of her old bedroom with a to-go cup in his hand. "I brought this for you, Miss Kelli," he said.

"You're a lifesaver." She took the coffee and inhaled the rich aroma of it before taking a sip. "How's it going in there?"

Her old bedroom was going to be a massage room. They needed water in the room though, and that had required some plumbing from the bathroom that sat across the hall.

"Good," Ian said. "Come check out the vanity." He stepped back into the room, and Kelli followed him. The glorious light poured in the front of the house, and Kelli closed her eyes against the brightness and warmth. It would be such a shame to put heavy black-out curtains over that window, and once again, her mind flashed to making this space a place to do pedicures instead.

Maybe it could be both, she thought. Massage tables could fold up and be put away. She turned toward the wall where her bed had been, and she could easily put three pedicure stations there. The windows took up the wall in front of her, and then to her right, the wall there could hold a television.

Her masseuse could play soothing music over the device, or they could put on daytime TV for women getting their nails done. The massage table could go right inside the closet when they weren't using it, and the vanity would be used for nails and massages.

"It looks great," she said, her eyes finally landing on the four-foot addition to the bedroom. She stepped over to the single sink, the cabinets below it a shocking white and the countertop a deep contrast in dark brown.

She could still see through the floor, and the boards they'd pulled up to run the pipes had been stacked in the closet. They'd put all of that back together, though, and Kelli could bring everything together with rugs, drapes, and linens. She knew the softer pieces of a room actually made it possess a certain feel, and everything she'd been looking at for her wellness studio came in shades of peach, gray, and blue.

She wanted soothing. Comfortable. Tranquil. A running water fountain in this room would be fantastic, and Kelli could see it in the front corner, the droplets all lit up by the sunshine.

She met Cal's eye as he came through the door and into the bedroom. "Remember how I said I might want to do pedicures in here?"

A wary look entered his eye, but Kelli forged forward. "How hard would that be to plumb?"

"It's a good thing I'm married," he said, giving her a smile. He stepped between her and Ian and pointed at the floor. "My wife has changed her mind a zillion times on things around our house. So I figured since you'd mentioned it, I'd go ahead and have Linus put in the pipes you need to fill the basins."

"On this wall?" Kelli asked, her vision shifting. She looked past him to the far wall.

"I know what you're thinking," he said. "It's an outside wall, ma'am, and it would cost you thousands to run the pipes over there. They're already here, as they go down to the bathroom below this and into the kitchen. Remember, it's like veins spreading out. You can't get too far from the source."

"Right," she said, turning in a full circle as her view for the room changed. "I could still do two chairs over here."

"Yep," Cal said. "If there's something you don't need water for, you can do that on the other side."

She nodded and gave him a smile. "Thanks, Cal. This is amazing."

"We'll have this room back together today," he said,

glancing at Ian. "The new cabinets for the kitchen are coming this afternoon, and we'll get started on installing those too."

"New fixtures for the bathroom downstairs by the end of the week," Ian said.

"Then we're on to cosmetic repairs and touches," Cal said. "We'll be out of your hair in less than two weeks."

Kelli couldn't believe how quickly they worked. The remodel and repurposing of the house would only take three weeks, and she reminded herself it was just the updating of two bathrooms and a kitchen, as well as this new plumbing into this room. They weren't tearing walls down and ripping out everything to the floorboards.

"Come see the new partition in the master," Cal said, and Kelli's heartbeat bumped strangely. She had to stop thinking about the large, long room that took up the entire western half of the upstairs as her parents' bedroom.

The room had a big picture window on the north side of it, as well as one that faced west. Since it was such a large room, and Kelli had two of those downstairs, she wanted this one to be sectioned off slightly.

She followed the two men down the hall and past the steps. In the meeting room, as she was calling it, she found the partition exactly as she'd pictured it. "Oh, wow." The light from the north windows came around the side of the wall as well as over it, as Cal hadn't connected it to the ceiling. "It really is just a partition."

"You weren't sure you'd like it," he said with a

knowing smile. "So we preserved the great height in the room that the vaulted ceilings give by not taking it all the way to the ceiling. The light you want is still there, from both windows."

He moved toward the bathroom. "We re-stained the wood in here to make it more modern, and the three-day bathroom fitters took care of the shower and tub. New toilet is waiting for install, and that's it."

Kelli had forgotten she was updating this bathroom too. She still had some sort of mental block about this room she needed to figure out. She took a quick look in the bathroom, nodded, and then faced the rest of the space.

She envisioned this as a great space for women to meet. She could have nutritionists and dietitians come do classes here. Clothing classes for how to wear the right type of clothes for a specific body type. Anything really, though she didn't particularly want to do aerobics or yoga up here, unless her schedule became so full she couldn't meet the needs of the people coming to the wellness center.

Around the partition, that space would host her office. She'd wanted a space specifically for that so she wouldn't take her work home with her, and she crossed the meeting space to the office area. Joy filled her at the quaint space with all that natural light. She had enough room for a desk and chair, a filing cabinet, and a lamp.

That was all she needed, and she turned back to Cal and Ian, who both wore questioning expressions.

Kelli had a hard time controlling her emotions, and she nodded as she grinned from ear to ear. "It's perfect. Thank you. Thank you so much." She went toward the tall, burly construction men and hugged them both, only worrying afterward if such a thing was appropriate.

They'd murmured words of "you're welcome," and "of course," and they all started downstairs.

"We'll be in and out," Cal said.

"I'm going to unbox and put things away," Kelli said. "Then I have interviews, but I can do those on the porch if I have to."

"We won't be in your rooms downstairs," he said. "Just back and forth."

She acknowledged that she'd heard him, and then she went toward the table holding all the boxes they'd brought in that morning. She removed fluffy Turkish towels the color of driven snow, a case of antibacterial wipes, and the new front doorknob from one box.

"Look what came," she said to Ian as he entered the house with his toolbox. "Can you put this on today?" The new doorknob came with an electronic code. That way, anyone could get into the center if they had the code. No keys required.

Kelli was planning to run an early-morning yoga class that started ten minutes after the first ferry arrived on Bell Island. She wouldn't run that one, but the one later in the morning after school started.

Right after that class, she'd do an aerobics class, and

then the juice bar would open. She honestly had no idea how many people would come all the way to Bell for yoga, aerobics, or wheatgrass, but she'd been working on the website and her social media for the past week too.

Eloise had promised to help her with the software needed for booking classes and clients, and even as a tremor of fear ran through Kelli, a stronger one of excitement overshadowed it.

"Sure thing," Ian said, taking the doorknob. "These are easy. Just the one?"

Kelli turned back to the boxes. "I actually ordered two, one for each door... Let me see if the other one is in another one of these boxes." She dove back into the boxes and found the second doorknob nestled among several boxes of teas.

She worked steadily, finding new homes for all of the things she ordered. Her phone rang near lunchtime, if the grumbling in her stomach was to be believed, and she swiped on the call from Shad.

"Hey, how's it going over there today?" he asked.

Kelli sank into her office chair and faced the windows that overlooked the front yard. "So amazing." She sighed at the gently waving leaves on the trees. "You'll have to stop by and see the progress. The bathrooms look great, and the new partition is fantastic." She continued to tell him about the pedicure idea, and then she asked, "How did your meeting go this morning?"

His sigh wasn't nearly as blissful as hers, and Kelli

immediately started to brainstorm ideas to cheer him up. Shad loved to eat, and Kelli always went to Diamond in the afternoons to pick up Parker from school.

"It was a doozy," he said. "So much so that I left work early."

"You did?" She got to her feet and started toward the front door. Something in her gut told her she'd find her boyfriend coming up the street toward the house on Seabreeze Shore. A smile filled her whole soul. "You're on Bell, aren't you?"

"Not quite," he said, chuckling. "But almost. Wondering if you could play hooky this afternoon."

"Why?" she asked, her pulse trembling as she stepped onto the porch. "What did you have in mind?"

"Me and you," he said quietly, because he probably stood nearby other people. "Lunch at The Kaleidoscope Café. A walk on the beach. Maybe a little gardening before you have to go back to Diamond…"

"Gardening?" Kelli giggled. "You're talking about going back to your place after lunch. Kaleidoscope will be busy at noon."

"I've called ahead," he said.

"Ah, so you're planning on me saying yes."

"Hoping," Shad said.

Kelli had the distinct thought he was hoping for a lot that day. Lunch, a romantic walk on the beach, and then taking her back to his place for some "gardening." Her lungs forgot they were supposed to inhale, and her head turned fuzzy.

She hadn't been with a man in a long time, and certainly not someone she wasn't married to. Her voice seemed to take a vacation as she reverted to the woman she'd been last year when she'd first come to the cove for Joel Shields's funeral.

Behind her, a door slammed, and Kelli jolted out of that scared skin. That woman who thought about her husband before herself in every instance. "I can play hooky this afternoon," she said. "But I think we should talk about...a few things before we do any gardening."

"Can't wait," Shad said, the smile in his voice obvious. "Should I get a RideShare and come get you? Or do you want to meet me at the ferry station?"

"How far out are you?"

"Ten minutes," he said.

"I'll meet you," Kelli said. "Give me twenty minutes, and I'll be there." The call ended, and Kelli hustled back inside to figure out where she'd left things. She gathered her purse and her wits and called good-bye to Cal and Ian.

The walk back to the ferry station always went faster, because most of it was downhill. She'd just reached the corner when she caught sight of a woman walking toward her, a little yorkie on a leash at her side.

"Mom," Kelli called, and her mother looked up from the ground. They smiled at one another, and instead of turning to walk the half-block to the ferry station, Kelli crossed the street to hug her mother.

"I was just coming to the house," her mom said, grinning as she stepped out of the embrace. "I have big news."

Kelli's smile tipped a little, but she managed to keep it in place.

"Devon proposed." Her mom's smile couldn't be contained, and her next words rushed out of her. "He proposed, and I said yes, and we're going to get married right here on Bell Island."

Kelli wasn't surprised by this news, and she laughed as she drew her mom into another hug. "I'm so happy for you, Mom," she said. "He's so great, and you deserve to be happy." She pulled away and held her mom by her shoulders. "Have you told Heather and Sabrina?"

"Not yet," she said. "I was coming to talk to you first."

"When's the big day?"

"That's what I wanted to talk to you about," her mom said. "I want all you girls to come. I want the whole family to come. Sabrina is busier than everyone else, and she probably won't be able to come in the summertime." Worry entered her mother's expression. "I was thinking the holidays. Thanksgiving or Christmas. Would that be terrible?"

Kelli frowned, trying to find a reason why that would be terrible. "I don't see why," she said. "It would be a good time for them to come, I would think. Celebrate the holiday together, then have the wedding."

"Right."

"Do you want me to text them?" Kelli asked, glancing toward the ferry station as the big boat blew its horn to signal its arrival. "Shad's meeting me for lunch."

"I won't keep you, then," her mom said. "And yes, if you could text them to find out what they think, that would be great."

Kelli nodded, her attention divided. Her mom turned and went back the way she'd been coming, as she lived on the west beach on Bell Island. Kelli walked toward the ferry station, her mind brewing over why she had to be the one to tell Heather and Sabrina about their mother's engagement.

There had to be more going on in those relationships than she knew, but she wasn't sure what. She knew her own relationship with her mother had been stilted and stalled for a long time, and neither Heather nor Sabrina had been back in the cove for longer than Kelli had.

She did know she didn't want to get in the middle of family drama, but she did want both of her sisters to come home and see how different things were.

As she caught sight of Shad, who burst into laughter when he saw her, she realized that the cove wasn't different. *She* was. She'd changed.

Just kissing Shad in public told the world that. "Sorry your meeting was hard," she whispered as people flowed around them in the ferry terminal.

"It's fine," he said. "Now, what has you glowing? Can't all be from the plumbing in the center."

"My mom is engaged," Kelli said, some of her earlier excitement returning. A natural worrier, she knew the anxiety over talking to her sisters and trying to get them to come to the cove for the wedding would return soon enough. Right now, though, she just wanted to enjoy the afternoon alone with her handsome boyfriend.

"Engaged," Shad said, giving her a sexy smile filled with insinuations. "That's an interesting idea..."

FOURTEEN

Eloise opened the glass door that had Cozy Cakes etched on it and faced the darker interior.

"There she is," Robin said, and Eloise saw a shape rise from a table deeper in the space. "I can't believe she made it. I told her she didn't have to come."

"I wanted to come," Eloise said. "Besides, I've been home for an hour." She walked toward Robin, her eyes adjusting to the dimmer light quickly. She hugged her friend and turned to AJ, who'd also risen from the table.

"My goodness," she said. "You all look so different." She couldn't believe the life she lived now, and while she knew the honeymoon was over, and she and Aaron had returned from their trip to Italy, she still felt like her hours were filled with dreams.

Tomorrow, she'd return to normal life. She'd get Billie and Grace off to school. She'd kiss Aaron good-bye and tell him to be safe at the station. She'd take the ferry to Sanctuary and work at The Cliffside Inn, catching up on everything she'd missed in the past ten days while she'd been gone.

"How was Italy?" AJ asked.

"Oh, we're not at the Wednesday Tell-All yet," Eloise teased. They better hurry up and taste this cake if they even wanted to make their weekly luncheon with the other women.

She stepped back and met Amy's eyes. AJ's sister looked so much like her, and yet so different at the same time. Her hair wasn't quite as golden, and her eyes seemed to hold more...life than AJ's. "It's good to see you, Amy," Eloise said pleasantly. "I didn't mean to interrupt. My RideShare got stuck in the detour."

She pulled out the remaining chair at the table and sat down as the others did too. Robin introduced Lana Mullen, the owner and baker of Cozy Cakes, and she went back to the binder on the table in front of her.

It hadn't been that long ago that Eloise had picked out her own wedding cake, and familiar excitement grew inside her. AJ had been waiting for this day for as long as Eloise, and she knew what it felt like, tasted like, and looked like to have such an amazing dream come true.

Lana went to get the first samples, and Robin met Eloise's eye. "Really, how was the trip?"

"The most amazing thing ever," Eloise said. "Such rich

history in Italy. So many old buildings." She sighed as if that could adequately explain an entire country.

"Did you do that gondola ride?" AJ asked. "The one you texted about?"

"Yes," Eloise said. "It's just as romantic as you see in the movies." She grinned around at the other women. "I'd go again in a heartbeat."

"Duke and I are thinking of doing a vow renewal next year," Robin said. "Twenty years. We never really got a honeymoon. Maybe we should go to Italy."

Eloise's eyes widened. "Robin, you would *love* it."

"I had a boyfriend from Italy once," AJ said, and that didn't surprise Eloise at all.

"Did you go to Italy?" Amy asked.

AJ shrugged, something mischievous in her eyes. "Not, like on a plane. But he was a good cook, and he'd serve me these perfect Italian cookies in bed."

"Okay," Robin said, rolling her eyes. "Going to Italy is not the same as eating biscotti with your boyfriend in a condo in Miami."

Everyone burst out laughing, AJ included, and Lana returned with a huge serving platter holding three different varieties of cake.

"Oh, wow," AJ said, her eyes widening as she took in the beautiful slices of cake on the plates. "I already know which one I want based on looks."

"Which one is that?" Lana asked.

Eloise could've picked for AJ, because she knew what

AJ liked. As the other woman pointed to the pale cheese-cake with delicate raspberries and blackberries perfectly positioned on top, she smiled. "I would've picked that one for you, AJ," she said.

"I want that in my mouth right now," Amy said.

"I'm not sure it fits with the schematics of the rest of the wedding," Robin said, drawing every eye to her. "What?" She shuffled some papers in front of her, and Eloise had forgotten how everything had to "flow" for Robin.

"You wanted casual, AJ," she said. "You're wearing a non-traditional dress, and Matt's not even wearing a tie. You're getting married on the golf course, and then everyone is moving to your backyard. You're serving seafood and steak bites from—" She cut a glance at Eloise, who raised her eyebrows.

Was Robin *judging* what AJ had chosen for her wedding?

"I don't want to give everything away," she said, clearing her throat. "I'm just saying I'm not sure a fancy cheesecake fits with the rest of the décor or the food."

AJ blinked and looked at the cheesecake as Lana put it in front of her. "I have plenty of selections," Lana said. "Let's start with this one. I can make it less..." She cut a glance in Robin's direction. "Elegant."

Eloise pulled in a breath, and Robin shook her head. "I didn't mean to say the wedding isn't going to be elegant."

Eloise picked up her fork as Lana put a plate of cake in

front of her. "I don't remember tasting this for my wedding."

"That's because you had the quintessential beach wedding," Robin said. "And a fruit platter for dinner. We didn't want fruit on the cake, remember?"

"Yes, I remember," Eloise said, giving Robin a wide smile. She took a bite of the cheesecake, her eyes rolling back in her head. "Mm, this is good."

"I do like this," AJ said. "What would you do to make it more...less elegant?"

"Let's say rustic," Robin said crossly. "I did *not* say your wedding wouldn't be elegant."

"I know," AJ said, a smidge of snap in her voice too.

"It's not woodsy," Amy added. "Does rustic work?"

"These are all semantics," Lana said. "People certainly serve cheesecake at all types of backyard events." She gave AJ a smile and sat down. "Eat, ladies. Let me find what I mean." She began to flip through her binder, and Eloise knew she shouldn't, but she ended up eating the entire slice of cheesecake.

She noted that Robin did too, but she'd probably put in a few miles on the beach that morning. Amy only had a few bites, as Amy was by far the most proper among them. "How are the girls?" she asked, and Amy lit up.

"They're great," she said. "Very excited to be flower girls in Aunt Ava's wedding." She beamed at her older sister, and Eloise knew they'd had a rough relationship for a while. It seemed AJ had done that to everyone as she'd figured out who she was and how to be around other people.

Eloise smiled at Amy and then AJ, who peered at the binder as Lana moved it closer to her. "Come look, Robin."

Robin got up from her seat, leaving behind her papers and folders. How she kept track of everything amazing Eloise and always had. She had the uncanny ability to hold tons of details and information in her head, as Eloise had watched her plan proms and dances in high school, and now weddings and other events, big and small, around the cove.

She stepped between Lana and AJ and bent down to see the binder too. Lana swept her long, beautiful auburn hair over her shoulder and leaned back slightly. "This is a cake I did for a July wedding. Their theme was patriotic, believe it or not, but we wouldn't have to go all-out with the red, white, and blue.

AJ studied the cake, a fine line between her eyes. Amy leaned toward the binder too, but Eloise just swiped her finger through the last bit of raspberry puree on her plate.

"I do like this," AJ said. "No flags, of course. But the berries are a nice touch. They make it casual and dressed up at the same time."

"No blueberries," Robin said. "Lisa's allergic, remember?"

"Yes," AJ said, though it was clear she'd forgotten. That was why people paid Robin what they did. She kept track of who and what they needed to make sure the wedding would go off without a hitch.

"I do like this," Robin said. "It feels more...appropriate for the event we're having for AJ. It'll be classy and sophisticated, of course. But not fussy. This cheesecake feels fussy."

"So this isn't a cheesecake," Lana said, pulling the binder back in front of her as Robin returned to her seat. She cast Eloise a look, and El gave her a quick smile, hoping that was enough to buoy her up and give her the confidence she needed.

"It's a vanilla bean cake with lemon curd filling," she said. "I didn't make it today, but I can whip it up in the next few days and give you a taste."

"You sold me at lemon curd," Eloise said with a light laugh. That broke the tension at the table, and AJ smiled at Eloise too.

"Show her," AJ said, and Lana slid the binder across the table to Eloise. Amy leaned closer to see it better too, and Eloise loved the brightly decorated cake.

"Would you do all the tiers?" she asked. "It feels like a lot."

"I think three or four," AJ said casually. "And I think if you put some twigs on it, and maybe some yellow leaves or something, it would be more appropriate."

"Oh, my word," Robin said, clearly disgusted. "Twigs? No, AJ. No."

AJ burst out laughing, and she reached over and took

Robin's hand in hers. "Robin, relax, would you? I was kidding."

Eloise tried to hold back the laughter building behind her lungs, but she couldn't. It too came flying out of her mouth, and she clapped one hand over it to try to stifle the sound.

"Okay," Robin said, her shoulders sagging. "I am a bit wound up." She exhaled and closed her eyes as she took a deep breath.

Eloise got out her phone and quickly sent a text to the group, though she sat with two of them. *We need to take Robin and Duke dinner for the next few nights until he leaves. Then she'll have tons of leftovers, and he'll eat like a king while she's still working a ton.*

She didn't check with Robin first. She didn't care if her friend got a little mad and then tried to refuse the meals—which Robin would do. Eloise could see and feel this need, and she was going to do something about it. If she had to order food and send it to Robin's address for the next week, she would.

She wouldn't need to, though, because only seconds after she sent the text, Kristen responded with, *I'll take tonight. I forgot about today's luncheon, and I put a whole chicken in the oven. I'll bring it by around six, Robin.*

Before Robin could even look at her buzzing phone, three more texts had come in. Eloise grinned to herself and kept her eyes down as Robin picked up her phone.

"Eloise," she said, disapproval in all three syllables.

"You're tired," Eloise said quietly, refusing to look at Amy or Lana. "Let us do this for you."

The extent of Robin's exhaustion must've been more than Eloise even knew, because Robin didn't even argue. Eloise looked at her and found her eyes shining as she nodded. "Fine."

"Fine," Eloise said, smiling at her and reaching to take her hand too. She squeezed once and moved the binder back toward Lana. "I love this cake. No twigs or yellow leaves though. Just strawberries and raspberries for miles."

"Four tiers," AJ said. "The vanilla and lemon is fine. You don't need to make it for me to taste."

Lana looked like AJ had suggested she frost a cake with manure. "Of course I do. I never serve a cake my client hasn't tasted first." She too picked up her phone and tapped a few times. "I can do it Monday morning if you'd like to come by for fifteen minutes to taste?" She looked back and forth between AJ and Robin, who both nodded.

"Just come around eleven-thirty or twelve," Lana said. "No appointment necessary." She grinned at Robin. "You bring me the best brides, Robin. Thank you for that."

Eloise didn't think Robin got thanked enough for what she did, and she was glad Lana had picked up on that. Her phone rang, and Marge's name sat there. "Excuse me," she said, getting to her feet quickly. "This is my manager."

She hurried away from the table as the line rang a couple more times and Robin said they might as well eat the chocolate cake so it didn't go to waste.

"Marge, hello," Eloise said pleasantly, heading for the tall wall of windows in front of her.

"Eloise, you're back in the cove, right?" Marge asked. "I thought you'd landed this morning."

"Yes," Eloise said, but she didn't elaborate. She'd told her staff at The Cliffside Inn that she wouldn't be back until tomorrow.

"Okay, good," she said, and the line scratched as she moved. "I just wanted to talk to you about the night janitor."

"Okay," Eloise said slowly. She'd hired an older gentleman in his late fifties to come in the evenings and clean up the kitchen and lobby areas. He did a little bit of maintenance around the property too, including taking care of the swimming pool and anything that actually needed to be fixed.

She employed a groundskeeper to maintain the lawns and gardens, and three housekeepers in addition to herself and Marge, who managed the kitchen in addition to living on-site for any issues that happened while Eloise wasn't there.

"I found him taking some food while you were gone," Marge said, her voice low and mysterious. "I didn't say anything to him, because I wasn't sure..."

Eloise frowned, her mind working quickly. "What food?"

"Oh, an extra pot pie from dinner last week. A few muffins from the morning before. Honestly, it was stuff I would've thrown away anyway, and I wasn't sure if you'd told him he could. He hasn't ever taken anything before."

Eloise had hired him about six weeks ago, as preparations for the wedding had amped up and her time to make sure cabinets didn't stick and the kitchen got thoroughly cleaned from top to bottom every night had dwindled.

"I'll talk to him," Eloise said. "Thank you for letting me know, Marge."

"It doesn't happen every day," she said quickly. "I don't want to get him in trouble."

"I know you're low-drama, Marge." Eloise smiled, because she'd tried to surround herself with as many low-drama people as possible. "Maybe he's just hungry sometimes, and he thinks the same as you. That the food will be thrown away anyway." She took a breath, her mind working fast now. "In fact, we should probably find a way to donate it to who needs it. There's no reason to throw away muffins and chicken pot pies if we don't have to."

"Is that why you sent Marilyn in last week?"

"Marilyn who?"

"Marilyn Benson," Marge said easily, as if everyone in the world would recognize that name. "She dropped by and said she wanted to talk with you about how the two of you could partner to help the community."

Eloise frowned as laughter rose from the table behind her. She turned back to her friends and the cake. "What does Marilyn do?"

"She runs the Cove Helping Hands organization,"

Marge said matter-of-factly. "She's been inviting us to the women in business meetings for a few months."

Suddenly, the bells chimed in Eloise's head. "Oh, of course." She gave a light laugh. "I think I need a major nap." She hadn't remembered telling Marilyn to stop by though. "I'll call her this week, once I get caught up with everything."

"She'd probably be a great resource for where the left-over food would be the most needed. She seems to have her hand in a little bit of everything around the cove."

"Sounds good," Eloise said. "Thanks, Marge." She hung up on her way back to the table and slid into her spot, which now held two pieces of cake—one chocolate and one almond. They were both delicious, and she let herself get caught up in the chatter at the table among AJ, Robin, and Amy.

In the back of her mind, her task list for The Cliffside Inn ballooned, and Marilyn Benson's name circulated like a black stain in clean water. She didn't know the woman very well, and she'd only spoken to her on the phone a few times. All of the invitations for the business meetings had come via email.

Aaron will know more about her, Eloise told herself, and with the idea to talk to her husband about the woman cemented in her mind, she was finally able to let go of the nagging feeling that she needed to find out what she could about Marilyn as quickly as possible.

FIFTEEN

Alice arrived at Sunshine Shores and stepped up to the hostess station. "Alice Kelton," she said. "I have a banquet room reserved." She was tired of eating out in the open and trying to hear everyone. With seven of them, she always felt like she sat really far from at least two people, and she didn't like it.

"Alice," someone said behind her, and she turned to see Robin, Eloise, and AJ arriving together.

"It's ready for you, ma'am," the hostess said. "Is your party here?"

"Some of us," Alice said. "Take them back, and I'll wait for the others." She grinned at Robin, who already had her eyebrows up. She looked pressed and sculpted today, with not a single hair out of place. She'd just gotten her eyelashes done, as well as the micro-blading on her eyebrows. She wore makeup today, which meant she'd had a meeting.

Her arrival with Eloise and AJ testified of that too, and Alice grinned at Eloise, who'd been gone for a week and a half. "You're back."

"I'm back," El said. "It's good to see you, Alice." She pulled back and studied Alice's face. "You look different, Alice. Are you okay?"

"I'm great," Alice said, though she did wonder what Eloise saw in her face.

"Spending all her time with Arthur," Robin said with a smile. Alice stepped forward and hugged her too, realizing the hostess was waiting.

"You guys should go," she said. "I'll wait for Kristen, Kelli, and Laurel."

"Okay," AJ said, and she went with the hostess. Robin gave Alice another look and then glanced at Eloise too.

"Okay," she finally said. "But we want an update on Arthur."

"I'm only saying it once," Alice said, smiling. She didn't even think she could say it once. She'd said nothing to the twins, though they'd enjoyed a nice dinner at her house on Monday night. At least Alice had thought it had gone well.

When she'd spoken to Arthur yesterday, he'd felt the same. Charlie and Ginny hadn't acted weird, and bless Ginny, she'd talked about the prom and their dress shopping escapades from that afternoon through almost the whole meal.

The bell chimed on the door, and Alice stepped forward to help Kristen enter. Jean came with her, and surprise darted through Alice. "Jean," she said. "How good to see you."

"It's okay, right?" the woman asked, her eyes filled with apprehension. "Kristen said it would be okay if I came."

"Of course it's okay you came." Alice exchanged a glance with Kristen. "You're welcome every week."

"I don't want to intrude on you girls," she said.

Thankfully, Laurel entered the restaurant in the very next moment, and Alice welcomed her into the trio. "You're not intruding," she said. "We let this one in, and you're safer than her."

Laurel looked like Alice had hit her with a frying pan instead of like she'd made a joke. Alice backpedalled quickly. "I was kidding, Laurel. You know Jean Shields, don't you?"

Laurel's eyes crinkled as she smiled. "Yes, of course. Hi, Jean."

"I sent some of the girls back to the banquet room," Alice said.

"Kelli was parking," Laurel said. "Let's just wait." She turned to Kristen and asked her something about the lighthouse that made Alice's ears perk up.

"What about deliveries at the lighthouse?" she asked.

"I was just wondering if they came by land or sea," Laurel said, her gaze as even as her voice.

"The lighthouse is on a cliff," Kristen said. "Boats can dock in the bay around the edge of the island. Sea Lion Beach? But they never do."

"Never?"

"I saw a boat down there a few days ago," Jean said, and Laurel focused in on her.

Alice squinted at Laurel, trying to figure out where this line of questioning was going.

"You did?" Laurel asked, and she might as well have pulled out her police notebook and flipped it open. "When? What day? Time of day?"

Jean looked at Kristen nervously, and Alice edged closer to Laurel in a silent attempt to get her to dial back the rapid-fire questions.

"Uh, maybe Wednesday or Thursday?" Jean guessed. "Had to be Thursday, because I'd just finished lunch, and I drove Kristen to your lunch last week."

"Jean," Alice said. "You should've come."

"I'm here now," she said, lifting her chin. "Getting out is...hard for me."

"But she wants to," Kristen said, smiling at her daughter-in-law. "Look, here's Kelli. Let's go sit, because I have some news for everyone."

Alice let them go ahead of her, and after hugging Kelli,

she stayed right next to Laurel. "What is going on?" she whispered.

"That obvious?" Laurel asked in an equally quiet voice.

"To me," Alice said.

"Well, you're a lawyer."

"You won't get behavior like that past Robin or El either."

Laurel's expression turned black, and alarm pulled through Alice. "Are you in danger?"

"No," Laurel said wearily. "I'm just so tired."

"That has nothing to do with why you were asking about a boat at Sea Lion Beach." Alice wasn't going to be put off by a comment about not getting enough sleep. She'd used that line plenty of times, and it was never true.

"I'll tell you later," Laurel said, shooting Alice a glare. "Please?"

"Okay," Alice said. "If you really will."

"I will."

They arrived in the banquet room, and as soon as Alice entered and closed the door behind her, the noise from the restaurant faded to almost nothing.

Relief hit her, and she smiled as she joined the others at the table. She sat in a spot next to Robin on her right and Kristen on her left, glad she'd thought to ask for a round table. She could see every face and hear all of their voices this way.

"I love the banquet room," Robin said.

"Me too." AJ sighed. "The noise in a restaurant wears me down in five minutes flat."

"Ditto," Laurel said, reaching for one of the menus in the middle of the table.

"News," Eloise said. "I'll go first. Italy was fantastic, and we had the time of our lives. I'm excited to get back to real life, though." She beamed around at everyone, no menu in sight.

Alice had eaten at Sunshine plenty of times, and she knew she wanted the sampler trio with a side salad, blue cheese dressing on the side.

Several of the women congratulated Eloise and welcomed her home, and as the chatter died down, Kristen said, "I'll go next. I bought a condo on the beach, and I'm closing in a couple of weeks."

A stunned silence filled the room, and then Robin squealed and launched herself out of her chair and around Alice to hug their Seafaring Girls leader.

"I'm so excited for you," Robin said. "You're going to love having more space and easier access to the beach."

"I think so too." Kristen smiled around at everyone, and Alice put her arm around her shoulders and gave her a squeeze.

"Where is it?" Laurel asked, and she seemed like a completely different person now that she'd sat down and had a glass of water in front of her. The storm cloud she'd walked in with had dissipated, and Laurel seemed her normal, cheerful self.

"Sandstone," Kristen said. "Rueben and Jean have already rented a truck for me, but I'd love to have anyone come help who wants to when I move."

"Just tell us when," Kelli said. "I can come help."

"Do you have news?" Robin asked, her eyebrows high."

"Not really," Kelli said with a slight shrug. "Things are going really well with Shad. Parker is leaving in another month to spend the summer with Julian. The wellness center is on track to open on June eleventh, and I hope you'll all come." She suddenly seemed nervous. "Then there will be at least six people there. Seven." She smiled at Jean. "Maybe eight. I think my mom will come."

"Please," Robin said. "It's going to be *amazing*. I heard a couple of ladies talking about it on the beach last week as I ran by."

"Really?" Kelli asked, her hope sky-high.

"Really," Robin said. "They said they wanted to try the yoga so they didn't have to wash sand off everything."

"It's a ferry ride," Kelli said, obviously worried about the location of the yoga studio.

"It'll be the first full-service yoga studio in the cove," Eloise said. "There's nothing like it here. The gym only does yoga three days a week, and you're going to fill a niche."

"I agree," Alice said, giving Kelli an encouraging smile. "I'll go next, if you're done."

"I'm done." Kelli gestured for her to go next.

Alice exchanged a glance with Laurel. "Arthur and I are talking more long-term." She cleared her throat. "He ate dinner with the twins on Monday night. It went well. I've, uh..." She had no idea how to tell her friends about the private parts of her life. It wasn't any of their business anyway, but she'd hoped that if she just told them, they wouldn't ask. She wouldn't have to lie.

"He's stayed over a time or two," she said, her voice grinding through her throat. That wasn't technically true, as there'd been no sleeping over for either one of them. But it got the message across, and Alice simply looked at AJ and Robin, sitting side-by-side.

"Your turn. Someone else's turn."

"Good for you, Alice," Robin said, acting as voice for the whole table. Alice caught their nods, and she was glad they hadn't made it into a squealing, big deal.

"Duke leaves in a week," Robin continued. "Thank you for bringing the dinners." She looked down, and Alice knew the moment Robin took to put her emotions back in their proper slots. She was better at it than anyone Alice knew, except maybe herself. "He'll take a bunch of it with him on the boat as he goes to Alaska, which is the part I hate the most. It's such a long journey, and he's all alone on that boat."

"He knows the way now," Kelli said gently. "And his friend goes with him."

"Yes," Robin said. "They do sometimes tie the boats together and have dinner together in the evening." She brushed at her eyes. "It was hard last year, and I thought it would be easier this year, but it's not. It's not at all."

Alice took Robin's hand in hers and squeezed. "You can come over any time. I'm just home by myself sometimes, now that the twins have jobs."

An unspoken conversation moved between them, and Alice saw the distance the break-up of Charlie and Mandie had put between them. Robin wouldn't leave her girls home alone, and she wouldn't want to bring Mandie over to Alice's, where she could run into Charlie, now her ex-boyfriend.

"Or I'll come to you," Alice said. "Easy."

"Sure," Robin said. "Easy."

"I ordered a baby bassinet," AJ said, moving the news along. The noise from the restaurant filtered into the room as the waitress entered.

Two women appeared, and they took appetizer and drink orders before leaving again.

"How are things with Matt's son?" Kristen asked, her eyebrows up.

"Getting better every day," AJ said. "He's warming slowly to me. This morning, he said he liked the way I made eggs." She grinned and shook her head. "Which is a miracle, because I can't cook anything, even eggs." She laughed, and it felt like the lighthearted kind Alice hadn't heard from AJ in a while.

She smiled at her friend, wondering if they should take some meals over for her too. She had Matt and Justin and herself to feed each night, and she might appreciate it.

"That just leaves you, Laurel," Kristen said. "What's new with you?"

She drew a deep breath, and Alice felt herself bracing for whatever came out of Laurel's mouth. The tension definitely increased at the table.

"I told you guys I got a new partner," she said, her voice its usual, quiet, even tone. She was always quiet and even and thoughtful, which was one of the things Alice liked best about her.

"But I got a whole new job. I'm not on the beat anymore. I got promoted to detective, and I'm in the narcotics division now."

"Narcotics?" Kelli asked. "Like, drugs?"

"Yes," Laurel said. "I've been assigned to a major case, and I'm currently trying to figure out how the drugs are arriving in the cove." She looked at Jean, Kristen, and then Robin. "By boat?" She glanced at Kelli and Alice. "Plane?" She met Eloise's eyes and then AJ's. "Packages to big businesses?"

"Wait, wait," Robin said, holding up one hand. "You think drugs are coming into the cove on fishing boats?" she asked at the same time Eloise said, "I'm not getting drugs at The Cliffside Inn in my soap packages, Laurel."

No one else said anything, and Alice needed a few seconds to make all the pieces line up inside her head.

"I don't think she's accusing any of us of bringing drugs to Five Island Cove," Kristen said quietly.

"I agree," Alice said quickly. "That's not what you're saying, right, Laurel?"

SIXTEEN

Laurel took a sip of her water and said, "Of course not," at the same time the door opened and the waitresses walked back in with their drinks. She didn't say anything as they approached, and no one else did either. At least nothing out loud.

Plenty of silent glances and exchanges happened without words, and Laurel had a conversation with Alice, and then a short one with Eloise.

"Are you ready to order?" one of the ladies chirped, and Laurel sat back in her seat while everyone went around and ordered their lunch.

Guilt cut through her, and she should've gone to bed before three a.m. so she'd be fresh for this lunch. She'd been at work by eight, and she'd barely been able to get out of the station to come to Sunshine today.

The moment the waitress turned to leave the banquet

room, she leaned forward. "No, I'm not accusing anyone of anything. I'm asking for your help." She looked at Robin, begging her to understand. "Maybe you and Duke could help me to know who I might talk to at the fishing docks to find out their schedules, where they sell their fish, and who the shadier characters are."

She switched her gaze to Eloise. "You're in the tourism industry now. That's a *huge* way to move products, El. I know that sucks, and *of course* I don't think you're participating in sex trafficking or drug smuggling. But that doesn't mean someone else in the hotel industry isn't. They could be, because you do get a huge amount of goods delivered that no one blinks twice at."

"I understand," Eloise said, nodding. "I'll help if I can."

"And your husband owns the golf course," Laurel said to AJ. "They have special packages with the Nantucket Steamer, and their own dock right there at the course. People can bring drugs in on their person, and they could be using that steamer and fronting as golfers, and you'd never know."

AJ blinked at her, her mouth falling open. "I don't even know what to say," she finally said.

"I'm not accusing Matt or his father or anyone at the golf course of doing it. I just need to explore every way on and off the islands, to try to find the holes and plug them." Her chest heaved, and she took a deep breath to try to calm everything. She was a cop, and she could maintain her cool. She also had very few female friends, and she did *not* want to lose these connections and relationships she now had. Her friends had practically fallen into her lap, because she'd been in the cop car that had been called to a scene with Kelli and her half-brother on Sanctuary Island.

Tears filled her eyes. "It's my first case. Everyone in narcotics is smarter than I am. I just want to do the best job I can."

"Of course you do, dear," Kristen said, and her smile held so much kindness that Laurel could breathe properly again.

"So I'd love to talk to you, Jean, about that ship. I'd love to talk to Duke before he leaves about the fishing docks." Laurel had a list a mile long of who she'd like to talk to. "I'd like to talk to Matt and see his bookings for anyone coming in on that steamer. I'd like to find out how to get in touch with other hotel owners. I'd love to talk to Shad about the town's policies on drugs."

As she looked around the table, she knew her case touched every single one of their lives. "And Alice, Robin, I'd love to talk to your kids and find out who's selling and buying at the high school."

Alice's face turned a shade paler, and her mouth dropped open too. "That's where the drugs end up? The high school?"

"One of the places," Laurel said evasively. "The biggest place, actually."

Alice looked at Robin, who looked somewhat

surprised as well. "Charlie has some sketchy friends," Alice said quietly. "At least, he used to."

"There was that boy who had pot last summer," Robin said, and Laurel perked right up.

"It's not pot I'm after," she said though. "It's meth and cocaine."

"Meth and cocaine?" Alice repeated, her voice too loud in the banquet room. "I've heard nothing of those."

"It's a growing enterprise," Laurel said. "We're trying to stem the tide before we're hemorrhaging." She met Eloise's eye, who nodded at her.

"Aaron's been worried about drugs in the cove for a year."

"We have a couple of people in custody, but their stories aren't...they don't hold up when the hard questions are asked. So I'm trying to push past their flimsy tales and find the real truth."

Laurel wanted to do that with her whole heart. Uncovering the truth and bringing justice to those who'd broken the law were two huge reasons she'd become a cop in the first place. She'd worked hard to pass the tests to become a detective, and she wasn't going to quit on this case just because it might be uncomfortable for several women in the cove.

"I'll help you," Eloise said.

"So will I," Robin said, and as Kelli said she'd talk to Shad, and Alice said she'd set something up with Laurel and her kids, Laurel's heart grew and grew and grew.

She'd already seen Robin brush the emotion from her eyes, and it took a whole lot to make Laurel cry.

She never let anyone see her tears, but today, she let them come, and she let them overflow. "Thank you," she said, allowing the hitch to clip in her voice. She ducked her head then, her face so hot now.

She wiped her eyes, and she looked up when Alice said, "Wow, Laurel never lets anyone see how she feels. I think we broke her, guys."

She half laughed as the others at the table started to giggle, but it was more of a sob than anything else. Actual tears splashed down her face, and she swiped at her cheek quickly.

"Group hug," Kelli said, and the next thing Laurel knew, every single woman had gotten up and surrounded her. Robin clutched her tightly on one side, as did Kelli on the other. Everyone piled on them, and their weight leaned into Laurel, who braced herself against the table.

"Okay, okay," she said, laughing.

"Do you get it?" Robin asked. "We love you, Laurel. You don't have to shoulder everything alone."

Laurel wanted to believe her, but it would take time for her to accept that. She'd relied so much on herself for so long, and it was hard to admit that she needed help— and that she had people she could trust to provide it.

"Thank you," she said as everyone laughed and backed up. "Really, thank you everyone."

"Just tell us what you need, Laurel," Alice said as she

walked around the table and sat down. She took a deep breath. "Okay, happy stuff. Good News Minute?"

"How about we just talk like normal people?" Kelli suggested, and that got another round of laughter.

"SO IT LOOKED LIKE A REGULAR BOAT?" LAUREL asked, keeping one eye on Jean as the woman leaned against the railing overlooking Sea Lion Beach. Laurel hadn't even known this beach existed, and apparently, the only way to reach it was to hike down the trail that led away from the lighthouse, or by boat.

"Yes," Jean said. "I've thought a lot about it since yesterday, and it was definitely Thursday. About twelve-thirty, because I'd already finished lunch. Rueben had gone back upstairs, and he's always back up there by twelve-thirty."

"Mm hm," Laurel said, watching the water undulate down below. It washed up gently on the beach, hardly any foam or white waves at all. She could definitely see an amazing afternoon slipping by on that beach, and she understood why the sea lions liked it. The privacy it afforded was good for sea mammals as well as drug deals.

She wrote a few sentences in her notebook about the beach, the weather, the date and time, as well as her witness's name. "Like a speed boat?"

"Yes," Jean said. "Like a normal boat you'd see on a

lake, pulling a water-skier."

"It's the wrong side of the island for that, right?" Laurel asked.

"Yes," Jean said. "The best place for water-skiing is between Bell and Diamond, on the southeast side of Five Island Cove. They even have an area roped off, almost like a lake."

"That's right," Laurel said. "The fishing boats go out on the southeast side of the island too, right?"

Jean turned and looked at her. "Yes," she said. "The fishing docks are over there. The best fishing grounds are south of Pearl, though. That's the rumor, at least."

"I'll ask Duke about it," Laurel said, as Robin had already texted her and said Duke could talk to her any evening before he left next week. In fact, she was planning to stick around and eat with Robin, Duke, and their girls when she showed up with dinner that night.

Her heartbeat bounced extra hard when she thought about the stew she was planning to make that afternoon. She'd been in the station by six a.m. specifically so she could leave by three o'clock today.

She certainly didn't have time to stand around in the sun, chatting with Jean Shields, even though she'd really like to. "Anything else you can think of? Did you see anyone on the boat?"

"Yes," Jean said, and Laurel noted how formal she was. She never said "yeah," but always "yes."

"A man was driving the boat. He was the only one I

saw."

"No one got on or off the boat? He stayed on the whole time?"

"For the minute or so I was watching, yes," Jean said. "I thought it was a little bit odd, seeing a boat down there, but it's not unheard of. I didn't stand there and watch for long. I'm teaching some sewing lessons in the afternoons now, and I had to get some patterns ready for my students."

Laurel gave her a closed-mouth smile. "Okay, sure," she said. "He didn't toss anything from the boat that you saw?"

"No."

"Thanks," Laurel said, snapping her notebook closed. "I'll let you go. Sorry to stay so long and make you walk out here with me."

Jean offered her a smile. "I don't mind, Laurel. I hope you get the information you need."

"Me too." Laurel returned the smile and together, the two women started back toward the lighthouse. Laurel's phone rang, and it wasn't her police radio, so it had to be a personal call. Sometimes Paul called her on her cell and not the radio, as everyone on the force could hear those conversations.

Eloise's name sat on the screen, and Laurel said, "Excuse me, Jean," and fell behind to answer El's call. "Hey," she said, turning her back on Jean's retreating form. "What's up?"

"I just had the strangest visit from Marilyn Benson," Eloise said, her voice hushed. "She's still poking around the property, in fact. I'm getting a weird vibe from her."

Laurel's hackles raised instantly, and not just because someone was messing with Eloise. "Explain more," she said, sounding very rough and very cop-like. "What did she say? What's she doing?"

"First off, my manager and chef—Marge?—she told me Marilyn had come by last week while I was on my honeymoon. She runs the Cove Helping Hands organization, I guess. She also hosts all the women in business meetings, which are apparently in the City Hall offices? I don't know; she's been inviting me since I opened the inn, but I've never gone."

"Okay," Laurel said, flipping open her notebook again and going to a clean page. She wrote Marilyn's name at the top of the sheet.

"I asked Aaron about her last night, because Marge had told me about her dropping by. He said he knows her, and she can be pushy. If I'm not interested in going to the meetings, I just have to be forthright and tell her. I didn't think I'd need to do that, because she invites me and Marge to the meetings via email. I've never answered them before."

"But she's now showing up at the inn," Laurel said, frowning out at the horizon.

"Yes," Eloise said. "She told Marge last week that she wanted to discuss ways we could partner to help the community. I have tons of leftover food most days, so I thought that might be something, but she seemed very disinterested in that."

"What was she interested in?" Laurel started walking back toward the lighthouse and the parking lot. She'd promised Thom she'd be back to the station by one-thirty to debrief and let him know about the various leads she wanted to pursue.

His wife had had a doctor's appointment that morning, or he would've come with her to interview Jean.

"She really kept pushing me to order all of my toiletries through the Helping Hands organization. She said it gives people jobs here in the cove, but when I asked her how, she couldn't explain."

"What did she explain? What's the benefit of ordering your shampoos and soaps through them?"

"Easy-to-schedule deliveries," Eloise said. "Lower prices. You know the spiel. I was actually starting to feel sold—until she said the delivery boy will stay and unpack everything for me. Then I remembered what you said about drugs coming into the cove in packages, and I thought, who really will unpack everything for me and put it away? They really do that for all the hotels in the cove?"

Laurel increased her pace, her pulse racing now. "That is interesting," she said.

"Marilyn made it sound like it was a benefit," Eloise said.

"Yeah, for them, if they're able to get drugs into the

cove without detection," Laurel said, her mind working overtime. "Thanks, El. I'm headed back to the station to talk to Thom. We're going to want to talk to Marilyn, I'm sure."

"Okay, good luck, Laurel."

Laurel arrived back at the station several minutes later, and Thom sat at his desk, poring over an open folder. As she approached, she recognized it as the one that held all the details from the air traffic controller.

"I think you're right about this," he said without glancing up as she sat down at her desk. "It's too perfect."

"We need to talk to Marilyn Benson," Laurel said, quickly relaying everything El had told her. "I talked to Jean Shields today too, and she saw a boat at Sea Lion Beach."

Thom frowned and sat back from the folder. "Marilyn Benson?" He reached up and put his hands on the back of his head. He gazed up at the ceiling, his eyes set on squint. Laurel had only been his partner for a few weeks, but she recognized this thinking pose.

"She runs the Cove Helping Hands organization, and that could be a *huge* front for drug movement."

Thom dropped his hands and looked at Laurel. "Good work, Baker," he said with a smile. "I know you're off early today, so I'll set up a meeting with Marilyn for tomorrow, if possible."

"Thanks," Laurel said, though she wanted to hold onto her leads tightly. She told herself it wasn't a competition.

"I'm talking to Duke Grover tonight too. He's going to give me some information on the fishing docks, the boats that come in and out of there, all of that."

Thom nodded. "Working those connections." He gave her a smile. "I'm talking to the mayor and the mayoral candidates this afternoon." He stood and reached for his credentials. "We'll meet in the morning, say eight?" He glanced at her. "Debrief and lay out all of our options. See which direction to go in from there?"

"Yep," Laurel said, giving him a smile. "Thanks, Thom."

"You're the one paving the way," he said, meeting her eye with his powerful gaze. "You're a good detective, Laurel."

"Really?" She stood up too, realizing how desperate she was for the praise.

He chuckled and shook his head. "I like the ones that don't even know how good they are." He leaned into his knuckles on his desk. "How many moves have you seen coming into narcotics?"

Laurel searched back through her memories. "I don't know," she said slowly, though she did.

Thom grinned at her. "See you tomorrow, Baker."

That was her cue to get out of there, and since Laurel knew how the station could suck a person back in, she opened her bottom drawer in her desk, extracted her purse, and left before she got pulled back to the next inter- view she needed to complete.

SEVENTEEN

AJ gasped and scooped up her last spoonful of raspberry sorbet. "You're kidding."

"I'm not," Laurel said, practically gleeful. "She demanded a lawyer and said she wouldn't say another word without a deal that included full immunity."

AJ couldn't even imagine living such a life as Laurel did. "And you arrested her."

"At that point, yes," Laurel said. "We were just questioning her about the beauty product delivery previous to that. She was cooperating too." Laurel reached for her frozen lemonade and flashed a smile around at the group. "It was really Eloise who tipped me off."

"I did nothing," El said. "Aaron said the arrest of Marilyn Benson could blow the case open."

"We'll see," Laurel said.

The reporter in AJ noted that Laurel had not given the

women at lunch this last Wednesday before her wedding any more details than the police had released to the public. Hardly anything had been said in the local paper or online, and Laurel was very careful not to say more than that.

AJ wanted to press her for more information, but Laurel wouldn't give it. She also didn't want to put her friend in that position, though she'd done it lots of times to other people she'd interviewed. As a columnist, it was her job to ask the tough questions and get the answers for her readers.

She reminded herself she wasn't covering this story in Five Island Cove, and she didn't need more information than she'd gotten from Laurel. Matt had also told her that Laurel and her partner had come to the golf course, and he and his father had opened their books to them. They'd made copies of them, asked a few questions about their contacts at the Nantucket steamer, the boat that ferried people between the two islands specifically for a day of golf in the cove, and left.

AJ hadn't asked Laurel anything more, and she hadn't volunteered anything. Perhaps there was nothing to tell, because the lead had gone cold.

"Are you two ready for the wedding?" Alice asked, directing the conversation away from Laurel's big news and toward AJ's.

"I am," AJ said, exchanging a glance with Robin and then Lisa, who'd come to lunch with her today. Her reception of AJ had gone at least three times better than Justin's, and once he'd seen the way Lisa treated AJ, he'd gotten better too. They ate dinner together most nights now, because Lisa liked putting together noodle dishes, grilling hamburgers and hot dogs, and baking a variety of treats.

AJ still had two and a half months left in her pregnancy, but she'd been packing on the pounds since Lisa had shown up.

"I think we'll be ready," Robin said. "There's been a slight hiccup with the band, but I'm handling it."

"What's the hiccup?" Lisa asked, and every time AJ looked at her, she saw Matt, as his eldest child and only daughter had gotten his eyes through and through. She glanced at AJ too, who experienced a trickle of trepidation as she waited for Robin to answer.

"You didn't say anything was going on with the band," AJ said.

"The bassist had his guitar stolen," Robin said. "We have three and a half more days. He's trying to get one here from New York, and he said he'll fly to the city and buy one before he'll miss the wedding." She waved her fork around as she spoke. "It's not a problem. Like I said, a hiccup I'm handling."

AJ nodded, and Kelli asked, "How are you handling Duke being gone?"

The life in Robin's eyes dimmed slightly, and she put her fork down. "It's okay," she said. "One week in, and only fifteen more to go." She flashed a smile made of pure determination and bravery, and AJ admired her so much. She possessed so much strength, and AJ wanted to be just like her when it came to holding her family together, working, and being such an amazing, supporting friend.

"How are Mandie and Jamie doing?" Kristen asked, and AJ's eagle eyes saw Alice take a sharp breath in, though she made no sound.

"Good," Robin said, her voice a bit too high for AJ's liking. "We're good, you guys. Honestly." She gestured toward Kelli and Jean, who sat side-by-side. "Someone else talk about something."

"The prom went well," Alice said, always so good at keeping the conversation going. "Ginny had an amazing time with Ray." She rolled her eyes. "I swear if I have to hear about it or that boy one more time..." She shook her head, though AJ knew she didn't really want Ginny to stop talking to her.

The individual conversations picked up then, and AJ watched as Kelli and Jean leaned their heads together and started talking. Jealousy surged inside AJ, and she tried to quench it with a big bite of her fish taco. Of course Kelli was going to have other friends. She took Parker to the lighthouse and Jean babysat him quite often. That didn't mean AJ and Kelli didn't still have a close bond.

The truth was, AJ still felt a bit distant from everyone currently sitting at the table, and Jean was just another reminder of it. Kristen alone knew how AJ felt about everything, as their morning walks had loosened AJ's tongue as well as kept her sane.

Lisa had been joining them, and AJ liked that too. She turned toward the younger woman and asked, "Lisa, you'll take me to pick up the bridesmaids' dresses this afternoon, right?"

Matt's daughter's eyes widened. "That's today? I thought it was tomorrow." She immediately started swiping on her phone. A groan came out of her mouth. "I scheduled a call with one of my professors." She looked at AJ with wide, fearful eyes. "I'm hoping he'll be the chair on my dissertation team."

"It's fine," AJ said with a smile. "We can go tomorrow too. I'm just excited to get them and pass them out."

"I can take you," Alice said. "And everyone should come get them from you, woman. You don't need to bring them to us." She reached for her phone, which she kept face-down near her at all times. "In fact, I'll text everyone right now to do just that."

"Alice," AJ started, but the woman had fast fingers, and the text went out before AJ could finish her protest.

"I can go this afternoon too," Robin said, as she checked her phone religiously the moment a text came in.

"Same," Eloise said.

"I'm sorry, AvaJane," Lisa said, and while she didn't say AJ's full name in the same throaty voice her father did, she did use the name more than the initials. Matt almost always called AJ by her full name, and thus, his children did too.

"It's okay," AJ said, smiling again. "Clearly, I have plenty of help."

"I wanted to do it, though," Lisa said, pouting a little bit. "I'm going to text him and see if I can push it back an hour." She glanced up. "We only need an hour, right?"

She was so eager to please, but she possessed a strong, almost intimidating air as well. AJ thought that came from her intelligence, as she definitely had a mind that most people didn't. She could be a brain surgeon or a rocket scientist in her sleep, and that did send a tremor of fear through AJ if she thought about it too long.

"Done," Lisa said. "It's at four now, so I can go too." She gave AJ a bright smile and turned to Alice. "I can drive if you want to go with us."

Alice smiled at her, and AJ liked how accepting and welcoming her friends had been to Lisa. This was her second luncheon with everyone, and AJ had thought she'd refuse to come last week. But she'd seemed excited when asked, and she fit right in with Laurel and Jean, though they were all wildly different ages.

AJ looked around the table at the eight other women, and her heart warmed. If she needed help, she had it right here at this table. If she needed someone to vent to, she could call on any of these women. If she needed someone's shoulder to cry on, she didn't need to look any further than her group text string on her phone.

"All right," she said, reaching for the dessert menu. "Who wants a piece of pie? On me." That caused quite the commotion, and AJ could only grin as Robin practically ripped the pie menu card away from Alice so she could look at it first.

A FEW DAYS LATER, AJ WOKE IN A STRANGE ROOM, her mind taking a few extra moments to catch up to where she'd slept last night.

Kelli's, she thought, and she pushed herself to a sitting position, her back aching. The light of the day hadn't started to come through the slats in the blinds yet, and she probably didn't need to be awake for another hour. She couldn't go back to sleep though, not in this bed which Parker usually slept in.

She took her time as she stretched out her back and arms, then she got up and padded next door to the bathroom. Due to the baby growing inside her, everything AJ did seemed to take longer than normal. She used to be able to shower, blow-dry her hair, slick on some mascara, and get out of the house in forty minutes or less. But now, she could barely get in the shower, get out, and get dressed in that amount of time.

By the time she did manage that, the scent of coffee wafted up the steps from the kitchen below, and AJ left her wedding dress in the garment bag and navigated down the steps. Kelli worked in the kitchen, putting together blueberry muffins while wearing her bathrobe, and AJ grinned at the simplicity of her best friend.

"Morning, Kel," she said quietly, as Lisa slept on the couch near the front door, and Kelli turned to face her.

A smile spread across her whole face, and she hurried toward AJ. "Good morning." She kept her voice down too. "I heard you in the shower, so I thought I'd put together some breakfast before I got in."

"You don't need to make anything," AJ said, hugging her tightly. "We have all those leftovers from last night." They'd gone to dinner with Lisa and Parker, and The Kitchen Sink on Pearl Island, where Kelli lived, gave the biggest servings AJ had ever seen.

As teens, she and Kelli would order one meal and share it for dinner before either of them could face going home. They'd done the same thing last night, ordering the crab cakes, clam chowder, and all the garlic cheese toast they could get. AJ knew a stack sat in the refrigerator, but she wouldn't say no to blueberry muffins either.

"We can have those for lunch right before we have to go to Diamond," Kelli said as she pulled away. She beamed at AJ, and she couldn't remember the last time Kelli had looked this happy. Maybe she never had. "How are you feeling, Ava? Good? Still want to marry Matt?"

"I've wanted to be Matt Hymas's wife since high school," she whispered, glancing over her shoulder to where Lisa still slept on the couch. She faced Kelli again. "So yes, I'm feeling good."

"Good." Kelli turned to go back into the kitchen. "Come have some tea. I know coffee makes the baby upset."

"He just gets a little too active for me," AJ said, sinking onto a barstool at Kelli's counter. "Thank you for letting us come here, Kel. It's been hard to get some separation for the big day."

"I understand that," Kelli said. "I live next-door to my boyfriend."

AJ smiled as she kept scooping the muffin batter into the tin. "And how are things going with that boyfriend? You don't sneak over there after Parker's gone to bed and sneak back here before he wakes up, do you?"

Kelli slid the muffins into the oven as she said, "Nope." She faced AJ, a semi-worried look on her face. "I don't know, AJ. I'm not like Alice or even Eloise."

"El and Aaron dated for a long time before she started sleeping over." AJ waved her hand. "I'm not pressuring you. I know who you are." She glanced toward the wall separating Kelli's twinhome from Shad's. "Does he?"

"He's learning, I think," Kelli said. "It helps that he's older, but I think he's definitely ready to take our physical relationship up a notch."

"And you're not?"

"I don't know," Kelli admitted, her voice lowering in volume. "I haven't really...done that with very many people, and I'm not sure I'm ready. I keep thinking about Laurel, and how she wasn't ready until she was. And Paul was so great to support her and just be what she could handle him being. Shad is like that."

"Well, that's a good thing, right?" AJ asked. "He's not pressuring you, is he?"

"Not even a little bit," Kelli said, sighing. "I just feel... abnormal. Shouldn't I want to be intimate with him?"

"Are you saying you don't want to at all?"

"I'm saying...I don't know what I'm saying."

In the living room, Lisa groaned, and Kelli clammed right up. From there, the hours passed in a flurry of showers, makeup getting applied, hair being curled and pinned, and clothing bags checked and then double checked.

Shad showed up just after noon and said their Ride-Share would be there in fifteen minutes. "Who needs help taking their things to the curb?"

AJ raised her hand. "All of this," she said, indicating her huge wedding dress in the black garment bag, as well as her carryon, which housed her shoes, makeup, and various other items she might need that day.

An hour later, she arrived at the golf course, where Matt's mother, Barbie, ushered her into a gorgeous bridal room. Champagne chilled in a bucket, and Barbie said, "I have sparkling cider for you, dear. How are you feeling?" She actually put her hand on AJ's baby bump, and AJ wanted to swat her hand away.

Instead, she said, "Good, Barbie. Thank you so much

for taking care of me." Matt's mother had been nothing but kind since he'd called and told his parents about the baby, the wedding, and everything else.

She'd brought AJ food during the bedrest week, and she'd never let more than a couple of days go by without texting her to see if she needed anything.

"All right, ladies," she called now, the room full of AJ's friends. She looked at Robin, who was already dressed in her stunning bridesmaid's dress. The pale blue accentuated her eyes and blonde hair, which she'd styled perfectly. Her makeup enhanced her beauty instead of creating it, and she'd told AJ she'd show up one-hundred percent ready so she could check on all the details.

"The room is yours," Barbie said. "The wedding starts in one hour."

The other women had to get dressed, and then they fiddled with their zippers, their hair, and their makeup until Robin returned to the room and said, "Ten minutes everyone. Let's get AJ into her dress."

AJ could get dressed herself, but she had asked all of her friends to help her. They crowded around, and AJ basked in their love and excitement, which they freely gave and which clearly shone on each and every face.

"Your something blue," Laurel said, lifting up a pair of blue heels. They weren't Americana blue, but a pale, robin's egg blue like the dresses the women wore.

"Something new," Lisa said, giving AJ a pair of

earrings in the shape of teardrops. "These are from me and my brothers."

"Are they real diamonds?" Alice asked, and Lisa nodded.

"We pooled our savings." She took them out of the velvet box. "Dad may or may not have added in a little too."

"You guys shouldn't have," AJ said, her tears pressing so very near the surface. She let Lisa put the earrings on, and she looked at herself in the mirror. She'd worked hard on her hair that morning, and Kelli had curled the back of it for her when AJ couldn't reach.

That was how her relationship with Kelli was. When AJ couldn't take another step, Kelli did it for her. When Kelli needed strength for just a few minutes, she borrowed it from AJ.

"Something borrowed," Alice said, passing AJ a pair of stretchy undergarments. "I washed these, and you'll be amazed at what they can do for your back."

"She's pregnant," Robin said, frowning.

"I know that," Alice said. "It's a pair of smoothers. It's not going to hurt the baby." She helped AJ step into the garment that went halfway down her thigh. It smoothed away all the bumps and lumps that AJ had been accumulating during her pregnancy—at least the ones that came from the clam chowder and chocolate chip banana bread that Lisa had been feeding her.

"It clips right there to your bra," Alice said, getting the last clasp done. "There. Look, she's still pregnant."

Robin ignored her, and AJ ran her hands down her body and over her baby bump. It was more like a baby ball now, but she didn't care. She loved the baby inside her with everything she had, and she couldn't wait to meet him.

Or her, she told herself, because that was what Matt would've done had he been there.

"Something old," Kristen said, and she lifted a weathered piece of paper. For a moment, the bottom fell out of AJ's heart, but Kristen's smile made everything better. "This is a note you wrote to me once. I've kept it all these years, and that's something, as I threw everything away last year."

She tucked the note against AJ's skin, just below her bra and under the stretchy smoothers Alice had just loaned her. "You can read it later." She kissed AJ on the cheek and fell back out of the way as Kelli and Amy, the two most important women in AJ's life, stepped forward with the dress.

AJ held Alice's hand to balanced herself as she stepped into the dress, and she let Kelli and Laurel tug it up over her waist, abdomen, and chest. From there, they started buttoning her into the dress, which fell off her shoulders in an elegant, but almost casual way.

The soft fabric definitely wasn't the shiny stuff a lot of wedding gowns were made of, but gave off a comfortable yet sophisticated vibe. There were no sequins and no glitzy things. The dress's sleeves puffed out, and the neckline scooped. The fabric clung to her body all the way to her hips, and then the skirt flowed to the ground in lots and lots of loose waves.

AJ felt like a tall, beautiful supermodel in the dress—if supermodels could actually take pictures while pregnant and wore sleeves as big as their arms.

"Your crown," Eloise said, and she came forward with the country-chic crown made of blue, green, and mauve flowers. This did have twigs in it, and no one said anything about that.

"You're ready," Barbie said, gripping AJ's shoulders.

"And not a moment too soon," Robin said. "Come on, ladies. It's time to be in the audience."

They hugged AJ one by one, and they left in the same fashion. She stood in the room with her sister, who handed her a bouquet of flowers that matched the crown. "Dad's right outside," she said, her voice thick and tight. "I'll get him, and then I'll get the girls in position."

AJ nodded, her own emotion too close to the surface to speak. Amy opened the door, and their father entered the room. A year ago, if someone would've told AJ that she'd be eating Sunday dinners with her dad, having him walk her down the aisle, and spending time with him, she would've laughed in their faces. Perhaps yelled a few choice words at them.

But now, she knew her father had cleaned up his life.

He'd tried to mend fences and make things right. He didn't drink anymore, and he'd been working with a couple of new fishermen to get their boats off the ground.

Today, he wore a suit in a deep charcoal color, his pale blue tie matching the dresses and her shoes. "Look at you," he said, whistling. "You're such a beautiful bride." He hugged her, and AJ clung to him tightly.

"Thank you, Dad," she whispered. "He's out there, right?"

"He's right by the altar," her dad whispered. "The girls are ready with their baskets of blooms. We're just waitin' on you." He pulled back and smiled at her. "You're ready, right?"

She hooked her arm through his, and together they faced the door. "Yes," she said. "I'm ready."

She'd waited her whole life for this wedding, and with every step she took, a new memory got made. She saw every flower her nieces, Mary and Darcy, tossed. She saw Amy's face filled with happiness as she stood next to her husband.

In fact, AJ saw every smiling face, from Robin and her girls to Alice and Arthur, to Kelli and Shad. Laurel stood with Eloise and Aaron, and Kristen steadied herself with a hand on her son's arm, with Jean right beside him. Matt's children waited in the very front row, and all three of them sent joyful smiles in her direction.

No one smiled wider than Matt, and when she

reached him, he took her right into his arms and kissed her neck softly. "Oh, how I love you, AvaJane."

He'd always loved her, and she'd always known it, even twenty-five years ago. She pressed her eyes closed as a relieved sigh moved through her body, and all of her anxiety simply dried up.

Her mind cleared somehow, and though it had been noisy before, she felt nothing but calm and peaceful as she faced the pastor who would marry her and Matt.

She hadn't wanted fussy, and the ceremony took less than ten minutes. The pastor said, "I now pronounce you husband and wife. You may kiss your bride and start your life together."

AJ faced Matt, and he faced her. The moment solidified, and AJ had never felt anything as serene and full of love as that single breath in time. He kissed her, and AJ laughed against his lips, her joy fuller than it had ever been.

"This is it," she said, clinging to his shoulders. "This is the beginning of our life and family together." A husband and a family—two things AJ hadn't anticipated wanting when she'd left the cove all those years ago.

"Together at last," Matt whispered, kissing her again as the crowd cheered behind them.

EIGHTEEN

Kelli entered the city building, leaving behind the bright June sunshine in favor of air conditioning. She did adore summers in the cove, as the temperature never really got above eighty, and a breeze always kept the beaches cool enough to sunbathe for hours.

Still, she sighed to be out of the sun for a few minutes. She'd dropped Parker at the lighthouse a few minutes ago, and the activity there had been intense. Everything Kristen owned sat on the sidewalk down the path from her cottage—or it would soon.

Moving day.

Kelli understood moving, as she'd done it twice in the past year alone, one of which had required packing up everything she and Parker owned and shipping it across twelve miles of ocean, from New Jersey to the cove. Kristen was only going a couple of miles, but she'd lived in the lighthouse or the adjacent caretaker's cottage for over fifty years.

That kind of deep root took a lot to pull up, and Kelli's chest quaked with emotion as she walked past the secretary's desk with a, "Good afternoon, Sandy. Is he in his office?"

"Just finished a meeting," she said with a smile. "You two should really come to dinner with me and Rex."

Kelli gave her a smile, but she didn't stop. "I'm sure we will." She hadn't spilled all of her secrets to Shad's secretary, but Kelli had stopped by enough in the past month since quitting at the high school to know the woman.

"Kelli," a man boomed, and she grinned at Nathan Baldwin, the city planner. Shad, as the finance director for Five Island Cove, worked with Nathan a lot.

She smiled at him and shook his hand. He wore the same thing she'd find Shad in—a pair of dark slacks, pressed into neat lines, a white shirt, and a tie. His salt and pepper hair never had a single piece out of place, and he had the brightest, whitest smile she'd ever seen.

"Hello, Nathan," she said, chuckling a little. He emanated power and prestige, but Kelli liked him. "How's your wife?"

"Good," he said. "She's trying every recipe in one of her cookbooks, but other than that seriously insane endeavor, she's good." He laughed, his blue eyes crinkling around the edges. "You and Shad off for a fun afternoon?"

Kelli chuckled as she shook her head. "We're helping a friend move," she said. "I don't think that counts as fun."

"No, probably not." His phone chimed in his pocket, and he frowned as he withdrew it. Suddenly, his attention was elsewhere, and he murmured, "Excuse me," in a voice that barely registered in Kelli's ears.

As he strode away, she wondered if his wife was really as good as he claimed her to be. Kelli had seen storms like that on a man's face before. Heck, she'd felt them inside her own soul.

"I hope he's okay," she said, continuing down the hall toward Shad's office.

Shad appeared in the doorway of that office, as if he'd just been waiting for her to finish her conversation with Nathan. "I'm just changing," he said, holding up a pile of clothes. "Then we can go."

Kelli slowed and stopped. "Okay, I'll wait out here."

"I want to ask you something," he said. "Come in. It'll be two seconds." He ducked back into his office, and Kelli glanced around as if a couple of cops would appear and arrest her for going into the office where her boyfriend would be changing.

No one appeared, and no one even looked her way. There wasn't anyone to even look her way, and behind her, in the distance, a phone rang and was answered.

She too went into the office, quickly pushing the door closed behind her. Shad had unknotted his tie and was swiftly unbuttoning his shirt. He stood facing his desk, and he glanced at her as she pressed her back into the door.

"What's up?" she asked, her voice slightly strained.

"How's Laurel's case going?" he asked, his fingers deft at such tiny buttons. They'd walked along the beach many times, but they'd never just laid out in the sun. Shad had a decent tan, though, and Kelli couldn't help staring at the muscles in his arms and chest as he switched his dress shirt out in favor of a T-shirt.

"Good," she managed to push out through her narrow throat. "At least, I think so. She doesn't say much about it."

"She and her partner came by to talk to me this week."

"Oh, really?" Kelli watched him unbuckle his belt, and she had the desire to look away and keep staring at the same time.

"Yeah," he said, stepping out of his pants. He wore a plaid pair of boxers beneath them, and his T-shirt hung down over most of those. He reached for the jeans sitting on the desk, and continued with, "Stayed for about thirty minutes, just asking questions. I told them what I could."

He shimmied into the jeans and zipped them up, finally meeting her eye. "I really don't think it's anyone in government. I know they were going to talk to Mayor Kent, and they've interviewed Greg Sherman too."

Kelli nodded, pressing her lips together. She didn't know all the details of Laurel's case, because while she updated them at their Wednesday lunches if she attended, she usually just said things were going well and progressing. Kelli assumed she was doing interviews and piecing together the case, but she didn't know details like who she talked to, when, and what information she'd learned.

"That's good, right?" she asked as Shad bent to pick up his running shoes. They looked well-used and well-loved, and he sat down in one of the chairs opposite his desk to put them on.

"It's good," he said. "We don't need a political scandal in an election year."

"Isn't that the definition of an election year?" Kelli asked, grinning.

Shad chuckled and stood. He met her eye again, this time with a hint of playfulness mixed with heat in his. "I suppose so." He scanned her from head to toe and back. "My, you look amazing this afternoon."

"I'm wearing a T-shirt and shorts," she said. "And they're not even clean, as I've been scrubbing the construction residue and dust from everything in the wellness center for hours."

"Mm." He approached and ran his hand along her jaw and back into her hair. "How are you feeling about us?" Before she could even comprehend his question, he kissed her.

Kelli pulled in a breath through her nose that sounded sharp, but she kissed him right on back. The windows looking into his office were frosted, and they had complete privacy here. Every stroke of his mouth against hers healed some part of Kelli she hadn't known had been quietly weeping.

Shad broke the kiss and moved his mouth to her neck. "I'm feeling really good about us," he whispered just before touching his lips to the sensitive skin along her throat. "I have a feeling it's going to be a great summer."

Kelli gripped his shoulders and ran her hands down his back, drawing him closer. "Me too."

He pulled away slightly but didn't go far. He searched her face. "Is that right?"

She let her hands linger along his waist, the nearness of him intoxicating. She looked up to the silver in his hair and smiled. "Yeah," she said boldly. "Because I'm feeling really good about us too."

"Good enough to talk about serious things?" Shad murmured.

"What kind of serious things?" She slid one hand up his arm and into his hair. "Kids? I can't really have more kids, Shad."

"That's fine with me," he said. "We'll have Parker to raise."

Adoration burst through her, and her eyes quickly moved back to meet his. "You want to raise Parker with me?"

"I'm falling in love with you," he whispered. "He's a great kid, and of course that's what I want."

Kelli took a moment to search her own feelings. "I suppose I'm falling in love with you too." A smile accompanied the words, because Kelli had not been in love very much in her life. At this point, she wasn't sure if she'd ever felt this giddy and secure with Julian, despite marrying him and trying to build a family with him for fifteen years.

Shad didn't smile, but a glow emanated from his very being. Though they already stood chest to chest, he somehow got closer to her. He pressed one hand against the door next to her head and pushed the other through her hair, bringing her mouth to his again.

This kiss felt different, and Kelli lost herself to the ebb and flow of it, letting Shad dictate how fast and how deep they went. Her pulse accelerated with her breathing, and by the time he pulled away, he was panting too.

"We should go," he said in a half-growl. "I don't think we can finish what we started right here or right now."

Kelli opened her eyes, feeling a bit woozy and wobbly. The moment she saw how red-faced and bothered Shad was, a new sort of power entered her bloodstream. She fisted her fingers in his T-shirt and brought him back for another kiss. One, two, three strokes and she said, "We can later."

"Tonight later?" he asked, backing up a step. Then two.

Kelli knew he wanted to stay the night with her. She thought about what AJ had said only a few days ago. They did live next-door to one another, and it wouldn't be terribly difficult for either of them to find their way into the other's bedroom.

Nerves marched through her, but Kelli said, "I think tonight would probably work. Depends on how tired you are after this move."

"How tired *I* am?" He chuckled and reached for his wallet. He stuck that in his back pocket and straightened up his dress clothes before picking them up. "Kelli, you invigorate me. I'm never tired when I'm with you."

She looked into his dark eyes and definitely felt herself falling. "Maybe one of the serious things we need to talk about is marriage," she said.

He smiled, but it was a soft, beautiful smile filled with love and kindness. "I'm absolutely okay talking about that."

"I don't want a big wedding," she said. "I'm not one who really likes the spotlight on me."

"You're kidding," Shad said in a deadpan. "I had no idea."

They laughed together, and Shad slung his arm around her, the other holding his clothes. "Kel, I would marry you anywhere you said, with just us there, or just your mom and Devon and Parker. Whatever you want is fine with me."

She put both hands on his chest and leaned into his strength. "You'd marry me right now?"

"Right now," he confirmed. "You tell me what you want, Kel, and I'll do it."

"I don't know what I want."

He smiled and touched the tip of his nose to hers. "I

know, sweetheart. That's why I'm moving at your pace. When you know what you want, we'll talk about it. Okay?"

"Okay," she whispered, wondering how she'd attracted the attention of a man as sweet as him. "Right now, I want to go help Kristen move. Then I want dinner at The Breakfast Club. Then...who knows what the rest of the night will hold?"

"Mm, I see how it's going to be," he said, his lips dangerously close to hers. "You're going to tease me all day in those sexy shorts, make me eat breakfast for dinner, and then kiss me on the couch and maybe kick me out before dessert."

"Maybe," she said, giggling against his mouth. "But maybe not."

He groaned and pressed into her, and Kelli held onto him as she laughed. They left his office and the building, arriving outside about the same time Alice pulled up to the curb in her SUV.

"Perfect timing," Kelli said, reaching for the front passenger door handle. "Hey, Alice."

"Sorry I'm late," she said, clearly flustered. "I have this new client who loves to tell me the same thing four or five times." She shook her head and reached for a couple of files sitting on the passenger seat. "She's impossible to get off the phone." She craned her neck to see into the back seat. "Sorry about the mess," she said to Shad. "I let

Charlie drive this to work, and he lives in here in the evenings."

"It's fine," Shad said, getting in behind Kelli. She heard him pushing some things out of the way and then settling as Alice got the car moving again.

"I can't believe Kristen is moving," Kelli said. "It's so exciting, isn't it?"

"I know she's thrilled," Alice said. "I went with her to sign the papers, and we got the key. She took me on a tour, and it's a fantastic condo. She'll be so happy there."

"I can't wait to see it," Kelli said. Working on Bell did keep her a bit isolated from the happenings here on Diamond Island, but she'd accepted as much. Eloise owned The Cliffside Inn on Sanctuary, and while she lived on Diamond with Aaron and the girls, she also had a separate life from the women on the main island.

"Uh, Alice?" Shad asked from the back seat.

"Yeah?" She made a turn that would take them out of the downtown area and up into the hillier part of the island where the lighthouse sat.

"There's a box of condoms back here." He held it up, and Alice yelped, hit the brakes, and jerked the wheel to the right.

Kelli cried out too as the SUV came to a halt. Alice jammed the car into park and twisted around. "You're kidding. Let me have those." She took the box from him, faced the front, and stared at it. "It's not open."

She looked up at Kelli, her eyes wide and filled with

fear. "It's not open," she repeated. "What does that mean?"

"Sorry," Shad said. "I just know you worry about your twins. I shouldn't have said anything."

"Are you kidding?" Alice said, regaining her sophistication and complete confidence in a single breath. "They left these in *my car*. They're either stupid or oblivious." She shook the box of condoms. "Both of which indicate they're not ready to use these."

She shook her head, her eyes blazing with anger now. "My word. These teenagers are going to be the death of me." She shoved the box under her seat and put her blinker on to move back out onto the road. "Were were this bad as teenagers? I don't think we were."

"Well, AJ did sleep with about fifty boys," Kelli pointed out, reaching for the handle above the door as Alice gunned the engine to get them back into the flow of traffic. "You went over to that boys camp a few times."

"I did not sleep with Billy Bridge," Alice said forcefully. "Everyone thought I did, obviously, but I didn't."

"Robin snuck out all the time," Kelli continued as if Alice hadn't spoken. "But that was just to spite her mom. I don't think she was out doing anything that required a condom."

"No," Alice said. "She wasn't. She'd just sit on her roof or wander the neighborhood."

"She's lucky she didn't get kidnapped, honestly." Kelli shook her head, her memories of her childhood streaming through her head now. "I didn't get in much trouble, even before things fell apart with my dad."

"That's because you were so *good*," Alice said, grinning at her. "What about you, Shad? Did you cause your parents to get ulcers?"

"Oh, yeah," he said casually, and Kelli turned to look at him, definitely interested in these stories. "Me and my brothers got in so much trouble." He grinned at her. "Nothing that required condoms, unfortunately. Well, my oldest brother, Wilson, he did have a fair bit of luck with the girls. But I didn't. I think they found me too intellectual."

"Mm," Kelli said. "Smart is sexy."

"Now," he said. "Back then, everyone wanted a big, buff athlete, and well, I couldn't put on weight as a teenager."

"Charlie can't either," Alice said. "But he doesn't seem to have a problem getting girls."

"Times change," Shad said, and Kelli gave him another smile and turned around as Alice made the turn into the parking lot at the lighthouse.

"Oh, wow," she said, and Kelli knew why. She got instantly overwhelmed at all the boxes, people, and movement at the lighthouse. Everyone had come to help, and only a quarter of them were actually needed. Shad probably hadn't needed to change his clothes, but an image of his bare chest and shoulders stole through Kelli's mind, igniting every cell in her body.

"All right," Alice said with a sigh. "Let's get through this." She got out of the car, Kelli a half-beat behind her. She felt like she'd spent a large portion of her life "getting through" things. She didn't want to live like that anymore. She wanted to experience life—the good and the bad. The hard and the easy. The wonderful and the awful.

"Hello," she called to Robin, who also wore a tank top and a pair of shorts. She had a box in her hand, which she passed to Rueben, who stood in the back of the moving truck.

"Hey," Robin said, smiling. "Look at you two." She cocked her hip and put one hand on it as Shad slid his hand along Kelli's waist. "You look so good together." She stepped into Kelli and hugged her, then did the same to Shad.

He looked surprised, but he went with it, and when Robin pulled away, she said, "Kristen is still in the cottage. Maybe you can see if you can get her to leave."

"Is she still packing?" Kelli asked.

"No," Rueben said from the truck. "Everything she owns is out here. She just...wanted a minute in the cottage alone."

"It's been twenty minutes," Jean said as she handed a lamp to her husband. "Parker's with Mandie and Jamie. They went for a walk down to Sea Lion Beach."

"Thanks, Jean," Kelli said. She glanced at Shad. "Well, it looks like we're going to avoid any of the heavy lifting." She took his hand and stepped up onto the sidewalk.

Several others simply milled about, chunks of sandwiches in their hands as they laughed and talked.

Kelli left the fray behind and went up the path that led to Kristen's cottage.

"She lives here?" Shad asked.

"Not anymore," Kelli said. "But yes, and you should've seen it after Joel died." She forced a fake shudder through her limbs, smiling at her boyfriend. "The man was a packrat and a hoarder. It wasn't pretty or fun to go through."

They arrived at the cottage, and Kelli rapped on the door. "Kristen?" she called. Getting no answer, she opened the door anyway. The cottage had been emptied of everything. It seemed so cavernous without the wall-to-wall papers, filing cabinets, folders, and furniture.

Kristen stood in the kitchen, in front of the sink, gazing out the window. "I can't get myself to leave," she said, her voice gravelly and nasally at the same time. "I've stood here so many times, just watching the wind play with the branches. If you listen, you can hear the ocean."

The window had been opened, but Kelli couldn't hear the ocean. She heard people talking from down the hill in the parking lot, and they covered any oceanic sounds that might have come inside.

"The birds calling," Kristen said, sniffling. "I love this place, and I'm so familiar with it."

Kelli reached her and put her arm around her, bringing her flush against her side. She didn't know what to say, so she said nothing for the time being. Shad stayed somewhere in the living room, silent as well.

"When I decided to leave New Jersey," Kelli said. "I did exactly this. It was so hard to let go, and so hard to walk out of the house where I'd lived for so long for the last time. The very air seems to have memories in it I thought I'd lose."

Kristen turned her head to look at her, but Kelli kept her gaze firmly out the window. "Only when I got here did I realize that the memories I wanted, the ones that really mattered, weren't tied to a house or a car or a place." She reached up and put her hand over her heart. "They're tied to me. They go with me, because they live inside *me*."

A set of tears pricked her eyes, and she looked at Kristen. They wept together for a moment, and then Kelli wrapped her in a tight hug. "It's time to go, Kristen. What you need and want will come with you."

"Okay," Kristen whispered. "I'm not sure I believe you, but I do trust you."

Kelli pulled away, wiped her tears, and took Kristen's hand. Together, they took the first step away from the window, then all the way out of the kitchen. Shad smiled at Kelli, one of his *I-see-your-heart-and-its-beautiful* smiles.

When they reached him, he too put his arm around Kristen as an added measure of support. She smiled at him too, and he said, "After I lost my wife, I didn't think I could ever leave the house we lived in. But I did, and I've been in that twinhome for a while now. It's where I met the second love of my life. This new condo is going to be a chance for a second breath of life for you."

Kelli heard the words he'd said—*second love of my life* —and she ducked her head and smiled. She'd forgotten what it felt like to be loved, and it sure did feel wonderful.

NINETEEN

A lice exited her office when she heard Ginny and Charlie's car pull into the driveway. She'd had the windows open for a few weeks now, because the weather in the cove was the balmy, beautiful high sixties and low seventies she loved. Days like the past few weeks were definitely a huge pull to keep Alice in the cove, if she'd needed one.

She rounded the corner that led into the dining room, kitchen, and living room, and her eyes went straight to the box of condoms on the kitchen counter. She hoped Ginny's and Charlie's would too. She hoped the sight of it froze them in their tracks. She hoped she could see their reactions and know which twin she needed to interrogate just from the look on their faces.

She'd had to wait a few days to stage this intervention, because the twins both had jobs. They didn't always come home together, and she'd wanted to see their faces at the same time. Alice was well-versed with twins, and they could easily pawn something off on the other if they weren't both present.

The back door opened, and Charlie led the way into the house. He turned to hold the door for Ginny, who was saying, "...that's it. You can't just expect her to be all hunky-dory."

"I don't," Charlie said. "Can we not talk about this? We're already going to have to spend all summer with her, and I don't want—" He turned and saw Alice, freezing instantly. "Mom," he said loudly.

Ginny nearly collided with him from behind, and Alice folded her arms. She knew who they were talking about: Mandie Grover.

Yes, they were probably going to see a lot of Robin, Mandie, and Jamie over the summer, because Robin was Alice's best friend. They'd spent last summer together, which was how Charlie and Mandie had started dating.

"Good afternoon," Alice said, hating that she'd stalled their arrival in the kitchen. Ginny could barely see past Charlie, a fact Alice knew from the way she bumped him and said, "Don't stop in the doorway, you idiot."

She muscled past him and came the few steps down the hall and past the laundry room. She arrived in the kitchen with a, "Hey, Mom," in her normal, cheery voice. All at once, she froze again, her eyes landing on the box on the counter.

Charlie followed her, shouldering her as he said, "Who's stopping in doorways now?" He looked at the box on the counter and kept on going. "Mom, can we order from Munk's tonight? It's fish fry, and we haven't had it for so long." He looked at her with puppy dog eyes and actually took her into a hug.

Alice didn't get to hug her son all that often, so she took advantage of it if she could, even if he was only doing it to get fish fry for dinner.

"It'll be like a celebration of the end of school," he said.

"You have another week," Alice said.

"But the last week is stupid," Charlie said, stepping back. "You can invite Arthur."

Alice smiled at her son. "Sure, baby. Do you want to get on and order it when you're ready?"

Charlie grinned at her, his eyes blazing with laughter. "Yeah, I'll do it. Arthur is a yes?"

"He'll be a yes, yes," Alice said.

Her son grinned and said, "Perfect," just as his phone buzzed. "That's Sariah. We have to go over the schedule for our summer Olympiad stuff." He looked at her. "I'm okay to talk to her in my room?"

"Sure," Alice said, barely looking at Charlie anymore. Ginny was sweating bullets in the kitchen, and while Alice was surprised the box of condoms belonged to her, there was no doubt they did. "Go ahead."

"Thanks, Mom." Charlie headed upstairs, leaving

Alice and Ginny alone. She still hadn't moved from where she'd grown roots in the kitchen.

Alice sighed, some of the fight leaving her body as she moved into the kitchen. She sat down at the counter, the box only a foot or two from her now. "Do you have something to tell me?"

"It was a joke," Ginny blurted out, her eyes wild. "For real, Mom. Some stupid guy threw them at Ray, saying something crude about how we shouldn't use them all in one night, and he tossed them in the back of the car, laughing."

Alice nodded, wanting to believe her daughter. She hadn't been in high school for a very long time, but she knew what teenagers were like.

"I forgot about them," Ginny said. "I swear, I haven't slept with Ray. With anyone."

"The box is unopened."

"Exactly," Ginny said, finally moving. She dropped her backpack by the cupboard where they kept the cereal and paper goods and stood at the end of the counter.

Alice reached out and curled her fingers around Ginny's. "I believe you. I worry about you, but I believe you."

"Ray's my boyfriend," she blurted out, tears filling her eyes. "We had such a good time at the prom, and he's so cute, Mom. He's smart, and he takes his classes seriously. He doesn't act like an idiot, but he likes to have fun. And bonus, he likes learning about World War Two as much as

I do, and his favorite flavor of ice cream is cookies and cream, just like me."

She swiped at her eyes and shook her head. "I don't know why I'm crying. This is stupid. I haven't done anything wrong."

Alice took a few seconds to absorb everything Ginny had spouted at her. "Except maybe not telling me he's your boyfriend. If that's not wrong, why did you hide it from me?" The prom had taken place a month ago. Ginny had been stunning in her black dress with a jeweled belt around her waist. Abby and Emily had come over to do her hair, and Alice had let them use her master bathroom, because the counter space was bigger. She'd enjoyed listening to them talk about school, summer, jobs, boys, and what they wanted to do with their lives. They were nice girls, at least it seemed so to Alice, and she'd enjoyed having them in her house.

"I don't know," Ginny said, her eyes still leaking. "I just see the way you're always on Charlie about his girl-friends, and I thought...maybe I shouldn't have a boyfriend."

"I worry about Charlie," Alice admitted. "Because he's a boy, and Ginny, boys aren't like girls."

"I know, Mom. I've heard this lecture before."

"Yes, well, maybe you need to hear it again, as someone who now has a boyfriend. Ray's not like you. He *will* want to be physical, and that's normal." She swallowed, because she had experience with boys and men.

"You'll have to decide when and if you're ready for that. I don't think it's wise to be having sex in high school."

She cleared her throat. "That's my stance for both you and Charlie, and I'm sticking to it." She picked up the box of condoms and stood. "I'll keep these for now, because I suppose if you do decide you need one, you should come get it from me. We can talk more then, if you'd like."

Ginny nodded, and Alice took the box into her bathroom. She sighed as she looked in the mirror above the sink. "I hope this is the right thing to do." Another breath went down easy, and Alice thought finding the condoms in her car was probably a blessing in disguise.

She went back out into the kitchen, where Ginny had put an English muffin in to toast. "I need to talk to you and Charlie," Alice said. "Do you have another few minutes?"

"Yes," Ginny said. "He knows about me and Ray."

Alice didn't say anything as she went to the bottom of the stairs. "Charlie," she called up. "I need you for a minute."

"Coming," he yelled down, and his footsteps sounded on the steps a few seconds later. "What's up?" He looked from where Alice had perched on the arm of the couch to Ginny, who stood in the kitchen with a butter knife.

"Okay," Alice said. "Ginny just told me she's dating Ray."

"It's not called dating, Mom," Ginny said, rolling her eyes.

"Whatever," Alice said, near to snapping. She pressed

her eyes closed and breathed in through her nose. She'd always been transparent with the twins. They knew things about her relationship with Frank she'd tried to shield them from.

They know, she heard in her mind, in Arthur's voice.

"I *am* dating Arthur," she said, her voice grinding on the first few words. "It's getting serious. We're talking about marriage, and that impacts you guys."

"Marriage?" Charlie asked, his voice pitching up toward the rafters. "Really, Mom?"

"It's been two months," Ginny said, clearly surprised as well.

"Yes," Alice said. "But I'm not sixteen years old. I've been in love before. So has he. He doesn't have any children, so it would just be the four of us. We wouldn't move or anything."

"He works at the high school," Charlie said as if Alice didn't know. "It'll be weird." He turned to Ginny. "Right?"

"I don't know," Ginny said. "I mean, we never see the counselors."

"*I* do," Charlie said, spinning back to Alice. "It's weird, Mom."

"It's been okay when he's come here for dinner," she said, watching Charlie's face for his real feelings. Arthur had been over for dinner with Alice and the twins three times now. "He's coming tonight. You like him."

"Yeah, but..." Charlie trailed off, and Alice knew he didn't really have any argument against Arthur.

She straightened. "We've been intimate, and I am falling in love with him. I love you guys with more energy than the sun puts out, and I guess I just need to know if this is going to break us."

"You're sleeping with him?" Charlie roared, his fists balling up. "Mom! Come on!" He paced away from her while Ginny stood stock-still in the kitchen.

"I'm not sixteen years old," Alice repeated, swallowing as Ginny continued to stare at her. "It's not the same as you and Ray at all. Or you and Sariah."

"How is it not different?" Charlie asked, plenty of sarcasm in his voice.

"For one," Alice said, piercing him with a glare. "I can't get pregnant. For two, Arthur and I are both gainfully employed, with careers and skills, and supporting ourselves. Three, I'm an adult, with plenty of life experience—including having sex with other men —behind me."

"Ew," Charlie said. "Mom, please stop talking."

"So you're saying having experience makes you wiser?" Ginny asked.

"No," Alice said quickly, seeing this conversation derail, and fast. "I'm saying I'm thirty years older than you guys. I'm not stuck in a constant cycle of hormones, and yes, I've had enough romantic experiences to know *exactly* how I feel. When you're young, like you two are, everything is new and wonderful, and you don't *really* know how you're feeling. You learn as you have innocent, *age-*

appropriate relationships." She folded her arms, the final punctuation mark on the conversation.

What she knew that they didn't was that sex took something from a person. There was a price to it, no matter what age a person was when it happened. She simply wanted them to be the smartest they could be when it came to their relationships, and she'd keep talking to them about that until the day she died. It was that important to her.

Both of them simply looked at her, but Charlie had taken the disgust off his face, and Ginny's stare had warmed considerably. "Well," she said as her English muffin popped up and she turned to butter it. "I guess those condoms will go to good use."

"Gross," Charlie said. "This can't be happening." He looked between Alice and Ginny. "Wait. What condoms?"

Alice grinned, the action only widening when she saw the smile on Ginny's face. Though she kept her head down, she said, "Charlie, you are seriously so clueless sometimes."

"What?" he asked.

"Mom had a box of condoms on the counter when we got home," Ginny said, picking up the twist tie that closed the bag of English muffins and throwing it at him. "They're the ones that idiot Lance threw at Ray last week. She found them in her car."

Charlie looked so confused, and Alice wasn't going to

be able to hold back her laughter for much longer. "Today? On the counter *today?*"

"Yes," Ginny said, starting to giggle.

"They're not mine," he said automatically, his gaze flying back to Alice.

"Of course they're not," Ginny said with plenty of exasperation. "They're mine—well, Mom took them and put them in her bathroom." She slid her gaze to Alice. "I guess now I know why."

Alice just shook her head as she started to laugh. Ginny joined in, but Charlie still seemed so confused. Alice opened her arms and gathered him up, moving him into the kitchen with Ginny, where they finished laughing together.

"This isn't going to break us, is it?" she asked, sobering. "Me and Arthur?"

"No," Ginny said. "I actually like Arthur."

Alice looked at Charlie, her eyebrows raised. He had to know she'd do anything for him, anything to protect him, and he finally lowered the tension in his shoulders. "No," he said. "It's not going to break us. I can't believe I'm saying this, but I like him too."

Alice hugged her children, pure gratitude that she'd been given such amazing kids filling her. "I love you guys," she said. "I will always love you, no matter what."

"Even if I want one of those condoms?" Charlie asked.

Alice pulled back and searched her son's face. "Even

if," she whispered. "You haven't been dating Sariah for very long."

"No," he said. "About as long as you and Arthur though."

"I'm not sixteen," she said.

"You forget we turned seventeen a couple of months ago."

Alice nodded, swallowing the biggest lump she'd ever tried to get down. "That's fine. But can we talk about it some more before I just hand one over?"

Charlie nodded, his Adam's apple moving too. "Maybe not right now," he finally said. "Okay?" He stepped out of Alice's arms and out of the kitchen completely.

"Okay," she said, turning to watch him go back upstairs. Her worry over him doubled, and then as if someone was blowing on the white tendrils of a spent dandelion, she exhaled, and all of her anxiety left her.

Her son was a good kid. The twins were almost adults. Alice couldn't control them the way she once had as children, and she had to trust that she'd done a good enough job educating them to make the smartest decisions.

"He's not Dad," Ginny said quietly, causing Alice to turn back to her.

"What?"

"He's not Dad," she said again. "I know you worry about him being this huge womanizer like Dad, sleeping with every female who walks by. Because that's what Dad did, but Charlie's not like that. In fact, he wants to be the *opposite* of that." She took a bite of her English muffin as if they were discussing homework or the bulbs Alice had planted a couple of months ago.

"He sees what Dad did to you, and he doesn't want to do that to anyone. Breaking up with Mandie almost killed him, and he's been trying to be so nice to her since." Ginny shook her head. "He really doesn't get some things."

"Is Mandie okay?"

"She is," Ginny said, her voice taking on a false quality. "I miss hanging out with her. She was a good friend."

"You can still hang out with her," Alice said. "He's right; we're going to see them a lot this summer."

"It's okay if it's just us," Ginny said. "But sometimes she wants to talk about Charlie, but I don't know. It's hard."

Alice nodded, because yes, sometimes life and situations were just hard. There was no other way to describe them, and they couldn't be circumvented. They just had to be gone through.

As Ginny picked up her backpack and said she was going to go do her chemistry homework, Alice pulled out her phone and typed up a quick message to her friends.

I love you guys. Thank you for being right beside me this past year.

She read over it once and then twice, and then sent it. She suspected Robin would call to find out what had happened, and Eloise would send her a private text to make sure she was okay. Kristen would too, and she'd offer to take the twins to a movie so Alice could deal with whatever she needed to deal with.

AJ was on her honeymoon, and Alice didn't expect her to answer, but Kelli would reply to the group and repeat the sentiment of love. Laurel would say she'd be over in ten minutes to make sure the twins were behaving, and Jean would send emojis with heart eyes and then maybe a chicken. She'd said she just loved the chicken emoji and couldn't help sending it whenever possible.

As all of those things happened exactly as Alice predicted they would, the love of her friends enveloped her from head to toe.

"THEY'RE HERE," ALICE SAID NEEDLESSLY AS THE doorbell pealed. "Ginny, get out the lemonade, would you? Charlie, take the salad out to the patio."

"Mom," he said even as he picked up the bowl of pasta salad. "They're cops. Not the queen." He rolled his eyes as he stepped out of the sliding glass doors that led onto their patio.

Alice exchanged a glance with Arthur, who picked up a stack of plates and followed her son as she went toward the door. She opened it to find Laurel and her partner, Thom Beardall, standing on the front porch. They wore identical looks of resignation and dread—at least until Laurel smiled.

"Evening, Alice," she said, moving into her personal space for a hug. "Relax. My word, you look like we're here to arrest you." She gave a light laugh and joined Alice in the foyer. "This is Thom, my partner."

"So great to meet you," Alice said, her Hamptons training returning in an instant. She shook the older gentleman's hand. "Come in. Come in. We've got dinner on the back patio all set up."

She stood back while Thom entered, and she then ushered him and Laurel through the house to the patio. Ginny was just finishing with the lemonade, and Alice made all the introductions. "Let's sit," she said after the last handshake. "These two just have some questions for all of us. No one's in trouble." She'd given this speech before, but both Charlie and Arthur looked a little nervous.

"I'll start," Laurel said as she speared a cucumber from her pasta salad. "We just want to know who buys and sells drugs at the high school."

"Names if you've got them and are willing to tell us," Thom added. "Everything is kept really confidential. No one will know you told us."

Charlie exchanged a glance with Alice, who gave him a slight nod. He reached for a slice of pizza she'd ordered from their favorite place and said, "I know a few guys who use."

"Use what?" Laurel asked.

"They smoke pot," Charlie said, lifting his chin. "Sometimes something a little stronger."

"Cocaine?" she asked, and how she could talk about such heavy subjects while she ate was a marvel to Alice. She seemed so at-ease, and while Alice had admired Laurel before, it now went off the charts.

"I think?" Charlie said. "Crack is cocaine, right?"

Thom nodded. "Different form. Same drug."

Charlie cleared his throat and took an enormous bite of pizza. Silence reigned over the table, but while Alice put food on her plate, she couldn't take a bite of it. The sun shone in the west as it arced down, and birds literally chirped around them. It didn't feel like the right setting to be talking about drug deals between teenagers.

She glanced at Arthur, who'd said nothing but hello to the cops.

"Paulie smokes crack," Charlie said. "Paulie King. As far as I know, he's the one who gets it and gives it out to his buddies."

"They're not really his friends," Ginny said, her voice almost a squeak. "I saw him push one of them up against the lockers and say if he didn't pay up, there would be a real problem."

"When was this?" Laurel asked, reaching for her notebook.

"Oh, a long time ago," Ginny said. "January, maybe?"

Laurel nodded and made a note while Thom said. "Do you see any drugs, Arthur?"

"I have a few kids on my list who clearly use," he said. "I can give you their names."

"Do you hear any rumblings from the teachers about it?" Thom asked.

"It's brought up in faculty meetings," Arthur said. "We're all trained to know what drug use looks like and smells like. It's supposed to be reported to the admin; students sent to call home. That kind of thing." He took a bite of his pizza, but a more normal one.

"We'd love those names," Laurel said. "Students and the admin over your drug-use enforcement."

"It's actually our on-site officer," Arthur said. "In conjunction with one of our vice-principals."

"Shawn Newmyer?" Laurel asked, exchanging a glance with Thom. "He's your enforcement officer, right?"

"Yes," Arthur said slowly, looking back and forth between Laurel and Thom. "He teaches a class on law enforcement, and does our forensics as well. Everyone knows if there's a problem at the school or in the community, and he gets called out, he'll just leave class." He took a deep breath. "But he's just got the two, and it's only happened a couple of times."

"Like when we had to shelter inside a couple of months ago, because there was that creepy guy trying to get in cars with girls," Ginny said.

"Right." Arthur nodded. "So Patricia called the police,

and Shawn is on-site. He's there immediately, and he can fill in the real police when they arrive."

"He's a real police officer," Laurel said.

"Right, of course," Arthur said, and Alice smiled at him. Seeing him flustered was actually kind of cute, because he was so supremely confident most of the time. "I just meant...yes, of course he's a real police officer."

"And Patricia, she's the VP that works with him?" Thom asked.

"No, she's the head secretary," Arthur said. "The VP is Marlo Benson."

"Benson?" Thom and Laurel asked at the same time. Laurel's pencil scratched at a mile a minute, but Alice couldn't read the chicken scratches on the paper.

"Right," Arthur said. "He's been there for years. Maybe close to retiring. He's a good guy. I've known him for a lot of years. Went through a nasty divorce a few years ago, but he's still a family man. Has a few grandchildren in the cove." He cleared his throat and finally stopped talking.

Both Laurel and Thom nodded, and another round of silence went around. "Okay," Thom said as he inhaled through his nose. "We'll just take the names if you've got them."

Arthur pulled a paper out of his pocket and said, "I typed mine up." He handed the list to Laurel, who didn't even look at it.

Charlie opened his mouth to speak when both

Laurel's and Thom's radios went off. A terrible screeching sound happened, and then a female voice, almost like a robot came over the airwaves.

Alice couldn't make out most of it, as it was a jumble of words and numbers, but Laurel and Thom instantly got to their feet. "Sorry," Laurel said while Thom simply hurried into the house. "We have to go."

"What's going on?" Alice asked, her brain still trying to catch up to the few words she'd heard come through the radio. She didn't understand the numbers or the order the instructions went out, but she had heard "fire," and "loading dock."

"I'll call you later," Laurel said, dashing after Thom. She didn't bother to close the sliding glass door, and Alice stepped over to do it so she wasn't air conditioning the back yard. She faced the table, suddenly feeling very cold.

"Sounded like a fire at the loading dock," Arthur said, standing and joining her. He put his hands on her arms and rubbed. "Come sit down, sweetheart. There's nothing we can do about it."

"True," Alice said slowly, and she let him tug her back to her seat at the table. "But why would two narcotics cops race off to the scene of a fire at the loading dock?"

She knew why; Laurel had said she was trying to find the conduit bringing the drugs into the cove. Could it be via the supply ships that came from the mainland? And what would happen if those shipments got delayed or stopped?

With summer arriving, Alice suddenly had the urge to get the grocery store and get everything she needed for the next three months. Instead, she sat down to a pizza dinner with her boyfriend and children and pretended everything was A-okay.

TWENTY

L aurel snapped on a pair of rubber gloves and adjusted her protective face mask. The ship still smoked, and not in the way a steamer should. This wasn't a steamer anyway; this was a large, commercial transport ship, with shipping containers full of food, goods, cars, building supplies, and everything else necessary for the thirty-five thousand people who lived in Five Island Cove.

Things weren't cheap here, because everything had to be shipped over from New York, Maryland, or Massachusetts. Their closest neighbor in the sea was Nantucket, and even that island was six miles away.

Laurel longed to escape to Nantucket right now. The Point would be beautiful right now in early June, and her mother would bake scones in the morning and fish pot pies in the evenings. Her mom and dad had moved there a few years ago, once her father had retired as a fire captain from the Five Island Cove department.

The familiar wails of those fire engines roared through Laurel's ears, and she knew the firefighters wouldn't let her and Thom anywhere near the still-burning ship. The possibility of it if exploding kept everyone on the dock as the engines pulled up and men and women jumped from them and got to work.

"This is a disaster," Laurel said.

"It's a day early too," Thom said, frowning at the ship. He hadn't put on his protective face mask yet, but Laurel found the scent of smoke terribly off-putting. Her ex-husband used to burn things in the back yard just for fun, and when she blinked, she suddenly stood in the spare bedroom, watching him through the slatted blinds as he took off his shirt and added it to the fire.

Terror ran through her, and she forced her eyes open again. She wasn't in that house. She wasn't trapped in that marriage. She wasn't going to get hurt that night, and her past was where it belonged—in the past. Behind her.

"You're right," Laurel said, catching up to what Thom had said. "The ship is a day early. I wonder why." She glanced around. "Do you think the manifest is here? The harbormaster? Maybe he can tell us why the ship is early." If anything, Laurel was more accustomed to shipments and deliveries coming late.

They'd already spoken with Philo Rock, the man in charge of the harbor. He'd given them the schedule of shipments, and Laurel's distrusting mind immediately started conjuring up reasons why he hadn't given them the correct one. "Perhaps Philo wanted to make sure the drugs go off the ship before we showed up."

"You think Philo's in on this?" Thom asked.

"I'm not ruling anyone out," Laurel said, cutting him a glance. "I think Marlo Benson has something to do with it. I want to talk to Shawn too."

"I really don't think Shawn is smart enough to pull off a drug ring like this," Thom said quietly.

"All the same," Laurel said. She'd be calling the Chief that night, and if it were up to her, she and Thom would be sitting down with Shawn Newmyer in the morning. First thing. In fact, why they hadn't thought to go to the enforcement officer at the school to find out about the drug ring intrigued her. "Did we miss Shawn?" she asked. "Why didn't we know he was at the high school?"

"He's only there in the morning," Thom said, shifting his weight as they both continued to watch the ship smolder. Spray went high into the sky, and the smoke coming off the ship turned light gray, and then white. "He runs the beat on Rocky Ridge in the evenings. That's where he lives."

"How do you know all this?" Laurel asked, realizing she didn't even trust her partner. She backtracked and took a deep breath to settle herself down.

"Shawn's an older cop, like me," Thom said, flicking a glance in her direction. "We have sons the same age. Trust me, he's not the brightest bulb in the box. That's why he's still on the beat and at the school."

"If you know him, why didn't we go to him?"

"Honestly?" Thom faced her, his frown lines deep between his eyes. "I forgot. He's a forgettable guy. And not smart enough to orchestrate a drug ring in Five Island Cove from his office in the high school."

"Okay," Laurel said, a little testily to match Thom's tone. "I just feel stupid, like we missed an important piece of the puzzle." She wouldn't have involved Alice's boyfriend or kids had she known there was an enforcement officer at the high school, that was all.

"We didn't miss an important piece of the puzzle," Thom said. "Unless you're talking about Marlo Benson."

"Yeah, what's with him? Are he and Marilyn married?"

"Once upon a time," Thom said. "I texted Cheryl, and she just confirmed it." He held up his phone for Laurel to take.

She did, and she quickly read the brief text exchange between her partner and the narcotics secretary at the station. She handed the phone back, her chest doing that weird vibrating, popping thing it did when she got really nervous. "This is crazy," she said. "Could the two of them be bringing in the drugs? A high school administrator?"

"He fits our profile," Thom said quietly. "A prominent figure if the case gets blown open. Heck, she's a prominent figure too, and there have been articles every day since we arrested her."

"Yeah, but they don't say anything." Laurel was proud of that, because it meant there were no leaks in the case. Nobody in narcotics talking to people they shouldn't be. She probably had the most occasion to let something slip to her friends, and she'd had to work really hard not to do that. The need to talk about the case ate at her and ate at her, until she finally talked to Paul about it.

But Paul was safe, as he'd demonstrated time and time again.

"No, but they're there. Can you imagine if an active school administrator was named as the ringleader? It also makes sense for why she's protecting him."

"Does it?" Laurel asked. "They're divorced. Most divorced people don't hold fond feelings for their ex-spouse." She certainly didn't, but once again, Laurel had to remove herself from the equation if she wanted complete objectivity.

"I don't know the extent of their divorce," Thom said. "We'll need to pay Marlo a visit tomorrow for sure."

"Absolutely," Laurel said. "I'd love it if we went in the morning and got Shawn in the room with him too. See who squirms."

"The Chief will never let us do that," Thom said. "We'll have to go through IA if we want to question Shawn as a suspect."

"But we can ask him what he knows about the drugs at

the school," Laurel said. "Like we did those kids tonight. They weren't suspects."

"Right."

Laurel really didn't want to go through Internal Affairs, because the paperwork alone could bury a cop. But if Shawn Newmyer was involved at all in the buying and distribution of drugs in the cove, Laurel would gladly swim through the red tape and mountains of papers to bring him to justice.

The firefighters stopped the flow of water, and Thom took a step forward. Laurel lurched after him, feeling very much out of her league in this partnership. She let him take the lead as he spoke to the Fire Chief, and then Philo, the harbormaster.

"We want it all," Thom said. "It's a crime scene, Philo, and no one's to get on that ship again, or take anything off of it, without first going through me or this young lady here." He indicated Laurel, who felt a sense of pride swell beneath her breast.

"A crime scene?" Philo asked. "You're insane. Some hand warmers got too close to one of those oil heaters, and they ignited. It was an accident."

"Yeah," Laurel said dryly. "And who's buying oil heaters and hand warmers in June in the cove?"

Thom smiled at her and nodded at Philo. "It's a crime scene. If it's in the way, we'll have the boat towed around to the south dock so we can examine it."

Philo growled, his frown taking over his whole face. "It's not in the way. I have other loading bays."

"Great," Thom said cheerfully. He turned to Laurel. "Well, you heard the Fire Chief. No one's getting on that boat tonight. We might as well turn in."

She saluted Philo, who simply glared at her as if it was her fault someone was trying to smuggle drugs through his port, and turned to leave. Struck with a sudden thought, she turned back to him. "Philo?" she asked. "Do you know where the hand warmers and oil heater were going?"

"To the department stores, I'm assuming," he said, starting to flip some sheets of paper. "I gave you the manifest last week."

"Right, I know," Laurel said. "But it just listed what was coming in. It didn't say where all those things go. Surely you know that too. Right, sir? Or do you just let anyone back up their van and start loading up boxes?"

He looked up sharply from his clipboard. "Of course not. I know where every box is supposed to go, and every single one is signed for by the company who ordered it."

"Of course," Laurel said with a smile. "Are those records digitized, or...?" She looked at Thom and raised her eyebrows. "We can come back tomorrow and start digging through your filing cabinets if that's where we'll find who's been ordering hand warmers and oil heaters for the past oh, nine months."

Philo's mouth dropped open, and Thom's expression

changed to one of pure delight. If he could applaud with just his eyes, he was currently doing so.

"I can pull up who ordered the hand warmers and heaters on the computer," Philo said. He glanced around and lowered his voice. "Do you really think they've been bringing coke in that way?"

"I think anything is possible," Laurel said. "We're just trying to follow-up on every lead." And frankly, she was utterly exhausted because of it. "If you can email me or text me the list of who's been buying those specific products in the last nine months, I'd be grateful," she said. "And if we need to see physical signatures of who signed for those items, we just ask you?" She blinked a couple of times.

"That's right," Philo said. "Those are physical copies, and I keep them in a filing cabinet in the control tower."

"Gotcha." Laurel grinned at him. "Thanks so much, Philo. You're amazing." She did turn then and start to walk away. Behind her, Thom said something, and then he caught up to her with a low chuckle coming from him mouth.

"Lady," he said under his breath. "You are *good.*"

Laurel glanced at him, glad for his praise. "If you picked up a hand warmer and felt it, would you know if the sandy stuff inside was what it was supposed to be, or cocaine powder?" She cocked one eyebrow, and watched Thom's expression roll through shock, disbelief, and then acceptance.

"I'd have no idea," he said.

"Exactly," Laurel said.

"You're *really* good," Thom said. "Your mind almost scares me."

"Join the club," Laurel muttered. They reached their cruiser, and she got in the passenger seat as usual. "What time do you want to pick me up to come back here to go through the carnage?"

"Well, we were having a whole crew come at three tomorrow afternoon," he said. "To search the ship. How about three?"

Laurel nodded and focused her attention out the windshield, the cool air from the air conditioner hitting her straight in the eyes. "That leaves the morning open to pay the high school vice-principal a visit."

LAUREL FACED THE WIND AND GATHERED HER HAIR into one hand. "This is amazing," she said, letting all of her cares and worries lift off her shoulders. Beside her, Paul laughed.

"Have you never ridden the steamer to Nantucket?" he asked.

She looked at him and released her hair. It went flying again, the wind trying to whip it right off her head. "Not for a long time," she said soberly. "Remember, I barely left the house for the last year of my marriage."

Paul's face changed in an instant too, and he said, "I'm such a jerk. I'm sorry. Of course I remember that." He gathered her close to his chest, and she wound one arm around his waist.

"My parents are going to love you," she said.

"What's amazing is that we got the weekend off together," he said.

"Aaron was in a really good mood after we talked to Shawn," Laurel said with a smile. "Heck, it made me happy too, knowing he's not involved in this drug case."

"You brought in the vice-principal, though," Paul said, clearly hinting for more information.

Laurel sighed. "Yeah," she said. "Just for questioning. He didn't have any new information, which is ultra frustrating."

"And what did you find on the ship?"

"Clothes, shoes, lettuce, milk, treadmills." Laurel could go on and on, but the ship that had caught fire earlier in the week seemed to be simply another boat bringing supplies to the cove. "Crib bumpers, strollers, meat, potatoes. We've released all of it that wasn't contaminated by smoke or burned by the fire."

She'd stood on the hard cement for days, watching as vendors picked up the things they'd ordered. She'd checked everything off the same as Philo, and she and Thom had gone home irritated, tired, and cranky.

They'd boxed up all the burnt items and anything left-over or unclaimed and taken it back to the evidence warehouse near the police station. Then Chief Sherman had ordered both her and Thom to take a three-day weekend, and he'd threatened to fire them if they so much as set a pinky toe on police property.

Laurel really needed this weekend in Nantucket with her fiancé and her parents. "I don't want to talk about the case," she said, exhaling away all of the stress. "I don't even want to *think* about the case."

Paul chuckled and nuzzled her neck, his voice quiet as he said, "I know you, Laurel, and you won't be able to stop yourself."

She brought his mouth to hers and kissed him for several long seconds. "I know, Deputy Chief Leyhe. That's why I brought you along. To distract me."

"Oh-ho," he said, chuckling as he kissed her again.

They arrived in Nantucket a few minutes later, and Laurel's heart took flight when she saw her mom and dad waiting for her on the hood of her dad's Jeep, which he'd parked facing the water right where the boats arrived and departed.

"There they are," she said, waving. "He's got the red windbreaker on." Laurel couldn't wait to hug her mother, and she turned toward the back of the boat so she could get closer to the ramp they'd walked up to get on. "Come on."

Paul went with her, and they managed to get off the steamer near the front of the crowd. Still, they had to walk slowly behind an elderly couple, so it took a few more minutes before Laurel cleared the station and ran toward her mom.

"You made it," her mother said, wrapping Laurel in the best of hugs. "I've missed you so much. You're so thin. Are you working too much?" She didn't release Laurel until her dad said, "You must be Paul."

Then Laurel stepped back and took Paul's hand in hers. "Mom, Dad," she said, though the water and the wind did make a noisy backdrop. "This is my fiancé, Paul Lehye. Paul, my mom and dad, Jim and Fae Baker." She beamed from her parents to the man she loved and back.

"It's so wonderful to meet you," her mom said, her voice pitching up. "We've prayed so hard for Laurel to find the perfect man for her, and she says it's you."

"Oh, well, I don't know about perfect," Paul said as he accepted her mother's hug. He grinned at Laurel over her shoulder, but Laurel got taken in another hug, this time from her father.

"Hey, Dad," she whispered, relying on his strength and power yet again in her life. Her parents had rescued her from her first marriage, and they'd been smart enough to take pictures and document everything inside the house —and on Laurel's body—that had allowed her to claim this new brand of freedom she enjoyed.

"You're not too thin," he said to her, and Laurel burst out laughing.

"Thanks, Dad," she said, stepping back. "The job's

been tough lately, but I do eat." She linked her arm through her mother's while Paul shook her dad's hand.

"All right," her mom said. "Since you made it on the morning steamer, we're just in time for lunch. There's this new pop-up at the Holiday House."

"Really?" Laurel asked. "Isn't that a boutique that sells Christmas decorations?"

"They still do that," her mom said. "But every day of the week, there's a new restaurant there. Your dad and I checked it out on the way here, and today, it's Lobster Legion. Every dish has lobster in it. Lobster for days and days."

Laurel grinned at Paul, who'd fallen into step beside her. "My mom loves lobster. It's her soul food. What she wants for her last meal."

He chuckled, and Laurel saw him sliding right into her family. He fit there, because he *was* the perfect man for her. "Lobster Legion it is, then," he said. He stepped forward and looked past Laurel to her mother. "Have you ever had lobster ice cream?"

Her mom's eyes rounded. "No, sir. Is that even a thing?"

"Oh, it's a thing," Paul said with a smile. "And delicious."

"If anyone makes it, I'm sure it'll be Lobster Legion," Laurel said.

"I didn't check the dessert menu," her mom said. "Now, Laurel, tell me what you decided to do about the food for the wedding. Wasn't your first choice unavailable? Something about not being able to get enough filet mignon for the whole force?"

"Oh, my goodness, yes," Laurel gushed. "They didn't want to put the steak bites on the buffet, so we had to either choose a different buffet—but all the protein choices were seriously lacking—or go with per-plate meals."

"And?"

"And I have the best wedding planner in the world, and she swooped in and saved the day." Laurel grinned at Paul. "We got the gold tier buffet—that's what they call it —with the steak bites for all those red-blooded men on the police force—by paying a little bit extra."

"How much extra?" Her mom paused by the Jeep while her dad unlocked the doors.

"We were already paying a premium fee in order to feed the number of people we want, so Robin said if we added another couple hundred dollars, couldn't they do the steak? They agreed, and done." She grinned and opened the back door. "You're going to love it, Mom. Robin's the best, and she managed to book The Glass Slipper for the ceremony. It's this *gorgeous* castle on the beach." Laurel sighed, feeling a bit out of her own skin, because she'd never really worried too much about what her wedding would be like.

But once she'd sat down with Robin, and the pages of those binders had been opened, it was like a whole new world had bloomed before her eyes.

"And you're still wearing your dress uniform to get married in," her mom said, not really asking.

"Yes," Laurel said firmly, reaching for Paul's hand as he slid onto the bench seat beside her. "I'm a cop, Mom, and it's what I want."

"Okay," her mom said airily, though Laurel knew she'd like her to wear a frilly, white dress to get married in. But because Laurel didn't need to fund a wedding dress, she'd been able to pay for the steak on the buffet.

"Does anyone care what I'm wearing?" Paul asked, and that broke the tension and got everyone to laugh.

Yes, this weekend on Nantucket was *exactly* what Laurel needed, and she snuggled into Paul's side, ready to escape the pressures of her new job back in Five Island Cove, if only for a few days.

TWENTY-ONE

I'm invoking the First Rights of Refusal to talk about Shad.

Robin gasped at Kelli's text and immediately reached for her phone. Never mind that she had strawberry jelly up to her knuckles. Phones washed, didn't they?

"Shoot, no," she said as the first smear of sticky stuff went across the screen. "Mandie, come finish these sandwiches."

Her oldest daughter got off the couch with a sigh. "I don't even like peanut butter."

"Then make what you do like," Robin said, stepping over to the sink. She quickly washed her hands and returned to her phone. She carefully wiped the jam off the screen to find that nearly everyone had responded already. Her heart pounded, because Robin hated missing things.

No way, Alice had said. *I was going to do that for*

Arthur!

Wow, Kelli, Eloise said.

I won't ask you anything about him, Kristen said.

What's this First Rights of Refusal you speak of? Laurel had asked.

"That means you have something to say," Robin muttered as she typed. She hit send right as Alice started to explain their ritual of calling the right to refuse talking about a topic. Only one of them could invoke the right at a time, which meant Alice would talk about Arthur today if she was forced to.

Robin didn't like forcing her friends to tell her things they didn't want to. She did like being in the know, and she disliked feeling left out.

No, Kelli said. *It means I don't want to answer a million question a million times.*

Just answer one then, AJ said. *How are things going with him?*

"She won't answer that," Robin said, watching as a couple more texts flashed on her screen.

You mean I could've just invoked this right not to say anything all this time?? Laurel asked, complete with the double question marks. Robin laughed out loud, because she did love having Laurel as a friend. She was level-headed and smart, and she'd experienced truly hard things in her life. Robin really related to people who'd worked hard to get where they were, and that fit Laurel to a T.

Sure enough, Kelli didn't say anything else in the text

string, while Alice, Laurel, El, and Kristen went back and forth in speculation about why Kelli would invoke this right. It was AJ who finally said, *Enough, guys. Leave her alone.*

Robin turned back to the spread of food on the kitchen island and sighed. "Ready?" she asked Mandie just as she put the top on a ham and cheese sandwich. "Is there room for that in the cooler?"

"Yep." Mandie smiled and put the ham sandwich on top of everything else Robin had packed into the cooler. "Did you get the shade?"

"Dad put it in the van for me before he left." Robin smiled at her daughter. They'd survived an entire month with Duke gone, and she could admit that the days had passed in a blur of activities, lists, phone calls, and five events in only four weeks' time. "I'll see if I can lift this."

She'd purposely not filled the cooler to full capacity, because while it had wheels, she still had to be able to lift it in and out of the car. She grunted as she got it from the counter, and it sounded like it had broken the floor for how hard it hit.

"Oof," Robin said. "You better come help me load it in the back of the van."

"All right." Mandie started to follow her, and Robin decided to take a chance on talking about Charlie. She'd tried in the past several weeks since he and Mandie had broken up, but her daughter had said very little.

"I see you decided to wear your suit," Robin said.

"Jamie," she called down the hall. "We're loading up. Bring me your phone and let's go." She continued rolling the cooler down the hall, where Mandie opened the garage door for her.

Together, they hefted it down the steps to the floor of the garage, and then into the back of the van. Mandie sighed and wiped her hand across her forehead.

"Yeah,' she said. "I decided that I can make this summer awkward whenever I see Charlie, or I can make it fun. I'd rather have fun at the beach." She gave Robin a weary smile that did show sadness around the edges. "I love the beach, Mom. He shouldn't get to take that away from me."

"No," Robin said, reaching out and tucking her daughter's hair behind her ear. "He shouldn't. I don't think he meant to take anything away from you, sweetie."

"I know." Mandie blinked a couple of times as her sister came out into the garage. "I know he didn't." She headed for the house adding, "I need to get my bag."

"Me too," Robin said, holding out her hand for Jamie's phone. "I'm not ready-ready to leave yet."

Her youngest put her phone in Robin's hand, scowling as she did so. "I don't see why you have to check my phone fifteen times a day."

"Because you send five hundred texts an hour," Robin said. "As soon as that slows down, I'll stop checking." She gave Jamie a raised-eyebrow look. "Did you delete any of these?"

"No, Mom."

"How about you take the sarcasm and sass down a couple of notches?" Robin asked. "Your sister and I have been putting together food and supplies to go to the beach for over an hour while you've been texting Damien." She hadn't even looked at the phone yet. "Or you can stay here while this phone and I go enjoy this glorious Sunday at the beach."

Jamie had the decency to look terrified and ashamed at the same time. "Sorry, Mom. I'll go get my stuff and help Mandie bring out the towels."

"Good girl." Robin watched her almost-fourteen-year-old trudge back into the house, as if being separated from her phone was akin to losing an eye.

She took a deep breath and blew it out as she started scrolling through the text messages. Jamie had found quite a group of friends, something Robin was grateful for. They'd been somewhat isolated last summer, as Robin had been so attached to her friends after Duke had left.

She didn't see anything nefarious or scandalous on the phone, and she never had. That didn't mean she was going to stop checking. She did look up as a car engine drew closer, and she frowned as her mother's car turned into her driveway.

Robin went to the back of the van and tucked Jamie's phone under her arm as she folded both of them across her chest. She met her mom's eyes through the windshield, and then Jennifer Golden took her sweet time getting out of the car. Robin didn't move a muscle to help her.

"Hey, Mom," she said, already tired and they hadn't even left the house yet. The sun, surf, and conversation with her friends would buoy her spirits, and she'd been looking forward to this beach day for over a week.

She'd suggested it as a way to celebrate the beginning of summer, and it turned out that a few hours on this Sunday was the only time all of them could make it. Laurel had been in Nantucket with Paul, but they'd agreed to catch the morning steamer back.

Kelli's ex-husband was coming to get Parker tomorrow, and then he'd be gone for two months. The twins had summer jobs, as did Mandie, and while they'd be able to attend beach days here and there, it wouldn't be every time. Even the Chief had taken this Sunday off.

It felt like the whole world just needed a break, and Robin felt that keenly deep down in her bones.

"Going to the beach?" her mom asked, still holding onto the car door.

"Yes." Robin didn't want to beat around the bush. "What are you doing here?" Behind her, the garage door opened, and she heard her daughters' voices. They stalled when they saw their grandmother, and that made Robin's heart hurt.

"I was just coming by to see how you were," her mom said, committing to getting out of the car and closing the door.

"Hey, Grandma," Jamie said, because she was the nicest of all of them. She put her backpack of stuff in the van and went to hug Robin's mom.

"We're doing great," Robin said, exchanging a glance with Mandie as she put her canvas bag on top of the cooler. She didn't bother to invite her mom to the beach. Jennifer Golden hated sitting in the sun, and she'd just say no. Worse, she might say yes.

For a few months there, Robin had thought she and her mother would be able to find a way back to each other. She'd worked so hard to forgive her mother, so hard to be patient with her, so hard to let her backhanded insults roll off her back.

But when she'd witnessed for herself how her mom had lied to her—and her girls—Robin had decided enough was enough. Just because they shared blood didn't mean they had to be friends.

"Good," her mom said as Jamie stepped away. "Great." She met Robin's eye again. "Maybe you three would like to come have dinner tonight at my place. After the beach."

Mandie coughed, and Robin shook her head. "I'll have work to do, Mom, and the sun always exhausts the girls."

"There's no school tomorrow."

"I have to be at work at seven," Mandie said. "Remember how I'm working on the grounds crew for the city?"

The look on her mother's face said that no, she had not remembered. Now, if one of Robin's sibling's children had told her mom they had a good-paying summer job, it would be all over social media, and Robin would've heard about it for hours straight.

"Of course," her mom said smoothly.

The last time they'd spoken, they'd argued—again—about how much Robin was working. She wasn't going to get into it again, and she turned back toward the garage. "We're doing fine, Mom. Sorry about dinner. Maybe another time."

"Robin, I know you're upset with me," her mom started, but Robin just kept walking. If she didn't, she'd say something she'd regret, and today was about golden sunshine and warm sand. They were going to Kristen's new condo, which had a sprawling beach that she visited every day. She'd told Robin hardly anyone used it, and once Robin had texted about this Sunday beach day, Kristen had invited everyone to her retirement community. They'd have a bathroom—two of them—nearby, and everyone had readily agreed.

Her mom would follow her into the house, but Robin didn't care. "Did we get the chairs?" she asked the girls.

"Right here." Mandie lifted them. "Mom, we could go to dinner."

"I'm not in the mood for dealing with her," Robin said quietly as her mom entered the house. She picked up her purse and her beach bag and headed out of the kitchen again. "Sorry, Mom, we told Jamie's friend we'd pick him up at ten, and we're late."

"Robin."

"I'm not upset with you," Robin said, pausing in front of her mother. She waited until Mandie and Jamie went back outside. "I simply don't want to have another fight. I'm doing what I think is best for my family, and that's that. I don't see why you think you get to have an opinion on it."

Her mom reached up and patted her perfectly styled hair. "Well, I—"

"Anna-Maria runs her own business from home," Robin said. "She works eighteen-hour days somethings *and* travels for shows. I have never heard you say a word about her or her schedule, and yet here you are—again— about to tell me I don't know what's best for my own family. Please, I'm begging you, don't."

Jennifer's eyes glinted with displeasure, but Robin didn't care. No, she couldn't care anymore. "Oh, and by the way, Duke and I will either be looking to buy this house by the end of the year or leaving it to buy one of our own. Maybe if I'm not renting my house from you, you'll stop feeling like you get to tell me what to do."

She took a step past her mom and then stopped. "Although, I'm not sure why you think that gives you any right now. We pay the agreed-upon rent, and we have not missed one time. Not once, Mother, even in the weeks Duke had no income coming in. So please, just go invite someone else to dinner and let me live my life."

Robin made it to the garage door before her mom said, "I'm sorry, Robin."

The apology made her freeze. Jennifer Golden didn't apologize. "For what?" she asked quietly.

"For trying to be part of your life when you don't want me to be."

"That's not it at all, Mom." Robin sighed. "I want you to be part of our lives in an appropriate way. That means you come to birthday parties just for us. If you say you're going to make crab legs, and you ask us to make something to go with, you don't lie and change your mind. It means you mind your own business, even if you don't agree with something we're doing. It means you don't put literally every other grandchild above the two you could see every single day—if only you cared enough about them." Her chest heaved, and she hated that she'd walked away and then gotten into the fight anyway.

"I have to go. I'm sorry too, for whatever I did that has never been good enough for you. I'm sure it's a long list that compounds and piles on top of one another. Please just know I'm sorry. I'm doing the best I can, and that's all anyone should be able to ask of me." With that, she left, her fingers trembling as she put her purse in the front seat and her bag in the back.

She reached up to close the back of the van, and she got behind the wheel.

"Is she leaving?" Mandie asked.

"I don't know," Robin said, putting the van in reverse.

"Let's see if we can get out of the driveway with her there." She managed it, as her mom hadn't pulled very far in. As they trundled down the road to pick up Damien, Robin said, "I love you girls, okay? Please don't ever let us get to where I am with my mother."

"You're nothing like her, Mom," Mandie said quietly, and Jamie just nodded in the back seat.

"I'm doing the best I can," Robin said, feeling her strength erode second by second. She did not want to cry on what was supposed to be a glorious beach day.

"You're doing great," Jamie said. "That's his house, Mom. The brown brick one on the right."

Robin came to a stop, and a teen boy who didn't look a day over ten came running outside. He climbed in the back with Jamie, said hello to Robin and Mandie, and they continued toward Kristen's new community.

———

AN HOUR LATER, THE GRAY CLOUD THAT HAD BEEN following Robin since her mother's visit finally dissipated completely. She trilled out a laugh at something Eloise had said, and she gazed fondly at her friend.

"I'm so glad this new family is working out for you." She reached over and took El's hand in hers, and the two of them watched Aaron splash through the shallow water along the shore, his girls laughing as they played with him.

"Billie's interesting," El said. "If a boy showed up that

she knew—or even another girl—she'd revert to her calm, quiet, more mature self. It's good to see her let go a little bit."

"Did anything ever happen with that boy she brought to the wedding?"

"They got their extra-credit in dance class." El shrugged. "I think they really are just friends."

Robin switched her gaze to where Mandie, Ginny, Jamie, and Damien were building a sandcastle. "I'm glad." She didn't want to talk about Jamie at the moment, and she watched her older daughter to make sure she was having fun. Mandie could hide a lot from most people, but Robin had a special vision for her kids. She could see and feel things others couldn't.

Charlie swam out in the ocean with Parker, Justin, and Derrick. Matt sat with AJ just a seat or two over, and every time she even moved a limb, he was right there, asking her what she wanted.

"How are your boys liking the cove?" Robin called down to him.

Matt turned toward her, his sunglasses a shiny, reflective blue. "I think they like it," he said. "Derrick and Justin are less than thrilled to get up at six a.m. to come work at the course, but the tips are good." He chuckled and turned his attention to the water too. "Justin's not that much older than Charlie."

"Don't remind me," Alice said with a groan. She and Arthur sat on Robin's other side, and Alice had both feet completely buried in the sand. She sipped a mocktail she'd whipped up right there on the beach, and Robin reached for the one Alice had made for her.

"Have you heard from Kelli?" Robin asked, and Alice looked toward her.

"She'll be here."

"She's late," Robin said, twisting to look behind her. Kristen, Rueben, and Jean had set up their shade back there, and she smiled at them.

"Yes, well, Laurel and Paul aren't here yet."

"They're coming from Nantucket," Robin argued. "Not Pearl."

Just then, a car pulled up and Kelli and Shad got out. "My word," Robin said. "He's wearing a dress shirt to the beach."

"He's not staying," El said. "Haven't you read your texts?"

"I turned off my phone," Robin said, and that was a mistake. She could feel El's eyes on the back of her head, and Alice's bored into the front. It was AJ, though, who said, "Did you get in another fight with your mom?"

"I don't want to talk about it," Robin said, rising to her feet. She left the others to gossip about her, though she knew it wouldn't be mean-spirited. She reached the curb and helped Kelli with Parker's bag.

"Hey," she said, giving Kelli a quick side-hug. "I was just asking about you." She switched her gaze to Shad. "Hello, Shad. Are you staying for the afternoon?" Maybe he just liked wearing slacks and shiny shoes in the sand. Robin knew of kookier things, that was for sure.

"Unfortunately, I can't," he said. "We've got a budget proposal due in the morning, and my team has misplaced half of it. Nathan's livid, and I have to meet with him."

"Nathan's the City Manager," Kelli supplied.

"Oh, right," Robin said. "I know Nathan Baldwin."

"Everyone knows Nathan," Shad said with a quick smile. "Some days, I wish I didn't know Nathan, and today is one of them. He's not pleasant to be around when things aren't going his way."

Robin exchanged a glance with Kelli, who wore a look of worry on her face.

Shad sighed. "Anyway, I have to go figure out what's going on and fix it." He wore a look of genuine dismay, and Robin offered him a smile.

"I'm sorry," she said. "We'll be here for hours, if you get done and want to come back."

"I just might," he said, leaning over to give Kelli a kiss. "You've got my suit, right, sweetheart?"

"Yes," she said, changing out her anxiety for a sunnier disposition. "Good luck."

He got back in the RideShare, waved, and the car drove off. Robin picked up the beach chairs from the sand, and together they started for the group on the beach.

"Nathan Baldwin isn't terrible," Robin said quietly. "Do you know him?"

"I've met him a few times," Kelli said practically under

her breath. "They're just stressed because the fiscal year starts on July first, and they have to have the budget approved at Tuesday's City Council meeting, or things will be messed up for the whole next year."

"Shad will find it, and fix it, and it'll be okay," Robin said.

Kelli nodded as they reached the group. She started setting up her chair between Eloise and AJ, and as she did, she said, "Okay, you're going to get a couple of sentences about me and Shad. If you want to hear this, you better come close enough to hear."

She waited while Kristen and Jean joined them, and while Alice wandered closer. Kelli stabbed her umbrella in the sand and started to twist it down in to anchor it. "We're talking about getting married."

Robin pulled in a breath and held it. She could see exactly the wedding she'd plan for Kelli and Shad. Something muted and off the books. Something that would only accommodate twenty people, because that would be all Kelli would want there.

"He hasn't proposed or anything, but we went ring shopping over the weekend."

"My goodness," El said. She got to her feet and moved Kelli's chair into the shade for her. "Did he buy something?"

"Not that I'm aware of." Kelli finished with the umbrella and faced everyone. "I'm a little freaked out, because Parker leaves tomorrow, and the studio opens on

Friday, and I just want one normal day. Okay? Just a day with sandwiches and too many chips, and oh my word, where did you get that mocktail?"

Alice held one up, her smile blinding, and Kelli practically dove for it.

"I think we can give her that day," AJ said. "Right, ladies?"

Robin murmured her assent along with everyone else.

"And I know what everyone wants to know," Kelli said. "And no, we haven't...done that yet. It's just one more thing I'm freaking out about, and I'm trying not to."

AJ patted her chair. "Come sit, Kel. No one expects you to be anyone but yourself."

Kelli sat heavily in her chair and faced the water, a long sigh escaping her mouth. After she took a drink of her cranberry and lime mocktail, she said, "Alice, you're a miracle worker."

Alice laughed, and Robin moved her chair back by Jean and Kristen to sit by them for a little while.

Half an hour later, Laurel and Paul arrived, and they looked fresh-faced and rested. Robin hung back while the others said hello, and then they piled under the shade made by Rueben's large tent.

"How's the case going?" Robin asked once Laurel had a mocktail and had sat down.

"Not great," she said, a frown marring her finer features. "But I haven't thought about it much this weekend. I got a text on the way back from Thom, and we're going to be going over all of our evidence again this week."

Laurel wouldn't say much else, and Robin nodded. She enjoyed the roar of the waves, and the chatter around her. She thought of Duke, and where he was right now. The clock would've just ticked to eight a.m. in Alaska, and he'd probably been out on the water for a few hours.

He was probably bringing back his first load of fish for the day, and he'd be headed back out after a spot of breakfast. She sent him her best thoughts, prayed for his safety, and watched as Matt's kids all came in from the water.

AJ started to pass out their lunches, and Robin sure did like that sight. It seemed that no matter how old children got, they'd still want someone to pack them a sandwich for the beach. She smiled at Charlie, who stood near his mom and toweled off.

She watched as Mandie and the others with her came in to get something to eat too.

"Look," Kristen said, as if Robin wasn't already looking.

"I see her," Robin murmured, and she actually blinked to make sure her eyes were working properly. Mandie had stepped over to Charlie and touched his arm. He'd looked at her, and now she said something to him.

She looked nervous as a rabbit among wolves to Robin, but then she smiled. Charlie smiled too, and he gave her a quick hug. That done, she got out her sandwich, a soda pop, and a bag of pretzels, and she and Charlie went about ten paces in front of the group, spread out their towels, and sat down to eat.

Ginny joined them, as did Jamie and Damien, and Robin could only shrug when Alice turned around and lifted both of her hands as if to say, *Can you believe what just happened?*

"Want something to eat, Kristen?" she asked. "I brought PB&J, and those dill pickle chips you love."

"Yes to the chips," Kristen said as Robin stood. "Rueben made me a salmon sandwich, though."

Robin had almost made it back to her cooler when AJ stood up. "I have terrible news," she said. "I just got an email that said my baby bassinet was destroyed in a fire and won't be delivered."

Robin paused and looked at Laurel. She got up and came closer too. "A baby bassinet?" she asked. "It must've been on the ship that caught fire last week."

"Must have," AJ said, frowning. "I had to special-order it, and they won't have another one in time for the baby."

"Must be one amazing bassinet," Alice said, and Robin shot her a look. She collected her lunch, including the dill pickle chips and a plastic container of shrimp salad, and returned to Kristen's tent.

"Chips, my queen."

Kristen laughed, but Robin noticed Laurel didn't chime in. "What's wrong, Laurel?" She offered her the sandwich. "I have tons of food."

Laurel took the sandwich, but it was clear she hadn't

even realized she'd done so. Her frown deepened, and then she turned to Robin. "She said *bassinet*, right?"

"Yes," Robin said, her stomach growling and her cooler ten steps away, across hot sand.

"I don't remember a bassinet on the manifest," Laurel said quietly. "And I've been through the ruined items three times. There was no bassinet."

"What does that mean?" Robin asked, keeping her voice low.

"It means there's a bassinet that was supposed to be on that ship...that wasn't. So where is it, and why would the shop say it had been destroyed in the fire?" She got to her feet quickly, despite Paul's protest.

"Sorry," Robin said, meeting his eye. "I do have more sandwiches."

"I'll take a couple," he said, watching Laurel. "She has more energy than anyone I know."

"She's just working through something," Kristen said.

Paul yawned. "Right, and I'm more tired now than I was when I went on vacation for the weekend." He chuckled, and Robin got up to go get more sandwiches.

She arrived just as AJ said, "Rock-A-Bye. I got the bassinet from Rock-A-Bye. Or I was going to."

"Perfect. Thanks, AJ."

"For your fiancé," Robin said, handing Laurel a few more sandwiches. She met Robin's eye before she took them, and Robin had seen that look before.

Laurel was back on the case.

TWENTY-TWO

Kelli stood with her son outside the twinhome, a couple of pieces of luggage on the sidewalk beside them. "You got your toothbrush?" she asked, though she'd asked ten minutes ago.

"Yes," Parker said.

"You have your phone and the charger?"

"Yes, Mom," he said.

Kelli looked down the street, expecting to see a Ride-Share at any moment. Julian had texted when he'd gotten on the ferry on Diamond, and they ran like clockwork. He should be here by now.

She told herself that the line for rides could be long, as it was officially the first day of summer vacation, and the cove had been filling with people for a couple of weeks now. Behind her, the scent of chocolate chip pancakes filled the air, as her mother had come over that morning to make them for Parker on his last day here for a while.

Once her mother left, Kelli would be alone in the house. Shad had already gone to work that morning, and he be in his budget meetings with Nathan until early afternoon. Then he'd get fed, and he'd go back for more meetings that would last until evening.

Kelli had plenty of tiny details to attend to at the yoga studio, and she'd probably spend her day there simply so she didn't have to be here.

"There he is," Parker said, and Kelli blinked her way out of her thoughts.

"You remember the code word if you feel unsafe?" Kelli said. "All you have to do is text me or call me and say it. I'll drop whatever I'm doing and come get you.'

"Yes," Parker said. "I remember it."

"Tell me," she said anyway, watching the blue sedan get closer. Sure enough, Julian sat in the back seat, and he was alone. Relief filled Kelli, because while he'd said he'd come alone, she hadn't quite believed him. Tiffany could be waiting in a hotel on Diamond Island for all Kelli knew. She had no idea when Julian had flown in, or when he and Parker would be returning to New Jersey.

"Spaghetti," Parker said, and Kelli dropped to a crouch in front of him.

"I love you," she said, taking him into a tight hug. "No matter what happens this summer, and no matter what your dad says, I love you."

"I know, Mom," Parker said. "I love you too."

She straightened as the car came to a stop. She pressed her palms to her thighs as the man she'd been married to for fifteen years emerged from the back seat. He didn't look at her, and he wore a giant grin as he jogged around the car toward Parker.

"Hey, buddy," he said, laughing as he lifted his son right up off the ground.

"Dad," Parker said, and he sounded so happy too. Watching them embrace did Kelli's heart some good, and she fell back a few steps to stay out of the way.

"Is this all your stuff?" Julian asked, setting Parker back on his feet.

"Yep."

"Let's get loaded up, then." Julian grabbed both bags and took them to the trunk, which the RideShare driver had opened for him. "Get in, bud. We're goin' swimming today, and then we'll fly out tonight."

Parker got in the car, and Julian closed the door before he turned to face Kelli. She looked at him, seeing all of the good things about him she'd liked so much. Those memories were strong as they sang through her.

At the same time, this man had cheated on her. He'd wanted a polyamorous relationship which included the woman he'd married only a few months after the divorce was final. He'd racked up debt to the tune of a million dollars in her name, and his.

"How's the business?" Kelli asked, tucking her hands into her pockets.

"Good," he said. "Listen, thank you for letting us—" He cleared his throat. "Me. Thank you for letting me have him for the summer."

Kelli swallowed. "Let me know if you need help with anything. He's not allergic to anything, and he's got his inhaler in case he runs a lot. It hasn't been a problem, though."

Julian looked like he might say something more, but he just nodded and started around the back of the car. "Our flight is at four-thirty tonight," he said. "We'll be back in Jersey by six. I'll have him text you."

"Okay," she said, and she switched her gaze from her ex-husband to her son. She waved to him through the window, and he grinned and waved back.

Then, with just the press of a foot against an accelerator, her son went zipping away from her. Kelli felt like part of her heart had been ripped out with a hot fork, and she struggled to breathe. She had no idea how long she stood there on the sidewalk, watching the empty street where the car had disappeared.

Her mom finally found her, and said, "Come on, dear. Come inside and have some tea."

Kelli did what her mother said, because she wasn't sure what else to do. Inside, she blinked against the cooler air and said, "That was horrible. I never want to go through that again."

"But you will," her mom said in a firm tone. "You *will* go through that again, Kelli, and it will be okay."

She looked up as she sat down. "What if he's not okay?"

"He'll be okay," her mom said. "You have to trust that he'll be okay. Otherwise, you'll drive yourself crazy. You prepared him. You told him the truth. You've done everything you can to make sure he'll be safe and taken care of. Now, you have to trust that all of that will be enough." She smiled and patted Kelli's hand. "Another pancake? I kept the buttermilk syrup hot just in case."

Kelli nodded, though she didn't really want another pancake. She wanted to be able to trust in herself and in the world out there that her son would indeed be safe and cared for in New Jersey this summer.

Please, she prayed, something she hadn't done in a very long time. *He's only ten years old. Bless him to be safe and cared for when he is not with me.*

Her mom put a plate of pancakes in front of her and sat down at the small, two-person table with her. "All right, Kel. Are we going to the studio today? Staying here?" She sipped her tea and watched Kelli.

"We?" she repeated.

"I know Shad is busy," her mom said. "If we stop by my house, we can grab Tina, and then she won't have to be alone all day."

"Mm," Kelli said, smiling at her mom. "Last time you

brought your yorkie to the studio, she tried to eat all the boba pearls."

That set them both laughing, and Kelli had never been more grateful for her mother than she was in that moment.

"Okay, Mom," Kelli said. "You stand right over there." She straightened her top, a floral, flowing tank top that felt like cool water against her skin. Her nerves skittered through her system, but Kelli tamped them down.

She'd been working to open her yoga studio and wellness center for seven straight weeks. She'd spent a small fortune, and she'd hired good instructors. She'd be working there seven hours each day, and a few on Saturdays too. Based on the surveys she'd been sending out to the people who'd signed up for any classes or her newsletter through her website, she'd decided to only do one yoga class on Sunday, and quite late in the day.

That way, she could sleep in. She could still go to the beach before noon with her friends. Kelli wanted this with every fiber of her being, but she also wanted to be a good mother, a good friend, a good daughter, and a good girlfriend.

Fiancé? ran through her mind, but Kelli didn't have room for it right now.

"Have you seen Heather or Sabrina?" she asked Devon, but he shook his head. Kelli looked at her phone and frowned. Her sisters had arrived in the cove yesterday, and because her mom's house was so small, they'd stayed at The Cliffside Inn. It was two ferry rides from Sanctuary to Bell, but Eloise's mother had been here for half an hour.

She didn't have the ferry schedule memorized, and she didn't want to start without her sisters. At the same time, she had a schedule to keep. After she cut the ribbon, she'd open the doors and let everyone walk through the facility on a self-guided tour for twenty minutes. Then she was doing a ten-minute class with yoga as she went over their classes and membership options.

"Kelli," Sori said. "It's almost time." She put a stack of paper cups next to the water dispenser on the porch.

"Yes," Kelli said, looking down the street to see if any cars were coming. Sori had come in for an interview and blown Kelli away with an amazing aerobics routine. Not only that, but she was a dietician, and she'd agreed to do their first class on proper vitamins for women for their optimal health.

"This is so exciting," Marina said as she mounted the steps. She wore a pair of leggings and a baggy tank top, because she would do all of the yoga moves with Kelli today. She'd been assigned the yoga classes, including the early-morning ones.

Right now, three yoga classes and two aerobics ones were all Kelli needed to keep up with those who'd signed up through her pre-launch promotions. She'd hired two part-time nail technicians too, and Sori would run the juice bar once the fitness classes concluded for the day.

The first week of appointments in the nail salon had been booked, and Kelli was hoping to get more today.

She'd also hired one masseuse—a mom who wanted to work a few hours each day while her kids were in school. Her youngest was starting into first grade this fall, and Wanda came with great credentials, even if they were a few years old.

Those appointments had gone quickly too, and Kelli had only opened them up for a month so as to not over-whelm Wanda or the studio. Eloise had been incredibly helpful with the software, and Shad had helped Kelli get everything integrated into her website.

She felt like she'd learned years worth of information in only a few weeks, and she reminded herself that it was just all new. The climb was steep in the beginning, but some things that had been hard the first few times, she could do without thinking now.

"Where's Wanda?" she asked. "I want everyone up here." She smiled at Erica and Toni, the two women she'd hired to do pedicures and manicures.

"Right here," Wanda said, pushing through the women standing back behind the gate, where Kelli had wanted them. She couldn't count everyone, but Shad would as they entered the studio. Kelli estimated there to be fifty or sixty people there, and she couldn't complain about that.

"It's time," Shad said in her ear, and Kelli shivered with excitement and nerves. He'd been nothing but supportive, and yes, they'd gone shopping last weekend for diamond rings. He hadn't brought it up again, and while Kelli had enjoyed snuggling with him and kissing him this week, she hadn't slept at his place, and he hadn't once asked to stay at hers.

She stayed awake as long as she possibly could. That way, she fell asleep the moment her head hit the pillow, and she didn't have any time to miss Parker. He'd texted her every day since he'd left the cove, and he hadn't used the word spaghetti once.

Kelli put her brightest smile on her face and took the large pair of silver scissors Shad had brought from the city offices. They used them for ribbon-cutting ceremonies for new government buildings, and he'd said she could use them for her grand opening.

"Welcome, everyone," she called in her loudest voice, and she somehow channeled her inner Robin, because her voice made everyone go silent out on the sidewalk. "I'm Kelli Thompson, and I'm thrilled you're all here for the grand opening of Whole Soul, a yoga, aerobics, and wellness studio destined to meet your fitness, health, and beauty needs."

A cheer went up, and Kelli would be forever grateful to AJ for helping her write the absolute perfect opening speech. She didn't want to be in the spotlight for long, so she lifted the scissors and added, "Once this ribbon is cut, I invite you to come forward and explore the building for a few minutes. Then I'll lead everyone in a short, simple yoga routine, and we'll have everyone who'll be working here around to answer questions about memberships and class options."

"Miss Thompson?" someone called just as she started to move the scissors.

Kelli looked up, her pulse throbbing in her neck. "Yes?"

"Can you tell us a bit about this location?"

She recognized the local reporter for the Cove Chronicles, as she'd contacted all of the press in Five Island Cove to try to get the word out about the studio.

"Oh, sure," she said, smiling. "This is the house I grew up in. My father was Guy Watkins, who was somewhat of a legend as a local artist. He poured all the stained glass windows you'll see in the house, and I bought it after his death, because I loved the flickers of color that came inside the house. They remind me of happy times, and they bring me joy. I hope they'll do the same for anyone who comes to Whole Soul."

She lifted the scissors, glad she'd been able to answer the question without getting emotional. "All right, everyone. Welcome to Whole Soul!" She sliced through the big, red bow that had been tied from one pillar to the other.

It drifted to the top step as the crowd cheered, and Kelli grinned out at everyone. She knew the reporter had a photographer with him, and she hoped her mother would be visible in the pictures. She nodded to Robin, who opened the gate, and the men and women who'd gathered on the sidewalk streamed onto the property.

Kelli stepped back to Shad's side, somewhere she felt very comfortable, and smiled and said hello to people as they went by.

"Seventy-seven," Shad said once they'd all gone inside.

"That's incredible," Kelli said. "I hope we get a lot of sign-ups today." She met Eloise's eyes, who grinned at her.

"You will," El said. "I've got the computer set up, and I'll go man it."

"Everyone to their posts," Kelli said, and her friends and loved ones entered the house too.

"Kelli," someone called, and she turned to find Heather and Sabrina hurrying up the street. "We didn't miss it, did we?"

"Yes," she said, irritated at her sisters. "Just the ribbon-cutting. We just started." She hadn't seen them in so long, and they'd only be here through the weekend. She didn't want to spend the time feeling frustrated and bitter, so she released her feelings into the sky as she went down the steps to greet them.

"The line for a RideShare was so long," Heather said. "We decided to just walk, but wow, that hill is steep." She huffed and puffed as Kelli drew her into a hug.

"It's okay," she said. "Go find Mom and make sure she's not hyperventilating in a corner somewhere."

"Why would she be doing that?" Sabrina asked. She

was the oldest of the girls, with lighter hair than both Kelli and Heather. She'd escaped most of the childhood trauma that had come in Kelli's teen years, but she still didn't like the cove much.

"Mom doesn't like this house," Kelli said, finding it odd that she knew more about their mother than either of her sisters. But at this point, she obviously did.

"I'll go make sure she's okay," Heather said, and she bustled off to enter the house.

Kelli linked her arm through Sabrina's, and said, "I'm so glad you guys are here."

"Me too." She grinned at her, and Sabrina had always been the sunniest of them all. She saw the good in people, and she believed she could do anything. She had done amazing things with her life, and Kelli looked up to her in many ways. "We're going to Kaleidoscope tonight, right?"

"If I'm still standing," Kelli said with a grin. She climbed the steps and entered the yoga studio, feeling as if her soul was indeed, whole.

Chaos flowed around her, and her first thought was to go right back outside. She overcame that, and she repeated, "If I'm still standing."

LATER THAT NIGHT, KELLI COULD BARELY STAY ON her feet as she climbed the steps to her twinhome. The grand opening of Whole Soul had been smashing success, and she had enjoyed the afternoon with her family and friends. They had eaten at The Kaleidoscope Café, and Kelli had introduced Shad to everyone important to her.

He held her hand as he patiently moved at her pace, and when they reached the top of the steps, Kelli said, "The code is seven-four-seven-seven."

"Too tired to enter your own code?" Shad teased, and Kelli gave him a warm smile. He released her hand and pressed in the buttons. The door clicked as the bolt moved, and he opened the door for her and gestured for her to enter.

"Do you want to come in for a drink?" she asked, because while she was tired, she didn't want to spend the rest of the night alone.

"Sure," Shad said easily. "Do you have wine or only soda pop?"

"I have a bottle of champagne I haven't opened yet," she said. "And one of red wine I have."

"Ah, I see. You've been over here drinking without me."

"A glass of wine before bed is *not* drinking," she said with a light laugh.

Shad entered her house and closed the door behind them. The electronic lock would twist itself after four minutes, so Kelli left it, kicked off her shoes, and sighed in bliss.

"Thank you for today," she said, leading him into the kitchen. "You spent your entire day off with me."

"Exactly how I like it," Shad said, and Kelli gave him a smile over her shoulder. In the kitchen, she got down two glasses—one champagne flute for her and one wine glass for him. He slid his hand along her waist, and Kelli melted into his touch.

"Kelli," he whispered, and she stepped into his arms to kiss him. Her heart pounded so hard, because she knew what she wanted to do. She wasn't very good at articulating how she felt or what she wanted, and she told herself to be brave. If she could employ just a little bit of courage, she could foster a relationship that was more open and more honest than the one she'd had with Julian.

She pulled out of the kiss, his touch so tender and so wanted. "Shad," she whispered, sliding her fingers through his hair. "Will you stay with me tonight?"

"Absolutely," he murmured, claiming her lips again.

She cradled his face in her hands, feeling the sexy roughness of his beard beneath her fingertips. She had one more thing to say, and she had to say it before they went upstairs. "Shad," she said again, tilting her head back for him to kiss her neck. "I'm in love with you."

He paused and lifted his head. His dark eyes searched hers, hope and desire mingling there. "I love you too," he said, a smile appearing on his face. "My dear Kelli, I love you so much."

Joy burst through her, and while she wanted to kiss him again, she said, "I want us to talk through everything before we get married. Money. Where we'll live. What we want our life moving forward to look like and feel like. Friends. Family, and the demand they put on us. How we'll deal with Parker, since he's my son and not yours, at least biologically. What we both want from the relationship. Careers." She cleared her throat, because she and Julian hadn't talked about any of the things she'd just said. If she'd known what he wanted, they might still be together. "What we want physically. All of it."

"I can do that," he said. "Does this mean we're engaged?"

"I don't see you down on one knee," she said with a grin. "Or any diamonds in sight."

He chuckled and pushed her hair back off her face. "All right. I'll get that done really soon." He gazed at her, pure love and tenderness in his expression now. "How about we start with what you'd like tonight to be?"

Kelli smiled at him and ran her hands down his arms to his, where she laced her fingers though his. "I can do that." She turned and led him toward the stairs, her heart rippling with every step she took.

TWENTY-THREE

E loise looked up from the registration podium as the door of The Cliffside Inn opened. It was almost three-thirty, and that meant Billie and Grace should be arriving soon. They came every afternoon about this time during the school year, and in the summer, she and Aaron juggled the girls between them, his parents, her mom, and even her friends.

Today, the girls had been with his mother in the morning, and she'd been planning to take them shopping for new flip flops, feed them lunch, and put them on the ferry to come to the inn.

The people entering the inn weren't her two step-daughters, and while Eloise wanted to frown and wonder where they were, instead, she smiled.

"Good afternoon," she said as the older gentleman

finished holding the door for the woman and they turned toward her. "Can I get your name?"

"Marlo Benson," he said, and Eloise looked at her tablet instead of him. She knew that name, because she'd seen the articles that had been circulating the cove for the past several weeks. Everyone in Five Island Cove knew the names Marilyn and Marlo Benson by now, but Eloise determined to be professional in public. She could freak out in private.

"Looks like I have you for the weekend," she said with a smile. "It's a great weekend to be at Cliffside." She picked up their holiday flyer and put it on the top of the podium. "We're doing a fireman's breakfast tomorrow morning from seven to ten, right outside on the front lawn."

She smiled and reached for a fresh keycard. Her mind spun around what she should do as soon as Marlo and this mystery woman checked in. It wasn't Marilyn, but then again, they'd been divorced for six years. The woman was a little older than Eloise, but not much. She wasn't as old as Marlo, that was for sure, and she had a head full of dark blonde hair that stopped at her shoulders. It almost looked like a wig.

"Tonight is seafood night in the lobby," Eloise said as she put the keycard in the coder. With a couple of taps, the machine would program the card to work on their room. "I have you on the top floor, in our corner suite. It's a great view to the west, across the island, for the sunset, and the balcony is available to you. You also have a fantastic view to the north, and we've had reports of whale sightings from the corner suite."

The machine beeped and Eloise took out the card. She put it on top of the flyer announcing their Fourth of July weekend events, which neither Marlo or his mystery woman had touched. "Do you want two keys?"

"One is fine," Marlo said in a gravelly voice. He gave Eloise a smile and reached for the key and the flyer.

"I just need to see the card you reserved with," Eloise said, putting a card reader on the top of the podium too.

Marlo turned to the woman, and she opened her purse to get out the credit card. Eloise could barely breathe while the woman's fingers fumbled through her wallet, and when she finally produced it, she caught the tremor in her hands. She gave the card to Marlo instead of trying to insert it herself, and he got the job done.

Eloise tapped on her tablet to complete the transaction, and the information came up on the screen. Adelle Spencer.

She touched the button to print the receipt, and said, "You can take the card out now."

Marlo did, handed it to Adelle, and signed the receipt for Eloise. "Welcome to Cliffside," she said as she gathered the receipt and tucked it on top of the pile of the others she'd generated that afternoon. "Do you need some help with your bags?"

The inn didn't have an elevator, and Eloise had been

considering putting one in. It would be expensive, and there was no way to do it inside the inn. She'd had a general contractor who worked on the commercial side of the hospitality industry in the cove, on Nantucket, and in Cape Cod come and look at the building, and he'd suggested adding it on to the outside of the inn.

The stairs went up right beside her, and he'd mentioned putting the elevator parallel to them, but on the outside of the building. It would take up some patio space, but then guests could go out to get on, and the doors would open on the other side, on the inside of the hallway at the top of the stairs on each floor.

"We're fine," Marlo said, the bag on his shoulder still in place. Adelle only had a small bag too, and she seemed to be able to lift it just fine.

Eloise didn't mean to stare, but she often wondered who the people were who came to the inn. What were their stories? Why had they chosen to come here?

She was grateful they did, because they paid her bills and allowed her the luxury to think about installing expensive elevators. The inn had been booked full every night for a month now, and while some of her more expensive rooms remained open until only days before, they'd been selling out eventually.

She fished out the receipt from Adelle and studied it. Would it help Laurel to know Marlo was here? Who was Adelle? She hadn't looked that much like him, as Marlo had darker hair, bushier eyebrows, and a face the shape of a box. Adelle had been more delicate, with blue eyes to go with her blonde hair.

"That hair was not real," she mused, and she tucked the receipt into her pocket just as the door opened again.

She looked up for Billie and Grace, but the woman who'd opened the door was taller than a junior high student. Still, Billie entered the inn, followed by Grace, and then Alice stepped inside.

Eloise grinned as she moved around the podium. "Hello, my babies," she said, wrapping Billie and Grace into a hug simultaneously. "I've been wondering where you were."

"We ran into this riffraff on the ferry," Alice joked, and she too took a turn hugging Eloise. "I insisted they ride with us, and we needed a bigger car because of the luggage." She stepped back and nodded toward the still-ajar door. "Arthur's getting it now."

"I have to admit I forgot you were coming this weekend." Her heart warmed at the sight of Alice in a pair of knee-length shorts the color of deep, dark eggplant skin. Eloise would never even consider buying a pair of purple shorts, but Alice pulled them off like she was a runway model.

She'd paired the shorts with a dark gray tank top that seemed simple, but Eloise was sure had silver thread running through it. Alice looked good in metallics, and she had several pieces that showed off her slim frame, her skinny arms, and the angles in her face.

With a pair of strappy sandals on her feet, Alice looked ready for whatever this summer day brought her. Eloise always felt frumpy next to her, and she told herself she had to wear the black slacks and professional blouses at the inn.

She was the owner, for crying out loud.

"Did Marge make cookies?" Grace asked, bouncing on the balls of her feet.

"There's always cookies during check-in." Eloise smiled at her.

"Can we go swimming, El?" Billie asked. "I brought our stuff."

"Yep." Eloise looked down the hall that led into the back foyer. Through a door that way, the patio expanded, and then the swimming pool took over the yard. "Go find Marge, and ask her if you can change in her suite. We're full today—Alice and Arthur are the last guests to check in."

"You can use our room too," Alice said. "If you can't find her."

"Okay." Billie smiled at Alice and then Eloise before she went with Grace to find cookies and Marge.

Arthur entered the inn, and he gazed around as if he'd just discovered some unknown land. "This is fantastic," he said. "I had no idea this was here."

"I told you Cliffside was a hidden gem in the cove," Alice said, smiling at him as she took his hand.

Eloise bustled back to the podium to get them checked

in, and she went through her spiel about the pancake breakfast in the morning, as well as the activities throughout the weekend. They were simple things like face painting, a pony ride on Sunday morning, and special discounts and coupons at the restaurants on Sanctuary Island and Rocky Ridge.

"Impressive," Alice said. "Nothing on Diamond?"

"I'm trying to keep people out here," Eloise said. "Diamond Island is amazing, don't get me wrong. But I want them to eat at our restaurants and sit on our beaches. They're less crowded, for one, and they're also just as good."

"Are you going to partner with Matt once he gets that golf course open?"

"Yes," Eloise said. "We've already talked about it. They're moving fast too. He wants it open before the baby comes."

Alice's eyes widened. "That seems hard to believe they'll get that done."

"Well, all three of his kids are working for him," Eloise said. "They just bought the old Sears center here on Sanctuary too. They're turning it into a miniature golf course."

"Wow," Alice said. "I'm glad someone finally bought that land. It's been an eyesore for a while now."

Eloise nodded, finding it almost comical that she and Alice were talking as if they'd driven by the abandoned retail center for years and years, when really, neither of them had been in the cove for very long, despite having grown up there.

"I'll take the bags up," Arthur said, reaching for the keys. He did just that, while Alice leaned her hip into the podium.

"So a weekend trip away," Eloise said, feeling shiny from head to toe. "Who's staying with the twins?"

"They're at my dad's," Alice said with a sigh. "And neither of them is terribly happy. But they both have a boyfriend or a girlfriend, and I didn't want to leave them alone at home. This way, if they're going to sneak out and do something naughty, it'll have to happen on Rocky Ridge." She smiled, but the gesture lacked its usual luster.

"I bet your dad is happy to see them." Eloise's mother adored Billie and Grace, and she often met them at the ferry and brought them up to the inn when Eloise couldn't.

"He's thrilled. They're going out on the boat for the whole weekend. Dad says he knows the perfect spot to be able to see the fireworks in New York City, Nantucket, and Five Island Cove without having to move a bunch of times." She grinned and shook her head, glancing up as Arthur's footsteps receded.

Eloise cleared her throat and started cleaning up the podium. She always filed the receipts, made a list of who was checking out the next morning by name and room number, and locked the tablet. In the evenings, she'd check the reservations for the next day's check-ins, make the housekeeping list, and send the texts and emails to the people who needed them. That way, the rooms got cleaned that needed cleaning. Welcome packets got made. Check-out documents were printed.

It had taken a few months, but going into month seven, Eloise finally felt like the machine was oiled and operating well.

"Have you guys talked about marriage again?" Eloise asked.

Alice drew in a long breath. "Yes," she admitted. "I mean, not as seriously as Kelli. I'd be shocked if she's not engaged by Monday."

"Me too," Eloise murmured. "It'll happen fast too, don't you think?"

"She won't want anything big," Alice said. "That's for sure. So yes, I think it'll happen fast. Probably before school starts for Parker."

Eloise nodded. "That's what I think too. He won't be back until mid-August, and I bet they get married in that two-week window between when he's here and when school starts."

"Mm, I'm sure you're right." Alice glanced at the stairs on her right again. "I don't know. I *really* like Arthur. Like..." She sighed. "It's hard to explain."

Eloise watched her closely. She seemed so happy when she was with Arthur. They'd spent afternoons on the beach together, and since he didn't work in the summer, Alice had told everyone that she saw him every day for hours.

"The twins like him," Eloise said. "Right?"

"Yes," Alice said. "He adores them too, surprisingly." She rolled her eyes. "Seventeen-year-olds aren't that fun, and yet, he gets along with them so well. They talk to him, and he talks to them, and there's no tension." She rubbed her hand down her face. "I'm not sure how he does it."

"He's a high school counselor," Eloise said. "He's trained to talk to seventeen-year-olds without judging them."

"I don't judge them," Alice said quickly.

"I know, sweetie." She rounded the podium and put her arm through Alice's. "Come get a cookie and tell me why you can't take a weekend trip to New York City and get married."

Alice made a choking sound and stumbled. "I could never."

Eloise laughed and kept walking. "But you've thought about it."

When Alice didn't respond, Eloise knew she was right.

"I don't know, El," Alice said as she sank onto the couch in the lobby. Eloise found the cookies on a table near the kitchen door and brought the whole plate over to the couch. She offered one to Alice, who took it and bit into it in the daintiest way possible.

She sat next to Alice and waited. She didn't have to

relentlessly question the way Robin did to get Alice to talk. Sometimes silence did the trick first.

"I couldn't marry him without the twins there," Alice said. "I think Ginny would be fine with it, but Charlie's still on the fence."

"Charlie acts like he's on the fence about everything," Eloise said, and that got Alice to laugh.

"In most things," she agreed, finishing her cookie. She dusted off her fingers and exhaled slowly. "I can see myself with him." She met Eloise's eyes. "That scares me a little. I was with Frank for so long—too long—and while this year has been hard, it's also been very liberating. I don't want to give up what I've found."

Eloise set the plate of cookies on the coffee table in front of her. "And what have you found, Alice?'

"Myself," she whispered. "Who I am, and what I want. I love my little law office in the front room of my house. I like that I can pay my own bills and provide a house for my kids where their friends can come. It's like..." She paused, and once again, Eloise just waited. So much of what Alice was saying, Eloise could've said for herself.

This past year had brought so many changes to her life. It hadn't been easy, despite having such amazing people at her side, supporting her. She'd always been herself, because she'd been alone for so long. But she'd found a new part of herself that had always wanted to step into the spotlight and hadn't been able to.

"It's like this open, honest life that I'm not afraid to let other people see," Alice said. "I was hiding in the Hamptons. Everything had to happen behind closed doors, and I was so unhappy."

"Arthur isn't going to steal you away to the Hamptons again," Eloise said gently.

"No, I know."

"It doesn't have to be a big affair," Eloise said. "Certainly not the wedding of the year." She grinned at Alice, who smiled back. "Think Kelli-style. Who would be there to watch?"

"My dad and Della," Alice said. "The twins. They'd walk me down the aisle." A dreamy smile touched her lips, and Eloise realized she *had* been thinking about this. Seriously.

"All of the ladies we eat lunch with on Wednesdays."

"And?"

"And that's it," Alice said. "I mean, your mother could come if she wanted to, but I don't need her there."

"Of course." Eloise heard footsteps coming from upstairs. "That's less than a dozen people, Alice. A few more if you let Duke, Aaron, and the other men come. Honestly, you could tell us all to meet here one afternoon, have the wedding, and Marge will feed everyone dinner. Done."

Alice's eyes widened again, and Eloise thought she might actually be considering what she'd just said.

"Hey, hon," Arthur said. "I swear I saw some whales

out the window upstairs. What do you say we drive over to the north shore and check it out?"

Alice got to her feet and stepped right into her boyfriend. He put his arms around her, and grinned as she said, "Yes, let's go see if your eyes are as good as you're always bragging about." They laughed together, said good-bye to Eloise, and left the inn through the front door.

Eloise stayed on the couch for a moment, enjoying the comforting feeling the couple had left behind. Alice looked good with Arthur. They got along well. She'd learned some things from her first marriage, and she'd learned a lot about herself in the past year.

"They'll figure out what's best for them," Eloise told herself, and then she got up and collected her phone from the podium. She pulled the receipt out of her pocket and looked at it, torn about what to do.

Then she dialed Laurel's number.

"I'M JUST SAYING I DON'T WANT TO TALK ABOUT Laurel during dinner," Aaron said. He picked up the salt and pepper shakers and turned to put them on the table. He faced Eloise again and took her into his arms. "I don't answer to very many people, but Nathan is one of them."

"I know," she said as he nuzzled his lips against her neck. She giggled and tipped her head back to kiss her husband, her life so different than it had been last year.

She hardly recognized herself at all, and she was so very glad for that. She hadn't even realized how miserable she'd been in her brownstone in Boston, and she'd started to think about selling it.

She wasn't going to go back there, and she didn't need to keep it. She hadn't wanted to sell it, because she'd had it for so long, and she did love the four-story house she'd lived in for decades.

"Perhaps we can take a trip to Boston," she whispered against Aaron's lips. "Just before school starts. Like we did last year."

He pulled back and looked at her. "Yeah? You want to?"

"Or after Laurel's wedding," Eloise said. "We could go for the weekend. Stay in the brownstone. Enjoy the city. Or just each other." She smiled at him. "Maybe your parents could take the girls for a long weekend. I could ask Kristen or Robin too."

Aaron held her tight against his body, and Eloise loved being encircled in his arms. "Let me look at my schedule," he said. "I'd love to take the girls, and we could go down into New York too."

"Sure," she said. "Maybe for fall break, if it works out. Going to the city would take a little longer than a weekend."

"Billie's always wanted to go to New York," Aaron said as he stepped away from Eloise. "Right, Bills?"

She exited the hallway, and she looked like she could kill her dad with her bare hands. "I hate this dress."

"It's two hours," Aaron said. "For my boss. We have him over once every few years." He swept toward Billie, and she squealed as he lifted her up off her feet.

"Dad, put me down." She laughed though, and Eloise liked the sight of the two of them.

Aaron set her on her feet and looked behind her. "Where's your sister?"

"I'll go check on her," Eloise said just as the doorbell rang.

Aaron jerked toward it; Billie smoothed down her skirt; he and Eloise exchanged a glance. "It'll be fine," Eloise said. "City Managers love me." She gave him a smile, ran her hand down Billie's hair, which had been slightly mussed when Aaron had picked her up, and continued down the hall to Grace's room.

"Gracie," she said when she reached the doorway.

The little girl sat on her bed, and she wasn't crying at the moment, but she had been. Eloise darted into the room and brought the door closed behind her. "Hey, hey," she said, hurrying toward the eleven-year-old. All of her stuffed animals, including the one Eloise had given her for her birthday last year, crowded around her.

"What's wrong?" She pulled the child onto her lap. "Why are you crying, Gracie-Lou?" She glanced toward the door. Aaron's boss was here, and he wouldn't want to deal with anything other than that right now. At the same time, Nathan knew he was a father—Nathan Baldwin was a father too, actually.

His children were all older and out of the house, like Matt's, but Aaron had been telling Eloise about them for the past week or two since she'd learned they'd be hosting Nathan and his wife, Polly, for dinner.

"I can't get my shoes on," she said. "And they're the ones that go with my dress. I don't have anything else to wear."

Eloise looked at the ground, where a pair of shiny, white shoes lay on their sides, as if Grace had thrown them there in frustration. She took a deep breath. "Okay, sweetie. Let's see what else you have. Maybe you could wear a different dress."

"I can't," she said. "Dad said I have to wear this one, because the lace makes me look pretty."

Eloise slid the girl off her lap and crouched in front of her. "Grace," she said. "You're pretty no matter what you wear. Let's find something, because your daddy's boss is here already." She stepped over to the closet and started going through the clothes there. She'd never concerned herself with the girls' rooms or clothes, but since she'd become their step-mother, the last two months had found her learning more and more about them.

Grace didn't hang up anything, and Eloise had put a royal blue dress in this closet last week. "What about this?" She pulled out the dress and held it up. "You have those white sandals you could wear with it."

"Okay," Grace said.

Eloise helped her change quickly, and they emerged from the bedroom at the same time Aaron called, "El?"

"Right here," she said, walking toward him with Grace in front of her. She met Aaron's eye and hoped she could tell him what had happened in the space of a single glance. "Her eyes are so blue when she wears this dress."

Aaron put his hand on his daughter's head in a kind, parental gesture. "You are perfect, Gracie-Lou. Come with Dad, okay?" He took her hand and led her into the kitchen. "You remember Grace," he said, his voice slightly different when talking to Nathan.

Eloise exited the hall while Nathan gushed over Grace's dress, and then he faced her. "Good to see you again, Nathan," she said, stepping forward to shake his hand. She looked at Polly, a properly polished woman, without a hair out of place. She reminded Eloise of Alice, when she'd first come to the cove last year for Joel Shields's funeral.

Expensive clothes, makeup applied by a professional, false nails to go with her false smile. "You must be Polly. I'm sure we met at the wedding, but it was a busy day for me." Eloise had never smiled so politely in her life, and Polly returned the gesture.

"You were the most stunning bride," Polly said, even her voice like rocks that had had all the edges smoothed off. "I told Nathan we should do a vow renewal just to have Robin plan a meal for us."

"And I told Polly that we should just do a twenty-fifth-anniversary party. It'll be the same thing." He grinned at her, and the love in his eyes wasn't hard to miss. He put his arm around her, and they chuckled together.

"Come sit down," Eloise said. "Would you like something to drink?"

They moved then, and Eloise played the perfect hostess by pouring wine, making chit-chat about the upcoming Heritage Fair the cove put on every August, and then serving the dinner Aaron had picked up an hour ago.

Billie knew how to play her part too, and Polly seemed charmed by her. Nathan spent most of his time talking to Aaron, and Eloise kept her smile in place while talking to Polly about her marketing company.

"It's called Cove Creations," she said. "We do everything from banners to billboards to boxes." Polly seemed quite proud of the endeavor, and Eloise supposed she should.

"How do you keep up with everything?" she asked.

"Well, Nate's not the mayor," Polly said, lifting her wine glass to her lips. "He even helps me sometimes, especially with shipments around the cove."

"That's wonderful," Eloise said, hardly recognizing her own voice. She was not used to dealing with political things, though she knew Aaron's job required it from time to time. Everyone know who he was; everyone had an opinion on the police and how they were doing.

She figured she could smile until her cheeks hurt a

couple of times a year, the same way Aaron could stand there and take family pictures when he didn't want to.

By the time the Baldwins left, Eloise thought she'd used all the patience the Good Lord had given her. Aaron laughed and closed the door, the sound immediately cutting off. He exhaled heavily and slumped against the door.

Eloise watched from her spot in the doorway between the living room and the kitchen. It was a large, arched opening, and one could see all the way from the front door to the back of the house.

"I'm exhausted," Aaron said, straightening and coming toward her. "Thank you, El. I know that's not fun."

She wasn't going to argue with him, though she had not enjoyed herself. "I can't believe your dad wants to be one of those guys."

He grinned at her as he took her into his arms. They danced in the kitchen, and he said, "Fits my mom, though, right?"

Eloise pealed out a string of laughter. "Your mom is only about half as fake as Polly Baldwin."

"Something for her to aspire to," Aaron joked. He stepped over to the sliding glass door and opened it, finally letting Prince back in. "Hey, buddy. Sorry to stick you out there for so long." He rubbed down the dog, who adored Aaron as much as everyone else seemed to.

"I'm going to go change and check my phone," Eloise said. "I'm afraid I've left Laurel hanging for too long."

He raised his eyes to hers. "I'm worried out you helping her with any sort of undercover thing, El." He straightened and approached her again. "You don't know what that's like."

"I know." She didn't know what it would be like to be in such a high-pressure, undercover operation. "But Aaron, I think I can help her. She said Adelle Spencer is a ghost, except for that charge at Cliffside. Doesn't that seem shady to you?"

"El." He smiled at her and gave her a sweet kiss. "Everything is shady to a cop. The important part is picking apart what is really shady and what's just your mind making things up."

"You think Laurel is making things up?"

"No." He sighed and looked over Eloise's shoulder. "I think Laurel is a brilliant detective. That's why I put her in narcotics. But I also think she's hunting for clues in this case, and she's hunting hard."

"She wants to get it right," Eloise said. "I know that much. She's not going to do anything without hard evidence."

"Which may or may not exist," he said. "We don't always get the hard evidence we need. She might be chasing a ghost."

"The drugs are here, right?" Eloise asked.

"Oh, they're here." He stepped back, and he did look so tired.

She didn't want to argue with him about the drug

problem in Five Island Cove. She hadn't even known there was a drug problem until Laurel's case, and she assumed most people on the islands didn't either. It was such a pristine, quaint place to live and explore.

"Come on, Mister Sherman. It's way past our bedtime." She led him down the hall, leaving all the dishes on the table and in the sink, where she'd do them tomorrow. She saw her phone flashing with blue and green lights, but she decided Laurel and whoever else had messaged her could wait a little longer, and she turned to unknot the tie at Aaron's neck as she kissed him.

TWENTY-FOUR

"The devices are tiny these days," Laurel said, flipping up Eloise's collar and barely touching her finger to the fabric there. "There's no wire to be found. No recording device. It's a mic, El. It'll broadcast everything that's said to us, where we'll be recording it."

Eloise nodded, because they'd been through this before. She still looked like she'd swallowed a bomb and was waiting for it to go off. Thom sat on the couch in the Chief's office, while Aaron himself sat behind the desk, glowering at everyone and everything.

Laurel knew he and Eloise had argued about her wearing the mic and going to the meeting Marilyn Benson ran for women business owners in Five Island Cove. She'd gone over everything with Eloise four or five times. Maybe six or seven. Perhaps even more.

The past ten days had been busy for Laurel, though

she felt like she and Thom were just spinning in circles. There'd been no bassinet on the ship manifest. Nothing in the evidence warehouse had indicated any infant products of any kind.

The manager and then the owner at Rock-A-Bye, the pediatric supply store where AJ had ordered the bassinet, said the fire was in their storage facility in New Jersey, one of the largest ports on the Eastern Seaboard. It hadn't even shipped to the cove.

Lucas Winters and Harold Marsden refused to change their stories, and even when Thom and Laurel had tailed Harold for seventy-two hours, they'd found nothing nefarious in his activity, the people he met, nothing.

She'd interviewed Marilyn again, but since they didn't have anyone else giving them any information, nothing she said could be corroborated. The city attorney wouldn't offer her a deal without some hard proof that what she said was true.

They'd released her a couple of weeks ago, but Laurel was sure she was running something illegal through the Cove Helping Hands organization, or through her toiletry delivery service.

She'd watched through the two-way glass while Thom had talked to Marlo Benson, but the vice-principal had seemed completely baffled by the line of questioning. Yes, he knew about the drug problem at the high school. No, he didn't know where they'd come from.

When they'd visited him again after his holiday

weekend at The Cliffside Inn, he'd said he'd taken his sister to Sanctuary, because her husband had just passed away. She was enduring chemotherapy treatments and needed cheering up.

Eloise had confirmed they'd stayed in the corner suite, which did have two beds, and Laurel had tracked down an Adelle Spencer in Louisville, where a Douglas Spencer had died two weeks ago.

On every turn, she'd been met with another dead end or the perfect alibi that actually checked out. All she had left was Marilyn Benson, and if this didn't pan out, Laurel had actually considered admitting defeat. She and Thom would start working a case with new, fresh leads, and this one would simmer on the back-burner until something different presented itself.

That felt like failure to her, but Thom had said that was how cases worked. Some of them went cold, only to warm up later.

"Okay," Laurel said, exhaling. "Remember what we talked about?"

"Yes," El said. "I'm just going to see what she says. If she approaches me, and we think she will, because she wants Cliffside to join her toiletry trade, I'm going to act interested and sign up."

"That's right."

"This is ridiculous," the Chief said, standing. "I still think I should go too."

"It's a *women* in business meeting," Thom said in a

deadpan. The Chief leaned into his palms and practically growled. In the past, Laurel would've shivered and scampered out of the Chief's office. Now, she just shot him a nervous look and focused on Eloise again.

She wore a look of pure determination on her face when she met Laurel's gaze, and Laurel admired her strength. When she looked at Aaron, Eloise softened. "Aaron, you're literally going to be in the next room over. What could possibly happen?"

"That's exactly what I don't know," he said. "It's nerve-wracking."

"It's going to be fine." Eloise reached up and patted her collar. "I can't even feel it. She's not going to pat people down before the meeting."

"There are metal detectors at City Hall," Aaron said.

"There's no way they'll get that," Thom said, now scrolling on his phone. "They get past airport security, Chief." He groaned as he got to his feet. "There's going to be six cops within twenty feet of that meeting. I understand you worrying, but we're being as careful as possible."

"It's time to go," Laurel said. That got everyone moving, and Eloise exited the office first. She stopped by the station sometimes, especially in the summer, and she collected the girls from Sally's desk, where they'd been eating Skittles and Starburst, and the three of them left.

When Laurel couldn't stand being in the tense presence of the Chief, she stepped out of the office and walked causally over to her desk, Thom behind her. They sat down, and she pretended to look through a couple of files.

To her left, back toward the Chief's office, a commotion drew her attention. The City Manager, Nathan Baldwin, laughed as he approached Chief Sherman's office, but Aaron certainly didn't seem happy to see him.

Thom stood and pocketed his wallet. "Let's go," he said. "Richard and Ethan are already in position. They have the recording device set up. We need to get in there before the ladies start showing up so we can tell Eloise where to sit."

He started for the exit, and Laurel did her best to copy the smooth, easy way her partner walked. She met the Chief's eyes, and he looked worried. He couldn't walk out on the man he reported directly to and who appointed him to his position. But his wife was wearing a mic at a meeting where she hoped to get information from Marilyn on a drug case.

Laurel's stomach felt like she'd swallowed bees. She couldn't believe she'd put her friend—one of her *best* friends—in this position.

Thom talked on the way to City Hall, but Laurel didn't respond once. "You're not one for undercover work, are you?" he asked as he pulled into the parking lot.

"No," Laurel said. It felt she'd suddenly been transported right back to her abusive past. She glanced around, knowing danger could walk through the door at any moment. "I'm not good at this."

Perhaps she wasn't cut out for narcotics. Or simply being a detective. She'd taken control of her life while on patrol, and maybe she should go back to that. This type of work, where she tracked down leads and talked to people who didn't want to talk to her, made her queasy

"You're a good detective, Laurel," Thom said. "Take a minute and get yourself together."

"What if I'm not cut out for this?"

"Then you'll know after this, and the Chief will put you somewhere else." Thom gave her a sad yet friendly smile. "I'd hate to lose you, but I do need you to be on your game here."

She nodded, tiny, short bursts of movement. "Yes," she said. "I'm putting on my game face right now."

Thom got out of the cruiser, and Laurel basked in the silence as it entered the car. The sun beat down on it too, and without the air conditioning, Laurel would bake before long. "You can do this," she told herself. "Get it together."

She didn't really want to go back on the beat, but she wasn't sure undercover work was for her either. She felt like she was trying to stuff herself—a round peg—into a square hole.

She got out of the car as Thom turned back to check on her, and she caught the concern in his eyes. He probably had children close to her age, and she appreciated the fatherly vibe he put off.

She also appreciated that he didn't ask her if she was

okay. He just nodded at her, and they walked into City
Hall shoulder-to-shoulder. She let him do the talking, and
they put their weapons on the security belt to walk
through the metal detector.

"Mornin', Buff," Thom said, nodding to the guard
standing there.

"Thom." The security guard smiled so fast, if Laurel
had blinked, she'd have missed it. He trained his eyes on
the monitors as Thom walked through, and then as Laurel
followed him. "You're good," he said, putting the bowls
with their keys on the counter.

Laurel wrapped the gun belt around her waist again,
latching everything tightly before she reached for her keys
and change. Thom tucked his wallet in his pocket, and
they continued toward their goal—the narrow room
behind the conference room, where most people stored
bottled water and the lunches they served to the people in
the bigger, more spacious conference area.

Thom knocked three times on the door and leaned
closer to where it met the jamb. "It's Thom," he said.

A moment later, the door opened, and Rich Foundling
stood there. He wore the same uniform Laurel used to don
every morning, and she smiled at how clean and crisp his
was. He looked from Thom to her to the area behind
them.

"Come on in."

They did, and the four of them smashed in the room

was almost too much. As Laurel was the only woman, the testosterone was definitely through the roof.

"This door won't open from the other side?" Laurel asked. "That's the last thing we need; someone coming in here during the meeting."

"It won't," Rich confirmed.

Laurel took a chair near the window, as they still had two more people coming. Technically, three, but she didn't think the Chief would make it before the meeting started. Nathan Baldwin stopped by the station from time to time, but the Chief usually knew about it in advance. Laurel remembered a time when he'd kept eight of his junior officers late one night just to make sure every wisp of dust had been wiped from the floors and windowsills. She'd been one of those eight, and a small smile touched her mouth.

She'd been so excited to have a job at the police station. She'd have stayed until all hours of the night to spray cleaner on glass and wipe it clean. Anything that proved she wasn't chained to anyone or anything, that she got to decide how she spent her time, that she could get a job and keep it.

She'd been spending a lot of time inside her old memories this summer, and she realized her new job had stirred up all kinds of things she'd stopped thinking about.

"Twenty minutes," someone said, and Laurel kept one ear on the conversation as she pulled out her phone and texted her therapist. She went back and forth with the receptionist and a few minutes later, she had an appointment for the next afternoon.

She sent a text to Thom to let him know, and then one to the Chief, as he'd always wanted to know when one of his cops was seeing a counselor. The department would pay for her to see one of their approved therapists, but Laurel had been seeing Dr. Adams for years, and she wasn't willing to change now.

In the beginning, her parents had paid for the sessions, as Dr. Adams only took cash, and it was fifty dollars for forty-five minutes. Laurel could pay it herself now, and that fact made her spirits lift.

Something came through the speakers, and Laurel perked up. "We've got live action," Rich said, fiddling with the volume button. "Are we gonna have Carolle stop in and see what's going on with the meeting?'

"Yes," Thom said, bent over the table. "They're prepped. They should be here in a minute."

A woman's voice came through the speaker, but it wasn't loud enough for Laurel to hear. Her heartbeat pounding in her ears probably had something to do with that, and she wished she could press a button and calm herself down.

"Just put that over there," a woman said in a saccharine-laced voice, and Laurel knew it. Marilyn Benson. "Yes, right there, Bitsy. Thanks." She sounded nice, and Laurel wondered how many ladies would attend today.

Marilyn's arrest hadn't seemed to deter her or anyone she knew from simply continuing on with their lives.

Voices kept filling the room, and Laurel had a hard time keeping them separate. Rich turned down the volume on the speakers one at a time, and then twisted toward Laurel. "Have her sit by the windows if she can."

"North or south?" Laurel asked as a text from El came in. "She's here."

By the windows, she sent quickly. *Waiting to see if you should be near the front of the room or the back.*

Her gut told her to put El close to the front of the room, because that would put Laurel only a few feet from her, on the other side of the door she looked up and stared at. *North end*, she typed out while Rich hummed and hawed about it.

"North," he finally said, but El had already confirmed.

"Oh, yes," came through the speakers, so loud it made everyone moan, groan, or cry out. "I'm Eloise Hall—Sherman." She gave a giggle, and thankfully, someone had turned down the speakers by then. "I just got married a couple of months ago. That last name still trips me up."

"You're the Chief's wife," someone said.

"Yes," El said, and she sounded so diplomatic that Laurel smiled to herself.

"I'm Sadie Flock. I own a dog salon near the restaurant district."

"I own The Cliffside Inn," El said, and several other women joined the conversation, asking her questions about business and how her booking software worked. They'd obviously been observing her website, and though Laurel had nothing at all to do with Cliffside, a swell of pride filled her chest for Eloise.

"Ladies," a woman said, and she sounded close. "It's time to begin."

"You guys okay in here?" a man asked, and Rich gave two thumbs up, though the two cops "checking in" on the women's business meeting couldn't see him.

We're a go, Laurel sent to Eloise just as a text from the Chief arrived.

I'm on my way, but I couldn't get Nathan out of my office.

She's good, Laurel said. *Set up in the right spot. We can hear her loud and clear.* Then Laurel settled in for a long meeting about stuff she didn't care about, and sure enough that was what transpired.

Two more cops piled into the room, and when the Chief arrived, it was standing room only. Marilyn led the meeting with a semi-iron fist that Laurel actually admired.

The moment the meeting ended, she sat up a little straighter, thinking, *Take the bait. Please, Marilyn, take the bait.*

"Eloise, right?" Marilyn asked, and Laurel's hopes flew toward the stratosphere. If they could get the sting set up, sitting in this claustrophobic room for an hour would've been worth it. She stared out the window, every muscle tight, as the blue sky, green grass, and white clouds outside created the picturesque setting for a small beach town.

"Yes," El said. "It's good to see you again, Marilyn."

"Again?"

Laurel could just see Marilyn cocking her platinum blonde head, her dark brown eyes telling the world her hair color came from a bottle. A lot of bottles.

"Yes," El said again, her voice a touch more guarded now. "You came by The Cliffside Inn a few months ago. Something about signing up for a...delivery service?"

"Oh, right," Marilyn said, and Laurel worked hard not to scoff. She couldn't jump to conclusions so easily. "What did you think of the meeting?"

"It was good," El said. "A little over my head, to be honest. But it was my first one, and one of the ladies I was talking to before it started said I'd catch on quickly."

"You will," Marilyn said, and she was being so nice. Maybe Laurel had read her all wrong. "We meet every second Thursday."

"Yes," El said. "I've got the schedule right here. I got it on the way in. Is it always here at City Hall?"

"Yep." A brief pause, and Laurel cocked her head, trying to envision what was happening on the other side of the door. Eloise was performing like a champion, that was what.

"Are you interested in learning more about the consumables delivery?" Marilyn asked. "I can't remember if you were going to call me and set up another meeting."

"Consumables," Eloise said, a snap following her words. "Yes, you would not believe how many bars of soap I'm going through. I think people take them for souvenirs."

Marilyn laughed, and Rich hurried to turn down the speaker again. She must be standing *so* close to Eloise, and Laurel itched to get out there and make sure she was okay. She met the Chief's eye, and he wore a thundercloud right there on his face. He was about to blow, and Laurel held up her phone and raised her eyebrows.

He nodded, and she tapped to get a call to go through to Eloise.

"Yes, that should work," Eloise said, and Laurel had missed the other part of the conversation. "Excuse me, this is my friend who's getting married, and I'm helping with the wedding." The ringing line came through the speaker, and then Eloise's voice entered the room and Laurel's ear at the same time.

"I'm leaving now," she whispered. "I seriously feel like I'm going to throw up."

"Aaron's on his way out," Laurel said loud enough for him to hear, and he practically shoved his cops out of the way to get from one end of the room to the other—and then to his wife.

Laurel hung up and collapsed back in her chair. "When are they meeting?"

"Monday at one," Thom said, his eyes glittering. "We got our sting, Laurel. Excellent work."

TWENTY-FIVE

"I love the cove," Lisa said, and AJ glanced over at her. She could definitely walk faster than AJ, but she seemed content to go whatever pace AJ wanted. "Dad didn't bring us here much. Usually once in the summer. Sometimes for one of the winter holidays." She turned her face into the sun and smiled.

AJ really liked Lisa Hymas, her new step-daughter. Out of the three of Matt's children, she'd been the easiest to connect with. She'd accepted AJ from the first moment they'd met, and she acted as excited about the baby as Matt and AJ did.

Justin was far nicer than he'd been the first time AJ met him, and Derrick lay somewhere in between Justin and Lisa—he was the middle child as well. AJ herself was a middle child, and she knew the subtle art of hanging out in the middle without too many spotlights on her.

"I couldn't wait to leave the cove," AJ said. "I left right after high school and didn't come back until last year."

"Really?" Lisa lowered her eyes to AJ's, and though they wore sunglasses, Lisa's weren't the reflective type. AJ could see her eyes through the shaded lenses, and she nodded.

"I hated it here. My...my mother left me and my siblings when I was only ten," she said. "My dad turned into a drunk, and things...I didn't like it here. I left as fast as I could, on a scholarship to Miami, and I never looked back."

"Is that why Dad says he's glad he didn't let you get away again?" Lisa smiled and reached for AJ's hand.

"Yes," AJ said. "He tried calling me and stuff after I left, but I never responded." She let a sad smile cross her face. "I feel bad about that, but life was...life. You know? I could only operate on what I knew at the time, and I absolutely didn't want to end up back here."

"And here you are."

"Time changes things," AJ said. "Time and experience changes people."

"Mm."

AJ took in a deep breath of the morning air and they made the right turn that would take them down the road that ran past Kristen's new condo. "What about you? What do you think of Derrick's new girlfriend?"

Lisa let out an exasperated sigh. "I think she's a bit

fake. I think she thinks Derrick is rich, and she wants a free ride."

"You think so?" AJ asked, though she had felt the false vibes from the woman. "Interesting."

"He won't see it, because he's a sucker for a blonde, but." Lisa shrugged. "Dad told us for years not to get pulled in by a pretty face. Handsome, in my case."

"So you're not seeing anyone?"

"Not at the moment," Lisa said. "But there's a man who'll be in my program next year that I've got my eye on." She grinned as widely as the ocean before them, and AJ laughed with her.

"I'm sure you do," AJ said, feeling like everything in her life had finally come together. "What's his name?"

"You're going to laugh," Lisa said, but her smile didn't hitch at all.

"Try me."

"Bart," she said, and Lisa herself burst out laughing. "It's such a cartoony name to me." She kept giggling, and AJ joined in. She thought happiness was made of two women walking in the morning, the bright blue sky above them, and a warm beach breeze in front of them.

"There's Kristen," AJ said, pointing ahead as the older woman stepped past the fence that marked her retirement community's property. When she reached her, AJ slowed and gave her a hug. "I wonder how things will go with El's meeting."

"She said she'd call, and that I could put you on speaker," Kristen said, holding up her phone. "It's not for hours, but I'm on the edge of my seat every time my phone so much as dings." She grinned, and AJ returned the gesture.

"Hello, Lisa, dear." Kristen hugged her too. "Are you ready for this bread-baking lesson?"

"I can't wait," Lisa said, and she sounded so genuine. "My mother wasn't great in the kitchen. I spend most of my expendable cash on take-out."

"Now you have a step-mother who can't cook either," AJ said. "Great."

"Hey, you put pizza and frozen lasagnas in the oven," Lisa said. "Mom doesn't even do that."

"What did you eat growing up?" Kristen asked.

"Cold cereal," Lisa said. "Peanut butter sandwiches." She gestured to AJ. "Frozen pizza. Mac and cheese. Ramen. Hot dogs. Grilled cheese sandwiches. Take-out." She shrugged again. "You know, we got by."

"Cooking is as easy as reading a recipe," Kristen said. "You'll see."

"I hope so," Lisa said. "I recall Jean saying the same thing about sewing. *It's as easy as reading a pattern.* And I couldn't do that." She laughed again, and AJ loved that she'd tried to integrate herself into AJ's life while she was here this summer.

"Jean has a sixth sense behind a sewing machine," Kristen said. "She's the same way on a boat. That's how she and Rueben met, you know. Yacht club in college."

"Really." AJ asked. "That's so cute."

"Yes." Kristen cleared her throat, and AJ just waited for her to continue. The older woman had claimed a place in AJ's heart years ago, and only cemented herself there in the past few months, coming to stay with AJ in the early days of her bedrest.

"I'm going to petition the City Council to re-instate the Seafaring Girls," she said. "I think Jean would be a phenomenal leader for the organization, and I can help her restart it. Of all the things I kept when I purged everything last year, I kept my files for the Seafaring Girls."

"Wow," AJ said, trying to wrap her mind around the idea. "I think that's a great idea, Kristen."

"Do you?" she asked. "I've been nervous to tell everyone."

"Why?" AJ kept her eyes on the road in front of her, because she only had one month left in her pregnancy, and her balance was a precious, precarious thing.

"I don't know," Kristen said. "I'm afraid Robin will think I'm going to try to do it myself. Or that Alice will be like, *you'll never be able to recreate what we have, Kristen.* Something."

"Oh, don't listen to Robin or Alice," AJ said with a wave of her hand. "I learned that when I was fifteen years old, and I've been so much happier."

"AJ," Kristen said in a chastising tone. Then she burst out laughing.

AJ joined her, and she decided that happiness was definitely *three* women walking in the morning, the blue sky above them, the ocean breeze accompanying them, and the conversation between them meaningful but light-hearted.

"I do love the cove," AJ said, hooking her arm through Lisa's. "Thank you for walking with me. Both of you. It does my soul so much good to get out of the house."

"Of course," Lisa said.

"I love it too," Kristen said. "It does my heart good to see you well, AJ."

"Being outside does free my thoughts," AJ said. She glanced at Lisa. "I struggle with depression and anxiety. I'm usually on medication, but I can't take it while I'm pregnant."

"And probably not while you nurse, right?" Lisa asked.

"Right." AJ had forgotten about that, and some of the fog that usually stayed out of her head on her morning walk tried to crowd in. She didn't let it, though, and she smiled at Lisa. "You'll come see the baby even after you go back to Baltimore, right? I want you to come as often as you can."

"I'll do my best," Lisa said. "I'm going to be in my first year of medical school."

"I know," AJ said. "No pressure. I promise. I'll bring him to you if you want."

"Are you going to keep writing?" Kristen asked.

"Probably," AJ said. "Matt says I don't need to, espe-cially once they get that second golf course open. And the mini-golf course will be pure profit, they say, but that's not until next year." She smiled into the sun as they turned and started walking east. "But I don't know. I do like putting together an exclusive story. I love interviewing athletes. There's a rush there I'll miss."

The truth was, AJ's life wasn't done shifting, and she didn't know exactly what the future would hold. As long as she had her friends, she thought she'd probably be okay.

Her phone rang, and she dang near jumped out of her skin. "It can't be El," Kristen said, pulling her phone out of her pocket. "It's not even me."

"It's me," AJ said, slipping her phone out from underneath her bra strap. "It's Kelli." She swiped on the call, her smile as real as ever. "Hey, Kel." She hadn't checked the time, but it couldn't be past nine yet, and Kelli taught yoga and aerobics from nine to noon.

"AJ," Kelli said. "I have some news, and I wanted you to be the first to know."

AJ's heartbeat sang in her chest. "Okay," she said. "I think I know what you're going to say, but go on." She didn't want to take the magic away from Kelli, who was the nicest woman in the world and deserved all the best things from life.

"Shad asked me to marry him, and I said yes!"

AJ lifted her free hand straight up into the air. "Yes," she cried. "I knew it! I'm so happy for you, Kelli."

"Is she engaged?" Kristen asked.

AJ nodded enthusiastically. "She's engaged," she practically yelled. "I'm walking with Lisa and Kristen. When are you going to put it on the group text?"

"I was thinking of waiting until Wednesday," Kelli said between giggles. "But that's mean, right?"

"You do what you want," AJ said, grinning like a fool. "I'll keep your secret if you want. I know Kristen and Lisa will too."

"Okay," Kelli said. "Well, we'll see. I guess if you see it on the group text, the cat is out of the bag."

"I want the full story," AJ said, a hitch in her side making her pull harder at her next breath.

"I have a class coming in," Kelli said. "But he asked me this morning, and I wanted you to be the first to know. I still need to call my mom."

"Okay," AJ said, though she wished she had more time to hear Kelli's excitement. In times like these, AJ hated the distance between the islands in the cove. She wanted to run to Kelli with her favorite cup of coffee, hold her tight, and congratulate her.

Why can't you? she thought, and she looked at Kristen and Lisa as Kelli said good-bye and the call ended.

"Would you guys be okay doing the bread-baking alone this afternoon? I want to go to Bell and surprise Kelli."

"Of course," Lisa said, in tandem with Kristen.

"Great." A pain ran down AJ's spine, and she groaned. "I need to slow down. I think I pulled a muscle in my back with that fist-pump." She shook her head in disgust. "This is what happens when you get old, Lisa. Don't do it."

"You don't know what old is," Kristen said, and she adjusted her pace to match AJ's snail-like walking. The three of them laughed, and even that hurt down in AJ's abdomen, but she couldn't help continuing to do it.

Matt wouldn't be happy about her going to Bell this afternoon, but AJ knew she needed to be there for Kelli if they were going to mend everything that had happened this spring and take the next step into the future together. She wanted that more than anything, so she'd get on the ferry and go visit her best friend.

"RIGHT HERE IS FINE," AJ SAID, AND THE RIDESHARE driver pulled over. "Thank you." She touched her card to the payment reader, collected her two Arnold Palmers, and got out of the car. It wasn't nearly as easy as it had once been, and AJ could say that about everything. Getting out of bed? Not nearly as easy as it used to be.

Getting on and off the couch? She actually groaned when she did those things now. Eating? She had two bites before she felt stuffed to the gills. Even this iced tea-lemonade combination would fill her to the brim with only a few swallows.

She'd taken one step through the gate at Whole Soul

when Kelli came out of the front door. "AJ," she said, her smile made of pure sunshine. "What are you doing here?"

"I come bearing refreshment for your after-aerobics workout." She lifted the Arnold Palmers, her purse sliding down from her shoulder. She couldn't shrug it back up without dropping one of the drinks, and Kelli hurried toward her to take one of them.

AJ got her purse back where it belonged and hugged her best friend. "I couldn't stand not hearing your engagement story, and I thought I could ride the ferry back to Pearl with you. Or we could go to lunch here. Or whatever."

She stepped back and looked at Kelli. "You have plans with Shad, don't you?"

Kelli grinned and shook her head. "Nope." She took a long sip of her drink and sighed. "Thank you for this. I've been drinking this wheatgrass stuff, hoping it'll get better, and let me tell you, it never does." She laughed, and AJ loved the sound of joy coming from her.

"I have an idea," AJ said. "But I can't walk very far, so we'll have to get a ride."

"Hurley Beach?" Kelli's blue eyes lit up, and she lifted her phone. "I'm already calling for a ride."

AJ tipped her head back and let her hair fall over her shoulders. "The sun is warmer on Bell," she said. "Diamond is so windy."

"Hurley will be windy too," Kelli said. "We'll see if we can get a spot by the only trees in the sand."

"In July?" AJ shook her head. "Not gonna happen, Kel."

"Hey, my boyfriend proposed to me this morning," she said. "Anything is possible." Her phone revved at her, and she added, "See? RideShare only two minutes away instead of the usual ten."

The same car AJ had just gotten out of pulled up a moment later, and she waved to the guy driving as if they were old friends. "He just dropped me off."

Xavier—if she remembered right—jumped from the car and opened her door. "This wasn't the right place? Just picking up?"

"I was meeting a friend," she said. "We decided not to stay here."

"I can tack this onto the other one," he said. "Save you the flat fee."

"That would be amazing," AJ said. "I feel bad I didn't buy you an Arnold Palmer."

"Oh, I can't have the caffeine," he said. "It makes my... it's better if I avoid it." He flashed her a smile, a pink tint coming into his face. He was probably a decade younger than AJ, and she found him cute and personable. "Where to now?"

"Hurley Beach, please," AJ said, dropping into the back seat. She used to slide into a seat, but not anymore. The moment Kelli joined her, AJ turned toward her. "All right. Start talking."

Kelli took a drink first and glanced toward the driver.

"Shad came with me to the studio this morning before he went to the office. The moment he insisted we get a Ride-Share instead of walking from the ferry station, I knew something was up."

"Do you normally walk?"

"Yes, but he said he had to get to work, and we should get a car, and I was like...okay." She sighed and leaned her head back, letting her eyes drift closed. "So we got in the car, and as we came up the hill, I could see the roses, the bows, and the balloons."

"Aw," AJ said. "You love balloons."

"I do," Kelli said, giggling. "It's kind of silly how much I love balloons. Anyway, he had them tied on every fence post. Flowers hanging from the eaves of the house. Bows tied around the columns and laced through the fence."

"Wow. When did he do all of that?"

"He said he got on the first ferry this morning to do it, then went back to Pearl to get me." Kelli glowed with happiness, and AJ could not be happier for her. "Anyway, he had the ring on the top step—he legit left a diamond ring sitting on the front porch of the house for two hours!—and he got down on one knee and said he loved me."

"This is so romantic," AJ said. "Kelli, he's an amazing man. You're going to be so happy with him."

"I hope so," Kelli said. "I do love him, and he loves me, and he loves Parker."

"Hurley Beach," the driver said, and AJ tapped her card again, thanked him again, and got out of the car again.

She drew in a long breath and faced the sand. Kelli had been right; the wind blew here too. At almost one o'clock, plenty of people had decided to come to the beach, and AJ waited for Kelli to join her so they could pick a spot.

"There's a patch by the trees," she said. "We don't have chairs or anything." She scanned AJ, who wore a rainbow-colored maxi dress, her baby belly very obvious. "If you get down on the ground, can you get back up?"

"I have no idea," AJ said with a grin. "Feels like an adventure, doesn't it?"

Kelli shook her head and led the way toward the patch of shade near the trees. "Can we sit here?" she asked a younger couple who'd put down a couple of towels.

"Yeah, sure," the woman said. "Oh, goodness, you're due any second. Marsh, go get her a chair."

"I'm fine," AJ said, but she eyed the sand at her feet, feeling like it was a mile if it was a meter, and she had no idea how to even sit down without something or someone to hold onto.

"I'll get you ladies a couple of chairs," the man said, and he dashed off to the rental hut on the beach.

"We could've done that," Kelli said. "We're fine, really. We're only going to be here for a little while.'

"We have friends coming," the woman said. "So we'll keep them all day. It's not a problem."

"If you have friends coming, we'll be in the way," AJ said.

"They won't be here for a while. You're fine."

Marsh returned quick as a whip, and he set up the chairs for them, steadied AJ as she sank into hers, and smiled at them. "Thank you," AJ said, that familiar groan coming from her mouth. Something sharp sliced through her abdomen, and she sucked in a breath. "Ooh, I aggravated something." She pressed her palm against her left side, and the pain ebbed into nothing.

She and Kelli sat in silence for a few minutes, and then Kelli said, "I do love him, AJ. I didn't think I even knew how to love, but I guess I do?"

AJ reached over and took Kelli's hand in hers. "Of course you do. You've loved me my whole life, even when I was completely unlovable."

Kelli smiled into the sky. "I just feel...I feel like Julian broke me. He told me how to do everything, and I let him. We tried to have Parker for so long, and it bonded us. But then...then, it was like he didn't really want me anymore. I didn't really want him."

"I understand," AJ said, though she didn't. Not really. The part about not being wanted, she got. She'd had plenty of boyfriends who only wanted one thing from her, and it wasn't to meet her at the altar and become her husband.

"But with Shad, I can *feel* that he wants me."

"It's nice to feel wanted," AJ murmured.

"I slept with him," Kelli whispered. "I haven't told anyone, and I'm not going to either. You're the only one, AJ."

"It's none of their business."

"They'll assume anyway." Kelli closed her eyes and sighed. "I guess I better put it on the group text."

"If you want," AJ said, another pain roaring to life, this time in her back. She shifted in her seat and held her breath until it started to fade. It only lasted a few seconds, and she wondered what she'd done to irritate the nerves in her back. Probably all that getting in and out of a low-riding sedan.

"I'll wait to see how things go with El today," Kelli said. "She'll have big news any minute now, I'd think."

AJ sipped her drink while Kelli checked her phone. "What time is it?"

"One-forty."

"Yeah, she should be done soon."

The breeze blew, and AJ listened to the man and woman behind them chatting, and she thoroughly enjoyed just sitting on the beach. Nothing soothed her as much as the sound of water trying to play with the shore, as children calling in the surf, as the steady white noise of the wind.

She must've dozed, because the next thing she knew, another pain had startled her, and then Kelli said, "Here she is. Oh, it's a long text."

AJ opened her eyes, trying to take in her surroundings quickly.

"Ready?" Kelli asked, and AJ nodded, though her head felt detached from her body.

"The meeting went well," Kelli read. "Marilyn Benson actually seems very nice. There are tiers to the delivery, and while I didn't know that, Laurel and I had talked about the possibilities of them trying to move in the drugs with such a new client. So I went for the gold tier, as it's called. I'll get three shipments per month, and while I don't need that and would never pay this much for it, if it'll help Laurel find out who's bringing the drugs into the cove, I'll do it."

Kelli took a breath, and AJ sucked at the air as her entire abdomen tightened. All at once, she realized what was happening.

No, she thought. *The baby's not due for another month.*

Kelli kept reading with, "My first delivery is on August eleventh. I guess we'll find out then if they're sending drugs with the soaps and shampoos." She looked up from the phone, and she must've seen something on AJ's face. "What? It's all good, AJ."

"I think I'm in labor," she blurted out, her panic starting to rise through her. She pressed both palms against the armrests on the flimsy beach chair and pushed. She couldn't quite get to her feet, so she fell back and then used her legs to get some momentum to get up.

"Labor?" Kelli jumped to her feet easily and put a steadying hand on AJ's arm. "Really? Are you having contractions?"

"My word, she's having contractions," the woman behind them said.

"I don't know," AJ said, her voice made mostly of air. "I've never had a baby before." Discomfort moved around her like someone had put a rubber band around the roundest part of her and tightened it. "Something's definitely happening."

"Does your back hurt?"

"Yes," she said, the pain intensifying now that Kelli had named it. "It hurt this morning too, on my walk."

"Let's go," Kelli said. "Even if you're not in labor, it's still probably an hour to the hospital. You don't want to be on Bell right now."

Tears filled AJ's eyes. "He's a month early, Kel. I'm not ready."

"Yes, you are," Kelli said firmly as she marched steadily away from the trees. "Thank you for the chairs," she called over her shoulder. "Keep moving, AJ."

AJ did what she said, every footprint in the sand sending her further and further into a tailspin. "We don't even have a name picked out."

"That's because you don't know if it's a boy or a girl," Kelli said.

"I can't do this."

"Hey." Kelli stepped in front of her, her eyes set on laser mode. "Yes, you *can* do this. You came back to the cove when you didn't want to. I left Julian in New Jersey. You broke up with Nathan. We have rebuilt our entire lives in the past year, and this baby is the pinnacle of that.

You've waited for him your entire life, and you can do this."

Nobody would argue with Kelli when she spoke in that voice, least of all AJ. She nodded at her as another wave of pain coursed through her. "It hurts," she said. "It feels like this tightening pressure. Pain through my abdomen and into my back."

"Yes, honey," Kelli said, and she got them moving again. "That's called a contraction."

TWENTY-SIX

K risten arrived at the hospital, having dropped her needlepoint the moment she'd seen Kelli's text. "AJ Proctor?" she said to the woman at the information desk. "Wait. AJ Hymas."

The woman looked up from her novel. "Do you know why she's here?"

Kristen noticed there was no computer at the desk. "She's having a baby."

"Maternity is on the third floor," the woman said, standing slightly. "Go down this hall to the elevator. Then up to floor three. You can't miss is when you get off."

"Thanks." Kristen's mind raced so fast, she was sure she could miss maternity. She told herself to calm down as she walked toward the elevator. She wasn't going to be able to do anything; she wasn't a midwife.

The baby was coming so early, though, and Kristen

sent up another prayer that everything would be all right. She told herself once again that infants could survive at thirty-six weeks, and that all an early baby meant was that AJ would be more comfortable sooner.

She stepped off the elevator on the third floor, and sure enough, she couldn't miss maternity. The hallway only went left, and a huge sign announcing the department stared her in the face. Sh didn't see Robin or Alice there, which surprised her, but she went straight to the nurses' station. "Do you know where I can find AJ Hymas?"

The woman frowned. "We don't have an AJ Hymas."

"AvaJane Proctor?" Kristen had to be in the right place. There was only one hospital in Five Island Cove. Sanctuary had a medical clinic, but Kelli and AJ wouldn't have gone there.

"She's still in delivery," another nurse said, looking over from a stack of folders in front of her. "They haven't brought her up yet. I'm not even sure the baby has been born."

"Oh." Foolishness filled Kristen. She probably hadn't needed to race out the moment Kelli had said AJ was in labor. She'd had two children herself, and Clara especially had been stubborn about arriving. That girl had been trouble from the start, but Kristen smiled to herself and said, "I'll go wait over here."

The nurses paid her no mind as she retreated to a sofa in a waiting area halfway between the elevator and the maternity wing. No wonder no one else had arrived yet. Kristen sat down, and she opened her notes app on her phone. She went over her presentation for the Assistant City Manager, a woman named Athena Cruz.

Kristen had known Athena for years, as she knew most people who'd been in the cove for a while. They tended to gather for events like the Heritage Fair on Diamond Island, or the hot air balloon festival that took place each year on Bell. Sanctuary had dances in the evenings every weekend in the spring, and Kristen used to attend anything and everything in the community.

Athena would then take the idea to the City Council, and they met on the third Thursday of the month. She still had another week and a half, but she was sitting down with Athena for lunch tomorrow. On Wednesday, Kristen would tell the girls what she'd done and why.

Rueben and Jean had put in their adoption papers, but there had been no movement on them. Their case worker, who operated out of Boston, in mainland Massachusetts, said it could take longer to place a baby out in the cove.

They were trying to be patient, but Kristen knew Jean needed something more than her two dogs, a couple of cats, and her few sewing lessons to pass the time. The Seafaring Girls would give her purpose, and it would allow her to work with kids. Kristen had enjoyed her time with the girls so much, and the skills of water safety, sailing, and watercraft general care and maintenance were just as important today as they'd been thirty years ago.

"Kristen."

She looked up at the sound of Robin's voice, and found her standing there with Jamie. She wobbled as she got to her feet to hug Robin. "Where's Mandie?"

"Work," Robin said, almost breathlessly. "Have you heard anything?"

"I rushed right over like a fool," Kristen admitted as she pulled away and smiled. "She was still down in delivery."

Robin glanced toward the station. "I'll go check."

Kristen checked her phone, wondering where Kelli was waiting. There were only texts with idle chatter about if the baby would be a boy or a girl from the others. Nothing from Kelli, Lisa, or AJ.

We're waiting on the third floor, outside maternity, Kristen typed out. *Should we be somewhere else?* She sent the message and met Jamie's eyes. "How's summer going, dear?"

"Too fast," Jamie said with a smile. "It always does."

"That's true." Kristen could see so much of Robin in Jamie's heart-shaped face and blue eyes. "I suppose that just means your dad will be home sooner."

Her countenance fell. "Yeah."

A glance toward the nurses' station showed Robin in conversation with one of them. Kristen retreated back to the couch. "Come sit down, dear." She patted the cushion beside her, and Jamie took the spot.

"Tell me what he's doing in Alaska."

"He called last night," Jamie said. "I think it's easier if he doesn't. I miss him more when I can hear his voice."

Kristen put her arm around Jamie. "I'm so sorry," she whispered.

Her phone buzzed, but she ignored it. "Is the weather nice? Does he get to see a lot of wildlife?"

"He saw a pod of killer whales yesterday," Jamie said, perking up. "He goes out really early in the morning to fish, while it's still dark. He brings back a whole boatload of fish before breakfast. After that, he goes out again and again. Every time he comes back full, he gets paid more."

"He must work a lot," Kristen said.

"Fourteen hours yesterday," Jamie said. "He sounded really tired, and I know my mom worries about him being alone on his boat." She too glanced further down the hall. "She hasn't been out on the boat with him in a while, but I have. He's real strong, and he knows what he's doing."

"I'm sure he does," Kristen said.

"Plus, he's not alone," Jamie added as Robin turned toward them. "He has a crew of three guys who go out with him. My mom only hears what she wants to sometimes."

Kristen smiled, because that was such a wise statement from such a young person. "We all do, dear." She looked up expectantly as Robin neared.

"They're bringing her up right now," she said, grinning from ear to ear. "They had a boy, but the nurses didn't have a name yet."

Kristen nodded, joy bursting through her. AJ had wanted a boy, and Kristen had been praying she'd get what she wanted. She checked her phone and found Kelli had responded with, *We'll come up. They're going to be moving her soon.*

The elevator chimed, and several people got off, including Kelli, Lisa, Justin, and Derrick. Matt was not with them, but Alice and Laurel brought up the rear.

Matt's three older children chatted enthusiastically, and they paused on the outskirts of the waiting area. Robin, ever the mother hen, went to welcome them and fold them under her wing to bring them in closer.

"What did we miss?" Alice asked. "Can we go see them?"

"They haven't brought her up yet," Robin said.

"How did she do?" Laurel asked, looking at Kelli and Lisa, who still stood side-by-side.

"So great," Kelli said with a smile. "I wasn't there, obviously, but Matt came out for a minute to say it was a boy. They're still trying to decide what to name him."

"I'm telling you, he's going to name him after Grandpa," Justin said, and he actually looked a little gleeful about it.

"Yancey is *terrible*," Lisa said. "No way AvaJane is going to let that happen."

Kristen kept her smile to herself, but she agreed with Lisa.

"AvaJane likes weird names like Ten," Derrick shot back.

"Ten?" Robin asked, horrified. That set Kristen to giggling—as did the very idea of naming a child Ten—and Alice burst out laughing.

"She does like strange names," Kelli said. "I wouldn't be surprised if he's Leonard or something from the forties."

"Or something like Ribeye, and they'll call him Rib for short," Justin said.

"Oh, you're being silly now," Robin said, but Kristen didn't think so. She could easily see AJ giving that baby a strange name, and she hoped Matt would at least try to tame her wild streak.

Kristen looked at her phone as the group continued to throw ridiculous names back and forth. It had been almost ninety minutes since Kelli had texted to say she'd brought AJ to the hospital, believing her to be in labor.

As she scrolled back down to the newest texts, Eloise's message arrived. *I just got off the ferry and the RideShare wait time is forty minutes. I'm going to walk, because it'll be faster.*

"She should call her husband," Laurel said. "The man has a car with a siren and lights on it." She shook her head and tapped before lifting her phone to her ear. "El," she said a moment later, then turned her back and walked away from the group.

Kristen admired Laurel, as the woman had been loyal, kind, and she'd really seemed like she needed Kristen's girls. They seemed to need her too, and she'd been enveloped and welcomed into the group easily.

Another chime of the elevator brought Arthur and Shad, Rueben and Jean, to the third floor. Kristen got to her feet to greet her son and daughter-in-law while Arthur kissed Alice, and Shad slid his hand along Kelli's waist.

They shared a secret glance, and Kristen's whole heart warmed at the sight of them. She almost said something before she remembered that Kelli had not announced her engagement yet.

"Look who's here," someone said, and a rousing cry went up before Kristen could turn to see who had arrived.

When she did, she saw Matt getting mobbed by his children, followed closely by Robin, Alice, and Kelli.

Matt wore pure happiness on his face; the glow only a new father—no matter his age—could possess. He passed the infant Kristen couldn't see to his daughter, laughing as he backed up. "Wow, you guys know how to turn out to support a person."

"What did you name him?" someone asked.

Matt gazed at his new son for another moment, his smile soft and caring. "Asher Proctor Hymas," he said. "Asher means blessing."

"Oh, that's perfect," Robin said.

"Asher's normal," Justin said. He stepped over to his dad and hugged him. Kristen knew things hadn't been smooth sailing for AJ and Matt and his older kids, and she enjoyed watching the two of them embrace.

The baby started to fuss, and Matt reached for him. "AvaJane said a couple of people could come back at a time." He glanced around. "Are my parents here?"

"Not yet," Robin said. "Want me to call them?"

"Would you?" Matt asked, and his eyes locked on Kristen's. "She wants you, Kristen. And Lisa."

His daughter squealed, and had Kristen been a younger woman, she would have too. Inside, she did, but she maintained her composure on the outside. Matt kept his son securely in his arms as they went back to AJ's room.

He gave her the baby and got out of the way. Kristen ran her hand along AJ's forehead, noting how tired and pale AJ looked. "You did it," she whispered, all of her maternal instincts firing. "Look at you, AvaJane. You're a mother."

AJ wept as she looked down at her son. "I did it."

"Yes, you did." Kristen knew how much AJ struggled. She'd seen it every day when the girl was in her teens, and she'd thought about her, worried about her, and prayed for her each and every day since the day she'd left the cove to this very day.

"Did you get to hold him?" she asked, looking up at Kristen with such hope in her eyes.

"Not yet," she said. "His sister did."

"He's so beautiful, AvaJane," Lisa gushed. "He looks just like you."

"No, he has your dad's chin. Look at that thing. It's

like a box." AJ laughed quietly, her son snuggled safely in her arms, no fussiness in sight. She lifted him toward Kristen. "You take him for a minute."

Kristen did, noting how tiny the baby was. "How big is he?"

"Only six pounds," AJ said. "He came early, the devil." Tears continued to flow down her face, and Matt asked her what she needed. Kristen's attention got consumed by the beautiful boy in her arms, and she couldn't look away from him. He grunted and snuggled into her too, and Kristen sighed in pure bliss.

There was nothing quite so wonderful and quite so perfect as a brand-new baby. "Hello, Asher," she whispered to the infant. "You have so many people who love you already."

"My parents are here," Matt said, and Kristen looked up. She gave him the baby, and she accepted Lisa's helping hand to stand from the hard chair.

"We'll go out so they can come in," Kristen said. She paused at beside AJ's bed and leaned down to give her a kiss. "You never cease to amaze me, AJ. I love you. Thank you for including me in this."

Kristen never wanted her girls to feel like they had to invite her to things. She wasn't their age, and she knew AJ particularly thought of her as a mother figure. Sometimes a daughter didn't want to do everything with her mother, and her thoughts once again lingered on Clara.

"I love you too, Kristen," AJ said. "Thank you for always being there for me."

"Your dad and sister are here now too," Matt said, glancing over to the bed. "Who should I bring back first?"

"Maybe my sister," AJ said, her eyes filling with tears again.

Kristen left with Lisa, glad she'd gotten a few minutes with AJ and a couple of minutes holding that precious baby. Out in the waiting area, she said, "She wants you, Wayne, and Amy."

"Can I take the girls?" Amy had both of her daughters with her. "Did she really have a boy?"

"Take them," Kristen said, though she didn't really know the visitor rules in the maternity ward. "And yes, she did." She smiled at AJ's family. "They gave him your last name, Wayne."

The man's chin trembled, and when their eyes met, absolute understanding passed between them. Kristen had gone out to Pearl Island a couple of times to try to talk to the man when AJ was going through her hardest times. Those visits had not gone well, as Wayne had been drunk most of the time, angry when he wasn't, and in complete denial about what his daughters needed.

AJ had reconciled with him over Christmas, and that meant Kristen couldn't hold onto the dislike of the man either.

"Thank you, Kristen," he said. "For everything."

She nodded, and the four of them went toward the

wing. Kristen faced her group of loved ones, old and new. She'd be there for any of them if she could, no matter what.

She caught sight of Jean, who clung to Rueben and seemed to be one breath away from a complete breakdown. Tears streamed down her face, and had the waiting area been quiet, Jean would've filled it with her sobs.

"Jean," she said, rushing to her side. "Oh, my dear, it's okay." She wrapped the petite woman in a tight hug and held her, as if she alone could stop the tide of hurt and pain at not being able to have a child.

She couldn't, but Jean gripped her too, and they held one another up for the time being.

TWENTY-SEVEN

"Shh," Alice said, pushing herself back and forth in the rocking chair as the back door opened, and Charlie walked in with his friends. "I have the baby." She smiled at the teens as they quieted down and got drinks out of the fridge.

AJ looked over at the boys too, and she looked exhausted. Alice had tried to take Asher for her for a couple of hours so she could sleep, but AJ had insisted on coming to Alice's house with her.

Charlie handed a can of soda pop to his friend, Tad, and then approached the living room. "Hi, AJ," he said with a smile. "Mom, can I have twenty dollars to go get those wheels for my skateboard? Remember you said you'd pay for them?"

"Yes, I remember." Alice tucked the snoozing one-week-old into the crook of her arm and stood. "Good morning, Tad," she said to the other boy. "Sam. Where's Ray?"

"He's working," Tad said. "He doesn't get off until one."

"Good for him," Alice said with a smile. She took her purse out of the cabinet where she kept it and rummaged through it with one hand to find a twenty-dollar bill. Asher grunted with the movement, but he didn't open his eyes. Even when he did, they were dark and unfocused, as with most newborns.

"Here." She finally just pushed her purse toward Charlie. "Find it and take it. If they're more than twenty, you'll have to fund it."

"Okay." He found the money in a flash, and Alice cocked one eyebrow at him. "Who's driving?"

"Tad," Charlie said. "Don't worry, Mom. He's a good driver."

"I am," Tad said.

"I'm a lawyer," Alice said. "Keep that in mind if you feel like doing something illegal. Even lawyers can't lie for their clients." She grinned at him, glad when Tad chuckled a little bit. Charlie just rolled his eyes, and the boys took their sodas and left. The house quieted again, and Alice opened the fridge. "Do you want something to drink, AJ?"

"No," she said with a sigh. "I should go. Matt's going to be home for lunch, and he loves to hold Asher too."

"Okay," Alice said, but she didn't want to pass over the

tiny boy. AJ had only been home for two days, as Asher had had some jaundice in the hospital that had kept him for an extra couple of days. AJ and Matt still put him under a light for a little while each day, but Alice could hardly tell the baby needed it.

She passed Asher to his mother, catching the look of love in AJ's eyes. She seemed softer all around, but if anything, becoming a mother made her understand her own mother's abandonment of her and her siblings even less.

"Thanks for taking him, Alice." AJ gave her a quick hug.

"You'll have to let me take him while you stay home," Alice said. "I will."

"I know you will." AJ gave her a tired smile. "I just... I'm so attached to him still. Matt says it'll wear off." She laughed a little and tucked Asher into his car seat. "There you go, my love. Let's go see Daddy, okay?"

She hefted the car seat with a groan and gave Alice another smile.

Alice walked her to the door and stayed there instead of accompanying her all the way to the car. AJ didn't want to be babied, Alice knew that. So she waved from the doorway and then closed the door behind her.

Ginny had gone to work at the ice cream shop, and Charlie would be gone for the afternoon with his friends. Alice faced her office, but she didn't want to work today.

Not when the sun was so bright, and Arthur didn't have to be in his office...

She called him and said, "Me and you. Rocky Ridge. Black sand beach. What do you say?"

"I say I'm grabbing my trunks and my keys right now." He laughed, and Alice smiled as she leaned against the doorjamb that led into her office. In that moment, with all the silence in her house and Arthur's sexy laughter on the other end of the line—and the fact that when she had free time, she wanted to spend it with him—told Alice that she'd fallen in love with Arthur Rice.

"Have you eaten?" he asked.

"No," Alice said quietly.

Arthur stayed quiet too, and then he asked, "What's going on?"

Alice smiled to herself, simply basking in the feeling. "Nothing. I'll tell you when you get here."

"I'll be there in five," he said, and the call ended. Alice felt like she was moving through quicksand as she walked down the hall and into her bedroom. She changed into her swimming suit and stepped into her coverup, which really just looked like a white maxi dress.

She'd just slipped on her sandals when her doorbell rang. She grabbed her hat as Arthur called, "It's just me, Alice."

"I'm in the bedroom," she called back, and she reached up to get her beach bag out of the closet. She heard Arthur, and she knew he'd have questions.

Her chest stormed, and tears pricked her eyes. Alice couldn't remember the last time she'd cried, and she told herself it was okay to be emotional about being in love. She just couldn't believe it.

"Hey," he said gently. "I'm coming in."

"Come in," she said, her voice breaking.

Arthur arrived at her side in a flash, which wasn't hard to do in her house, as small as it was. "What is it?" he whispered. "One of the kids? AJ?"

Alice turned and wrapped her arms around him, hoping she moved fast enough that he wouldn't see her glassy eyes. "I just...I feel ridiculous."

"Why?" he whispered.

She clung to him and he to her, and Alice could feel *every*thing in that moment. She only needed a few seconds to tell him, and she did want to tell him. She drew in a deep breath and stepped back. "AJ left, and the twins are busy today, and I didn't want to work." She reached up and brushed her hair back out of her face, then let her hand drift down the side of his face.

She looked into his dark eyes. "My only thought is when I can see you again, and I called, and you seem to want to spend all your free time with me too."

"I do," he whispering as he leaned into her touch.

"Listening to you laugh, I realized I'm in love with you." Alice smiled, the gesture wobbling a little bit as her eyes burned. "I love you, Arthur, and it's just got me a little emotional."

Arthur took her face in his hands and leaned toward her. "I love you too." He kissed her, and Alice liked that he led the action but let her participate in it. He didn't try to rush, but he took his time, really showing her how much he cared about her.

When he finally broke the kiss, Alice nearly stood in the closet. "What do you want to do now?" he asked.

"Go to the beach," she said. "I love the black sand beach, and I don't think you've ever been."

"I haven't." Arthur smiled at her and ran his hands through her hair. "I was talking about life in general. Do you want to get married? We could move in together. Or just keep doing what we're doing."

Alice smoothed down the collar on his polo. "You don't want to just keep doing what we're doing."

"No," he said. "That wouldn't be my first choice." He backed up, taking Alice with him. "What's your first choice?"

Alice knew what she wanted, and she'd already said the hardest words. "I'd like to get married."

A grin burst onto Arthur's face. "Let's do it then." He wrapped his arms around her and lifted her off her feet. "Best email I've ever sent."

Alice laughed and kissed him again as he held her up. "Maybe we should skip the beach and stay here for a minute."

He set her on her feet. "I'll do whatever you want,

sweetheart." He nuzzled her neck. "You're dressed for the beach already."

"Mm." Alice ran her hands through his thick hair. "I want you to meet my dad and Della."

"Let's go to Rocky Ridge," Arthur said. He bent to pick up her floppy hat. "I'd love to meet your dad and step-mother."

"We can talk about a real wedding on the way," she said.

"I bought a ring," Arthur admitted, casting her a look out of the corner of his eye.

"You did?" Alice paused in stuffing a towel in her bag. "Arthur. You didn't need to do that. I'm fine with this being more casual."

"I am too," he said. "But nothing about how I feel about you is casual, and I know you like diamonds."

Alice wasn't sure if she should be exasperated about the money he'd spent or pleased that he knew her.

"I want you to know that I'm serious about you," he said. "If the diamond is the only way I get to do that, so be it."

Alice faced him again, and she found him holding the diamond. Shock moved through her, and her gaze flickered from the gem to Arthur's face. "You have it with you?"

"You said black sand beach," he said, grinning. "You've told me how much it meant to you, and I don't know. I just thought..." He shrugged and stepped toward her. "Will you marry me?"

"Yes," Alice said, her immediate though of Charlie and Ginny. How would they react to this news? She'd need to talk to them before she told anyone else, which meant she couldn't text this news out.

Her hand shook as Arthur slid the ring on her finger, and she kissed him again. "We'll tell my dad and Della, but I need to talk to the twins before the news can spread faster than that."

"Fine with me," Arthur whispered. "My mother will be thrilled." He grinned at her and reached past her to her beach bag. "Let's go. Are you going to text your dad?"

Alice looked around for her phone, wondering where she'd put it. "Yes," she said. "As soon as I find my phone, I'll let him know we're coming and that I have some news for him."

"Knock, knock," Robin said as she opened AJ's front door. "AJ? It's Robin, Mandie, and Jamie." She stepped into the house, noting how completely silent it was. She'd arranged with AJ to come by today, but if AJ was asleep, she could take the girls to the beach.

Behind her, Mandie carried lobster and sushi rolls, but those would keep until later.

"Let me check on her," Robin said, adding, "You two wait here." She went further into the house and around the corner to the office. AJ lay on the couch there, and sure enough, she was fast asleep. Her baby slumbered in a playpen, and Robin gestured for Mandie to bring the food.

"Let's just leave it," she said. "They're both asleep."

Jamie's face fell, because she wanted to see the baby. Things had been hectic at the hospital a couple of weeks ago, and Robin had only got to hold Asher for a couple of minutes. She'd been by AJ's a couple of times since, but the girls wanted to meet the baby too.

They'd been spending their Wednesdays on the beach, so all the kids could come too, but AJ hadn't ventured out into the sun with her son yet. So Robin had offered to bring lunch today, and her daughters would get to see the baby, and AJ would get a little break.

Mandie unloaded the sushi and put it in the fridge, and Robin kept an eye on Jamie, who stood in the office doorway and peered toward the baby.

"AJ," someone called, and the door slammed closed. At the same moment, an alarm started ringing in the office. Robin barely knew which way to look—toward Matt, who'd just come in through the front door—or into the office, where AJ was sitting up.

"Can we stay, Mom?" Jamie asked, and Robin waved her off for a moment.

"Oh, hey," Matt said, grinning as he walked further into the house. "I forgot you guys were coming today."

"We don't have to stay," Robin said.

"Stay," he said. "I just came by to see if AJ was awake. She sometimes sets her alarm at the wrong a.m. or p.m."

He laughed and went straight into the office. "Oh, she's up."

"I set it for a.m.," she said, rising to embrace him. "How did this morning go?'

"We passed," he said. "The course opens on August tenth, and if that baby had played things the way he was supposed to, we would've gotten it done before he came." He grinned and the two of them laughed.

Robin liked watching them, but they also reminded her that she went home to an empty house every day, no matter what.

"Come get Asher," AJ said. "Whoever wants him."

"I do," Jamie said, practically leaping toward the playpen. She bent over and picked up the baby, who made a cute infant squeaking noise.

"Hold his head," Robin said. "Find a seat, Jamie."

"I can hold a baby, Mom." She took a seat on the loveseat, her attention on the baby boy in her arms.

"Come eat," Robin said. "We brought sushi and lobster rolls."

"Oh, bless you," AJ said. "I've been craving sushi for days, and Matt's kids don't like it."

"Matt doesn't like it," Matt said, grinning as he joined them all in the kitchen.

Robin laughed with him and then asked him about the golf course on Rocky Ridge.

"We're already booked for tee times for the next three weeks," he said. "We're trying to get the steamer from Nantucket to put on a special route to Rocky Ridge instead. Our customers don't want to come to Diamond, and then get on another boat and go north again. But they're not sure they want to do it."

"Do they even have the ferries?" Robin asked.

"Oh, they have them," Matt said, taking two lobster rolls. "They just don't want to use them."

"Why wouldn't they want to use them?" Robin asked. "They'd make money on it, wouldn't they?"

He bit into his lunch while AJ grinned at the sushi. Robin took a sushi roll and a lobster roll, and she put them on a plate for Jamie. After setting that aside, she took one of each for herself too.

"They'd make money, yes," Matt said. "I don't know what the hang-up is. They've explained it to me, but I don't understand it."

"It's because it's not about the boats," AJ said. "It's about the manpower required to run the boats. They don't have the people. They have to get insurance on those boats. They'd have to fuel them. You're not bringing them that much business."

"They could stop at the Ridge before continuing to Diamond," Matt argued.

"Did you propose that to them?" Robin asked.

"I did," Matt said with a frown. "I even said we'd increase the fee. Our polls said people would pay it." He shook his head. "There's something going on there I don't understand." He filled his mouth with more lobster roll while the storm vibrated in his expression.

"Thank you for the sushi," AJ said, smiling.

"Thanks for letting us come hold your baby." Robin smiled at her and picked up her sushi roll.

"When does Duke come home?" AJ asked.

"Not until September," Robin said. "But we're on the final stretch." She put a smile on her face, because she didn't like being negative about Duke behind gone in front of the girls. They helped her immensely around the house, and Mandie cooked dinner more than half the time these days.

Robin had been busier than ever this summer, which had made the time go by faster. "Laurel's almost ready for her wedding," she said. "We have the food, the flowers, the cake. She's not wearing a dress, and we did our final walk-through of the venue this week." She smiled at AJ, hoping she didn't noticed the topic shift.

"That's great," she said. "I really like Laurel."

"I do too." Robin liked Laurel a lot. She hoped everything went well with the first delivery at The Cliffside Inn, because while neither she nor Eloise spoke much about it, Robin knew it was a pivotal day.

"Are you going to the Heritage Fair?" she asked next. "You two should come. Bring all the kids. We're going on Sunday afternoon."

"Sunday afternoon?" AJ repeated. "That's the busiest time."

"No, the busiest time is Friday night," Mandie said. "When all the teens are there."

AJ grinned at her, but Mandie barely broke into a smile. "Then all those teens get forced into going again with their families on Sunday afternoon."

Mandie did smile then, and Robin appreciated her daughter so much. She'd been mature about spending time with Charlie this summer, and she never complained when Robin asked her to do something. She got up and went to work every day, and she didn't blow through her money by buying jewelry and makeup, though she loved both.

"When do you want to go?" Robin asked, refraining from suggesting a time. She had a big event on Saturday, so if AJ chose that day, she'd have to bow out. Mandie and Jamie could still go though.

"Sunday morning?" AJ suggested. "It'll be cooler, and we can leave once the big crowds show up."

"Sure," Robin said. "I can do Sunday morning."

"Should we invite everyone else?" AJ asked.

"Sure, put it on the text." Robin finished her lobster roll, the creaminess of it making her mouths so happy.

"All right, I'm headed back to the course, babe." Matt leaned over and kissed his wife. "What do you want me to bring home for dinner?"

"Lisa's making those hand pies," AJ said. "She'll be home in a little bit. She just ran down to the coffee shop to do her orientation calls with her team."

"Oh, right." Matt waved good-bye to Robin and added, "Thanks for bringing lunch and checking on my wife."

"Of course," Robin said. "I'm hoping to get a minute with that baby too."

"Good luck," Mandie said. "Jamie's going to hog him until you force her to give him up." She looked toward the office, and Robin grinned at her.

"Don't worry, Mandie," she said. "I'll make sure you get to hold him too." She turned back to AJ. "What do you think about Kristen's proposal to the City Council about the Seafaring Girls?"

"You know what?" AJ straightened and left the rest of the sushi in the tray. "I think it's a great idea. I think Jean would be amazing in that role, and I think it's a worthwhile program."

"You didn't when we were kids," Robin said, smiling.

"What was worthwhile when we were kids?" AJ challenged. She shook her head and put the lid on the sushi. "Besides, I was really sick back then."

"Oh, honey, I know." Robin took her into a hug. "I wish I'd known then how hard things were for you. I didn't know, and I'm sorry."

"You have nothing to be sorry about," AJ said into Robin's shoulder. "Even I didn't know how bad I was." She stepped back, her eyes focused on something a bit far away. "I guess she'll text after the meeting tonight?"

"I suppose," Robin said. "She made it sound like they'd

just be bringing it up tonight. She's not sure if they'll vote on it right away."

"Even if they do," Mandie said, meeting Robin's eye. "It seemed like she wouldn't get to decide who ran the program or anything."

"No," Robin said, putting her arm around her daughter. They'd had Kristen, Jean, and Reuben—and their dogs —over for dinner a few nights ago. Kristen had practiced her proposal, something she'd told the group about at lunch last week. She'd only gone into surface details then, but Robin had gotten the nitty gritty over fish and chips.

"I know she's worried about that," Robin said. "But she'll have some influence, and I don't think she needs to worry too much about it." She flashed a smile at AJ. "Okay, I'm going to go see if I can pry that baby away from my baby."

KELLI FOLLOWED AMY AND HER GIRLS UP THE STEPS to the house where Wayne Proctor lived, feeling like she shouldn't be there. AJ had insisted she come to breakfast though, and Kelli was no good at telling AJ no. She didn't want to spend this Saturday morning alone, and Shad had gone in for another emergency meeting.

She hadn't realized how important he was in the city government, but he was the Financial Director for the entire town of Five Island Cove. Only the City Manager,

JESSIE NEWTON

the Assistant City Manager, and the Mayor sat above him, and he had been taking quite a few afternoons off this summer.

"Mary, hold the door for Kelli," Amy said to her daughter. She flashed Kelli a smile. "Smells like Grandpa has his maple omelet bake. Darcy, go see if he needs this milk out here."

Kelli walked past the crated milk bottles, and she'd been contacted about the home milk delivery. She didn't like milk, and with Parker gone and not eating it on his cold cereal, she couldn't remember the last time she'd actually bought milk.

Kelli stepped past Mary, who looked mostly like her mother—with a tiny bit of AJ's nose in there. "Thank you," she said.

"You're welcome," the girl said, and Kelli blinked as she looked around the house. It was the same one AJ had lived in growing up, but so much had changed. The shape of the house remained, but even the layout had been altered.

The wall between the front living room and the back, where the kitchen sat, had been removed. Light streamed in the huge back windows, reflecting off the newer hardwood floors, new appliances, and comfortable-looking furniture.

"Wow," Kelli said under her breath. Wayne Proctor had terrified Kelli as a teenager, but now he turned from the stove, a flowery apron tied around his waist.

"Hey, there's my girls." He laughed as he scooped Darcy into his arms, and she asked him about the milk. "Yeah, we should bring that in."

"I'll get it," Kelli said, but Amy's husband, Donovan, entered the house with the crate in his arms.

"Where's AJ?" Amy asked, stepping over to her dad and giving him a quick kiss on the cheek. "She's here, right?"

"They're all out back," Wayne said. "She wanted to show Matt and his kids the deck and the beach." Wayne looked past Amy to Kelli. "My goodness. It's Kelli Watkins. I hear congratulations are in order for you."

He wore a smile the size of a yacht, and he came toward her with a spatula in his hand. "Getting married soon, I hear?"

"Yes," Kelli said, plenty surprised as Wayne hugged her.

"When's the big day?"

"We haven't actually set a date yet," Kelli said, feeling such a difference inside Wayne. He stepped back, and she loved this real-life example that people could change. They could take a life that seemed so hopeless and turn it around completely.

She grinned at him as he stepped back. "It's so good to see you."

"How's your mom?" he asked. "AJ said she's engaged too."

"Yeah, mm hm." Kelli nodded. "She's good. They

don't have a date either. Well, actually, I think they're aiming for Thanksgiving. That's when my sisters can come." Kelli didn't want to wait that long; what she was waiting for to set a date, she wasn't sure.

Something *was* holding her back, as she hadn't even asked Robin to plan the wedding yet. She'd talked to Robin about it, who said she'd clear her schedule and give Kelli the event she wanted, even if the guest list wouldn't top fifteen.

The back door opened, and AJ entered with her husband right behind her. Matt carried the baby, and his adult children filed in behind him. The house felt really full after that, and Kelli thrived on the energy of AJ's family.

She'd always loved being anywhere but at her house growing up, and she and AJ had often holed up under the back deck here at her house, as it stood several feet off the ground and offered a great view of the ocean.

AJ reached her and hugged her, saying, "I'm glad you came, Kel."

"Me too," Kelli said, embracing her back. "You look great."

"Asher's going almost six hours at night now," AJ said, pulling back to beam at Matt and her son. "Lisa will get up and give him his morning bottle, and she lets me sleep for a few more hours."

Kelli watched as Matt's sons joked with Wayne, and

AJ said, "It's amazing how much one summer can change things, isn't it?"

"Oh, yeah," Kelli said, thinking of last summer. She'd left the cove in June, and by the end of the summer, she'd decided to move permanently back to Five Island Cove. This summer, she'd started dating a man *and* gotten engaged to him.

"Justin actually said he was sorry, and that he misjudged me," AJ said quietly. "He said he can see that I'm perfect for Matt, and that he's just glad his dad is back to who he used to be."

"Wow," Kelli said.

"Yeah." AJ sighed and leaned her head against Kelli's shoulder. "How's Parker? You don't say much about him."

"He's good," Kelli said. "He hasn't used our safe word once this summer, and every time I talk to him, he seems upbeat and happy." She smiled at the people in front of her. "Older. His voice is changing a little already."

"Only a couple more weeks until you get him back."

"Yeah," Kelli said. "On the same day Eloise is getting that delivery." She looked at AJ. "Are you worried about that?"

"I don't know if I should be or not," she admitted. "Laurel doesn't seem to be, and honestly, neither does El."

"When is Laurel ever ruffled by anything, though?" Kelli asked, grinning at AJ. "That woman is like a rock."

AJ started to giggle. "She is, right?"

"Except when she's with Paul. She melts a little then."

"Yep," AJ agreed. "He's perfect for her." Her baby started to cry, and AJ stepped away from Kelli to attend to him.

Kelli sat down to a yummy maple bread pudding breakfast, and though she didn't share blood with anyone in the room, it was exactly where she was supposed to be.

She couldn't wait to see Shad again, though, and she called her son on the way back to her twinhome just to feel connected to him too. August eleventh—the day she'd pick-up Parker in New Jersey—couldn't come fast enough.

TWENTY-EIGHT

E loise didn't need a hidden camera; The Cliffside Inn had security cameras on the front door, the back door, the patio, and the foyer. That didn't include the storage room, but part of the consumables delivery service offered unpacking, so she wouldn't be in there anyway.

"Are you sure?" Laurel asked. "You could go in and pretend like you didn't know. Help put things away."

"Or show him where to put things away," Aaron said.

Eloise looked at her husband, wishing he hadn't made the trip to Sanctuary that day. At the same time, knowing that he lurked right here in the apartment behind the inn comforted her.

"What will it look like?" she asked, already confused by the array of items on the kitchen table. She'd given Marge the day off and asked to use her suite. Marge had agreed and gone to Pearl Island to visit her sister, so she shouldn't be interrupting them.

"It's actually a pair of glasses," Laurel said, reaching into a box and pulling out a case. "Whatever you look at, we'll see."

"Oh, well, I can wear glasses." Eloise looked at Aaron, who nodded. They'd left the girls with Robin and Alice and their kids, all of them planning a trip to the beach that morning. Kelli had flown to New Jersey last night to pick up Parker today, and they'd both be home by nightfall.

Everyone on the group text wanted information from Eloise or Laurel the moment they had it. Eloise knew Laurel wouldn't tell them anything, especially if it pertained to the case. Eloise herself had sworn up and down and even signed an agreement that she wouldn't either.

"Okay," Laurel said, slipping the glasses onto Eloise's face. She adjusted them, and Laurel added, "Let's see if they've picked up the WiFi."

She tapped on the laptop she'd already set up, and when she grinned, Eloise assumed everything was working how she wanted it to.

Eloise drew in a breath and smoothed her hands down her blouse. She wore the same thing she always wore to work. She'd left the house at the same time. She'd checked out her customers the way Marge usually did.

She'd ordered food for that night, since her cook would

be gone. She'd insisted the delivery come between noon and two p.m., as that was her slow time in the lobby and at the front podium. She didn't want to be dealing with check-in or check-out while the delivery boy was there.

She wasn't even sure it would be a boy. Marilyn Benson herself could bring the toiletries for all Eloise knew.

"All right, love," Aaron said. He got up from the couch and took her into his arms. "You're fine. We're right here, and we can see and hear everything." His voice reverberated on Laurel's computer, and she muted it. "There's not going to be any snakes in the box, so you have nothing to be afraid of." He smiled at her, and Eloise put her hands on his chest, focusing her attention there so he couldn't see how nervous she was.

"Look who's being all calm this time," she murmured. "And a lot of people are afraid of snakes."

He chuckled and hugged her, and then he said, "All right, El. Let's see what happens."

Eloise nodded, locked eyes with Laurel, then Thom, who stood near the door of the suite, and she left. A few people played in the pool, and she heard evidence of a volleyball game going on down on the lower terrace. She ignored all of that and went inside the inn, down the hall, and stopped to check something at the podium.

The clock had barely ticked to noon, and her stomach roared at her to eat something. She still hadn't figured out what to do with her leftovers, and she'd spoken with her night janitor about taking whatever he wanted.

When she'd met with Nick, she'd learned that yes, his wife had lost her job. They didn't have much to live on, and they were caring for their five-year-old granddaughter. Once Eloise had heard that, she'd told him to take whatever he found in the fridge at night that had clearly been served to guests. They wouldn't re-serve it, as they legally couldn't, and Eloise had been thinking about donating it.

Nick had been so grateful, and Eloise had crossed off the idea of finding a place to donate the food from her never-ending to-do list.

In all honesty, she wanted this sting to be over too. It felt like a weight had been hanging over her head for a month, just waiting to drop. She wanted to see what came in the delivery, so Laurel could get her man—or in this case, woman—and move on. She could focus on her and Paul and their wedding that was less than a month away now.

Eloise simply wanted everything to go back to normal.

Thankfully, she didn't have to wait long for someone to walk through the door. The woman carried a large box that seemed to cause her trouble, and she dropped it on the floor only a few feet inside the door. "Phew," she said, wiping her hand across her forehead.

She grinned at Eloise as if they were old pals, and said, "I'm Hillary Henson. I have a delivery for you?" She held out her clipboard, and Eloise was a little surprised it wasn't electronic. "From Benson Beauty?"

"Right," Eloise said, reaching for the clipboard. The woman stood about as tall as Eloise, so not much more than five-foot-three. If that. She weighed probably half as much as Eloise, so she gained a bit of confidence that she could overpower her should it come to that.

She balked at the thought, her mind spinning over a possible physical altercation. That wouldn't happen, would it?

"And you unpack it for me?" she asked.

"Gold Tier members get the unpacking," the woman said.

Eloise glanced up and took in the name tag on her shirt. Hillary was spelled with two L's, which Eloise found interesting. "I am Gold Tier," she said.

"Are you?" Hillary consulted the clipboard and even flipped a page. "Huh, okay. Sorry, I didn't realize." She looked at the box on the floor, and Eloise realized she would've left it there had she not mentioned the Gold Tier. "Show me where you want this. I'll get it put away for you."

"I've got a wall of cupboards right back here." Eloise wasn't going to touch that box. Number one, Aaron, Thom, and Laurel had told her not to. Number two, she was paying an enormous amount of money for the Gold Tier—an amount she would've never agreed to if the situation were different. She'd have blown off Marilyn's proposal and never gone to another women in business meeting again.

She led the way past the podium, ignoring Hillary's grunt and groan, and into the storage room off the back of the inn.

Hillary huffed and puffed as she brought the box back. She put it on the counter and pulled a box cutter from her back pocket. She wore a navy blue uniform from head to toe, almost like the scrubs a nurse would wear in the hospital.

Eloise kept out of arm's reach of her, proud of herself for doing so. Aaron would be happy about that too. She opened the far cupboard and looked inside. "This is where the soap goes. Shampoo and conditioner in this one."

She kept opening cupboards and saying what was in them as Hillary began lifting boxed of soaps—body and hand—from the box.

"Oh, these are so much nicer than what you've been ordering," Hillary said. "You've been going through Hotel Amenities?" She looked at Eloise with surprise, as if no one in their right mind would order from the largest hotel supply company in the country.

"Yes," Eloise said simply. "How are your products better?" she asked.

"Our bottles are eco-friendly, for one," Hillary started, and Eloise wanted her to stop talking immediately. She just kept going on and on until she reached the last item in the box. "That's it," she said, and Eloise's heart fell all the way to the floor.

She'd been standing back by the far wall while Hillary got the job done, and she'd seen everything the woman had removed from the box and put on the shelves. None of it resembled drugs in any way, shape, or form.

"Wait," Hillary said. "You've got an extra case of hand soap." She actually stepped back from the cupboard and counted. "Yeah, there's three, and on a thrice-monthly delivery system, you only get two." She reached for the closest box, but Eloise darted forward.

"I'm almost out of it," she said. "Could you leave it, and just bring me one next time?"

"No," Hillary said, and not in a very friendly voice either. "We do the tiers and the monthly deliveries a certain way so it's easy to pick and pack. You'll still get two next time, because it's too hard to do special orders."

"I'll pay for it, then," Eloise said. "À la carte."

"We don't do à la carte." Hillary gave her a smile that wasn't really a smile and plucked the case of hand soap from the shelf. She picked up the bigger box and moved to step past Eloise.

"She's taking that case with her," she whispered, not quite sure where the camera or mic was in the glasses. She pushed them up on her face. "What if that's the one with something in it?"

She wasn't wearing an earpiece, and she had no way of communicating with anyone in the suite. She glanced that way, saw no one, and then started down the hall after Hillary. "Will you come every time?" she asked, nearly yelling at the woman. "Or will I have to show a different person where to put things next time?'

Hillary turned back to her, the large box flapping from her hand. Eloise could see all the way inside it, and she froze at the stamped logo she saw there.

Cove Creations.

It's called Cove Creations, Polly Baldwin had said. *We do everything from banners to billboards to boxes.*

"Where did you get that box?" Eloise asked, her throat so dry. Hillary said, "It'll be me every time, ma'am," right over the top of her, but she dropped her eyes to the box in her hand. She looked back at Eloise, obviously confused.

"I, uh, need some big boxes like that," she said. "I'm moving soon, and everything I have only holds bottles of mini shampoo." She forced a laugh through her throat, catching movement on the lawn behind Hillary. Someone in a black uniform, and Eloise yanked her eyes back to Hillary's.

"Could I keep that one?"

She looked at it again. "Sure, I guess. I don't know where we get them." She stepped forward and put the box on the ground a few feet from Eloise.

"Do you do the picking and packing yourself?" Eloise asked, watching someone come up the front steps behind Hillary.

"No," Hillary said. "It's done at the warehouse. I just pick up the boxes in the morning and deliver them."

"Mm." Eloise nodded as if she understood their system. "Is it the consumables warehouse?"

Hillary frowned. "I don't know, ma'am. I really need to go. I have more deliveries to make." She turned to leave, but she came chest-to-chest with Laurel Baker. *Detective* Laurel Baker.

She said, "You're going to need to call in to get someone else to do your deliveries." She held up her badge and indicated Thom, who'd stepped into the inn and now stood beside her. "My partner and I have a few questions for you."

Eloise grabbed the box and stepped backward. She smelled Aaron before she knew he was there, and she turned to find him in the back of the inn, where Hillary had just put away all of the boxes. He had two of his K9 cops with him, and all three of them wore rubber gloves as they started removing the new items and letting the dogs smell them.

"Aaron," Eloise said, hurrying toward him. "Have them look at this. Look at this!" She shoved the box at him.

"What is it?" He frowned down at the empty box. One of the German shepherds barked, the sound so loud in the small space.

Eloise flinched, and she looked past him to where the dog had alerted on the case of hand soap that had been next to the one Hillary had taken. The officer turned it over, and the same stamped logo sat on the bottom of it that beamed out at them from the inside of the larger box.

"That box says Cove Creations on it," Eloise hissed at Aaron, pointing. "So does this one. Do you know who owns Cove Creations?"

"No, who?" Aaron searched her face, and Eloise's pulse moved so fast, she thought her heart would explode.

"Polly Baldwin."

TWENTY-NINE

Laurel did wear an earpiece, and she heard everything the Chief and his K9 officers said.

"Where's the warehouse where you pick up your deliveries?" she asked, notebook out and pen at the ready.

"It's on Diamond," Hillary said. She'd started with attitude, but she'd calmed down once Thom had said they could talk on the lawn for a few minutes, in the shade, or they could get on back to the station and chat there. "Down by the shipping yard. Tons of warehouses down there. It's 12-B."

"12-B," Laurel repeated, writing it down. "You never go inside?"

"My deliveries are brought out onto the dock. Loaded up by Benson Beauty workers. I sign a paper. I leave."

"So you own the delivery van."

"Yes," Hillary said. "I deliver anything anyone contracts me to."

"Primarily Benson Beauty products, though, right?" Thom asked. "They partner with you exclusively?" He held up his phone. "Says so right here on your website."

"Yes," Hillary said slowly, her eyes rounding though he pulled his phone back so only he could see it. "I deliver for them three days a week, to about a third of the hotels in the cove. Tuesdays, I come to Sanctuary. I've got the Beachfront Bay hotel, and now Cliffside. Everyone wants their delivery when it's not check-in or check-out. Makes timing difficult."

"I bet," Laurel said with as much sympathy as she could muster. She took Thom's phone as he offered it to her. She gasped, her mind racing in a contest with her pulse suddenly.

"What?" Hillary asked.

"How do you know Marilyn Benson?" Thom asked, because Laurel still had a vice-grip on his phone and was staring at the two of them, both smiling, on Hillary's delivery website.

"She owns Benson Beauty," Hillary said, frowning.

"That's the only way?" he pressed.

"And she's..." Hillary exhaled and looked north, her expression troubled and dark. "She's my mother, okay?"

"Hm." Thom took his phone back from Laurel, who thought she should be writing something down, but she didn't know what.

Laurel blinked, trying to formulate her next question. In her ear, she heard that the drug dogs had alerted on something. They wanted the box Hillary had taken. It sat on the top step on the porch, and Laurel reached up and pressed the button on her radio. "Ten-four on that item. It's on the top step for you."

She focused on Hillary again, who turned and looked over her shoulder. "What's in the box, Hillary?" she asked.

The other woman spun back to her, pure fear in her eyes. "Hand soap," she said.

"Yeah, I don't think so," Laurel said. "See, I've got drug dogs here, and they've already scented something on the toiletries you put in the cupboards. Tell me what I'm going to find in that box. Is it dangerous for my guys to open it? Are my dogs going to start barking when they come outside?"

One of them did emerge from the inn, and Laurel held up her hand. His handler yipped at him, and the dog sat. She put her arm around Hillary and turned her around. "There they are. If that dog even so much as whimpers, I know there's drugs in there. If my dog gets hurt, that's assault on a police officer. If my guys get hurt when they open that box, same thing." She kept her voice low and her mouth close to Hillary's ear.

"So you better tell me right now what's going to happen, and if there's any reason at all we shouldn't open that box."

Hillary started to cry, and that caused Laurel's heart to

bleed a little bit. She told herself calloused detectives didn't cry when they caught their criminals. Perhaps she wasn't so calloused yet. Perhaps she wasn't cut out for this job.

"He's going to bark," Hillary said. "That's all I'm saying without my lawyer."

Laurel reached for her handcuffs and held them up. The K9 officer edged his dog forward, the German shepherd eager to work. He got within a foot of the box and barked. His handler moved him closer, and the dog started barking and barking and barking.

"Is it coke or meth?" Thom asked.

"I don't know," Hillary said.

"How did you know which box to take?" Laurel asked.

"It's marked," Hillary said. "Not every shipment has a marked box, but the ones that do, I take back."

"Take them back where?" Thom asked.

"I..." Hillary cleared her throat. "I want a lawyer."

"I'm going to put these on you for your own safety," Laurel said, stepping in front of her while the K9 officer backed his dog away. The second one came out, and they had their second dog positively ID the box for drugs.

Once he'd stopped barking, Laurel said, "You're under arrest until we get to the bottom of where those drugs came from. You have the right to remain silent..."

An hour later, Laurel stood in the evidence warehouse, Thom at her side, both K9 officers there, and Chief Sherman pacing the length of one of the stainless steel tables. Thom sliced open the top of the box, which bore no markings at all. Not on the top, not on the sides, not on the bottom. Nowhere.

Hillary had said it was marked, but if that was true, none of the cops could see how or where.

The Chief picked up one of the other boxes that had been in the shipment too and turned it over. "This one has a stamp on it."

Laurel ignored him, because Thom had opened the flaps on the box. She leaned closer to see what was inside. "Dear Lord in Heaven," she whispered.

Bags of methamphetamine sat there, not a bottle of soap in sight.

Relief spread through her faster than wildfire on dry brush, and she honestly felt like slumping to the ground and sobbing. If Paul had been there, she'd have clung to him and bawled like a baby.

"This one has a stamp on it too," the Chief said, and Laurel looked past Thom, who was now poking back the plastic in the box with the tip of a pen. He said something to the K9 officers, who converged on the boxes to weigh the drugs.

"What are you going on about?" she asked the Chief.

He held up a box. "This one has a stamp on it." He indicated all the boxes. "They all do." He nodded down to the one where the first zippered bag of meth was being removed. "That one doesn't. So it's marked by *not* being marked."

Laurel picked up one of the boxes and looked at the bottom of it. Sure enough, a deep, dark stamp sat there, curling letters that spelled out *Cove Creations*.

She read the name aloud. "It's not Benson Beauty." She met the Chief's eyes, and oh, he had something brewing there.

"Eloise said it's Polly Baldwin's company," he said under his breath. "We had them over for dinner a few weeks ago, and apparently Polly told her all about it. Billboards, banners, and—" He lifted the box. "Boxes."

She searched his face, too many thoughts filling her mind to seize onto any one of them. "Do you think...Nathan?"

"I don't know what to think."

"I think this better be handled delicately," Thom said, and Laurel jumped, as she hadn't realized he'd come up beside her.

"Delicately?" Aaron growled, his fists balling at his sides. "He's the blasted City Manager. He was in my office three weeks ago—oh, no. No, no, no." He ran his hands through his hair and paced away.

Laurel exchanged a glance with Thom. "What?" she asked, as she could definitely handle the Chief with a softer pair of gloves than Thom.

"I told him about the case," Aaron said, spinning back to her and Thom. "*That's* what got him out of my office."

"What do you mean?" Laurel asked, frowning.

"Remember how I was late to the women in business meeting, because Nathan showed up? He just wanted to shoot the breeze about nothing, so I started telling him about some of our cases. He doesn't really care, but it does make him feel important. I know how to play to Nathan Baldwin."

"Okay," Laurel said slowly.

"The moment I mentioned this case, he jumped to his feet and said he'd just gotten an important text. He had to head back to this office. I was so relieved, I didn't think anything of it."

"What are you thinking of it now?" Thom asked. "You think he knows about the drugs his wife is peddling?"

"No," Laurel said, keeping her eyes on the Chief's. She'd always been able to read him very well. "He thinks *Nathan's* peddling the drugs, using his wife's company." She faced Thom, her chest seizing over and over with every beat of her heart. "We need an appointment with the City Manager, Thom."

LAUREL SWIPED AWAY THE CALL FROM PAUL. SHE quickly tapped out a text that she'd call him later, and she looked up at Thom came to a stop in front of City Hall. "I have a bad feeling about this," she said, shoving her phone in her pocket.

She wanted this drug case solved and done before the wedding. She had three weeks to go, and the paperwork alone on the ten pounds of meth they'd found that morning would eat up her free time between now and then.

And that was just one box in one delivery, Laurel thought. Thom had not gotten out of the car yet, and Laurel wasn't going to move until he did.

"You were right," he said with a sigh. "This is big. This is the kind of story that breaks the trust of a small town like ours. No one will believe it, and people will be afraid."

"I know," Laurel whispered. "What do we do, though?"

"At least it's not the Mayor," Thom said with another sigh. "Can you imagine?"

"But Nathan Baldwin's office is right next door to the Mayor's. He's friends with the Chief." She didn't want to say the next part, so she just thought it. Nathan Baldwin lived next door to Arthur Rice. He golfed at Matt's course. Shad Webb's office sat on the other side of Nathan's—and Laurel knew through Kelli that they'd been having a *lot* of weekend meetings.

Could Shad be in on the drug ring too? Did Matt look the other way for the City Manager? Did his father? Had Arthur Rice ever seen him moving boxes out of the house late at night? Bringing in a lot of packages at odd hours?

How could he have done this all these months without *anyone* knowing?

Even if they didn't know, Laurel believed there would've been signs. They'd all simply chosen to look the other way. She'd spent so much of her life looking the other way, and she wasn't going to do that anymore. Oh, no, she was not.

She got out of the car first, Thom following her this time. "Laurel, Laurel," he called. "We have to time this right. Wait, would you?"

She slowed and stopped. "How long does it take them to secure the warehouse?"

"We can't have Marilyn or his wife tipping him off," Thom said. "Wait. He's the kingpin, Detective. You take down the pawns first. Then go after him."

She nodded and waited. Minutes ticked by as they stood out in front of City Hall, with every available officer in Five Island Cove converging on the warehouses by the loading dock, getting the other city officials out of their offices, bringing in hotel owners, as well as any acquaintances of Nathan Baldwin. It was practically the whole blasted island.

Laurel hadn't said a word to her friends, and her stomach writhed. They'd be livid with her, as Matt and his father were definitely being brought in. Eloise would need to appear at the station. Arthur was getting contacted. Shad was probably already with a couple of police officers.

"Guess who owns Marilyn's warehouse?" Thom

asked, holding up his phone. Laurel read the text quickly. *City records show Nathan Baldwin as owner of the warehouse 12-B,* one of their narcotics cops had texted. "So we've got him on having drugs at a property he owns or rents."

"Possession," Laurel murmured.

Finally, a bleep came through the radio, and Laurel heard, "City Hall is clean. You're free to go in."

"Unit five-two. We're finishing up at the warehouse," someone else said. "All suspects in custody, phones removed."

Once all the reports had come in that everyone else— all the other players in the game—had been secured, Thom nodded. "It's time."

She kept her temper in check as they went through security. As they rode the elevator to the fifth floor. As she marched down the hall and right past his secretary's empty desk to his office.

"Nathan Baldwin?" she asked, entering the office while pulling out her badge. The man stood with a golf club in his hand, and he turned toward her surprised. "Detective Laurel Baker. Can you put down the club, please?"

Nathan did as she asked, his brow furrowing. "What's going on?"

"We have a few questions," Laurel said. "Can we sit?"

Thom flashed his badge too, closed the door behind him, and locked it. Nathan went around his desk and sat down. Laurel could barely contain herself to a chair, but she managed it by perching on the very edge.

"Your wife owns Cove Creations, right?" she asked.

"Yes," he said, still obviously confused. "Has something happened to her?"

"No, sir," Laurel said crisply. "Do you know who she sells her boxes to?"

"Boxes?" he repeated. "She doesn't sell boxes."

Thom swiped on his phone and held it up for Nathan. "That's not one of hers?"

Nathan peered at the photo. "Obviously it is." He looked at Laurel and then Thom, keeping his eyes there. "What's going on?"

"Are you bringing drugs into the cove?" Laurel blurted out, tired of the cat-and-mouse game.

Beside her, even Thom gasped.

"Of course not," Nathan said, but he laughed afterward, and it sounded nervous.

Laurel *sensed* the lie, tasted it, and she leaned toward him, feeling dangerous and nearly out of control. "Sir, I was held captive by my own husband and forced into things you know nothing about. I can sense a lie from a mile away, and you sir, just lied to me."

"Officer Baker," Thom said, but Laurel held up her hand.

Nathan Baldwin looked like a caged alley cat, and Laurel knew his claws were about to come out. She didn't care. She actually craved the fight this time. "How long have you been bringing drugs into the cove, using your wife's stamp to mark the boxes after they'd left her warehouse, and distributing them through Marilyn Benson's beauty company?"

"Marilyn Benson," Nathan said, his expression taking on some of his normal swagger. "There's the person you should be after. Or that police chief of yours. All he does is look the other way." He scoffed and then laughed again. "Everyone does. Shad Webb, Athena Cruz, even Bertha out there. Heck, everyone looks the other way, even my own neighbors."

"What are you saying, sir?" Laurel asked, glancing at Thom. He had his tape recorder out and running, and Laurel was glad for that. Politicians talked in such circles.

"What evidence do you have that I'm the one bringing in the drugs?" Nathan challenged. "Am I under arrest?"

"No, sir," Thom said quickly, though they could easily arrest Nathan on possession, as he owned the warehouse where drugs had been found.

"Then I'm done talking." Nathan stood and buttoned his jacket. "If you'll excuse me, I have a meeting with the Mayor."

"To go over your resignation?" Laurel asked, standing too. "This isn't over. You can't just walk away."

"Unless you're going to arrest me, yes, I can." He looked right into her eyes, and Laurel blinked, sure she'd see her ex-husband glaring back at her when she focused on Nathan again. He did appear, but on the next blink, Nathan was back.

"Nathan Baldwin," she said, taking out her handcuffs for the second time that day. "You're under arrest for possession of a class B drug, with the intent to sell or distribute that drug." She clipped the first cuff around his wrist and stepped behind him. "You have the right to remain silent. Anything you say can and will be used—"

"This is preposterous," Nathan bellowed, trying to rip his remaining arm free.

Thom stepped to Laurel's side, and together, they got him cuffed and walking toward the door while Laurel continued to read him his Miranda rights.

THIRTY

"You're where?" AJ asked, sitting up as Matt's words sank into her head. "Jail?" She met Lisa's eyes, hers suddenly as shocked as AJ felt. "Slow down, babe. Slow down. What's going on?"

"They brought me in for questioning," Matt said. "They have twenty-four hours to arrest me, and they're going to keep me here." His voice grew softer. "Laurel is everywhere, AJ. There's not enough cops to do all the interviews, and there's over a dozen of us here."

"Laurel?"

"She arrested Nathan Baldwin," Matt said, his voice still buried under his breath. "He says my dad and I are part of his drug ring."

"What?" AJ got to her feet. "I'm coming down there."

"You can't come down here," Matt said. "No way. Stay with the kids. I'm fine."

"They're going to keep you in jail overnight." Hysteria crept into her voice, and she honestly didn't know which way to look. "For nothing. I can talk to Laurel."

"I don't think so, babe," he said. "Shad's here too. The Mayor. Greg Sherman. They even put Aaron in a holding room down at the end of the hall by himself."

AJ turned in a full circle, not sure what to do next. "You're kidding. Aaron?"

"Nathan is naming everyone," Matt said. "It's a lot for them to sort out, but I'm sure they will."

"Laurel *knows* you," she said. "She knows you're not smuggling drugs into the cove through the golf course." The very idea was laughable, though AJ had been a little worried when Laurel and her partner had interviewed Matt and Yancey earlier that summer.

"They can only keep us for twenty-four hours," he said. "I just wanted you to know and not to worry."

"Not to worry?" AJ couldn't even comprehend that. The back door opened, and Justin and Derrick walked in. They wore horrified looks on their faces, and AJ wanted to fold them into a hug and tell them everything would be all right. Somehow, she'd make everything all right.

"Your kids just got home."

"They watched us get taken away," Matt said. "Me and Dad. The cops said they had to stay at the golf course for another hour, and they'd let them go once the threat had been contained."

"Threat?"

"Is that Dad?" Justin asked.

AJ nodded and handed the phone to him. "Dad?" he asked. "Are you all right?"

She paced while Justin, Derrick, and Lisa all spoke to Matt. Once she got the device back, she said, "I love you, Matt. Tell me you'll be home tomorrow night."

"I'll be home tomorrow night, my AvaJane," he said. "Take care of the kids for me, would you?"

"Yes," she whispered.

"I love you," he said, and the call ended.

Numbness spread through AJ. She wanted to throw her phone through the window and rage into the cheery, summery sky outside. How could Laurel do this to her?

Bitterness coursed through her, and AJ stabbed at her phone, trying to get to Laurel's name. She called the woman, but of course she didn't answer.

AJ screamed as tears started to flow down her face. Lisa took her phone and said, "AvaJane, look at me."

She did, and she started to calm instantly. "This isn't going to help Dad."

"You're right." She opened her arms and drew Lisa into a hug. She gestured for Justin and Derrick to come join in, and they did. The four of them stood there, breathing in and out and holding one another.

"It's going to be okay," AJ said after a few moments. "Your dad is not guilty, and he'll be home tomorrow night. He doesn't want us to panic, so we're not going to." Asher began to whine in the office, and AJ went to get him. With the baby in her arms, she could see Matt so clearly in his face, the shape of his forehead, his chin, even the way his voice sounded.

"Daddy's going to be home tomorrow," she said softly to her son. "It's okay, baby. It's all going to be okay."

She didn't know how, but AJ *believed* that the mess happening at the police station would get sorted, and Matt would come home.

She had to believe that, or her anger would eat her alive, and all she'd be able to do was think about all the nasty things she wanted to say to Laurel Baker.

"I don't understand," Alice said as she folded up her beach chair. "Why are we leaving?" She looked at Robin, who'd actually started to cry. "Who was on the phone?"

"El," Robin said, stuffing things into bags in the most unorganized fashion. "They found drugs in the shipment to the inn. They made an arrest there. She obviously couldn't say anything to us, so she didn't. Except now, they've gone to the inn to get her too. Or they did. Something."

Robin wiped her face, and Alice turned back to the water and called, "Charlie! Ginny! We have to go." She wanted to call Arthur, because he could come sit with the kids and watch movies while she went to the police station to help Eloise. The twins would be fine home alone together too, but since Robin literally never cried, Alice's anxiety had shot toward the moon.

"Come on girls," Robin said. "You'll be staying with me tonight."

"Why?" Billie asked, rubbing a towel through her hair. "Where's Dad and El?"

"They're tied up at the station," Robin said, wiping her face. "They're not going to be home tonight."

Alice met Robin's eye. "They're not?"

"There is something huge going down," Robin said, shouldering her bag. "Get your things, girls, and follow me. I'll be right back for anything we can't carry." She stepped away from Aaron's kids, and Alice went with her.

"Talk to me," Alice muttered.

"Eloise isn't under arrest, but she was escorted from the inn by a pair of cops. Aaron's been detained in a room by himself. They won't let her see him. Laurel's case went all the way to Nathan Baldwin."

Alice pulled in a breath. "Wow. You're okay with the girls?"

"Yes," Robin said.

"I'll go to the station," Alice said. "I'm an attorney. I should be able to talk to Eloise and Aaron." The tension in her chest solidified, and Alice's lawyer skin slid easily into place. She'd trained for this, and in fact, she *lived* to make sure her clients got fair treatment.

The twins caught up to her, both of them panting.

"What's the rush?" Charlie asked. "You just left us back there."

"I have to get to the police station," Alice said. "Eloise and Aaron need me." She met her son's eye. "I'm going to send you two in a RideShare, and you're to go home and stay there. Do you understand me?"

"Yes," Ginny said for both of them.

"I'll send Arthur to stay with you," Alice said. "It sounds like things are a real mess at the station." She'd told the twins about her engagement to Arthur Rice. She hadn't mentioned it to Robin yet, and her eyes flitted in that direction. She didn't want to tell Robin that she didn't want a huge wedding.

However, if she didn't talk to her soon, Robin's feelings would be hurt. Alice looked at her phone, praying for a message from Arthur. She had none. She tapped to call a RideShare while Robin loaded all of their beach things in the back of her van and headed back out onto the sand.

"Five minutes," she said. "Put your things in the van. We'll sort them out later." While Charlie and Ginny did that, Alice followed Robin, jogging the last few steps to where they'd set up for the day.

"Hey," she said, out of breath. "I know it's not a great time, but I have to tell you something."

Robin looked up, her bright blue eyes almost clouded with her emotion. "What is it?"

"Arthur and I are engaged," Alice said, unable to contain her smile. "I haven't told anyone, because well, I don't want it to be a big deal." She hooked her thumb over her shoulder. "The twins know. We told my dad and Della, as well as Arthur's mother. I just haven't told anyone else."

Robin's eyes widened, and she dropped the towels she'd been picking up. She grabbed onto Alice and held her tightly. "Congratulations."

"I'd hire you, Robin. You're my best friend, and I love you, but honestly, I don't want the type of wedding you do."

Robin stepped back, those electric blue eyes searching Alice's face now. "What do you want?"

"Honestly?" Alice looked up into the sky, wishing this day didn't hold so much tension. "I want a backyard cere-mony with my friends and family. I'll wear one of my expensive dresses from the Hamptons, but I don't need a new one. Then, I want to go inside and have a huge spread of food set out on the counter, and I want to eat. That's it."

Even as she spoke, she could see where she wanted all of this to happen. "Your house would be perfect."

"What?" Robin asked, scoffing. "You're kidding."

"I'm not," Alice said. "You have that huge patio. We could put tables out there. Heck, you already have that picnic table that seats all of us. You have a big island. So we'll put out all the food—I'll buy it, of course. No one should cook on their wedding day." She grinned, her tongue rushing ahead now. "And we'll chit-chat before the ceremony. Go get that done under those amazing trees you have, and then, we'll eat. Done."

"Oh my word, you're serious."

"Dead serious," Alice said, grinning. "Don't think about it now. You get home and take care of the girls. I'll go to the station."

"Your twins could come to my house," Robin said. "Mandie's fine with Charlie."

"I know," Alice said. "She's such an amazing girl, Robin." She bent to get the towels and toys Aaron's girls couldn't handle, and together, they walked back to the van.

The RideShare for the twins pulled up, and Alice asked, "Do you guys want to go home, or go with Robin?" She looked from Ginny to Charlie, and they each wore a different expression.

"There's not room in the van," Charlie said. "I want to shower and change." He looked at Ginny, who nodded.

"Then maybe we can go to Robin's," Ginny said, looking from Alice to Robin. "Is that okay?"

"Of course," Alice and Robin said together, and when they looked at each other, they both managed a smile.

"Alice Kelton?" the RideShare driver asked.

Alice herded her teens into the car with a, "Text me when you get home, and when you get to Robin's. I hope I won't be late, but I don't know what I'm dealing with yet."

"Okay," Ginny said. "Love you."

"I love you both. Stay together." She closed the door

behind them, and immediately booked the next car—the one that would take her to the police station.

Twenty minutes later, the RideShare driver said, "I don't think I can get you any closer."

Alice could not believe the activity at the police station. Robin had not exaggerated when she'd said something big was going down. No less than seven TV vans had been parked along the street. The parking lot had been taped off and closed, and four uniformed officers kept waving traffic by.

"Stop here," Alice said, gathering her purse. She probably should've gone home and showered and changed too, but her white maxi dress coverup would have to do. "I'll get out." She paid and stepped from the car, a very angry-looking officer coming toward her.

"Ma'am, you can't be here."

"Oh, I beg to differ, sir," she said. "I'm Alice Kelton, attorney-at-law. You have two of my clients detained inside, without arrests. I have every right to be here." She swept her gaze down his chest to his name tag. "Now, Officer Lundy, will you kindly escort me to Aaron Sherman or Eloise Sherman?"

Officer Lundy visibly swallowed, and he turned and gestured for someone else to come. "This is Alice Kelton, the Chief's lawyer. Will you take her inside?" He turned toward Alice. "I just can't believe the Chief is involved in this."

"He's not," Alice said. 'Thank you, Officer Lundy."

"Officer Burlbury will get you where you need to go."

Alice looked at the other officer and gestured for him to lead on. She followed him in her strappy sandals, getting overwhelmed by the number of people, the shrieking of telephones, and the sheer chaos inside the station.

"My goodness," she said, looking around and trying to find something to latch onto. Everything seemed to be in constant motion, and Alice got a little seasick.

"This way, ma'am." The officer opened a door on his left and started down the steps. She tore her eyes from the fray before her and followed him into the basement.

Dozens of people had been put in holding cells down here, and Alice looked at them as she walked by. Her pace slowed as she went past the first one, easily holding twenty people. "What is going on?" she asked.

No one answered her, and the noise didn't extend down here. The people here looked to be from every walk of life. They wore suits and ties. Board shorts and T-shirts. Dresses. Jeans. There were men and women, and Alice couldn't make sense of it.

Everyone watched her, and as her gaze switched to the second cell, a commotion started near the back and surged forward.

"Alice," someone said, and her eyes locked onto Matt Hymas.

"No." She rushed toward him, her heart flying to the back of her throat. "Matt," she cried. "What are you doing here?" He'd curled his fingers through the grate, and she put her hands on his, searching to see if he was hurt.

"It's Alice," he yelled over his shoulder, and a couple of men moved for someone else. Shad came forward, wearing his very business-like clothes, and Alice gasped again.

"What is happening?" She couldn't believe her eyes. What had Laurel done? How could Alice fix it? "Shad, talk to me."

"You need to talk to the Chief first," he said with a smile. He really was the kindest, most gentle man. There was no way on this planet he was involved with any drugs coming into the cove. No way.

"Does Kelli know you're here?"

"I haven't gotten my call yet," Shad said. "Matt called AJ a few minutes ago. The police are overwhelmed, and doing the best they can."

Several people nearby shifted, and Alice sensed that Shad's opinion wasn't the most popular one. "I'm going to make sure they attend to you first," she said. "You're now my clients too, understand?"

"Can I be your client?" someone else asked, and Alice threw them an acidic look.

"Alice."

Her world spun, because this could not be happening. She knew that voice, and it did not belong in a crowded holding cell, where Arthur had to wait to defend himself.

Instant fear and fury combined in Alice's soul, and

both Matt and Shad parted to show her that yes, indeed, Arthur had been brought in too.

"Arthur," she choked the name out. "Why are you here?"

He came as close as he could and leaned his forehead against hers through the squares in the bars. "I live next door to Nathan Baldwin," he whispered. "Apparently, I got some of his boxes one day, and I should've known what he was doing because of that."

"That's preposterous," she said, no real power behind the words. She sniffled, and she hated the sound of it. She hated the weakness it fostered inside her. She straightened and met his eye. "I'm going to get you all out of here tonight."

"Ma'am," the officer said. "You can't talk to them."

"Like hell I can't," she barked at him. "These three. Matt Hymas, Shad Webb, and Arthur Rice. I want them in a room by themselves right now. They're my clients, and I demand to be able to speak with them privately."

The officer looked like she'd hit him with a brick. "Uh..."

"Now," she said again, marching toward him. "Get them out of there now, or I'll be filing a lawsuit against you personally and against this entire department for mistreatment."

"I don't have anywhere to put them," he said, and Alice could see he was trapped between a rock and a hard place.

Alice looked at him and then back to the important people in her life. "Let's put them in with Chief Sherman then. I'd like to hear all of their stories at the same time anyway."

"Alice, my dad," Matt said, and Alice frowned at the older gentlemen now standing at Matt's side.

"Yancey Hymas is now my client as well. Bring the four of them with us."

Kristen watched in complete horror and disbelief at the images playing on the television screen in front of her. The reporter kept saying he didn't know what was factual and what wasn't, but that "reportedly, over thirty people have been taken in for questioning in one of the biggest drug stings in Five Island Cove history."

She changed the channel, only to see similar footage. "...the police aren't saying anything, and there is no official statement from the department, the Mayor's office, or anyone at City Hall. Rumors are that the police emptied the building before two detectives went in and arrested the City Manager, Nathan Baldwin. He's been arrested on charges of drug possession and the intent to sell drugs, after over ten pounds of methamphetamine was found in a box at a local inn."

Kristen clicked off the TV and got to her feet. Laurel was not one of her girls, but she had become a close friend and someone Kristen loved. She'd found her phone, called for a ride, and put on her shoes before someone knocked on her door.

"Mom?" Rueben called through the door. "Let me in."

She hurried to the door and unlocked it, letting her son spill into the house. "Mom, AJ called and said I should come get you and take you to her house. She'll explain everything once you're there."

"AJ?"

"They have Matt at the station," Rueben said, and Kristen gasped. "And his father, and Shad, and Arthur."

The world fell out of the bottom of Kristen's life. "You've got to be kidding."

"Eloise and Aaron are there too," Reuben said. "Robin called on the way over. Kelli's on her way to AJ's, as is her sister. Jean and I came to get you." He put his arm around her. "Come on, now. Your friends are going to need your strength and wisdom."

Kristen wasn't sure where either of those things were at the moment, but she dug down deep to find them on the drive over to AvaJane's.

THIRTY-ONE

R obin woke when light rapping penetrated her flimsy slumber. Her eyes flew open, and from her position of lying on the couch, she could see straight down the hallway from the living room to the front door.

Her phone lay on the coffee table in front of her, and Robin reached for it at the same time she sat up. A sense of spookiness ran through her as she thought of someone standing on her front porch at two-thirty in the morning.

Eloise had texted since Robin had checked her phone last. *We're done here. We're coming to get the girls.*

Robin bolted to her feet when the knocking happened again, this time a little louder. She flew down the hall in her bare feet, unlocked the door, and opened it.

Eloise and Aaron stood there, both of them looking like they'd been run over by a truck. "Robin," Aaron whispered, and she flew into his arms.

The navy blue midnight sky was a little spooky with the moon throwing her silver light around, and Robin hurried to back up and let them in. "Come in," she said to urge them along. "You shouldn't take the girls. Just sleep here for a while. They're fine."

"I want to see them," El said as she entered. Robin closed the door and relocked it. When she turned, Eloise took her into a hug that said so much more about what had happened that day. Robin felt El's shudder move from her chest into Robin's, and while she wanted to cry and she wanted the whole story right now, she simply held Eloise together for a few moments.

She cleared her throat and said, "I put them in my bed. I wasn't going to sleep anyway, and they didn't want to be on the second floor. It worked out, because then Charlie and Ginny came. They're upstairs."

El stepped back and nodded. She faced Aaron, laced her fingers through his, and together they padded down the hall and turned left. Robin followed them, wrapping her arms around herself.

She couldn't believe what had transpired today. She'd talked to AJ, who'd spoken to Matt on the phone from jail, for over an hour. She'd tried texting Alice, but she only got back a terse response that had said, *Yes, they're all here, and yes, I'm getting them out.*

She hadn't heard from her since. She'd learned about dinnertime that Kristen and Kelli had gathered at AJ's house, but she didn't want to pack up six kids and join them. She'd ordered pizza, which had taken forever to come, and she'd stayed glued to her phone while Mandie and Ginny spearheaded game night to help everyone stay calm and have fun.

"Robin?" Charlie whispered, and she turned away from the hallway and back toward the stairs.

"What's going on, Charlie?" she asked. "Are you okay?"

"I heard someone knocking." He finished coming down the stairs, and though he stood a foot taller than Robin and he'd turned seventeen a few months ago, right now, he looked like a frightened rabbit. She got a healthy reminder that he was just a kid, and she wrapped him in a hug.

"It was Aaron and Eloise," she said. "They went to check on their kids, and then I hope to talk to them."

"Have you heard from my mom?"

"No, sweetie. I'm sorry."

"I'm sure she's all right," Charlie said, grinding his voice through his throat. "If Aaron and Eloise are here, she can't still be at the station, right?"

Robin's phone began to buzz in her hand, and she stepped back from Charlie to look at it. "It's her now," she said. "Should I put her on speaker?"

The blue light from her phone illuminated Charlie's hopeful face, and he nodded. Robin swiped on the call and tapped the speaker button. "Alice," she said, her voice still somewhat muted. She stepped into the office to hopefully keep the call from echoing up the stairs and back to the bedrooms. "Charlie was just asking about you."

"He's still awake?" Alice asked, and she sounded like the same old Alice she'd always been.

"Eloise just got here," Robin said, avoiding the picture window that looked out over the front yard. The deep of the night scared her for some reason. "I think the knocking woke him up." She glanced at Charlie, who remained standing in front of her desk as Robin sat behind it.

"Where are you?" Robin asked.

"I was hoping to go with Arthur," Alice said, finally sounding a bit uneasy. "I wanted to know how the twins were. How everyone is."

"I think we're all about the way you'd expect us to be. Shocked."

"It's all worked out," Alice said. "I mean, it's not all worked out, but Yancey and Matt left a half an hour ago. They should be home by now. Shad went with them, because Kelli is staying at AJ's."

"Mm."

"Arthur stayed with me, but he could've left a while ago. Aaron and El were the last to leave. I mean, besides their night crew."

Robin heard footsteps, and she and Charlie looked toward her office door at the same time. Eloise entered first, followed by Aaron. "It's Alice."

"What happened?" Robin asked.

Eloise started the story with the woman who'd arrived

to unpack her toiletries. Aaron filled in most of the vital police bits, especially after they'd arrested her and taken her to the station for questioning.

The dots had connected to Marilyn Benson, and then to Polly Baldwin, and then to Nathan Baldwin. "Because of his position in the city," Alice said. "They decided to bring in everyone who even touched him. So Arthur is Nathan's next-door neighbor. Shad works in the office right next door to him, and they have a close friendship. They run money through the city—and to be honest, I'm not sure Shad's completely out of the woods yet."

Aaron shook his head and said, "I don't think he is," in a quiet voice. During the story, he and Eloise had taken the two chairs in front of Robin's office. Charlie had retreated to the couch and sat down. "I don't think I am either," Aaron said.

"What?" Robin asked. "Aaron, that can't be true."

"They've put me on administrative leave," he said. "Paul's going to run the investigation into what I knew— what anyone in the department knew—and when. I mean, El and I had Polly and Nathan over for dinner only a few weeks ago. We could've been conspiring with them, you know?"

"We weren't," Eloise said firmly. "That was the most mind-numbing night of my life."

"Yes, but then we knew about Polly's company, right?" Aaron smiled at Eloise, and it seemed so out of place that Robin found it romantic.

"Anyway, they brought in everyone who'd been getting deliveries from Marilyn," Alice said. "Every employee in her beauty business. Everyone from Cove Creations—"

"That's Polly's company," Eloise said.

"Everyone who Nathan Baldwin started naming— that's how Arthur got picked up," Alice continued. "Matt and Yancey had already been questioned in the past, and they hadn't mentioned that they'd taken a delivery from Benson Beauty several months ago. I guess someone thought that might be them trying to hide something." Alice sighed. "In short, they brought in over sixty people, and they have a fraction of that in terms of manpower and interviewing space. It took a while to get through everyone."

She paused, and Robin sensed something else needed to be said, but no one wanted to say it.

"Laurel insisted on talking to everyone, even if they'd been interviewed by someone else," Aaron said. He cleared his throat. "She's a good cop."

Alice and Eloise remained silent, and Eloise even folded her arms.

"She did her job," Alice said. "I just...she seemed so cold, Aaron, don't you think? And I honestly don't think she believed anything anyone said. I think she thinks they're all guilty in some way."

"Detectives have to detach themselves from the case

and the elements in it," Aaron said softly. "That includes the people."

"I—We know her," Eloise said. "She knows us. She's been spending time with us for months. Almost a year. I just don't see how she could've looked at Shad the way she did, demanding to know if he'd been laundering money through the city budget and accounts to hide the drug activity."

Robin sucked in a breath. "She did that?"

"She accused Matt and Yancey of the same thing," Alice said. "In the end, I told her she better charge them with something and there better be evidence, or we better get to leave. She has no evidence."

"Yet," Aaron said. "It'll take her some time to go through everything they took from City Hall and those two warehouses."

"They're not going to find anything on Shad or Matt," Eloise said. "They're not money launderers." She shook her head, her disgust at the very idea apparent. Robin couldn't imagine either one of them doing anything illegal either, but she remained silent.

"Where's Laurel now?" she asked, because she did care about Laurel. Eloise had spoken true; they'd been friends with her for a while now, and Robin had a particularly close relationship with her that had bloomed and strengthened as they planned her wedding together. She knew Alice was close with Laurel too, and Eloise had been making an effort to get to know her well, since she worked with Aaron so closely.

"She was still at the station when we left," Aaron finally said. "She and Thom were in my office with Paul."

"I'm going to petition that Paul be removed, by the way," Alice said. "It's not right that he and Laurel are dating *and* they're leading this investigation together. It's a conflict of interest."

"Internal Affairs will do it," Aaron said, reaching up to rub his hand over his eyes. "Paul will just get debriefed."

"And he'll tell Laurel," Alice said firmly. "No, that's not happening. Who's behind him?"

"Uh, Lester Stone," Aaron said. "He's a good cop too." He sounded so tired. "They're all good cops, Alice."

"I'm sure they are," she said briskly. "Listen, it's late. We just got to Arthur's. You're with your girls. Let's all get some sleep and talk later."

"Yes, I'm exhausted," Eloise said.

"Robin, the twins are okay there?"

She looked at Charlie, who raised his head and nodded. "They're fine, Alice. They're so great to have around. They kept the younger kids busy with games tonight, and Charlie ordered pizza and cleaned it all up." Her heart squeezed with love for Alice and her children. "They're fine here. We'll sleep late tomorrow, and I'll make pancakes and bacon around ten. Everyone should come."

"Text it out," Alice said. "Everyone's on Diamond, so I'm sure they'll all come."

Even Laurel? Robin wondered, but she didn't ask. The call ended, and she took Eloise and Aaron upstairs to the last remaining guest bedroom. Once they were settled, and Charlie had gone back to bed, Robin retreated back to the couch.

She wanted Duke's strong arms around her. She wanted his comforting voice in her ear, whispering that everything would be okay. She wanted to have his anchoring spirit near her, because without him, she tended to spin wildly out of control.

Breakfast at my house at ten, she texted to the group thread, not removing Laurel from it or starting a new one. If she wanted to come, she should.

Robin didn't think in a million years that Laurel would show her face at breakfast in the morning. A sigh pulled through her whole body, and she lay back down and repositioned the blanket over herself.

She kept her phone in her palm, both of them pressed to her chest. The vibration from a text snapped her eyes open, and she lifted the device to read Laurel's message.

It had come only to her, and it read, *I'm so sorry for everything, Robin. I understand if you don't want to finish the wedding. I can't imagine anyone will talk to me again. That's okay, and I don't blame them. Sorry again.*

Robin's fingers flew across the screen, and she sent

reassuring text after reassuring text. Surely everyone would forgive Laurel. She was only doing her job.

But Robin hadn't had a loved one take to the station, held for hours, and then questioned and accused of helping move drugs through the cove. How would she feel if she had? Her chest tightened at the mere memory of Laurel saying that Duke could be bringing in drugs on his fishing boat, and she swallowed the lump that had formed in her throat.

Laurel never texted back.

THIRTY-TWO

E loise moved through her days as if underwater. Everything seemed blue and gray, and people's words seemed to take a long time to enter her ears and make sense of. She got up and went to the inn, as she usually did.

Aaron came with her for the first week, and they brought the girls too. He'd take them to the beach during the busy times, and they'd stay and eat dinner with the guests. Life seemed so normal in some ways, but completely warped in others.

AJ had started a text string without Laurel on it, but Eloise texted her privately and told her the location of the Wednesday lunches. Two had passed now, and Laurel hadn't come to either. She hadn't even responded to any of Eloise's texts.

"Back today," she said as she entered the kitchen, her

voice sounded warbled, as if she'd tried to speak to her husband under the water. "How are you feeling?"

He looked up from his breakfast of toast, eggs, coffee, and the latest Internet news on his tablet. "Good," he said. "It's going to be fine, El. I'm cleared now."

"Took them long enough," she said.

"Internal Affairs doesn't do anything quickly." He got up from the table with a groan. "Things are settling down. Laurel and Thom will make their case, and they're working with the DA now. There's no more spotlight on me, or Matt, or Shad, or anyone." He put his empty plate in the sink and slid his arm around Eloise.

She poured coffee into her mug, feeling as hot and boiled as it was. "She won't return my texts." She didn't have to name who "she" was. They'd discussed Laurel at length.

"She's embarrassed," Aaron whispered. "She needs time. You *know* Laurel."

"Yes," Eloise said, looking up at her husband. "I do know Laurel, and I know what running away looks like and feels like. I know she's done it before. I know she'd rather just stand in the background than talk. I know she misses us." Her voice cracked, and Eloise shook her head and focused on loading her coffee with sugar. "I know she'd like to come to lunch. I know she'd want to hug Kristen and confess how nervous she is to get married. And I know she wants us all at her wedding, but we haven't even gotten an announcement."

Eloise turned in his arms and held him. "I know she has them, because Robin said they went out last week. I know I hate feeling like this. I know I hate it when you tell me her schedule, so I can come to the station and not run into her." She wetted his shirt with her tears, and to Aaron's credit, he just stood still and held her with all the strength he had.

She gained control of herself and stepped away from him. "I'm sorry to ruin your morning. You're probably nervous too."

"A little," he said. "But El, you never ruin anything for me." He brushed her hair back. "You're going to see your mom today?"

Eloise took a deep breath. "Yes," she said. "The girls have gifts for her for Grace's birthday."

"Tell her happy birthday from me," he said, kissing Eloise's forehead. "I'll bring dinner home tonight for everyone."

"She's coming with us," Eloise said.

"I remember." Aaron reached for his keys and wallet, kissed her again, and walked out into the garage.

Eloise slumped against the counter, her coffee forgotten. She'd sent a lot of texts to Robin over the past couple of weeks, until finally Robin had asked her to stop asking about Laurel. It put Robin in an awkward spot, and Eloise had never felt so bad. She'd taken lunch to Robin and apologized, and they were fine now.

Her phone rang from behind her, and she reached for

it. "Did you forget something?" she asked, already moving toward the garage door.

"No," Aaron said. "I just wanted to let you know that today is also Laurel's day off. She didn't want it to be awkward for me on my first day back."

Confusion ran through Eloise. "Okay," she said. Hadn't she just told him she hated it when he told her Laurel's schedule? Plus, she already had plans to spend the day with her mom on Sanctuary. "I can't bring you lunch today."

He chuckled, and said, "I know, love. Have a good day." He ended the call, and Eloise looked at her phone to make sure the call had been real. For a man of not many words, Aaron calling to tell her Laurel wouldn't be in that day made no sense.

"Eloise," Grace said behind her, and Eloise turned back to the house.

"Yeah, sweetie?" She let the garage door close behind her as she approached the girl. Grace had gotten dressed, which was surprising all on its own. Eloise had learned that the child had to be prodded and poked to do everything, from getting dressed to finding shoes to getting in the tub.

"I can't find my card for your mom."

She also lost things left and right. Eloise smiled at her. "Let's see," she said. "I think you were working on it with your dad last night. It's probably on his desk." She led the way into Aaron's study, a place she didn't normally go. He kept an array of pictures and papers tacked to the back wall, and she could distinctly remember when he'd laid out the evidence of how much money Kelli's father had been taking from women around the cove.

She didn't look at the things hanging there now, and instead, focused on his desk. Outside the window to her left, a lawn mower started. She glanced that way and saw the lawn care company Aaron paid to keep up with the yard.

All at once, a flash of lightning hit her smack dab in the brain. "Lawn care," she said, the card for her mother forgotten. Laurel wouldn't be at the station today, and when she had days off, she spent them in her yard.

"Here it is," Grace said, but Eloise barely heard her.

"Billie," she called, but the teenager probably wasn't up yet. She hurried through the house to her room and knocked as she opened the door. Billie lay in bed, her eyes closed, frowning. "Billie, you don't have to get up. I have to run out for a few minutes, and I'm going to leave Grace with my tablet. Can she watch in here?"

"Yes," Billie said in an annoyed, groggy voice.

"I'll give her headphones."

"Fine, whatever." Billie rolled over, and Eloise turned. She left the door open and rushed to get Grace, the tablet, and the headphones. With the girls all set up for a while, she called a RideShare, quickly changed out of her pajamas, and ran her fingers through her hair. She'd taken one slurp of coffee, though what she was about to do had her heart racing already, when the ride arrived.

She got in the back seat and repeated the address she'd already put into the app. Ten minutes later, the car pulled up to Laurel's house. "Thank you," Eloise said. She got out and stood on the sidewalk, soaking up the sight of the house. The front yard hadn't been mowed yet, and in fact, a few weeds had infested the front flowerbeds.

Somewhere in the neighborhood, a machine ran and it could've been a lawnmower or a chainsaw for all Eloise knew. She started up the driveway and went to the front door. The doorbell rang through the house, but no footsteps accompanied it.

Eloise frowned, her mind spinning. "She's obviously not here," she muttered to herself. "Now what are you going to do?"

"Eloise?"

She spun toward Laurel's voice, the sight of the woman standing there in long jeans, a ratty T-shirt, and gardening gloves the best thing Eloise had seen in weeks. A sob flew from her throat, and she rushed down the stairs and straight into Laurel's arms.

"It's enough," she said through her tears and the lump in her throat. "You can't keep hiding from us. From me. I'm done letting you do that." She stepped back and kept her grip on Laurel's shoulders. "You're coming to Sanctuary with me today. It's Grace's birthday this weekend, and the girls made gifts for my mom. We might go swimming at the inn, or we might go to the beach, or we might just sit on my mom's back deck and sip lemonade. But you're coming."

Laurel hadn't smiled or said anything else yet. She shook her head, everything about her so *sad*. "I can't." She swallowed and cleared her throat. "I have so much yard work to do."

Desperation clogged Eloise's throat as it moved down into her stomach. "Please," she said. "I hate not seeing you. I hate that you won't respond to my texts."

"Eloise." Laurel sighed and stepped back. She focused on her gardening gloves as Eloise let her hands fall back to her sides.

"I'm coming to the wedding," Eloise said, clearing the tears from her eyes. "I'm going to keep texting you until you come back to the group."

Laurel looked up and over Eloise's shoulder. "They don't want me back."

"Of course they do. They just needed some time to process it all. It's been long enough."

"AJ won't forgive me."

"I'm sure she has already," Eloise said, though she hadn't spoken to AJ in almost a week. She'd still been upset at last week's luncheon, but Eloise dismissed that thought. "They know you didn't mean to hurt anyone; that you were just doing your job. You didn't directly accuse any of them or Shad or Matt or anyone of doing anything wrong. You just asked questions. None of them even got arrested."

Laurel shook her head again. "I've had news crews on my lawn for days. They've only just now started clearing out. I need to get the weeds pulled and the grass cut."

"Laurel," Eloise said sharply. "Look at me."

She did, but her gaze didn't hold for long. "I'm sorry, Eloise. Maybe I'm the one who needs more time to process."

"Process what?"

Laurel took a deep breath and blew it out. "What you said is right," she said slowly. "I was just doing my job, and I'm really good at that job. I'm a good cop."

"You are."

"But in order to be a good cop, I have to distrust everyone. I did distrust Matt. And Shad. And Arthur. I thought they could be involved. That's what a good cop does—they look at everyone the same. Anyone could've done it, even if they're the nicest guy in the world, and even if they're engaged to your best friends."

She spoke slowly, deliberately, as if she'd gone over this speech several times before delivering it. "I don't trust anyone, and that's what makes me a good cop. But it also makes me a terrible friend."

"No, it doesn't," Eloise said.

Another car pulled into the driveway, and Eloise watched as Paul got out of the cruiser. He looked at Laurel, wiped his hands down the front of his jeans, and then smiled at Eloise. "Good morning, El." He moved right to Laurel's side and put his arm around her. "You okay, baby?"

"Yes," Laurel said, lifting her chin and meeting Eloise's eyes fully for at least a couple of seconds. "I'm sorry, Eloise. Tell them I'm sorry, but I'm not...tell Grace happy birthday from me." With that, she turned and went into the garage, leaving Eloise to face Paul.

"She's seeing a counselor," he said quietly. "This has been really hard for her."

"I know that," Eloise said, not bothering to keep her voice down. Tears filled her eyes again. "She doesn't have to punish herself like this. Everyone would welcome her back, I just know it."

Paul smiled and wrapped her in a hug. "You're an amazing friend," he whispered. "It's so good to see you."

"Aaron's back at work today," she said against his shoulder.

"I know," Paul said. "I'm here to try to get Laurel to go in for the party at lunch." He pulled back and grinned at Eloise. "You might have broken the ice for me to do that."

Eloise looked into the garage, but Laurel had walked right through it and into the back yard. "Good luck, Paul." He'd need it, and Eloise added a prayer to that as she rode back home to get the girls up and ready to go see her mother.

THIRTY-THREE

R obin would need bionic fingers by the time she finished texting everyone who needed a text. *Can't wait*, she sent to her husband, along with a few heart emojis. Duke would be home next week, and Robin couldn't wait.

Laurel's wedding was the last big event she had before the calendar moved into winter. She'd gotten the girls off to school alone, just as she had last year. Once the wedding finished today, Robin planned to wear pants with an elastic waist, drink all day if she wanted to, and count down the minutes until Duke docked in the cove.

Then, she'd have to sober up, put on real pants, and get back to work. She had a Halloween party to plan for the largest corporation in Five Island Cove, a female-owned and run candle company, and then she was looking forward to a slower holiday season.

Any news from you and Arthur? she sent to Alice. They hadn't spoken of much else besides Laurel and the arraignment of Nathan Baldwin since Alice had told her she was engaged. She'd announced it at the next luncheon, and Robin had dutifully told Laurel.

She opened that text string next and said, *I'll be at the Slipper by ten. Everything we need is there, so just bring yourself and your police dress, and we'll be good to go!*

She smiled and added, *You're getting married today, Laurel. It's going to be so amazing.*

Laurel would respond to business texts, but she'd clammed right up over the personal ones in the past few weeks. Robin sighed as the message she got back was, *Thanks, Robin. See you at ten,* and nothing more.

Everything felt stuffed and stilted when it came to Laurel, and Robin didn't know what to do about it. Eloise had tried going over there. She texted Laurel every day now.

Her fingers flew as she sent a text to the group. *Everyone should be at The Glass Slipper by eleven-thirty, ready to go. If you want to get ready there, that's fine. There's tons of room, and you can show up any time after ten. Laurel and I will be there then.*

She sent the message, and when she didn't get immediate responses—besides Eloise, who said, *I'll be there at ten!*—Robin suspected the others might not come to the wedding at all.

That horrible thought had been gnawing away at her

for days. Weeks. She couldn't shake it, and she couldn't fathom it at the same time.

She sent another text to Alice. *You're coming to the wedding, right?*

I don't know, Alice sent back, so she'd seen the other messages. *And I don't know about Arthur either. We need to make a plan.*

Yes, Robin said. *You do.*

She navigated over to Kelli's individual text string and send the same message to her she'd sent to Alice. *You're coming to the wedding, right?*

Kelli didn't answer, and Robin repeated the message to every single person, individually. Kristen. AJ. Jean. Even Lisa.

Robin was an excellent lecturer, and this distance and silence between them and Laurel was honestly exhausting. She tapped out what she hoped would be something to make them feel guilty for the way they were behaving, and she sent it to every single one of them. She didn't care if they didn't want to talk to her after this. She would *never* abandon a friend on her wedding day.

She silenced her phone and got in the shower. When she got out, she saw Eloise had called, and she called her back. "You sent a lecture to Alice?" Eloise asked in lieu of hello.

"She deserves it," Robin shot back. "I sent one to everyone. They're all acting like babies. You and I are the only ones who seem to understand Laurel was *doing her job*. Nothing bad happened to any of them! It's time to move on, for crying out loud."

Eloise said nothing, and Robin decided she didn't care about that either. "I'm getting dressed," she said. "I have to check on the girls and about fifty pieces of glassware. I'll see you at the Slipper."

"Okay," Eloise said quietly, and Robin ended the call. Maybe she'd gone a little overboard in the lecture. Part of her cared, but another part of her simply wanted everyone to come together and make things right. They couldn't do that if no one would *talk*.

Tears filled her eyes, and she pressed them back. She finished getting ready, right down to her flawless makeup and her new, shiny red heels. She went out into the kitchen to find Mandie and Jamie already dressed as well, and she drew them both into a hug.

"Oh, I love you guys," she said. "Promise me that we'll never stop talking. If things go bad, if something happens, we *have* to sit down and talk about it." She drew back and looked at them. "Okay? Without conversation, things die."

"Okay, Mom," Jamie said.

"They're not coming to the wedding?" Mandie asked.

"I don't know," Robin said, helplessness clouding her thoughts. "I honestly don't know."

Half an hour later, she arrived at The Glass Slipper. She parked her van right out front, and the three of them started unloading. By ten, she had everything in the bridal room. Everything was getting put together in the main hall, where the ceremony and buffet would take place.

She stood in the doorway of it, the wall of windows down both sides bringing in brilliant sunshine that made The Glass Slipper the treasure it was. Claudio, the owner, worked on a ladder to hang flowers from the ceiling, and the whole place would look like a scene straight out of *Cinderella* when he finished.

Across the hall from her, Robin focused on the altar. Laurel and Paul had chosen a pattern for the fabric that emulated their jobs, and all the peach-colored police badges did was remind Robin why so many of her friends wouldn't be there that day.

She'd gotten several texts back from them after she'd laid into them, but she hadn't read any of them. Cowardly, she supposed, but she had a job to do that day too, and she wasn't going to let their negativity and refusal to forgive infect her.

"Everything is okay?" Claudio asked, and Robin put her professional smile on her face.

"Yes, everything is wonderful," she said, turning as the first scent of food met her nose. "The buffet goes along the left side," she said, pointing the way for the chefs as they came streaming in.

The windows on that side actually opened out onto a gorgeous patio and then the beach, and as Robin watched, someone began setting up tables outside too.

Everything was going to be perfect for this wedding—

except the fact that Robin and Eloise would be Laurel's only friends there.

"Where is she?" Robin asked, pacing in the bride's room. Her daughters stayed busy on their phones on a couch in front of the windows, but Eloise paced with her.

"Why won't she answer?" Eloise lowered her phone. "You try again."

"She's not going to pick up," Robin said, about to crack. "I can't believe Laurel isn't here. I can't *believe* she'd do this to Paul."

"When's the last time you talked to her?" Eloise asked.

Robin sighed, because they'd been over this already. "This morning. She texted this morning. She said she'd be here at ten." A quick glance at her phone told Robin the time had ticked past eleven. The wedding started in less than an hour.

"Is Aaron with Paul?"

"Yes," Eloise said, her voice a ghost of itself. "Should I go tell him?"

"I honestly don't know anymore." Robin stopped walking and faced the beach outside. She simply wanted to fly away and never come back. This wedding was supposed to be the second-biggest event of the year, behind Eloise and Aaron's wedding. The entire police force was coming, as they didn't seem to have any problem with what Laurel had done to bring down the biggest drug conspiracy the cove had ever seen.

They'd found over five hundred pounds of meth in the Cove Creations warehouse, and Nathan Baldwin was facing a dozen charges, as was Marilyn Benson, and a handful of hotel owners. Laurel had literally cracked the case and provided a safer environment for kids of every age, their parents, and the whole community.

And yet, her friends remained silent.

Unbelievable, Robin thought. "What if she doesn't show up?"

"I'm calling her again," Eloise said, but Robin had lost hope. All she could see was waste—a waste of her time and energy on this wedding. A waste of Laurel and Paul's money. A waste of food.

The complete waste of a year, as Laurel had become such an integral part of all of their lives. How could everyone just throw that away?

Behind her, the door opened, and Robin spun that way, her heart pounding like a jackhammer. Kristen walked in, with Jean and Rueben right behind her, and Robin sobbed as she ran toward her.

"You came," she said, wrapping Kristen into her arms. "My goodness, you came. Thank you for coming."

"Of course I came," Kristen said. "Didn't you read my texts?"

Robin couldn't admit that she hadn't, because she was

still so stunned Kristen had come. Of course she would, though, because Kristen was the ultimate example of forgiveness and kindness.

"Where's Laurel?" Jean asked, and Robin released Kristen to face her.

"We don't know," Robin said, searching their faces. "You haven't seen her, have you?"

THIRTY-FOUR

Laurel sat in her police cruiser, wishing she'd driven another car. At the same time, everything she needed for the wedding had been loaded into this car last night, and it made no sense to drag it all out and into a RideShare.

She saw the curtains flicker in the window, and she closed her eyes. *Make it right, then.* The words ran through her head in Dr. Adams's voice, and Laurel couldn't put off what she needed to do for another day.

She did want her friends back; she'd told her therapist that several times. Finally, Dr. Adams had told her to *make it right, then. Do the work, Laurel. You don't get anything if you don't do the work.*

Drawing a deep breath, Laurel focused on this moment. The one right in front of her. The one where the car was too hot, and the radio too loud. The one where her throat itched, and her eyes burned. The one where everything relaxed, and her shoulders finally went down.

Leaving her phone in the car, Laurel got out of it and headed for the porch. The front door opened before she even reached the steps, and Matt Hymas came out of his house. For a moment, Laurel thought he'd turn her away, but instead, he smiled.

"It's about time you came by," he said, leaning against the top pillar.

"I'm so sorry, Matt," she said. She climbed the steps while he watched her, and while she knew Matt, she couldn't say they were best friends. She stepped toward him awkwardly and hugged him. "I hope you can forgive me."

"There's nothing for me to forgive," he said.

She stepped away and nodded. "How's AJ?"

"She's right through there," he said. "Go see for yourself."

Laurel braced herself, feeling every muscle from her heel to her shoulder tense. She relaxed them one by one as her breath whooshed out of her mouth. "Okay." She walked inside while Matt stayed out, and the scent of sausage met her nose.

"She's here," Lisa said, and she tossed the kitchen towel in her hand on the counter. "Hello, Laurel." She approached and sort of grabbed onto Laurel in a second awkward hug. "AvaJane, she's here."

445 WEDDINGS AND A BABY   445

"I heard," AJ said, coming down the hall with her son in her arms. "Would you?" She passed Asher to Lisa, who cooed at him as she grinned at the baby. She sighed and looked at Laurel.

Her heartbeat quivered at the sight of the tall, beautiful woman. "I'm so sorry," she said, her eyes darting to movement in the office. Alice appeared, with Kelli right behind her. "Oh, you're all here."

"You asked us to come," Alice said.

"I just...I did, yes." Laurel missed Alice with a strength she didn't understand. "I'm so sorry, Alice. I didn't know Arthur lived next-door to Nathan. I didn't mean to get him in trouble, or cause you so much work."

Alice sighed and looked at Kelli.

"I'm sorry, Kelli," Laurel said. She'd been practicing her sorry's for days. She'd said it in a text, and she'd left the group message to give people time and room to find their own way through the chaos the case had caused.

Right now, all she could do was apologize. "I'm really sorry," she said again. "I didn't know it would go to Nathan, and I didn't know it would paint Shad in a bad light." She faced AJ, who intimidated her the most, though she wished someone else would say something.

She told herself she didn't expect them to say it was okay, because it wasn't. "I'm not great at being friends," she said. "That's an excuse, but it's also real, because if we weren't friends before all of this, I wouldn't be here apologizing. I'm good with cases. I'm good with not letting personal feelings get in the way." Her voice broke, so maybe she wasn't all that good at that.

She cleared the emotion away. "I've had some experience with putting my feelings aside and soldiering on. But I wanted to apologize. I wanted to explain that everything happened way too fast. The whole force was called in, and the next thing I knew, we were bringing in anyone who'd even looked at Nathan Baldwin in the past year."

She tucked her hands in her jeans pockets, noting that none of them were dressed for a wedding. Her heart thrashed painfully against her ribcage at the thought of getting married without them there to see it. She owed so much to this group of women who'd taken her under their wing, loved her, and healed her.

"I hope you can forgive me one day, but I know better than most that relationships aren't the same after something like this. They might mend, but they also might not, and no matter what, it won't be the same." She nodded, her piece said. "That's all. That's all I can say."

She smiled at Lisa and Asher, and surprisingly, they both smiled back. "Okay, well, I'm sure Robin's beside herself that I'm not at The Glass Slipper. She's probably called a dozen times." Laurel took a step toward the still-open front door. "I'll...see you around."

Her foot had just touched the porch when Alice said, "Laurel, get back in here."

She turned, unsure of what she'd just heard. "What?"

Alice rushed at her and grabbed her in a hug. "Robin

can wait," she whispered. When she pulled back, Laurel saw the hint of tears in her eyes and a smile as wide as the ocean. "Come help me pick my shoes to go with my dress. You were going to do that, remember?"

Laurel's mind spun. "What?" she asked again.

"I forgive you," Alice said. "I've been trying to figure out how to text you or call you for a couple of weeks now, and I'm sorry I haven't figured out how."

"Me too," Kelli said, her voice wavering. "It took me a while to realize that of course you had to look at Shad as closely as you did. He could've been hiding money in all kinds of places. He understood what you were doing more than I did." She exchanged a glance with AJ, and when Alice stepped back, Kelli took her place and hugged Laurel.

"He's almost here, and he's bringing my clothes for the wedding."

"What?" Laurel wasn't ever going to say anything different again. "You're coming to the wedding?"

"I wouldn't miss it," Kelli whispered. She stepped back, her chin wobbling. "I'm just so bad at talking to people after a conflict. Or before. Or during. I'm getting better, but I'm bad at it."

"I'm worse," AJ said, her smile flashing so fast Laurel barely saw it. "I was *so* mad at you, Laurel. It felt like you were trying to take something from me I'd waited for and worked for for *so* long."

"Babe," Matt said, but AJ held up her hand. "It took

me the longest to understand that you weren't. And then, I found myself in the same boat as some of the others. I wasn't brave like Eloise, and I couldn't figure out how to talk to you."

Laurel stared at the three of them. "I don't know what to say."

"You're going to come help me with my shoes," Alice said, grinning. "Arthur's going to be here soon, and I need to at least be dressed." She hooked her arm through Laurel's, who stumbled forward to go with her.

"Look," Kelli said. "Shad's here, so you can help me get dressed too. I still don't know how to zip up that gown."

Laurel looked over her shoulder as Shad came up the steps, several bags swinging from his arms and draped over his shoulder. "That ride from Pearl was a bear," he said. "I'm about to drop these."

Matt lunged toward him to help, and Kelli stepped past Laurel and Alice too.

"I'm really sorry," AJ said, taking Laurel from Alice and hugging her. "You're a good person, Laurel. You did the right thing. Please don't feel bad about it anymore."

"I don't know how to not feel bad about it," she whispered.

"Did you take down the drug lord?" AJ asked, turning as her son started to fuss.

"Yes," Laurel said.

"Then you don't have anything to feel bad about."

"I made a lot of people's lives hard," Laurel said. "Including yours."

"For less than a day," AJ said. "And yes, I was scared, and yes, I was mad. But I got over it. You should too."

"You make it sound so easy," Matt said, chuckling. He shook his head as he passed. "I'm putting this stuff in the bedroom."

"Come on," AJ said. "Let's go get ready, and I'll catch you up on everything Asher's been doing the past three weeks."

"Oh, boy," Alice said in a dry tone. "I think Laurel would rather hear about the new restaurant going in by dress shop. They did cause the pipe to burst right before El's wedding, but it's all fixed up now, and there's a new Southern barbecue place going in."

"Wow," Laurel said. "Do you think they'll stay in business?"

"Who knows?" Kelli asked from behind Laurel. "People here don't eat anything but lobster, I swear. They need to branch out."

Laurel smiled, and it felt so good to do that. "Guys," she said as she got herded into the master bedroom. "I have to get my phone and call Robin."

"Nope," Alice said, stepping out of her khakis. "Kelli will text her. Now, which of these shoes is going to look better with my dress?" She shimmied into the dress and then put on one bright blue heel and one white one.

"Blue," Laurel said, and Alice nodded to herself in the mirror.

"Yes, I think so too." She met Laurel's eyes, and while everything didn't magically go back to the way it had been before she'd sat across the table from Alice and Arthur and asked him questions about the packages he'd taken in for Nathan, it suddenly improved.

She detected no malice in Alice. No disappointment. No deceit. She'd truly forgiven Laurel.

Kelli laughed as she said she'd give Alice a hundred bucks if she'd wear one of each shoe as she walked down the aisle, and Laurel found herself joining in with a giggle.

"Thank you," she said as they all quieted. "Thank you for forgiving me."

They converged on her and hugged her, and Laurel closed her eyes and basked in the friendship and love from these three women.

"My word," Alice said. "Is that the time? Robin is going to rip you apart." She bent and hurried to get her shoes in the right boxes.

Laurel saw the clock, and how close it had gotten to eleven. "I thought Kelli texted her."

"I forgot," Kelli said, picking something up off the bed. "I'm not even sure where my phone is..."

"Let's go," Laurel said. "I'll call her from the car."

"I'm sorry," she said the moment she entered the bride's room. She'd already apologized to Robin in the car, and she grinned as she pushed the door all the way open and held it for AJ, Kelli, and Alice to walk through.

"That's my cue to leave," Rueben said, and joy filled Laurel that he and his wife had come. She grabbed him in a hug as he tried to pass, and neither of them said anything.

Laurel hugged Jean too, and then Kristen—the woman who'd been so accepting, so caring, and so loving—enveloped her in a hug. "I'm so glad you're here."

"I am too," Kristen said. "You'll answer my texts now, won't you?"

"Yes," Laurel said, another wave of guilt cutting through her. "I'll answer texts now."

"Good," Eloise said, practically punching the word at her. "Because I'm tired of texting into an abyss." She took Laurel from Kristen, her smile as genuine as they came. "I've been so worried about you. You do know I drive by your house every day, right? Just to make sure you're still alive? Aaron is *so* sick of me asking about you."

Laurel let her eyes fill with tears as she nodded. "I'm sorry, Eloise. Really, I am. I just...didn't know how to build the bridge."

"Yes, yes," Robin said, arriving on the scene. "Eloise is an excellent bridge-builder. Let's get you dressed." She was all business, and Laurel didn't want to cause her more stress.

Everyone she wanted to be at the wedding was there, and her mother entered the room a moment later. "Oh, good. She's here."

"Mom." Laurel turned away from Robin and the policewoman skirt she held to hug her mom. She'd told her where she was headed that morning, and the relief she felt at the forgiveness of her friends overcame her.

She sagged into her mother's hug as she said, "Paul is so excited to marry you."

Paul.

"Yes," Laurel said, trying to focus her thoughts on Paul. "Let's not make him—or anyone else—wait longer than we said they'd have to."

From there, a flurry of activity happened around Laurel. Robin helped her get dressed. She sat in a chair and let her mother braid her hair into a crown while Alice and AJ applied her makeup.

"We're five minutes late," Robin said, rushing over with the bouquet. She handed it to Laurel and backed up, a fond smile filling her face. "You are simply stunning. It's time to get married, Laurel." She turned on her heel and said, "Places, everyone. Get in line, please. It's time."

Laurel stayed near the windows while everyone else filed into place. She met her father at the door, where he kissed her forehead and said, "I'm so happy for you, Laurel."

"Thank you, Dad," she said. Everything about this

wedding was different than her first. Just having her parents there was a huge difference, as she'd been forced into a previous marriage against her will. The whole thing had taken a few minutes at some city building in mainland Massachusetts.

Now, she stepped into the mouth of the hall and looked out into the vast space before her. Everyone had gotten to their feet, and some marching, police music with a hint of bagpipe played over the speaker system. White, yellow, and peach flowers drifted from the ceiling, creating an ethereal feel to the room.

"Ready?" her dad asked while Laurel was still scanning the faces in the audience. She saw her friends down at the end of the aisle, all standing in the first couple of rows now. She saw Eloise's mother, and Robin's, and all of AJ's family members.

Every cop she knew—and every one she didn't—stood there in their uniforms, their hats tucked under their arms. They wore gloves and dress stripes, and Laurel absolutely felt like she belonged to the department.

Thom stood with his wife right in the very back row, closest to her, and he saluted her with a giant smile on his face.

Her eyes traveled down the length of both walls made of windows, where the oceanic breeze came in to keep the air cool and touch everything with the scent of sea and salt.

She saw Paul standing at the altar, and her view narrowed to just him. His smile. His dark eyes shining with joy. His pressed and perfect uniform.

"Yes," she said through a dry throat. "I'm ready."

THIRTY-FIVE

"Here's what I think," Kelli said as she set down a plate with two pieces of wedding cake on it. She sat in her chair and looked at Alice. "You and I should get married together."

Alice picked up her fork and took a bite of one of the pieces of cake. She leaned closer to Kelli and further from her fiancé. "What are you talking about?"

"You don't want a big wedding," Kelli said. "You haven't scheduled anything. I don't want a big wedding. I haven't scheduled anything. I just want to get it done."

"Okay," Alice said slowly, glancing around the room where people danced. Laurel and Paul looked like they'd been haloed in heavenly light, and Kelli loved the feelings of happiness and bliss she could only find at a wedding.

"So we do it at the same time. Get one pastor. Set up

one wedding. I'll go first it you want. Then you can get married. Then, I don't know. We move on with our lives."

Alice trained her eyes on Kelli again. "I've already talked to Robin about doing something in her back yard."

Kelli's heart fell to her toes and then rebounded back into place. "Perfect," she said. "Can I just tag along?"

A smile spread across Alice's face. "I don't see why not." She leaned back and looked at Arthur. "And it wouldn't be tagging along."

"You two look like you're planning a bank heist," he said, also glancing around as if they were doing something heinous. "What are you talking about?"

"Having a dual wedding in Robin's back yard," Alice said.

"Next weekend," Kelli added, and Alice swung her head toward her, her eyes wide and filled with shock.

"Next weekend?"

"What are you two waiting for, honestly?" Kelli speared a bite of the chocolate cake and put it in her mouth. She watched Alice and Arthur have a silent conversation, and then she turned to Shad. "Would you marry me next weekend? In Robin's back yard?"

"Sure," he said easily. "I can go get my parents on Friday night. Fly back with them." He looked at Alice and Arthur. "Are they joining us?"

"This is even more insane than what I proposed to Robin," Alice said, but her smile had returned. "I told her I just wanted to get it done, and then we could eat in the yard and celebrate together."

"Sounds perfect," Kelli said. "I'll order the food if you want."

"Do you even have a dress?" Alice asked.

"No," Kelli said. "I figured I could find something...somewhere."

Alice started to laugh, and Kelli joined in. She really didn't want anything fancy, and she'd talked to Shad several times about just meeting him in City Hall and tying the knot one afternoon, just the two of them.

Then, the idea to ask Alice to do a dual ceremony had occurred to her. Seeing Laurel and Paul and their big extravaganza... Kelli did not want that. She'd told Shad that twenty minutes ago while they'd been dancing.

"There's Robin," Kelli said. "I'm going to ask her right now."

"Kel," Alice said, but she'd already gotten to her feet. She waved at Robin, who came walking over in her professional stride, heels a-clicking against the stone floor.

"What's up?" She surveyed the table. "How's the cake?"

"Good, great," Kelli said, not wanting to talk about cake. Her heart raced, and she felt a little out of control. "Alice and I want to get married next weekend."

"Not to each other," Alice said quickly. "But a dual ceremony. In your back yard. Like we talked about."

Robin's eyes bulged to the point that Kelli giggled. "What do you think?" she asked. "Alice and I will arrange everything." She met Alice's eye, who nodded. "I'll even send a housekeeper."

"I have housekeepers," Eloise said, arriving at the table. "What are we doing with them?"

"Cleaning Robin's house," Alice said, popping another bite of cake into her mouth.

"For our weddings." Kelli indicated herself and Alice. "Next Sunday. We'll all gather there. We'll get married. We'll eat. It'll be glorious."

"Oh, I like this idea," Eloise said, smiling around at everyone.

"Duke is coming home Saturday," Robin said, and Kelli saw her wedding-in-a-week plunge toward the earth.

"Then the Sunday after that," Alice said, and Kelli whipped her attention right back to Robin.

She started to nod slowly. "The Sunday after that would work."

Kelli jumped to her feet and hugged Robin. "Thank you," she said. "Thank you, thank you, thank you." Breathless, she stepped back and added, "We'll take care of everything, right, Alice?"

"Yep," she said, reaching for another bite of cake. "Though, Robin, you might want to help Kelli with a dress. She literally said she could find something...somewhere."

Robin turned toward her, a look of pure horror on her face. She snapped her mouth closed and then opened it again to say, "Oh, no, honey. That won't do. We'll go shopping tomorrow. I know just the place that will have something for you."

THIRTY-SIX

Alice stepped into her silky, silver dress, a blip of rebelliousness creeping through her at not wearing a white dress to get married. She'd decided she didn't want to spend much money on this wedding, and that wasn't because she didn't love Arthur with the strength of her whole heart.

It was because she did.

She didn't need fancy clothes, fancy food, or fancy flowers.

She only needed him.

And the twins, of course. She'd bought Charlie a new tie to go with his suit, and she'd bought Ginny a new pair of shoes to go with her prom dress from last spring. But Alice had selected her wedding attire from the back of her closet, from the things she hadn't been able to bring herself to throw away after she'd left her life in the Hamptons for this new one on the beaches of Five Island Cove.

The old her would literally be stepping into the future as a new woman in her metallic dress and bright white high heels.

"You're dressed already," Kelli said as she ducked into Robin's bedroom.

"Zip me up," Alice said, grinning at Kelli in the full-length mirror. "I just started, besides."

Kelli's chilly fingers slid over Alice's shoulders and then did up her dress. "This is a gorgeous dress."

"Thanks," Alice said, smiling at herself in the mirror. "I wore it to a fundraising dinner in the city once, with Frank." She could remember that night as vividly as if it were yesterday, and it hadn't been a bad night. Frank had actually spoken to her, and they'd danced a few times. She'd stood with a couple of other wives from her neighborhood, and while she wouldn't call them friends in the way Kelli was, it hadn't been a terrible night.

She stepped into her shoes and reached for the teardrop diamond earrings she'd put on Robin's dresser. With those on, she declared, "Done," and turned to help Kelli pull her dress over her slip.

She wore the traditional white for a wedding, but her dress wasn't frilly or froofy. It would fit through the door just fine, and in fact, it looked a lot like the dresses they'd worn for Laurel's wedding, with lace upon lace, but in white instead of peach.

"Did you get this at Judy's?"

"Yes," Kelli said. "They took off the straps to make it a little more formal."

Alice buttoned up the back of it and brushed invisible dust from her bare shoulders. "You're so pretty," she whispered, pressing her cheek to Kelli's.

Kelli smiled, and she seemed happy and confident, both things Alice knew she'd struggled with.

"Okay, shoes," Kelli said, her voice wavering slightly. "Hand me that box, would you?"

Alice handed her the box, and Kelli pulled out a stunning pair of ruby red slippers. They even sparkled with jewels on every surface, and Alice gasped. "Kelli, those are amazing."

"There's no place like home," she said, putting the shoes on the floor and stepping into them. "Are you sure your dad isn't upset he can't walk you down the aisle?" She titled her head to the side to put in her earring—a single silver hoop that nearly touched her shoulder.

"He's already done it once," Alice said. "He's fine, Kel."

"Okay."

Alice faced the door, waiting for Robin to come through it. "She'll come get us when it's time, right?"

"Yes," Kelli said, perching on the edge of the bed. "Thanks for doing this with me, Alice."

"Are you kidding?" Alice turned back to her. "This is the greatest thing that's ever happened to me."

The door opened, and Robin poked her head in. "Everyone is sitting down. Mandie's playing the music. She'll switch it when she sees you." She smiled and then committed to entering the room. "Wow, look at you two."

Alice cocked her hip and struck a pose. "Don't we look amazing?" She dissolved into laughter. Robin hugged her and Kelli at the same time, and then Eloise came into the room.

"I knew you'd stay and chat," she said. "Just going to get them real quick, my right eye." She joined the group hug, and so did AJ, Kristen, and Laurel. They sighed together, the seven of them, and that only set them all laughing in the next moment.

"Go on, go on," Robin said, stepping back and causing the huddle to break up. She wiped below her left eye. "You're making me cry, and now dinner is going to be late."

"Oh, my goodness," AJ said. "You need to take a chill pill."

"Well, I will once all these blasted weddings are done," Robin sniped back at her. Alice looked at Kelli, and they laughed together again. It was usually Alice and Robin trading jabs, but Eloise joined in as the rest of the women left the bedroom.

They linked arms, and Alice and Kelli followed them into the kitchen and to the back door.

They paused there while their friends took their places up near the altar. There was hardly a front row and a back row, as there were only four rows total. Less than two dozen chairs, though they were all full.

Charlie came to Alice's right side, and Ginny to her left. Parker took Kelli's hand, and they stepped out of the house first.

"I love you guys," Alice murmured as Kelli took her trip down the aisle to a waiting, glowing Shad Webb.

"Love you too, Mom," Charlie and Ginny said together. Then they stepped toward Arthur, who wore pure joy in his smile.

A dozen steps later, her children passed her to him, and he touched his lips to the spot right behind her ear. "You're a stunning bride, Alice."

"Thank you," she murmured, and then they faced the pastor together.

KELLI LOVED WEDDINGS, AND THERE WAS NONE better than her own. She listened to the pastor talk about open communication and forgiveness, both things every marriage needed to succeed. He turned slightly toward her and Shad, and her grip on her soon-to-be-husband's arm tightened. Her legs had been shaking for the past ten minutes, and the moment the pastor said, "I guess you two are first," she calmed.

"Kelli Anne Watkins, do you pledge yourself to Shad

Michael Webb, for now and for all eternity, to be his lawfully wedded wife?"

"I do," she said, and she giggled as she met Shad's eyes. She had never envisioned getting married again, but as the pastor asked him if he'd pledge himself to be her lawfully wedded husband, and Shad said, "I do," Kelli's whole future expanded.

What she'd thought would be there vanished, and the entire slate got wiped clean. She could be anyone now. Go anywhere. Find the joy and happiness and love she'd thought she'd lost when she left New Jersey last year.

"I love you," Shad said, and that brought her back to the present, where she wanted to stay.

"I love you too," she said.

The crowd cheered as they kissed, and Kelli's face heated. She really didn't want the spotlight to shine too brightly on her, and definitely not for too long. Thankfully, there was one more wedding to complete, and the pastor turned to Alice and Arthur to get the job done.

Alice's voice barely rose above the slight breeze playing with the leaves in the trees, but Arthur's "I do," boomed throughout the yard.

"Wow, okay," Alice said, laughing. The pastor barely held it together while he pronounced them husband and wife, and then Arthur dipped Alice practically to the ground to kiss her.

She squealed, and the crowd did too. Kelli laughed along with everyone else, especially when Alice very nearly toppled to the ground as Arthur tried to get her back to a standing position and almost couldn't manage it.

He turned to their small circle of family and friends and raised their joined hands. "I love this woman!" he called, and everyone surged forward to give hugs and congratulations.

Kelli's mother reached her first, and she said, "This was so perfect, Kel. I think we should do something like this for my wedding at Thanksgiving."

"I'm sure we can, Mom." The moment she released her mother, she hugged Shad's mom, who was quite a bit older than her own. "Thank you for coming," she said.

"Oh, honey," his mom said. "We wouldn't have missed this for the world. Shad's been looking for someone like you for so long, and he's been talking about you for ages."

Kelli pulled back and looked into her watery brown eyes. "He has?"

"Oh, yes," she said. "He's so in love with you."

"She's not wrong," Shad said, his arm sliding along Kelli's back. "Come on, Mother. The food is out already, and it's time to eat." He escorted both of them into Robin's house, where sure enough, the food had been laid out, along with all of the fanciest paper goods available.

There was no china, no sterling silver, and no bows. But it was the most perfect wedding in the world to Kelli.

LAUREL WATCHED AJ HUSTLE THROUGH THE CROWD to catch up to Kelli, who hadn't stayed near the altars for very long. Alice still stood there, talking to her dad and step-mom, to Robin's mother, and then stepping over to give Kristen a hug.

Baby Asher babbled in Laurel's arms, and she looked down at the infant. "Your momma will be right back," she said. "She just went to tell her best friend congratulations."

"Look at you with that baby," Paul said, his eyes full of light. He wrapped them both up in his arms. "We want one of these, don't we?"

"You know what?" Laurel asked. "I think I do, and I don't think we have to wait if you don't want to."

"No?" He swayed with them, and Asher *ga-ga-ga'ed* as he reached for Paul's tie.

"No," Laurel said, smiling up at him. "I love you, Paul. You didn't leave my side for a moment when things got really hard, and I think you'll be the best dad in the whole world."

"Mm." He grinned and leaned down to kiss her.

"No kissing now," Robin said, and Laurel broke the kiss. She laughed as she tucked herself into Paul's chest. "We're doing the dancing and kissing later." Robin gave her a bright grin as she went by, Duke stuck to her side.

"Is that true?" Paul asked.

"I don't think Robin jokes about the schedule at a wedding," Laurel said.

"I heard that," Robin called over her shoulder.

"And she doesn't," Alice said as she approached. "We really are dancing later, and I told Robin I wanted to kiss Arthur while we did. So now she's saying it's the dancing, kissing moment of the wedding."

Laurel stepped out of Paul's arms to hug Alice. "You looked better than any bride I've ever seen."

"Even Eloise?" Alice whispered, holding Laurel the way she'd always wanted a sister or a friend to hold her.

"You and Eloise tied," Laurel said, because if there was someone she loved as much as Alice, it was Eloise.

"Boo," Alice said, laughing as she pulled away. "Don't make me cry, Laurel. Today is a happy day."

"Mom," Charlie called, and Alice's attention moved to the back entrance of the house. "Mandie can't find the frappé."

"It's in the freezer in the garage," Alice called. "Come on, you two. We're eating now."

Laurel nodded, but she let Alice and Arthur go by, as well as the rest of Alice's and Kelli's families.

"They love you, Laurel," Paul said, as if he knew the doubts and worries in Laurel's mind.

"I know they do," Laurel said, bouncing little Asher in her arms.

AJ came to the back door, and said, "Laurel, come on. Alice and Kelli want to do toast, but they won't do it without you and Paul." She gestured for them to hurry, and Laurel did finally take the first step out of her row and toward the house.

Toward all of the women she loved, who'd welcomed her into their lives. Who'd forgiven her, and who'd shown her what it meant to be a true friend.

Inside the house, she found everyone gathered around the island in the kitchen, where Kristen lifted her glass first. "To the next round of the Seafaring Girls," she said.

"No way," Laurel said. "Did they vote on Thursday?" Kristen hadn't said anything, but of course, they hadn't had a luncheon yet either.

"They did," Kristen said. "And they voted to bring back the program, and they asked me to be the consultant on the board as they organize the program over the next few months."

"Kristen, that's wonderful." Robin hugged her and raised her glass. "Hear, hear!"

Everyone repeated it, and Laurel picked up a glass of champagne and handed it to Paul before taking one for herself.

"Any other announcements?" Robin asked. "We usually do these at our Wednesday lunches." She looked at Duke as she said it.

"Jean has one," Kristen said, but Jean just shook her head. Laurel's heart went out to the woman, as she didn't possess a mean bone in her body.

"I'll tell it," Rueben said. "We've had a birth mom select our portfolio as the adoptive parents of her baby.

She's not due until February, but we're already going over paperwork, and we'll be flying to North Carolina to meet her in a few weeks."

"That's so great," Laurel said as others gave similar exclamations of joy or congratulations. She lifted her glass again and took another sip.

"Nothing else?" Robin asked. "Okay, let's eat."

Read on for the first couple chapters of The Seafaring Girls, the next book in the Five Island Cove series, for more great friendship and sisterhood fiction that brings women together and celebrates the female relationship.

Alice Kelton got up from her desk when she heard the back door open. The twins were home from school. Or at least one of them was, as Alice glanced at the bright pink sticky note on her computer. *Ginny's working today!* had been scrawled there, in her daughter's handwriting.

She smiled at it and tapped it as she went by the computer on the other side of the desk. "Charlie?" she called as she stepped into the hallway. Down and around the corner into the back of the house showed her that her son had indeed arrived home from school, but he wasn't alone.

His girlfriend, Sariah Page, had come with him, and she currently had her fingers fisted in the collar on his jacket, kissing him.

Alice cleared her throat, and Sariah and Charlie

jumped apart. He looked at her, plenty of panic in his eyes. "Hey, Mom." He cleared his throat too, and she dang near rolled her eyes.

"Didn't think I'd be home?" She folded her arms and glared. "Hello, Sariah."

"Hey, Alice." She hovered half a step behind Charlie. "I should go, Charles. I'll see you tomorrow."

"Okay," he said, following her to the garage exit. They didn't kiss again, and the pretty blonde slipped outside. He faced her again, his usual devil-may-care expression on his face. "I knew you'd be home."

"You seemed surprised."

"I'm a little surprised." He sighed and opened the fridge. "I don't know what to do about Sariah."

Alice scented blood, and she moved in for the kill. "What do you mean?" She strode toward him, telling herself to calm down, move slow. Big movements could scare the teenagers away.

"I mean...I like her. She's pretty. She's smart." He closed the fridge and opened the cupboard, obviously trying to do anything he could not to look at Alice. "But she's also going to NYU in the fall, and...I'm not."

"Ah, I see," Alice said. Charlie had never particularly excelled in academics—except for chemistry. He loved the stuff, and he had applied to Boston University. He'd gotten in too. No scholarship. No nothing. He'd have to pay for all of it, and Alice had helped him look into getting grants to help fund it.

Truth be told, he hadn't even decided if he was going to go or not. She knew one of his New Year's goals was to make a decision for the fall, but only a week into January, and he hadn't done it yet.

Alice was trying not to put any pressure on him. A pressured, cornered Charlie usually wasn't a good thing.

"Plus," Charlie said, and he turned his back on her. Alice sat at the bar, ready for anything. Or so she thought.

"Mandie and I have been talking again," he said, and Alice so wasn't ready for that. She almost toppled off her barstool she flinched so hard.

"What?" she asked, her voice mostly made of air. "Mandie Grover?"

"Yes." Charlie pulled down a box of popcorn and turned toward her. "Can I make this?"

"Sure," she said. Arthur wasn't home from the high school yet, but he loved popcorn as much as Charlie did. Alice was just glad they had something in common, though Arthur got along very well with the twins. He was one of those special breeds of human who actually liked and understood teenagers, and they liked and understood that he just wanted them to be the best they could be.

He'd helped Ginny a lot with her college applications, and she'd gotten into NYU, BU, Yale, and Towson. Charlie had only applied to Boston, and he'd gotten it, so that had spared him from feeling like a failure compared to his sister, something Alice knew he did a lot.

"And?" she prompted. "What about Mandie?"

"I'm thinking...I don't know what I'm thinking."

Alice watched him put the popcorn in the microwave and start it. Her mind whirred like the machine, and she drew a breath. "I think I know what you're thinking."

"What's that, Mom?" He finally faced her, plenty of challenge on his face. He looked so much like his father, but he was much gentler, and much kinder. Alice thanked God for that every day.

"I think you're wishing you didn't have a girlfriend," she said. "Then it wouldn't be so confusing to be friends with Mandie. You might even be able to take her to a dance this spring, and hang out with her in the summer."

Charlie didn't make a face and sigh, which meant Alice was right. He'd never admit it right away, and he simply turned to get out a big bowl for his popcorn. The buttery, salty scent of it started to fill the air, and Alice let the silence fill the spaces between what she'd said.

"Maybe," Charlie said as he opened the microwave and shook the bag of popcorn. "And Mom, you were right about girls."

"Which part?" Alice got to her feet and approached her son. She curled her hand down the side of his face and around to the back of his head.

"They're aggressive," he said. He shook salt all over the popcorn and looked at her again. "Sariah wants to, you know. Do it before we graduate. I told her you'd be home this afternoon, and she still sort of attacked me when we walked in."

Alice narrowed her eyes. "She's being aggressive with you?"

"I mean, I think so," Charlie said. "Maybe it's just because you've talked to me and talked to me about sex, and girls, and I don't know." He did the hefty sigh she'd heard before and walked into the living room.

Alice stayed in the kitchen, almost afraid to move. His girlfriend wanted to sleep with him, and he hadn't done it yet? She wasn't sure if she should rejoice or panic. Usually, the guy had to convince the girl that everything would be okay. Not having that barrier would make everything easier for Charlie.

Her stomach churned, and now the popcorn smelled slightly charred instead of delicious and buttery.

She turned as the garage door opened again, and this time, her husband of four months walked in. "Hey, beautiful," he said, a smile curling the ends of his mouth instantly. He took her into his arms, and Alice pulled on Arthur's strength and stability to use in her own life.

"Hey," she whispered into his shoulder.

He pulled back and looked at her. "Everything okay?" His gaze skimmed further into the house, obviously searching for what had upset Alice.

"Yes," she said firmly. "Everything's fine."

Arthur took his briefcase over to the counter that acted as a credenza and said, "Hey, Charlie. How was school?"

"Great, Arthur," Charlie said, flipping through the channels without looking at his step-father.

Arthur turned back to Alice, and she shook her head. Her son was sitting here, bored out of his mind while he tried to find something to watch on TV, when he could be with his girlfriend. It wasn't that hard to find somewhere for two teenagers to go, not if they were both properly motivated.

Charlie obviously wasn't, and Alice didn't want to disrupt something in the cosmic universe by freaking out about nothing.

Yet, she told herself. She didn't have anything to freak out about yet.

A WEEK LATER, ALICE HUMMED TO HERSELF AS SHE went around the house, picking up socks, shoes, and dishes. No one seemed to be able to get anything where it belonged except for her. She'd needed a break from her case—a nasty dispute between two parents fighting over their kids—so she didn't mind the clutter that had accumulated this week.

She usually made everyone go around on Saturday for a few minutes and help her put the house back together. This week, they'd been busy with Arthur's mother, who didn't have very much time left on this earth. She'd been sick for a while, and Alice would miss her once she finally passed.

The silence in the house filled Alice with peace,

where it had once struck her with fear. She knew now that no one was going to ring her doorbell and judge her the way they did in the Hamptons. She had no images to protect or uphold here. No pretenses to live up to.

She was a busy lawyer who worked from home, with two kids who'd graduate from high school in six short months, a new husband to dote on, and plenty of household chores to keep her busy.

Her phone chimed in her back pocket, one notification after the other, telling her that her friends had started a lively conversation while she'd been in a dead zone picking up plates with dried cheese on them from Ginny's nachos last night.

The device continued to sing at Alice until she put all the dirty dishes in the sink and pulled it from her pocket. "My goodness," she said, swiping to see what was so important.

I'm dying, Eloise had sent. *Billie got asked to Sweethearts today. She's fourteen. Aaron's going to go ballistic. I need all the chocolate I can get to sweeten him up.*

Who asked her? Robin had asked immediately. Now that she wasn't swamped with clients, she had more free time to respond to texts quickly. Not that she hadn't before. Her cellphone was practically sewn to her fingers.

Alice's was too, so she wasn't judging. She did so much business with her phone, and it was easy to get absorbed into it for long periods of time and not even know it.

A boy named Luke Howard, Eloise said. *He's a year older than her, and Aaron's not going to like that.*

It'll be okay, AJ had said. *The Howards live right by us, and they're a good family.*

Agree with AJ, Robin said. *The Howards are good people.*

Aaron's looking them up right now, Laurel sent as Alice watched. She sent a winking emoji, but Alice didn't think she was kidding at all. The Chief of Police would probably run a background check, call them in for finger-printing, and do a deep dive into their past going back generations. He had all the resources to do it.

How wonderful for her, Kristen sent.

Jean chimed in with, *I can help with a dress if she needs one.*

I don't even know if it's formal or not, Eloise said.

It's not formal, Robin said, and she would know. Robin knew everything that happened in the cove, and some-times she irritated Alice. At the same time, there was no one Alice loved more than Robin Grover. *But it's not casual either*, she said. *It'll be best dress. Not jeans. Not prommy.*

Alice didn't really have anything to add to the conver-sation, but she tapped out, *It'll be okay, Eloise. He's got a month to get used to the idea, right?*

Good point, Eloise sent. *I just wish they got along better. He's so protective of her.*

There could be worse things, Kelli said. *How exciting*

for her to be asked. How does she know Luke?

The conversation went on from there, but Alice had work to do. She rinsed the dishes and put them in the dishwasher. She wiped down all the counters and the stove. She straightened all the pillows in the living room and took the kitchen trash out to the big, black can Charlie towed out to the street on Thursdays.

She started a load of laundry, taking Ginny's clean clothes upstairs to her room. She peeked in the twins' bathroom and frowned. She didn't clean their rooms or do their laundry, but she would come up here to make sure the toilet and tub weren't going to rust through or be stained permanently.

Obviously, no one had cleaned this bathroom for a while, and Alice couldn't even remember whose turn it was. The garbage can lid bulged open, and she stepped into the bathroom to collect that.

She opened the lid, her hand already reaching for the sides of the bag that had been pulled over the can. She froze, her breath wheezing into her lungs, at the sight of the pregnancy test sitting there.

It had been used, and it showed only one line.

Not pregnant.

Her heartbeat sounded like a bass drum as it banged through her whole body. Whose was this?

Her mind raced; Sariah had been over to the house just yesterday, along with the rest of the Academic Olympiad team she was on with Charlie. She'd asked to use the bathroom, and since someone else had been in the half-bath off the kitchen, she'd gone upstairs.

Ginny had a boyfriend, but to Alice's knowledge they hadn't slept together.

She pulled in another breath, and the extra oxygen reminded her of the conversation Charlie had had with her last week about Mandie. They'd been talking and texting again—Alice checked his phone regularly—and Mandie had dropped by two or three days ago. She'd talked to Charlie and Ginny together on the front porch for about a half-hour, left a loaf of lemon zucchini bread, and gone home.

Alice didn't recall her coming in the house. Charlie couldn't be sleeping with her...could he?

She reached for the pregnancy test, dislodging some used make-up remover wipes. In her mind, teenagers were so very stupid, because whoever had put this in the trashcan should've done a better job of hiding it. Even if it had been under the make-up remover wipes, Alice probably wouldn't have seen it.

With the stick in her hand, Alice felt like she was swimming outside of her body. Nothing made sense, and questions formed her whole world. Her feet felt like they were slipping down a muddy slope, and she couldn't catch herself.

Bottom line, she needed to know who'd used this pregnancy test. No matter who it was, Alice felt like everything was about to change.

SNEAK PEEK! THE SEAFARING GIRLS CHAPTER TWO:

Jean Shields could not stop crying. Every time she managed it for even a moment, her mind would attack her, and the tears would flow again.

I'm so sorry.

There were so many things those words couldn't make up for. Having a baby taken from her was one of them, and Jean reached for another handful of toilet paper as a fresh set of tears ran down her face.

At least her crying had gone down a notch from the howling sobs she'd dissolved into earlier that morning.

I'm so sorry, Jean.

She was so sorry too. She'd used the same words to cancel her sewing students for that afternoon, and she honestly didn't know how to even leave the bathroom. She had no idea how to tell her husband. Rueben had been as excited and as anxious as Jean to finally have a human baby to take care of.

Outside the bathroom, both of their dogs lay on the carpet, watching her. If she even twitched, they lifted their heads, and Jean had sobbed into Timber's neck for a good twenty minutes right after receiving the horrible text from her adoption case worker.

The birth mom has a relative who said she'd take the baby.

Jean brought her knees to her chest and set her forehead on them. Her own mother had been so excited. She'd come to the cove twice in the past four months to help Jean set up a nursery. Kristen, Rueben's mother, who lived only fifteen minutes away on the other side of Diamond Island, had sat with Jean in the afternoons while she made baby dresses in a variety of sizes.

They'd spent a small fortune on bedding, a crib, diapers, bows, a stroller, and every other baby item on the market.

Jean knew this was her only chance to raise a child, as she'd turned forty-one in December. Rueben would be forty-four in March, and their case worker had already admitted their age might keep a birth mom from selecting them.

She'd had no idea that the adoption could be stolen from her at any moment. Had she known that, she wouldn't have painted the walls a soft pink. She wouldn't have sewn baby giraffe curtains, with the cutest zoo animals in the background. She wouldn't have been shopping online for blessing dresses and scrapbooks and digital picture frames.

Jean wanted to scream. She wanted to shake her fists to the sky and bellow at God for His cruelty in allowing her to love the baby that she'd never even get to see now. She wanted to pound the earth the way hail did, and she wanted to whip her fury against the cliffs the way the wind got to.

As it was, Jean, a woman of only five-feet, three-inches and barely a hundred and twenty pounds, sat on her bathroom floor and sobbed into her arms.

This was hell, and Jean had no idea how to find her way out of it. There was no ladder tall enough to get her to the top. There was no floatation device that could keep her from drowning.

The dogs—she and Rueben had parented several over the years—lifted their heads, both of them looking down the hall and toward the microscopic kitchen on the bottom level of the lighthouse where Jean lived.

It had taken her some months to warm up to the idea of living underground, but Reuben loved the lighthouse, and Jean loved Rueben. They'd had many years on the mainland near her parents, and it was time for him to be here, with his mother.

"There you are," his voice said, and Jean wanted to disappear. She didn't want him to find her like this, but she couldn't get herself to move.

He bent down and patted the dogs. "What are you guys doing--?" He'd spotted her, and Jean didn't have anything to say.

"Honey." He stepped into the tiny bathroom and knelt in front of her. "Are you hurt?"

In so many ways, yes. The kind where she bled? No.

She cried so hard she couldn't answer him, and Rueben ran his hands down her arms, his eyes searching for injuries.

"Hon," he said again. "Talk to me. Calm down a little and talk to me." He wrapped her in strong arms that could pull in heavy, wet ropes from the sea. He smelled like coffee and peanut butter, what he'd likely consumed for his afternoon snack. The man loved a good peanut butter cookie, and Jean had nothing better to do than perfect her recipes and provide food for her husband.

She needed something to do. Something to give her purpose in her life.

She clung to him, feeling the soft quality of his cotton shirt against her face and giving him some of the agony that had plagued her for hours. "My phone," she managed to say, and Rueben picked it up from where it sat on the closed toilet seat.

He kept her close, and the damning messages didn't take long to read. "No," whooshed out of his mouth, and Rueben sat down heavily on his knees, no longer trying to kneel up. He probably couldn't, because Jean knew that feeling of suddenly carrying the world on her back.

That was how Miranda's texts had felt. Like she'd tossed Earth, then Mars, then Jupiter onto Jean's back with the words, "I'm so sorry."

She also knew it wasn't Miranda's fault that the birth mom had changed her mind. Jean supposed they'd been warned that birth moms could do that, especially young ones. The one that had chosen them was in her early twenties, though, and Jean and Rueben only had five weeks to go until their baby would be born.

Not your baby anymore, she told herself, finally feeling some semblance of peace enter her heart. That came from Rueben, because while the man was tall and a bit bear-like in the breadth of his shoulders, he possessed a marshmallow heart. He was kind, and good, and loyal. He was hard-working and strong, and Jean loved him with everything she had.

"I'm okay," she said, taking a breath. Air felt like cement in her lungs. "You're here. I love you." Tears leaked down her face as she pulled back. "We're okay, and that's all that matters."

Rueben cried too, and she hated seeing the broken, anguished look on his face. "I'm so sorry, Jean. I—I don't even know what to say or do."

"I don't either," she whispered. "Maybe you could help me up? I've been in here for hours."

After crying for those initial twenty minutes, Jean had gone into shock. She'd wandered the lighthouse living levels—there were two—and once she'd realized what was happening again, she'd needed to throw up. Pure devastation could make one nauseous, she supposed.

Rueben stood and lifted Jean easily into his arms. "Do you want to lie in bed?" he asked, his voice low.

She nodded and clung to him. He laid her on her on her side of the bed after pulling back the blanket, and he tucked her in tightly. Jean started to cry again, and when Reuben slid into bed with her, his boots and jeans off now, they held each other and wept. Both dogs jumped up onto the bed, but Jean didn't find their presence as comforting as she once had.

"I love you," he whispered. "You're enough for me."

"I love you too," she whispered back. "You're enough for me too."

"It still hurts," he said, his arms around her gently, but with plenty of pressure so she'd know how very much he wanted her to be close to him.

"Yes." She closed her eyes and tucked her face right against his chest, where she could hear this heart beating and smell the scent of his skin. "It hurts so much."

"I CAN'T CRY ALL DAY TODAY," JEAN SAID THE NEXT morning. Reuben looked at her over the top of his coffee mug. "Can I come up top with you?"

"Of course," he said. "No sewing today either?"

"I canceled all week," she said, looking away now.

"That way, my students will still be even." She stirred her coffee absently, and she still hadn't taken a sip. "Did you tell your mother?"

"Yes."

So Kristen would be coming by today. Jean was surprised she hadn't arrived yet, actually, though she supposed it was only five-thirty in the morning, and Kristen was seventy-eight years old now.

She'd probably told all her girls, and Jean's eyes filled with tears. She didn't want to see anyone. She didn't want to talk about it. She didn't want cards, gifts, food, or sympathy. It would only make her feel weak.

Her phone sat on the table in front of her, and she swiped it on.

"She's going to bring lunch," Rueben said, his voice so quiet. Everything about living underground was so quiet, and Jean found that urge to scream some sound into their living space increasing once more.

"I don't want her to bring lunch," Jean said, plenty of bite to her tone. "I don't want to cry all day today." She met her husband's eyes, and he nodded.

"I'll tell her." He picked up his phone and started typing.

Jean looked at her texts. None of the women she'd spent last summer and fall, then the holidays, with had texted her. The group text had gone quiet after Eloise had told everyone about Billie getting invited to the Sweethearts dance. Either Kristen hadn't told them, or she'd used a different group text—one with Jean not on it.

That idea made bitterness surge up her throat, and Jean started typing a message to the whole group.

I don't know if you've heard, but Rueben and I lost the baby. I don't want to talk about it right now. It's too raw for me. We don't need any food. I don't want to push you away, but I really don't want to cry all day today, so it'll just be easier for me if everyone just gives me a little space and a little time to process it.

Jean didn't think there was enough space in the universe, or enough time left in her life, for her to get over this. Her mother had told her she was over-dramatic growing up, and Jean pulled back on the reins of her drama. Perhaps she would find a way through this confusing maze of disappointment and grief.

But right now, she just wanted to be alone.

"I'll bring my eReader up to the top," she said as she finally lifted her coffee mug to her lips. She couldn't remember if she'd eaten yesterday or not, as everything felt hollow and strange inside her. "And I'll just read by you. Is that okay?"

Rueben got up and came around to her side of the table. "It's absolutely okay," he whispered, dropping into a crouch beside her. "I'm worried about you, Jean. Do we need to go see the therapist again?"

She traced her fingers down the side of her husband's face, enjoying the soft quality of his salt-and-pepper beard, and the concern in his dark eyes. She'd seen a mental health professional for years, off and on. She'd had trouble accepting her infertility, and she often suffered from depression.

Moving to the cove permanently had actually been wonderful for her, as she'd learned to rely on herself and on Reuben, instead her mother and sister in New Haven. Forging a friendship with Kristen had buoyed her up, and when Kristen started bringing her to the Wednesday luncheons with the other ladies, Jean's outlook on life had improved drastically.

Those women cared about her, and she cared about them. She loved being involved in their lives, and she looked down at her text again. It was all still true, and while she knew Robin, Alice, Eloise, AJ, Kelli, and Laurel would be at the lighthouse in two minutes flat if she asked them to be, she really didn't want to cry all day today.

She sent the text and focused on her husband again. "Yes," she said. "I think I need to see someone again." She appreciated that he'd said "we" when he'd asked her, but the therapy wasn't for him. Sometimes he did attend her sessions with her, if her doctor wanted him there, or Jean did.

He'd dropped everything for her over the years, and Jean felt like such a failure. She couldn't get pregnant. Couldn't give him the children he wanted. Her body literally couldn't do what it was meant to do, and she'd never felt so broken before.

More tears pressed behind her eyes, especially when her phone vibrated. That was probably Robin or Alice, as they had older children who got up early for high school. Jean suddenly didn't want to see their replies. Even reading how sorry they were about the loss of the baby would make her cry.

"All right." Reuben drew her into a hug. "Leave your phone here, hon. Get your eReader. Let's go up top and watch the sun rise together."

She nodded and left her phone right where it was on the table. She'd have to deal with the messages later. Or maybe she wouldn't. Maybe she'd just delete them all and pray someone else would have something to talk about soon enough.

When she returned from the bedroom with her eReader, Reuben took her hand and raised it to his lips. "What about the Seafaring Girls?" he asked, his voice low and kind. "My mom's been asking you to do it, and you couldn't because the baby was coming."

Jean heard the unspoken words. *Now there's no baby coming, Jean. What are you going to do with your life? Who cares that you're even on this planet?*

She'd resisted becoming the Seafaring Girls leader, because the program was starting the first week of March, and she was supposed to have a baby the second week of February. With that out of the picture, perhaps she could take on the nautical safety and education program.

"I'll think about it," she told Rueben, and he nodded.

FOUR WEDDINGS AND A BABY   493

They started up the steps, and by the time they reached the top of the lighthouse, Jean knew what she wanted to do. "I should do the Seafaring Girls," she said. "Maybe then I'll have a purpose to my life."

"You bring me joy," he said, smiling at her. She marveled how he could be so strong. He had to be suffering too; he was. She could see it in his face. She'd felt it in his pulse last night. She'd heard it as he'd cried with her.

She managed a smile for him too, and his eyes did light up a little more. "If I had someone counting on me for something, it might help," she said. "Doctor Hill has always said to pour myself into service whenever I'm feeling worthless."

"You're not worthless, Jean."

"But I *feel* that way," she said, turning away from him. "I'm okay." She sat down in one of the chairs on the balcony and faced the cool, gray water. The sun had started to light the day, but none of its gold had kissed the earth yet.

Rueben sat beside her, and she slipped her hand into his. Yes, she should take on the Seafaring Girls if the position was still open. That would definitely give her something to focus on, something to do, and something to help her feel like she wasn't perfectly inconsequential.

"Will you text your mom?" she whispered as the first rays of light started to glint over the water. "Maybe she's already filled the leader position."

"I'll text her and find out," he said, reaching into his pocket for his phone.

Jean nodded, because Kristen hadn't mentioned the Seafaring Girls in a while, and she didn't know if she'd found a leader yet or not. She wanted to pray that she hadn't, but Jean's heart felt like a piece of wood in her chest. Praying for a baby had never worked. Praying for this birth mother hadn't either.

She wasn't going to pray to have the Seafaring Girls job, because God didn't listen to her anyway.

Jean didn't know how to hope anymore. That ability felt as cracked and as crumpled as her ability to bear children.

So she simply sat in her chair, her hand in her husband's, and watched the sun come up. *Whatever will be, will be,* she thought.

"She hasn't read it," Rueben said, tucking his phone away. "She's probably still asleep."

"Probably." Jean kept her focus on that moment. The very one in which she lived and breathed. Every inch the sun moved, she saw it, because if she let her attention wander forward or backward, her eyes would fill with tears, and she *really* didn't want to cry all day today.

Read THE SEAFARING GIRLS soon - coming August 10, 2021.

BOOKS IN THE FIVE ISLAND COVE SERIES

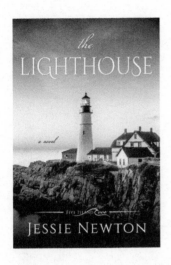

The Lighthouse, Book 1: As these 5 best friends work together to find the truth, they learn to let go of what doesn't matter and cling to what does: faith, family, and most of all, friendship.

Secrets, safety, and sisterhood...it all happens at the lighthouse on Five Island Cove.

The Summer Sand Pact, Book 2: These five best friends made a Summer Sand Pact as teens and have only kept it once or twice—until they reunite decades later and renew their agreement to meet in Five Island Cove every summer.

BOOKS IN THE FIVE ISLAND COVE SERIES

The Cliffside Inn, Book 3: Spend another month in Five Island Cove and experience an amazing adventure between five best friends, the challenges they face, the secrets threatening to come between them, and their undying support of each other.

Christmas at the Cove, Book 4: Secrets are never discovered during the holidays, right? That's what these five best friends are banking on as they gather once again to Five Island Cove for what they hope will be a Christmas to remember.

BOOKS IN THE FIVE ISLAND COVE SERIES

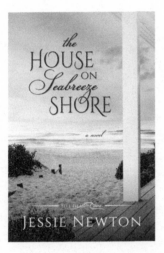

The House on Seabreeze Shore, Book 5: Your next trip to Five Island Cove...this time to face a fresh future and leave all the secrets and fears in the past. Join best friends, old and new, as they learn about themselves, strengthen their bonds of friendship, and learn what it truly means to thrive.

Four Weddings and a Baby, Book 6: When disaster strikes, whose wedding will be postponed? Whose dreams will be underwater?

And there's a baby coming too... Best friends, old and new, must learn to work together to clean up after a natural disaster that leaves bouquets and altars, bassinets and baby blankets, in a soggy heap.

BOOKS IN THE FIVE ISLAND COVE SERIES

The Seafaring Girls, Book 7: Journey to Five Island Cove for a roaring good time with friends old and new, their sons and daughters, and all their new husbands as they navigate the heartaches and celebrations of life and love.

When someone returns to the Cove that no one ever expected to see again, old wounds open just as they'd started to heal. This group of women will be tested again, both on land and at sea, just as they once were as teens.

Rebuilding Friendship Inn, Book 8: *Description to come!*

ABOUT JESSIE

Jessie Newton is a saleswoman during the day and escapes into romance and women's fiction in the evening, usually with a cat and a cup of tea nearby. The Lighthouse is her first women's fiction novel, but she writes as Elana Johnson and Liz Isaacson as well, with over 175 books to all of her names. Find out more at www.authorjessienewton.com.